The Mysterious Fall

Angus Silvie

First published in Great Britain 2019
Jan 2021 revised edition
Cover illustration by William Hallett

With many thanks to my mother, for her hawk-eyed attention to detail in unearthing errors, and to others too, who know who they are.

FOREWORD

You may be familiar with the following phrase: "The events, characters and places depicted here are fictitious. Any similarity to actual persons, living or dead, is purely coincidental." They often say that at the end of movies, sometimes even the beginning if the needle on the 'possible litigation' barometer is pointing to stormy. The fact that I am mentioning this here now, however, is thankfully not for fear of being sued. It is instead to prepare the reader for what is to come. I'll explain.

The people in this book are fictitious but the geography of this tale makes use of some real places that are not fictitious at all. Although almost all of them are described as accurately as possible, occasionally the book does sprinkle in a dusting of imagination, allowing me to take a few liberties with the descriptions. Anyone who knows and lives in the areas mentioned will no doubt be surprised to read that there is a forest or road or field in some place where there never has been one, or a street with a name that does not exist, but if I hadn't done this then the storyline would not have worked. After all, this is fiction, isn't it? So please put down your Twitter pen, and go with the flow. Just pretend you have never visited the places described (this will be easier if you already haven't) and the result will be that you can enjoy this tale in the same state of laissez-faire that I was in when I wrote it.

PROLOGUE

Rules govern everything. There are rules in life, there are rules of life. And if you believe there is an after-life, then there are also rules after life. No-one alive really knows what the after-life rules are, although it is not difficult to find a great many people who are convinced that they do know, and claim this knowledge through faith even though faith is by definition not based on what we know, but what we believe, and believing is not knowing, just thinking and often hoping that you know.

When believers die, one of four things could happen: they will either have their beliefs enacted, or those of a different faith applied (and imagine what a surprise that will be), or experience no after-life of any description, or discover that the rules of the after-life are in fact completely different to anything they or any other person had foreseen. Which of these is it to be?

CHAPTER 1 : THE DIARY

"Lillian! **Lillian!** *Grab the rope!" he screamed, but the wind, swooping up and over the cliff top, immediately caught his words and threw them back behind him. Far below, Lillian, fighting to see through the soaked and matted hair plastering her forehead, strained to look up. Had she heard something? Was that Walter?*

Desperation was enveloping her; she could not hold on much longer. The light was fading, smeared darker by the shakes and slaps of hard-blown rain, but now, thank God, out of the gloom she could just see the knotted end of a rope snaking and bumping down the steep slope towards her. She could imagine Walter frantically playing it out from eighty feet above, strands of shaggy black hair jumping like wild horses in the battering wind. She willed him to go faster, but the rope kept sticking, getting caught on bits of foliage or scree and forcing him to flick it up and down like a slow whip to dislodge it. Blinking away the rain, she kept focused on it – it was her only hope now, the only thing that could save her.

Her fingers were painfully numb, yet somehow still clinging to the little chunks of solid rock that poked from the crumbling wet stone and patchy earth. She knew that if she let go, that was it: her life was over. Her left leg hurt so much she feared she must have broken it as she slithered down the steep, wet, chalky cliff slope – the pain was excruciating. On top of that her arms and legs were scratched and bleeding and her palms badly grazed.

Below her, the slope became a sheer drop and she could hear the sea lashing the rocks, huge waves exploding in flourishes of spray that whooshed up through the rain in plumes of mist and drenched her in a wet, salty drizzle.

She had no energy left to scream; instead tears streamed down her face and merged with the rain as death pulled with increasing force on her shoulder. The rope was coming though; she could see it getting closer now. Twenty feet, ten feet, then, just as it had nearly reached her, as she readied herself to lunge for it in one last all-or-nothing effort, it got caught on a small stubbly plant and stopped again. The delay was enough, her strength was gone. She knew that she could not hold on, and a slow horror overwhelmed her; she knew what was coming.

What should have been a scream came out as a despairing grunt as her left hand slipped from its weakened grasp. Immediately the instant additional weight applied to her right hand jerked it free, and with resigned dismay Lillian watched it let go, as though it belonged to someone else. A million thoughts burst into her head but she just wanted to ignore them and think of nothing. She watched the rope getting smaller and more indistinct and waited for the impact.

Marlo Campbell stopped typing, closed his eyes, and sat still for a moment. He breathed in as deeply as he could, hoping that this would infuse his brain with even more creative energy to help him sustain this storyline. Then again, was he getting a bit carried away with the drama of the incident and introducing too much artistic licence? A bit too much flowery prose? He wasn't sure whether you could have a shake of rain but it sounded clever even if it wasn't. No, it was all good. This was such an important element of the story – he had to make it exciting and vibrant.

But it also had to be believable. Would there really have been a rope on the top of the cliff? Very handy for Walter and for the ensuing drama, but ropes don't grow on cliff tops. He would have to try and think of a way to explain that. Just because wherever you look people are churning out novels like they are baking a cake doesn't mean it is easy.

He exhaled loudly, opened his eyes and sat back in his cheap old faux-leather swivel chair, allowing it to rock gently and hoping as he always did that the flexes and creaks were not signs that it was about to collapse beneath him.

Rather than generate inspiration, all his breathing-in exercise had done was present him with questions that needed answers. An old cracked biro lay on the desk in front of him, and he picked it up and twirled it in his fingers. Predictably he dropped it and it bounced on the floor and rolled under a side unit. Of course it did, where else would it go? That just about summed up the way his life went really. Well it could stay there, he didn't care. Something for those little invisible spiders to weave their webs round.

He reached instead for the small, battered object which had become his inspiration. It was a diary, about the size of those Ladybird books he used to read as a child, with a page for each day. The once bright red and gold patterned cover had now faded into a peculiar blotchy crimson, the edges of the pages brown and scuffed. It smelled faintly of times past, like the interior of an antique writing bureau; hints of old leather and mustiness. On the inside cover, in fading black ink, was a carefully written but brief introduction:

1886. This is the private diary of Lillian Jones, of 31 Challenor Street Brighton. Should anyone find themselves reading this, I implore them to return the diary to the above address without reading further. Thank you.

Marlo could imagine Lillian sitting at her bed table as the diary year began, dipping her pen in a small, stained inkwell to write the inscription, a year of empty pages ahead of her, so innocent of the events that were to befall her.

Thereafter was a neatly-written and comprehensive account for every day, meticulously completed right up until Tuesday September 21st, where the entry ended with:

"I am so happy Walter has invited me out tomorrow, it
seems we shall likely go to the sea and take some air!
He knows that I have been wanting to stroll along the cliffs
and watch the evening sun so I very much hope we
might go to Seaford Head."

But September 22nd and every page after that was blank. Why was that?

The diary had come from his father's house. He had spent countless weekends travelling down to the outskirts of Brighton to clear out the small terraced house after his father died of a sudden heart attack two years ago, and had found the diary stored in a bureau amongst some old photographs. Why it was there was something he hadn't been able to establish.

His mother had died of cancer when he was fourteen, an event he had never really recovered from and which made the death of his Dad all the more shattering. As an only child, and with just a few other distant relatives, he didn't really have anyone else to query the diary with. He'd spoken to a few of his father's friends at the funeral but none of them knew. Maybe Dad had got it with a box of books in a boot sale – boot sales had become a bit of a hobby for him in his later years.

As soon as Marlo started reading it, though, he felt a connection, an involvement, and he knew he could not just leave it there. Who was Lillian Jones? What kind of life had she led up to the point at which she had started her diary? Why did she write the diary? What was her life like? And of course, why did she stop writing the diary on September 21st?

He felt he needed to know, but wasn't sure why it felt so important to him. Maybe it was because this was history coming to life, not a dry school lesson. Perhaps it was because he was quite possibly the first person to read it all, other than her.

So, his interest piqued, he had made some initial investigations and found Lillian's name on the 1881 census: she was born in 1866 to Thomas William Jones, a milliner, and his wife Mary. She had two younger siblings, William and Alice, and an older brother, Frederick.

At the time of the census, and indeed when the diary was written, the whole family lived above the shop at 31 Challenor Street, Brighton, except for Frederick, who had taken lodgings of his own closer to where he worked, down by the seafront.

However, a check of the 1891 and 1901 census records revealed no mention of Lillian. Intrigued, he had spent an afternoon at the National Archives in Kew trawling through death certificates and eventually found what he had somehow hoped he would not find, yet which still shocked him.

Lillian Jones had died unexpectedly on Wednesday, September 22nd, 1886, the day the diary entries stopped.

The death certificate showed the cause of death as 'accident' and gave no clues as to what had befallen her. She was just one of many people who lived, died, and were forgotten in the sinking sands of inconsequential history.

This suddenness of her death was a horrible discovery and Marlo was dismayed and saddened that a girl he thought he had come to know, even if it was only through nine months of her thoughts, had died so young. Such a waste. But what actually happened on that fateful September day in 1886? What was this mysterious 'accident' that she had?

So his next port of call had been the Sussex Daily News archives, as this was a regional local newspaper with records from the time and could be accessed from the British Library. It did not take long for him to find what he was looking for.

The Friday September 24th edition had a paragraph on page five under the heading 'Two Deaths On Seaford Head'. It was dispassionately factual and brief, but in no way what Marlo had been expecting:

"The death of Miss Lillian Jones of Brighton, twenty years of age, has formally been announced following her disappearance after a fall from the cliffs during a storm near Seaford on Wednesday. Her attempted rescue by her companion Mr Walter Threadwell ended in tragedy as he was unable to save her. She fell into the sea and was washed out in a heavy swell, and searches by police yesterday were unsuccessful in finding her. Her death in the prime of her life has caused much grief for her family and great sorrow in her neighbourhood. The police are investigating in case foul play was involved. As her body has yet to be recovered the funeral date will be announced in due course. In a singular coincidence, yesterday also saw the discovery, a few hundred yards from where Miss Jones fell, of the body of a man. The name of the man is not yet known. A coroner's report is awaited but police advise that the man's death was suspicious. It seems possible that the two deaths are linked but no-one has yet been able to suggest how this might be the case. Mr Threadwell has been helping police with their enquiries but as yet no charges have been brought and the police have advised that they have no reason to suspect him at this stage."

So she had died violently, and in unusual and mysterious circumstances given that the death of another man appeared to be involved too. Marlo sat back, slightly stunned. The diary was an even more poignant legacy then, those last words of Sept 21st holding an unknown portent of what was to come.

The following Monday's edition confirmed the name of the dead man as Jed Attleborough, a drifter, and revealed that the cause of death was by 'stabbing with a knife'. This was another surprise and gave an added twist to the mystery.

Really intrigued now, he painstakingly searched through all of the following editions for the year but surprisingly found no further mention of Lillian, Walter, or Jed. This seemed odd, as surely they would at least have reported on the questioning of Walter, the conclusions of the investigations into any foul play, the funerals of Lillian and Jed, and any potential murder trial.

Yet there was nothing, it was as though it had all been brushed under the carpet. Something didn't seem right.

At home that night, thumbing through the diary again, an idea formed. He could write a novel! Why not? It was quite a thing for a girl of twenty to die falling off a cliff, and if he could make something out of the strange case of the older man who got stabbed at the same time, it could prove to be a tale worth reading. He would base it on Lillian's life, and fill in that blank page of September 22nd with imagination and drama.

English had been his favourite subject at school, and maybe he was now finding his true calling. He'd read loads of books and he knew what clunky writing was. If he managed to avoid that, and make it interesting, at least it shouldn't be unreadable and who knows, it could sell millions, assuming each copy came with a free diamond or something. Without the diamond, maybe a few dozen if he was lucky, but that didn't matter. He'd got nothing else in his life worth caring about, and this could give him a purpose.

With purpose comes enthusiasm, an attribute that creates energy but sometimes fails to wait around for preparation. And so it was that, with a beginner's mindset, Marlo ploughed into page one without even considering the finer details of his plot.

He did a lot of research though, and became quite fascinated with life in Victorian Britain, more so than he ever had at school, because it had so much more relevance now.

He wrote about Lillian's life and everything around it, weaving the diary entries into what he had hoped was a historically accurate tale of the life of a young Victorian girl, working hard and discovering romance for the first time. For someone who didn't know what romance was, this was quite difficult. But then he wasn't a girl either, and, taking these key factors into account, some might argue that he wasn't particularly qualified to be tackling this subject matter at all.

Yet he felt a strange affinity with his heroine, and anyway in these modern times why should his gender be an issue? He could always ask a girl at work to read through it to make sure he had not made any obvious blunders with regard to the enigmatic secrets of the female psyche.

And now, months later, he had reached the point that he hoped the reader wouldn't be expecting - the drama and excitement which was now unfolding. Yet even at this stage he still hadn't mapped out an ending. This was seat-of-his-pants stuff, and he was beginning to feel like a man who had built an expensive boat in his garage only to find that he couldn't get it out of the door.

So what would happen now? He'd described Lillian slipping off the cliff, but was she actually pushed? The trouble is, if she was pushed, why would Walter be trying to rescue her? That didn't really make sense.

He put the diary down. He would go back later and deal with that and the whole issue of how Lillian fell; for now he just wanted to describe what was going to happen to her.

The impact never came. Instead there was a loud ripping sound, and a sudden and frightening deceleration as Lillian brushed past a thorny bush jutting at an unlikely angle from the cliff face, her billowing dress catching on the branches and practically wrenching it from her body, biting into her as it violently halted her descent. Instantly she found herself hanging upside down beneath the bush, her dress now virtually ripped to shreds but miraculously still holding her weight as she swung precariously in the wet wind.

Marlo paused once more. He had to confirm his decision now; he was prevaricating. He didn't want to go there..... but he had to do it. But once Lillian had died, was that it? Would the story just end there? No, there had to be more to the way that she died. There needed to be a twist.

He looked at the diary again, hoping without reason that it would give him some inspiration on how to do this, how also he could then perhaps complete the story through the rest of that year to explain the impact of her death and how her family, as well as Walter (assuming he had not pushed her off), learned to cope without her.

Sure, that sounded about as exciting as a paper plate of stale bread on a plastic table, but that was the challenge: to throw the ingredients into the literary word mixer in his head and somehow emerge with a plate of exquisite chocolate truffles that everyone would coo over. If the writing was chocolaty good and sweet to read, was it as important to have a gripping storyline too?

Although..... if Walter did push her off, then the book would turn into a much more exciting crime thriller, with perhaps a chase, and a tense court case. Yes, that did sound better. That meant he was definitely going to have to rewrite the bit about the rope, but that was probably more believable anyway, and at least it wouldn't affect the rest of what he had written up to that point.

The first chapters of the book, he reflected, were probably a little dull. Based on the diary entries, they had introduced Lillian and her family and set the scene for their daily life running a small but well-frequented hat shop on Challenor Street. Business was steady and good enough to provide a living, but no more than that. Lillian helped out in the shop whilst also assisting her mother in looking after William and Alice, who were fourteen and ten respectively.

She began a relationship with Walter in late July and Marlo had followed Lillian's description of their blossoming romance through August and September, to the point where she was confiding in her diary that she felt Walter might be her future husband, even though she had not known him that long, and that she hoped that he may be considering a proposal.

Walter was five years older than her and all Marlo could glean about him from the diary was that he first approached her in a tavern when she was in the company of her friend Edith, he was tall and dark with thick black hair, bushy eyebrows and a large nose which gave him a distinctive yet quirkily handsome air, and that he worked for an accountancy firm, regularly making use of the firm's horse and trap to come and visit her, as he lived on the other side of town.

Apart from that, Lillian's diary described mostly what they did together, where they went, and her romantic feelings for him. It sounded as though he had swept her off her feet. Marlo was curious as to whether this was her first serious boyfriend, as prior to that she had made no mention of any others, and this could explain why she was so besotted with him.

He wondered again what Lillian had looked like as a young girl of 20. He had read, over and over again, every word Lillian wrote that year, and subconsciously formed a picture of her in his mind. He was aware that he was just imagining how he *wanted* her to look and in reality she could look like anybody, but in his head he saw a strongly defined yet feminine mouth, a small nose, large dark eyes and curly auburn hair. The diary gave no clues, though, and so it was just intuition influenced by old Victorian portrait photographs he had seen over the years.

Not having ever had a girlfriend, he knew he was probably creating a fictional one; making Lillian into who he wanted his girlfriend to be. Was that wrong? Probably.

But now here he was. September 22nd 1886, and the story was getting exciting. So far he had described how, having spent the day journeying all the way along the coast and across to Seaford in the horse and trap, Lillian and Walter had headed up to the Seaford Head cliff for an afternoon stroll. The plan was to then take a late afternoon tea in Seaford town before heading back to Brighton, ideally arriving as dusk fell.

But it had not worked out as planned, and Marlo had described how, as they hurried back along the cliff tops, caught out by a sudden storm, Lillian had gone to have a closer look at the crashing waves and stumbled near the edge, slipping and falling off.

Marlo was pleased with his description of the fall but the role of Walter in her death wasn't the only challenge that he had given himself. He'd stated that the reason she and Walter had chosen to walk along the cliffs on a darkening autumn afternoon was to watch the sunset, but he had described Lillian's fall as being in the middle of a raging storm. Why would the couple have set off for a cliff walk if a storm was coming? That didn't really make sense. Once again this novel writing business really wasn't proving to be easy. There were potential logic traps everywhere, and the irony was that he was the one who was laying them for himself.

He got up and walked over to the window of his 14th storey East London flat. The sun was pulling the last vestiges of warm light with it over the horizon and a damp darkness was moving in and taking over. Glittering meshes of window lights and street lamps were multiplying in the city below, repainting the greys of the day with yellow, white, and black.

'That's enough for one day', he told himself. 'Sort it out tomorrow. Time for food'.

A rummage in the lukewarm fridge confirmed that he had given too much thought to his novel during the last few days and not enough to food shopping. He dined that evening on 6 slices of garlic sausage, a tub of ripening cream cheese, and a shrivelled apple, and the following day was pleasantly surprised that he was not ill.

CHAPTER 2 : WORKING LIFE

For a few seconds she hung there, shock turning to relief, then fear. She could no longer hear Walter, far above, his cries blown back and forth by the wind, his voice calling but dying before it reached her. She shouted upwards but was so exhausted that no sound left her lips. Her dress suddenly ripped again and she jerked downwards, nothing between her head and the pounding waves below.

Frantically she grabbed upwards and caught hold of the mossy trunk of the bush, ignoring the pain of the thorns as she swung her other hand round and pulled herself upright and towards the cliff face. Having saved her life, her dress was now a hindrance as it blew round her in the wind, flapping in her face and tangling itself round her legs as she desperately tried to gain a footing on the cliff face despite the intense pain in her leg.

Her right foot, scrabbling upwards, found solid rock, and she realised that the bush that had broken her fall was jutting from another small ledge, big enough to get half her body onto. Her hands already slipping from the stem of the bush, she strained to lever herself up and onto the ledge, pulling her shredded dress away from the thorns and collapsing onto the small slippery outcrop in a state of shock. She lay still but breathing heavily, not daring to believe that she was still alive, but aware that she was still in considerable danger, completely unable to save herself, and with virtually no chance of rescue.

Not far below her now and ever louder, the waves bit angrily at the cliff, and shards of spray were whipped off by the wind and tossed upwards, battering her relentlessly. She peered up into the stormy blackness, hoping to see or hear some sign of Walter or the rope, but now there was nothing. All she could see above her was the sheer white rock of the cliff. Her breath returning, she tried again to call out, but her weak cry was snuffed out in a blanket of wind. She screamed again, louder this time.

Walter was still there some two hundred feet above her, his eyes scouring the vista below him for any sign of Lillian. The black clouds had blocked out the last embers of light from the sinking sun and it was hard to see anything now. Once more he shouted out her name, then listened intently. Almost as the words died he thought he heard a sound which could have been Lillian.

He strained to hear above the wind and the sea. There it was again - a faint cry from far below. Was it her? Or was it just a seagull?

Marlo paused. He realised that as he was writing he was subconsciously giving Lillian a chance of survival, which was not how it should be. As the archives stated, she dies. But a night's sleep had re-charged his creative juices and he had got a little carried away in his efforts to squeeze in a few paragraphs before work.

This was getting a bit messy. He glanced at the clock - it was 8:05am and his shift started at 8:30am. Damn, he thought, late again; it can wait now, I need to get to work. He switched off the computer, took his old canvas jacket off the hook in the hallway, grabbed his backpack and left the flat, pulling the door closed behind him as he stepped into the concrete passageway. As it clicked shut, he felt a cold shiver run through his body and heard a distant noise that was like air rattling through a vent. He glanced round quickly, but there was no-one there. Must have been the wind, it often shook some of the windows at this height.

He hitched his backpack over his shoulder, and headed for the once shiny and now grimy metal lift which as usual seemed to find it quite an effort to ratchet him down to the ground floor.

It wasn't a bad commute. Marlo had used the inheritance money left by his mother to help buy his small Bethnal Green flat before London prices sky-rocketed, so had ended up with a fairly well-positioned city base from where he could use the Tube and buses to easily access most of the jobs that the capital city could offer him, without having to spend a fortune on travel.

It was not the most luxurious apartment block in the area, indeed from the outside it looked as though it had been built with the word 'stark' as its guiding design principle, but it was functional and well maintained, mostly populated by long-term and reasonably affluent residents or young professionals like him who had taken over from the long established older, poorer residents as they, well, died off. He even had a parking space in the gloomy underground garage where his little used and elderly VW Polo sat patiently collecting grime and waiting for some attention.

He emerged onto the pavement through the metal-framed entrance door, its wire mesh glass scuffed with ground-in traces of scrubbed graffiti. He breathed in the semi-sweet early morning air that bore the rising sound of London traffic and general hubbub, hitched up his backpack, and turned left.

A hundred yards on and the noise opened up into a crescendo as he headed onto the busy arterial highway; traffic queuing, buses stopping and starting, bicycles weaving. The pavements were thronging with determined commuters competing for space, repeatedly quickening then slowing their stride in their attempts to pass each other, wasting no time. Already most had their mobile phones clamped to their ears or clutched in their hands, early e-mails being read and replied to in a multitasking maelstrom of mission-focused movement. This was what London had become. Marlo stepped into their world and immediately became one of them, a man with only one aim, intent on getting to work as quickly as he could, so that later that day he could leave work on time and get home as quickly as he could, even if he did not really have anything important to rush home for. It was just what you did.

He had been in his current IT support role at Convestia for 4 years now. It was just five stops on the Tube and a short walk either end – 25 minutes at a leisurely pace and he was at his desk. But that assumed no delays and of course that morning an earlier defective train had slowed everything down. 'Typical!' thought Marlo angrily as his train ground to a halt once more, 'absolutely typical. Always when I am late. Damn it!' Some passengers looked round and Marlo realised that the last part of his thinking had inadvertently become audible muttering and his face was now partially screwed up with frustration.

Getting angry at delays is something the mature commuter does not generally do, as weary experience tells them the only thing this does is make you more stressed than you already are whilst also indicating to everyone else that you are an idiot for hubristically thinking that showing your displeasure will make any difference. Huffing and tutting marks you out as either a new commuter or a bit of a prat. Marlo knew this, so cursed his involuntary lack of control and quickly and more traditionally began a quiet yet intense study of the shoes of a randomly selected fellow commuter, internally reminding himself to calm down, blend in, and carry on.

'Half day, Marlo?' came the expected greeting as he hurried into the office and past one of his grinning colleagues who was perhaps unaware that he had just won a prize for lack of originality. But Marlo just replied 'Morning, Matt', with an artificial half-smile, not rising to the bait but adding an explanatory 'defective train' once he was past him to make clear it wasn't his fault. Everyone working in London knows that, unlike most other world cities, this is a perfectly viable un-challengeable explanation that is used, often truthfully, by at least one worker in every office on every day, and not worth a further retort unless you are creeping in a few hours after your contracted start time, at which point it is often wise to upgrade your excuse to 'signal problems'.

Ten minutes isn't a lot in some jobs, but when you are late on the helpdesk you're increasing the number of outstanding calls your fellow workers have on their stack and contributing to poorer response time statistics, which of course was not what managers want to see.

Now, where was the shift manager? Ah, excellent, over there tied up with a production problem, hopefully unaware that Marlo had only just walked in. With a bit of luck he wouldn't scrutinise the day's stats too closely, but in any case Marlo would work through 10 minutes of his lunch break to compensate. He was like that, such a goody two-shoes, but he couldn't help it. Within a minute he had his headphones on and was taking his first call, all thoughts of Lillian and Walter in their Victorian world pushed to one side as modern London real life took over from the fictional world he was creating.

CHAPTER 4 : IT STARTS

It had turned into an unusually warm and sunny day for early April, a slight breeze hurrying lazy fluffs of cloud across a pale blue sky, so at lunchtime Marlo went out, bought a sandwich and sat on a bench in a nearby park, watching humanity as it passed by. All those people, so many people, all enveloped in their own little worlds, all with their own troubles and emotions. Was there one, amongst all the others, just one, who might be his soul mate? Given his experience with women to date, and the small matter of his ridiculously unattractive face, it seemed unlikely. Thirty two already and not a sniff. Nothing.

It is hard to explain what makes an ill-favoured face. All humans have the same core features: a couple of eyes, a nose and a mouth, yet the variety of ways in which these components can be assembled, and enhanced or distorted through visual garnishes such as eyebrows, ears, hair and chins, indeed hairs *on* chins, is infinite. A planet of billions of people, yet almost all have a face that no one else has. Astonishing when you thought about it.

Sod's law that Marlo had ended up with one of the least helpful faces, or so he thought. He considered himself hideous. Perhaps he could have secured a role as an amusing pug-nosed criminal in a 1940s Ealing comedy, gurning for the camera to accentuate his suitability for the role of comedy thug, were it not for the fact that he was too skinny and too effete to be believable in such a role. He would also have had to overcome the additional handicap of being born in the 1980s, perhaps a deciding factor in this case.

Ok, everyone struggles to mitigate and overcome any bad hand that has been dealt to them, whilst at the same time thankfully taking advantage of all randomly inherited superiorities. That's just life. But wherever there is difference, there is comparison, and where there is comparison there is judgement, and where there is judgement there is someone who ends up at the bottom of the ladder looking sharply and sadly up at everyone looking judgementally down at them from the safety of the rungs above. When it came to looks, Marlo was the one who felt that he only ever saw the soles of feet.

Often a strong personality can overcome physical handicap, and many aesthetically challenged humans have played this card very successfully, but Marlo didn't have this either and try as he might, could not manufacture one. He was naturally quiet, very polite, obsessively non-confrontational, and by dint of comparing his behaviours with those of the more confident, outgoing, testosterone-charged chaps around him, had become extremely self-critical and lacking in self worth.

A couple holding hands went past. That didn't help either. That or any signs of physical affection, it was all just rubbing his face in it. So he tried to ignore the look-how-lucky-we-are couples, and instead focused on individuals who might have potential as an 1880s character in his book. As they walked past he imagined them behaving as that character, acting a part. If he was fortunate something would click and he would quickly jot down details of the person he had just seen, ready to slot into a storyline as needed. Who he really wanted to see was someone who looked like his vision of Lillian, so that he could use their appearance to add three dimensions and colour to the flat black and white image in his head. But he never saw Lillian, and today was no different.

At home that evening he made some tea and settled himself into his home office chair in front of the computer once more. It didn't take long to check his emails. That was one of the few benefits of having no real friends other than at work, and therefore also no need to engage in social media - he did not have to waste time wading through barrages of mails, tweets, posts, updates and whatever else people feel obliged to launch at each other on a regular basis these days, so that was good.

And wasn't social media these days mainly about taking the mouldy cake of your life and placing a beautiful silver cloche over it? Look at my shiny, fabulous lifestyle! There's nothing under the cloche, really there isn't! Well there wasn't a cloche man enough for the job as far as Marlo was concerned so he couldn't be bothered to try and invent one. Anyway, why on earth would anybody be interested in his life? Why shine a light onto something best left in the dark? The trouble was, ignoring social media just cemented his exclusion.

It was a small compensation, but at least he had the distraction of Lillian's diary now, and writing his novel had given him a reason to wake up the next day, a point to his existence. He was creating something that with a bit of luck would rank as an achievement, and at the same time he was enjoying it – he liked writing, and maybe this was a way forward for him.

Then if by some miracle he managed to get it published, he would have made his mark on society. He could be proud of what he had done and as a published author it might get him some admiration from afar, or even aclose, if that could be made a word. Admittedly not the kind of attention he would have got if he had a different face and was moodily strumming a guitar and flicking back his messy hair on a boy band concert stage, but given that he had no musical ability, this could be the next best thing. Could be, probably wouldn't be, but at least it gave him a reason to build the rocket that would take him to the star of fulfilment. God, what an awful metaphor. He would not be using that one in his book; only a fool would do that.

He sighed, turned his attention back to his story, and ploughed on.

Walter, now lying face down on the wet grass with his head peering over the edge of the cliff, shouted Lillian's name again, convinced he had heard her through the howling wind. But there was no reply. It was really dark now, and he could see nothing below other than the distant white froth of the waves. He had expected to see rocks down there at this part of the cliff, but the water had covered them and from what little he could see looked as though it must be right up to the chalk face.

Perhaps the last cry he thought he heard was as she fell into the sea, where she would surely have been thrown against the cliff by the waves, especially with the rocks just underneath the surface. He looked around him – it was gloomy and wet and the cliff top was unsurprisingly deserted.

There was nothing more he could do now; he would have to get help or at least let local people know what had happened. With a last look down, he struggled to his feet, turned to face inland, and checked his bearings. To his right was the path they had just come along as they headed back to Seaford, and he could make out the lights of the small house by the beach that they had both noticed earlier. To his left was Seaford town itself, but it was still some distance and out of sight beyond a cliff top. He decided to take the closer option of the small house, and scrambled off down the footpath towards it, eyes straining in the gloom to ensure he did not slip and unwittingly fall off the edge as well.

Lillian lay precariously and barely conscious now, clinging to the crumbly chalk ledge but knowing that she did not have much longer. "Come on girl, you have to stay awake, don't give up now," she urged herself, "don't give up, don't give up!"

Marlo felt a breeze brushing his neck and got up to close the window. He paused – the window was already closed. He remembered now that he had been so keen to get on with his novel that he had forgotten to open it as he normally did when he got home in the evening. It must have been a draught from under the door, he reasoned, with questionable logic given that the door had a draught excluder. He sat back down and stared at the words he had written.

He knew that Lillian would die – that was a matter of record and he was committed to his book reflecting that – but he still didn't really want her to. After all, this was a work of fiction so he could change his mind, couldn't he? But it would be a bit hard now she was about to drop into the sea and get dashed against the rocks; he had sort of written himself into a corner. What to do? The guidance Lillian had given him so far through her diary evaporated after 21st September, so from this point on it was no longer her words and spirit helping him shape his story, it was just down to him.

He picked up the diary, thumbing through the pages as his brain mulled over his dilemma. He came once more, as he had so many times already, to the last page and stared at the final five lines of careful handwriting.

"I am so happy Walter has invited me out tomorrow, we shall
likely go to the sea and take some air! He knows that
I have been wanting to stroll along the cliffs so I
very much hope we might go to Seaford Head and watch the
evening sun"

Something wasn't right. The words looked different this time somehow, in a different order than he remembered. He stared at them, puzzled, then suddenly started back in his chair, his eyes wide open. The first letter of each line spelled out.... I LIVE. No, surely not. He checked again. Yes, it did, it really did. That couldn't just be coincidence, could it?

Was this a message? Was it Lillian telling him that she lives, she doesn't die after all? No, that would be stupid, she would not have known that when she wrote the diary.

Also, it is a matter of public record that she did die. But then the words really did look different; he couldn't put his finger on it but he was sure they were not quite the same as before.

Aware that he might not be thinking rationally in the excitement of the moment, he let himself calm down and waited until his heart rate felt steady again. So, if Lillian were to survive, he could complete her diary for that year and beyond, describe the life she supposedly never had in reality, and turn the climatic tragedy of his novel into a plot twist, knowing that perhaps, just perhaps, it was closer to fact than fiction after all. Yes, how about she swims to safety only to be kidnapped into servitude so the authorities just assumed she had perished at sea..... perhaps that is what actually happened. His mind was racing with the possibilities.

He looked again at the diary entry. No, he was being silly. It must just be coincidence. And yet....something odd was happening. I LIVE. It was there, it was speaking to him – could it be Lillian speaking to him, still guiding him? No, he was reading too much into this. Or was he? This had scrambled his brain, he couldn't think straight. He knew that he should probably work the implications through before going back to the story, so he forced himself to close the document and switch off his computer. He would let his mind lull over it all before typing anything else.

That night his dreams were different. Vibrant, thrilling. He could not remember exactly what they were, he just knew that he had had them, through that immediate post-sleep memory that leaves ethereal traces from another area in your brain but will not reveal any detail however hard you try to recall. He guessed that they must have had something to do with Lillian's story as before he went to sleep he had struggled to focus on anything else.

CHAPTER 5 : A DIFFICULT CHOICE

Marlo wasn't very productive at work that day. He couldn't tell anyone as he wasn't going to reveal that he was writing a book until he had finished it, especially given the subject matter. But as the day progressed he started to wonder whether he had got a little over-excited last night. After all, it was only five letters so the chances of them forming a couple of words at the beginning of those lines were perhaps not as astronomically small as he had first thought. Maybe it *was* just an amazing coincidence. Outrageous coincidences happen all the time, don't they? He remembered once humming an old tune that had been a minor hit fifteen years previously but he had not heard since – it had suddenly come into his head but he didn't know why, and he was struggling to remember who sang it. Then five minutes later he had turned on the radio and they were playing that exact song, the DJ then helpfully announcing who sang it as well. So perhaps some first letters of words spelling some other words wasn't so incredible after all.

But he wanted to believe it was her. He decided that he would get back home and start to turn Lillian's situation around, and, with all the power of an emperor judging gladiators at the coliseum, let her live. The minor shortcoming in this plan was that he had no idea how he would do this, as he had managed to get her into rather a difficult position from which escape seemed unlikely.

His dilemma was interrupted, though, when he remembered that there was a leaving-do that night. Unusually, it was on a Wednesday. It had been scheduled to avoid the packed crush that afflicts most London pubs in office areas towards the end of the week that means each trip to the bar ends up taking at least twenty minutes. The flip-side to this strategy was that you still had to come to work the next morning and managers knew that many of the heavier drinkers would suddenly and surprisingly be struck down by a temporary heavy cold or migraine the next day and be far too ill to come in, with all of them miraculously recovering with no residual symptoms the following day.

Of course this was not really an issue for the leaver as they only had two more days left and no reason to impress anybody. If they didn't turn up for work the next day there wasn't really anything the employer could do. For everyone else, it was a bit of a pain.

As anyone who works in a large office in a city will confirm, leaving-do's are not uncommon, but when the leaver in question is someone from your team it is seen as pretty poor form if you do not attend. Also, Sophie was a very pleasant girl upon whom Marlo had occasionally secretly bestowed some wishful thinking, but she was just attractive enough to be well out of reach to him yet gregarious and available enough to be well within reach of all his better-looking and more outgoing colleagues. He knew that however much drink Sophie consumed, it would not be enough to make him appear more enticing than his rivals. There were always better men around him. That should be inscribed on his gravestone, he reckoned. 'Marlo Campbell – always surrounded by better men, even now'.

So he didn't really have a huge incentive to go.

At 5:00pm the exodus to the Dog and Sparrow began.

"Coming Marlo?" asked Dominic, a large jovial balding man in his late thirties who routinely wore bright red T-shirts that didn't suit him, "should get a few free drinks out of this!" "Yeah, sure," replied Marlo weakly, immediately berating himself for not just saying no, "I've just got a few loose ends to tie up then I'll be over."

He didn't really have anything to tie up; none of his ends were loose. But he still didn't want to go and now his can't-say-boo-to-a-dead-goose personality had tripped him up again. Then again, after a few drinks Dominic, like everyone else, probably wouldn't care or remember whether he had turned up as promised or not, so all was not lost. He resumed his task of opening and closing a few files on his computer to make it look as though he was still busy. If he got up to go home now he would draw attention to himself and more questions would be asked than if he left after everyone else had gone. There was a noise behind him and he felt his seat being briefly wiggled as James, the unfeasibly young looking trainee, brushed past. "Come on matey!" he said, "no ducking out of this one, beer awaits!"

"I know," smiled Marlo, amused at the young man displaying a level of enthusiasm rarely seen during working hours, "I'll see you over there."

"Right you are," James nodded and dashed off after his colleagues.

Marlo sat back. Maybe he should go after all. That was two people he had given assurances to now. It was almost as though someone was pulling on him with a thin twine that was not enough to drag him off his seat but was forcefully nagging him to take a chance and go. Forget about finding a girl, just go and have a night out with friends. But there were always girls there, that was the problem, and he was constantly hyper-aware of how they were looking at him, their body language, their natural ease with other blokes but not with him. He couldn't ignore it. It would bite away at him all evening.

Yet despite constantly convincing himself that he would never find that special person and it was pointless looking, human nature dictated that he would always have an underlying ultimate goal of finding her, that elusive creature who might be his future partner, and tonight could be the night. What if his girl was sitting even now at a table in that pub, hoping to meet someone like him? Yeah right, as if that was even remotely likely.

It is all well and good being a babe magnet, but not if you are pointing the wrong way round and repelling rather than attracting. To be fair he might as well have been the wrong way round, and directing his backside at them all evening, for all the success he had had. So heading down to the pub now would once again put him in that situation, and he knew in his heart that it would only bring disappointment as it always did. But now two people might be telling everyone that he would be along in a minute, and if he didn't he would have to come up with some excuses for tomorrow that were unlikely to be plausible. Sophie herself would probably be a little upset if he didn't bother to turn up. Or maybe she wouldn't – after all, she was a girl and most girls seemed to have a 'who are you again?' opinion of him so she probably wouldn't even notice. And she was leaving so it didn't matter anyway.

Of course he really wanted to get back to his novel now that he had seen that possible message from Lillian - this leaving-do was really bad timing. What to do.....

As he dithered, five people - the last of the day shift - emerged from the cloakroom on the other side of the office, and he noticed that Sophie was one of them. She looked up and caught his eye. "Hey Marlo!" she called across the office, "you joining us?" That was it, he couldn't back out now. "Sure!" he called back with false enthusiasm, "hang on, I'll come with you..."

CHAPTER 6 : THE DRINKS

Marlo looked round at the group of drinkers he had ended up with. James was there, first pint already almost finished, his trainee 'responsible' mind switched off now that he was in happier surroundings and able to express himself like the student that he no longer was. Mark and Surav were two colleagues in their mid-twenties, with long-term girlfriends. They liked football, cars, women and beer and were therefore very much at home in this environment. They were both intelligent and quick-witted, and always up for a pub debate. Lisa, Jane, Amy and Vicky he knew only from afar – they were part of the new intake who had only been at Convestia for a few months now and had not yet lost their eagerness to impress. Pub outings were a good way for them to get to know some of their colleagues a little better.

Atif was there too. He was originally from Chennai in India but had been in the UK for 6 months now, had a long-term visa, and was hoping to further a career in customer service. His English was good enough for phone calls but not quite lively enough for him to overcome his reserved and very gentle nature, and contribute anything more to the conversation than a constant grin and an attentive air, which as many pub bores will attest, can be a very useful attribute when everyone else has wandered off to find better conversations. It makes it easier for those wandering off, too – if the bore has someone to drone at, he won't miss them.

And then there was Ben, tall and thin and with the look of a man older than his years but only in his late twenties. His Harry Potter glasses and slightly greasy side parted hair summoned the word 'geek' to mind and Marlo secretly empathised with him because if anything he appeared even less likely than Marlo to be able to lure a lady. But he still felt sure that should, in some unreal world, he and Ben be competing for said lady, knowing his luck the girl would choose Ben.

"So how did you get the name Marlo?" shouted Amy, a small but feisty character who was known in the office for her raucous laugh and explosive sneezes, and despite her diminutive stature had no problems in holding centre stage in a noisy pub.

"Well, my parents gave it to me," he smiled, making sure as always that he kept his mouth almost closed, shielding his brownish teeth from the world. "Anything else you would like to know?"

Amy gave a sarcastic grin. "No, that's just what I wanted to know, thanks for filling me in. Who'd have guessed, eh?"

Marlo relented. "Actually, there is a reason. My parents admitted once that I was probably conceived in a hotel in Marlow in Buckinghamshire, so that's where they got the idea. They chopped the 'w' off for me."

"Well, I like it, it's unusual, sounds a bit Scandinavian," said Jane, cradling her fast-emptying first glass of white wine, "better than having a dull name like mine."

"Thanks!" Marlo said, before remembering to add "but Jane's a nice name too." Unfortunately they both knew that he would be hard pressed to justify that hasty assertion, but Jane smiled at him and he smiled back. That was a nice feeling for him.

"More drinks guys?" Surav had stepped forward, to the relief of those whose wallets were less used to daylight. No-one refused, more drinks arrived, and the evening wore on. Marlo learned that Ben had once been to China and liked it. Lisa played the flute. Mark had climbed Mount Kilimanjaro for charity three years ago. Vicky had a degree in engineering and couldn't really work out why she had ended up in IT. Atif smiled and nodded a lot but said almost nothing.

Half way through the evening Sophie – who had been in another group - had come over and said hello and thanks for coming, even though most had come for the drink more than the opportunity to talk to Sophie; there were a fair few there who had not spoken to her all evening and would only do so in order to say goodbye, or perhaps not at all if they felt they could get away with it. Just turning up was enough, wasn't it?

Some pleasantries were exchanged and some brief work tales recounted that more often than not shed the management in a bad light, but it was clear that she was enjoying the company of her closer friends in the other drinking group and after a while she returned to them for the rest of the evening. Marlo's pointless hopes of kindling a flame there were short-lived.

Drink changes people, everyone knows that. They lose their inhibitions, say things they wouldn't when sober, and, on occasions, fall over, or get angry. But it affects some more than others. Marlo had seen with his own eyes a team-mate from a few years back who had the remarkable ability, once completely laddered, of being able to sleep standing up. William would be standing with fourth or fifth pint in hand, as far as everyone thought listening to the conversation, when suddenly someone would hold their hand up and loudly whisper "William's asleep!" Everyone would go quiet and sure enough, although still standing and holding his pint, his eyes would be closed, his breathing regular, and his mind completely oblivious to his surroundings. To all intents and purposes, he really was asleep. Yet he did not fall over or even drop his glass. And when he 'awoke' he would have no recollection of the period during which his eyes were closed.

For Amy, it only took a couple of gin and tonics and she was no longer Amy the Office Worker, she was Amy the Party Animal. She would laugh at everything, start nudging people, slur her words, repeat herself, and comment inappropriately on colleagues she only vaguely knew.

Concerned friends would soon start suggesting she didn't partake in the next round, or better still, went home while she was still capable of doing so. Amy would always respond with a grin and a slurry "yeah, right," and ignore them.

The next morning Marlo would wait to hear which fellow late drinker had been obliged to help her to the station, and more often than not, onto the train. Once, two worried colleagues had actually gone out of their way to accompany her on her train and see her all the way back to her front door. This was just as well as she had spent much of the journey insisting that every stop was where she got off and then each time trying angrily to get out of the wrong side of the train.

Marlo found this amusing but also hard to comprehend. If he drank too much alcohol, yes, he would be unsteady on his feet, but he would also make every effort to force himself to continue to talk as lucidly and sensibly as the fog of alcohol would allow, however tempting it might be to suddenly wave his arms around and announce that he was a potato.

His brain, however sozzled, would always retain an over-riding motivation to ensure that common sense and rational behaviour overcame any latent but admittedly hard-to-find exhibitionism. Captain Dull ruled, even when drunk. He felt superior yet at the same time disappointed that he couldn't just let go of his inhibitions completely and be as raucous and socially carefree as everyone else. Apart from bumping into things, the main side-effect of over-indulging for him was an instant need to sleep. In other people's eyes, particularly girls - boring. To him – responsible, and better than acting like an idiot. Yet all girls seem to prefer the idiot, even if they said they didn't. It made no sense.

He did not possess the ability to sleep standing up, but on two occasions in the past he had woken up in the morning on the bathroom floor in his flat, face imprinted with red lines from the floor tiles, having presumably managed to stagger home from the pub in the fresh air – he didn't remember doing it - but finding the fifteen foot journey from bathroom to bed in the stuffy air of his flat defeated by the urge to immediately sleep.

Despite his usual pre-arrival determination to resist temptation and moderate his alcohol intake, this approach never took into account the generosity of others and the addictive lure of the stuff he was drinking, and so at 10:45pm he found himself on his fifth pint, far more than was good for him, hazily sitting at a table with Ben, Atif and Jane. A few small groups remained but most people had sensibly gone home. "How do I always end up with the losers?" he mused despondently, answering his own question very easily with the realisation that that was probably what the others were thinking too.

But at least Jane was there and although she was no Marilyn Monroe (Marlo doubted that she would have been sitting in this group if she was), she was about his age, had been very pleasant all evening and a good conversationalist, and Marlo was enjoying her company. He had no idea if this was reciprocal but he hoped so. He had made her laugh a few times and although his recollections of the later stages of the evening were starting to merge into each other, he thought he had been good value overall and hoped Jane had developed the same opinion. And she had a nice crinkly smile too, where her eyes did half the work and made you feel as though she really was enjoying the moment.

Ben and Atif mainly listened, Ben occasionally making a tenuous observation but clearly struggling to pay attention following a regrettable failure to back out of a Sambucca challenge earlier and now suffering the after-effects. Atif had avoided the Sambucca press-ganging through strategic use of the washroom facilities and was still nursing his second pint, watching and smiling but enigmatically saying nothing.

"It's getting late," said Marlo purposefully, "what are everyone's plans? Work tomorrow!"

They all groaned. "I had... better go," said Ben, easing the words out slowly to ensure that they came out in the right order, "I told my .....missus I would.... be..... home by midnight."

Marlo nearly choked on his beer. Missus?? Ben? He couldn't help spluttering "I didn't know you were married, you kept that quiet!"

Ben just grinned proudly and nodded, as that was easier than speaking. Although it took Marlo longer than usual to find and focus on Ben's fingers, as he seemed to have more of them than usual, once checked he could plainly see that there was no ring.

"Where's your ring?" It was meant to be a question but sounded more like an accusation. Fortunately Ben was too far gone to notice and just held up his bony hand, waved it around a bit and said "Allergy. Can't wear metal on my skin. She doesn't mind." He laughed. "She knows I'm not Casanova. Can't be anyway, he's dead. Ha! Also, also..." he made a wavering effort to fix Marlo in the eye "she trusts me. Yep, she does." He nodded emphatically, confirming to himself that what he had just said was true, and returned his gaze to a stain on the table.

Whether it was true or not, Marlo was still reeling. The one person he knew who he had comfortably assumed would be even less likely to have a girlfriend than him had done considerably better than that and married one! This was the ultimate proof of his own abject failure.

"How long have you been married then Ben?" he asked in a way that he hoped would sound politely interested rather than insanely jealous.

Ben looked up and smiled slowly at him in the steadily unsteady way that only drunk people do. "Hang on," he said, and it was clear that he was thinking. His eyes moved around a bit then managed to re-focus on Marlo. "This year, ten years. I should have known that," he grinned. Then, to explain: "we were... childhood sweethearts. Married young."

"Aah, how nice," said Jane, "that's really sweet." Marlo didn't think so, he felt anything but sweetness and light just now, in fact that had soured his whole evening. But Jane was still there at least so he turned to her, keen now to change the subject.

"Where do you have to get back to, Jane?"

"I'm in Chertsey. Bit of a trek, and I have to make sure I don't miss the last train. How about you?"

"Oh, I'm just down the road really. Five stops east on the Central Line."

"Wow, that's handy, lucky you. If I could afford it I would probably look to get closer to work but the house prices keep going up, you just can't keep pace with it. It's mad."

Marlo suspected that at this stage the Successful Chat-Up Line for a normal man could be something along the lines of 'well, you can try out my flat if you like!', as, even if accepted as the joke that it clearly was, it would hoist a small flag of possible interest which might be detected and noted positively by the recipient. But he had no idea what response that would bring in Jane's case or whether that would in fact immediately cross the 'gone too far' line for even a normal bloke, let alone a no-hoper like him. In any case Atif was still there watching as well as Ben, and he did not want to make a fool of himself. So he just nodded.

"You're right," he said "I got in just at the right time when it was more affordable." He groaned inwardly - what a dull and responsible thing to say, that would really impress her. He paused, then took, what was for him, quite a plunge. "Would you like me to walk you to the train station?"

"Aw, thanks mate," interjected Ben, momentarily overcoming his alcoholic haze to display a commendable sense of humour, "but I think I can manage."

Jane laughed. She was merry but not drunk and Marlo had noticed that after the first glass, she had subsequently been careful to drink sensibly. He wished he could have said the same for himself. Normally he stopped at three pints so he was finding the fifth hard going and couldn't have started another even if someone had plonked it in front of him.

"Well I'm only going to the nearest tube station," said Jane, "then I'll get to the train station from there, but thanks for the offer, that's very nice of you."

"No problem," said Marlo, a little disappointed but not at all surprised. It was a slight variation on the answer he always got. "We had better head for the Tube, then!" At least he could walk her there and who knows what might happen from there – she might change her mind and decide that some company on the train home would be a good thing after all. And after that, who knew?

He knew Ben lived in North London somewhere and would be taking a bus. He turned warily to Atif. "Where do you have to get to Atif?"

For almost the first time that evening, Atif spoke. "I am in Stratford," he announced. Marlo cursed his luck. Atif would need to get to the same tube station as Jane and himself. It was always the same, he just never got the opportunities, ever – there was always something that stopped him, every time. If he had not felt sorry for Atif, if he had just ignored him, if.... but it was too late now.

The three of them emerged unsteadily from the Dog and Sparrow into the chilly night air and headed for the tube station. The cold was like a dose of smelling salts but Marlo was still having trouble walking in a straight line and his legs seemed to be only half-attached to his pelvis. He hoped Jane was not noticing his unusual gait, but his rational brain was also telling him that when you are drunk, you can sometimes think that you are striding confidently along like a soldier on a march when in reality you look as though you have rubber bones in your legs and the pavement is a different height every time you put a foot down.

"Bit chillier than when we left work, isn't it?" he ventured to Jane, hoping to divert attention from his legs yet desperately wishing he could have thought of something a little more interesting to say. He knew that they both knew that this was better than silence but only just.

"Yes," replied Jane, "quite nippy." Looking straight ahead, not even a glance at him. Already the defences were coming up.

Before he could change tack, Atif piped up next to him, suddenly talkative now that he was out of the pub.

"Mr Marlo, you have been working Convestia for some years I believe, is this correct?"

"Yes, 4 years now," replied Marlo cagily.

"What in your view are the opportunities in this company, what additional skills would be helpful to progress? I would welcome your advice because in my opinion you are well-respected."

Marlo sighed. Poor timing, Atif, such poor timing. But how could he not take time to answer after being paid such a compliment? He also felt a little sorry for poor Atif as many colleagues felt that, despite management assurances, he represented the toe in the murky waters of outsourcing, offered up by the Indian resourcing company, through which he had got his visa, as a sweetener for a big deal that could result in off-shoring and job losses. You couldn't blame Atif for this, but at the same time if he was given lots of help and encouragement that could backfire in the long term if the managers were impressed by his performance and this convinced them to outsource everything. Then again, there would almost certainly be other far more tempting incentives and promises which would lure those managers to a decision irrespective of Atif, so what was the harm in helping him a bit.

By the time Marlo had formed his tired blurry thoughts into what he hoped was an appropriately professional answer and replied cautiously to Atif's supplementary questions, they had reached the station without Marlo having had a chance to think of anything else to say to Jane. She had just walked silently along beside them.

Now she was heading west and he and Atif were heading east. "Are you going to be ok at the other end?" Marlo asked Jane, "can you get home ok from the station?" As soon as he said it he wondered whether he should have done. Had he just been patronising? Why wouldn't she be able to get home, when she did it every day? Having a drunken Mr Timid stumbling along next to her would hardly be helpful. In time-honoured fashion, he had clumsily tried to disguise an option for her to accept an invitation by wrapping it up as solely a concern for her well-being but had that backfired? Had he been too obvious? How did you do this stuff? His brain felt as though it was swimming loosely in a bucket of alcoholic chat-up befuddlement so he stopped trying to think.

"Yes, it's fine thanks Marlo," she smiled "I texted my boyfriend while you were talking with Atif and he is going to pick me up."

The arrow of despair struck true and hard into Marlo's back. Although he had been half-expecting it, it was no less painful than all the previous ones.

"Great!" said Marlo a little too loudly. "Fine, good! I'll see you tomorrow then."

"Yes, bright and early I hope!" Jane rolled her eyes and wobbled her legs. "Easier said than done though!" she laughed.

"You're right there." Marlo's legs were already wobbling, he didn't need to pretend. He guessed Jane had noticed that.

She headed off down the escalators leaving Marlo with Atif. They looked at each other. "Come on then," said Marlo, trying to disguise his feelings, "let's go."

Marlo didn't remember much of the journey home, but he did remember closing the front door when he got home, launching himself on the sofa and punching it as hard as he could before waking up some 3 hours later for a call of nature and from there dragging himself to bed. When his alarm clock shocked him awake right in the middle of a dream where he had successfully brought a girl back to his flat, his misery was complete. He seriously thought about not going to work that day and breaking his proud record of never having taken a day off sick. But despite his internal despair and a fierce headache that only 4½ pints of beer with not enough water can give you, he still went into work. He was Captain Dull, remember.

CHAPTER 7 : REFLECTIONS

Thursday was not a good day, and Marlo wasn't the only one suffering. Three colleagues failed to make it in, and most of those who had celebrated Sophie's leaving were looking the worse for wear. Had they known, Convestia customers may have been better served by waiting until Friday before phoning in for support. Call waiting times were a little longer that day, and the advice given may have been less mentally agile than it should have been.

Marlo saw Jane, she smiled and waved at him and he waved back. She would now be a recognised acquaintance, but as always that would be as far as it went.

At lunchtime Marlo went for a walk. He looked without seeing, his mind elsewhere. The revelation about Ben's wife had reminded him of Duncan, a chap he vaguely knew who worked in a different department. He had noticed him mainly because of his strange and frankly off-putting shape, whereby his lower half expanded upwards and his upper half expanded downwards to meet in a waist of extraordinary proportions totally out of keeping with the rest of him. He looked as though he had provided the template for the first comedy sumo wrestler inflatable costumes.

On top of that he had short curly brown hair that looked as though it belonged on a yak, and wore ill-considered glasses with white side arms that he was always pushing back up his nose, so although providing some visual amusement Marlo did feel sorry for him if only out of empathy for someone who he deemed to be even more visually unappealing than he was. This empathy vanished one evening when in the pub after work he found himself at a table next to another group that contained Duncan.

It transpired that Duncan, despite appearances, was a chap full of confidence in his own opinions and possessed of a remarkable lack of self-awareness and the mandatory loud voice that complements this condition. He was the perfect illustration of a pub bore, a man capable of loudly recounting a truism as though he was the first person to have thought of it.

Marlo couldn't help but hear him droning on about his work project, pointing out how badly the project had been run before he came along and inserting small but cutting digs at everyone but himself and those listening to him. Then he started telling jokes, and although he was quite a good story teller and set the joke up nicely, when the punch line came his audience could usually see why they were supposed to laugh but didn't always want to.

"Did you hear about that Communication Skills course they had the other week? I didn't go." "Why not?" a colleague obliged. "They didn't tell me it was on. Eh? Eh? Ok, here's one. There's this couple, right, going into hospital to have their first child. The husband, he's with his wife when she starts, you know, doing the business. So the baby's coming but there's no midwife. So the husband runs out into the corridor trying to find a midwife. Someone asks him what he's doing and he says 'I'm having a mid-wife crisis!' Midwife, you see? Like mid-life. Alright, alright, try this one..." and before any of his audience could excuse themselves, he was telling the story of the man who tried to sell his car to a man from China, which added a touch of potential offence to his already dubious oratory and had his captive audience looking round nervously and wishing he would keep his voice down, even in a noisy pub. But Duncan did not pick up on any visual cues and ploughed on regardless, revelling in being the centre of attention yet unaware that his colleagues only had to humour him because they worked with him and couldn't really avoid seeing him the next day.

Marlo smiled as he listened, realising that his sympathy for this boorish fellow was mixed with a degree of admiration that someone with such physical and social deficiencies was managing to overcome them through a complete lack of insight as to what others were thinking of him, something Marlo knew he would never be able to emulate.

Duncan had now run out of jokes and after someone else mentioned their train journey that morning, Duncan leapt in and began a less than original yet amateur theatrical speech on the outrage of paying a king's ransom for being herded like cattle every morning, with no guarantee of a seat but a guarantee of being late. This was a tired, oft repeated subject, yet Duncan was relaying it as though it was conversation gold. Then he delivered what was to Marlo the sucker punch. "I had to help get a refund once," he revealed, "one of my ex girlfriends was delayed by over three hours because....."

Marlo didn't hear the rest. His ears had stopped working when he heard the words 'one of my ex girlfriends'. One of? That means many! Duncan – this large pretentious chump, with seemingly no redeeming features, physically unattractive and with the social skills of an ox – had enjoyed a number of previous girlfriends. HOW?? And more to the point why? Why on earth were girls attracted to this man? Could they really be attracted to a 'character' no matter how repulsive that 'character' is? If Marlo suddenly started boasting uncontrollably in a loud voice would girls come flocking? Of course they wouldn't. It just didn't add up. How was Duncan able to attract women when he wasn't?

This really was the final straw. It seemed obvious that women must have some inherent chemical or psychological revulsion switch that only activated when he was around, and although he sort of knew why, he still felt unjustly treated. Surely he wasn't as loathsome as Duncan? That man was indisputably an oaf. Things were even worse than he thought. This depressed him so much that he could not concentrate on what his own group were saying so shortly afterwards made his excuses and left. The sofa had got a real pummelling that night.

So as far as his Convestia colleagues were concerned, though, he was just a quiet, genial and pleasant guy, moderately intelligent, polite, and never one to lose his temper. He just blended in, anonymously turning a small and insignificant cog in the engine of London life, the same as all the other insignificant cogs. The fact that he hated himself was of no consequence. He did not have low self esteem, he had *no* self esteem. Then again, half the people in his office might hate themselves too. It is no secret that everybody has secrets. It is just that no-one admits it until it is often too late.

He realised he had walked further than he had planned, and hurried back to the office, arriving slightly out of breath but with his professional mask back in place.

CHAPTER 8 : THE MESSAGE

As Marlo opened the door of the flat that evening the sun was streaming into his lounge, spreading a warm golden light which drew his attention to the beginnings of what would probably be a really impressive sunset given the ribbons of wispy pink cloud that were settling on the horizon and gilding the distant skyscraper windows with warm colour. Aside from the view of the city, this was one of the key advantages of living on the 14th floor – if there was a good sunset, he would see it in all its glory.

A good sunset. That was what Lillian had been hoping to see from the cliff top. His mind had been so tied up with work and colleagues over the last couple of days that he had completely diverted his attention from the novel, but now more than ever he needed something to take him away from reality.

He sat down at his desk and turned on his computer. He knew that thanks to that hidden message he would now have to work out how Lillian was going to live rather than die and how she could escape from the perilous situation he had written her into. This death was so mysterious that it wasn't even a death now.

He glanced at the diary. It was open. This was odd. He always left it closed; it was a routine for him to close the diary at the end of every session to indicate to himself that his writing for that day was done. It was open at July 7th and read:

"Papa has a big order to work on so asked if
I could help with the ladies' hats by attaching a
band of black silk ribbon under the brim. All
twenty hats are for Wimbledon House girl's school
which has just opened last year in London. From what I
hear they need them for a fete and Papa only has seven
days to have them all ready so I also helped pin roses
to the crown which were white and mauve. They are
very pretty and smell nice! I hope the girls enjoy their gala.

Marlo looked at this rather innocuous entry. It wasn't quite as he remembered it but he hadn't got a photographic memory so he couldn't be sure. Was this another sign? Why was the diary open at this page? He excitedly checked the first letters of each line: PIBTWHDTV. No, this time nothing, no message. There weren't even enough vowels to swap them round to make a word or sentence.

He closed the diary and opened up his document on the computer. Then something made him go back. He opened the diary again at July 7th.

He had definitely closed it on Wednesday morning, how could it have opened itself? So if there was no obvious explanation for that, then perhaps there was a chance that July 7th did indeed have a hidden message there somewhere and someone or something was helping him find it. He tried moving the words around, reading every other word or reversing their order. Still nothing. Then he saw it. The last letter of each sentence seemed to form... yes! It was there again, a message – it had to be! He wrote down the letters to make sure he had got it right... FALLINSEA. Fall in sea. Lillian must fall into the sea. So she wouldn't hit the rocks and she definitely wouldn't somehow scramble back up the cliff either. It had to be the sea.

Stunned, his heart racing, he sat back and digested what he had just seen. Once was incredible, twice was not feasible. This could not be coincidence. It was telling him what to write and was so specific to the exact point he had reached in the story that it could not be chance.

He looked up at the ceiling - he wasn't sure why - and whispered "Lillian?"

His head was swimming and he didn't know why he was trying to talk to someone who had been dead for well over a century, but he was in a place he had never been before and all the rules of logic and rationality that had governed and defined his life to date were being challenged by what was happening to him now. It had to be her, surely, but how could it be?

Yet the ceiling remained where it was, his computer screen continued to stare squarely at him, the diary remained open at July 7th, and Lillian did not answer him. He suddenly realised that he was completely tensed up and gripping onto the chair as though his life depended on it, so forced himself to relax a little. He was being silly, there must be an explanation. He stretched his arms, but as he did so he shivered, and wondered why it had suddenly got cold.

He glanced at his indoor thermometer. 21° and that wasn't even with the sun on it. Why was he so cold? There were goosebumps on his arms, but that shouldn't happen at this temperature. Perhaps it was the nervous excitement. Irrespective of the cause, he was still cold so went to the bedroom to get a jumper. As he put it on he heard a small thump which seemed to come from outside his front door. He walked swiftly back into the lounge and peered through the front door peephole, a little on edge as crime was not unknown on this block.

There was no-one there. He opened the door a little and felt a rush of warm air. He looked both ways along the corridor – it was empty. Maybe he was hearing things, or maybe it was just kids playing then running away. He closed the door again, feeling very uneasy, and went to open the window, having forgotten once again to do this when he first came in. It was noticeable how much warmer it was outside than in, even though this had not been the case when he had arrived home just 10 minutes previously, and the indoor thermometer still read 21°. Perhaps he was ill - something definitely wasn't right. But what with that and the message, all happening at once, there must be more to it than that.

Back at his desk he realised that the two messages he had found were somewhat contradictory. For her to fall in the sea and then still live seemed unlikely. Especially since she has injured her leg and there is a storm whipping up the waves. Although at least the sea would not be too cold – it had been a long hot summer that year and the sea temperature although chilly would not have been freezing. He would need to mention that. With the tide in she could certainly hit the water not the rocks as he had planned, and she was now a lot further down the cliff with less distance to fall before hitting the water so less chance of injury. He needed to write.

So, charged with a new, burning excitement, he set to work.

Lillian must have briefly passed out as she had the sudden sensation of waking up. She felt cold, wet, weak and her leg hurt. She did not know how long she had been lying there, half clinging, half resting on the precarious ledge. The rain had eased a little but gusts of wind were still buffeting her as though she was on the receiving end of a pillow fight. She did not know how much longer she could hold on. That question was almost immediately answered for her as a sudden tremendous blast of wind came out of nowhere and slammed into the cliff face. It shoved her sideways, loosening her grip and forcing her weight onto a smaller area of rock which instantly gave way.

As the rock disintegrated beneath her, she knew that this was it, the final fall. Her stomach whooped up towards her lungs as she plunged, but she knew to take a deep gulp of air before she punched into the water with a painful and chilling slap. That was followed by a whoosh of suction as she was dragged deep below, then sucked by underwater currents out and away from the cliff face as the wave receded. Miraculously the incoming swirl of water had been high enough to cover the rocks at that point, and her fall avoided them. But her lungs were exploding, she had no air left in her and no control over where she was in the water. Her innate refusal to die was useless against the force of nature that was not allowing her next breath. All she could feel were the harsh, pounding forces propelling her back and forth, and the physical battering of water being meted out prepared her for what she was sure would be the moment of final impact as she was launched back into the rocks.

But then suddenly she surfaced, gasping, spluttering, sucking in air mixed with cold seawater as she bobbed up and down in the dark, rough sea, now riding the spattering waves as they gathered themselves up to attack the cliffs again. Somehow she had survived so far, but she realised she was still far too close to the now exposed hard, chalky rocks and just one swell of crashing water would churn and throw her straight back at them.

With only her arms and one useful leg to propel her, she summoned up every ounce of energy she had and fought frantically to swim further out to sea. She was a strong swimmer and so despite her condition she ploughed furiously into the white laced waves, her arms rotating as fast as the heavy water would allow as she bobbed up and over the crouching, roaring walls of water that were rolling in towards her.

Rising up and over each incoming wave, she began to notice less foam and the motion becoming less violent. After five minutes, and completely exhausted, she turned to look back and realised she had done enough and was far enough from the shore to take a rest. Out here the swell was huge but gentle, heaving her naturally over each arch of the waves without her needing to do anything. She rested by floating on her back for a while, grateful that the long hot summer had ensured that the sea temperature, although still shiveringly cold, was still a little less freezing than normal for *this time of year. This would give her more survival time to find a safe place to get back to shore, but she couldn't hang around as the cold was already starting to bite into her core and numb her limbs. She had to keep moving.*

She resumed swimming, occasionally stopping again to float for a rest, just for a moment, no more than that. She had swallowed sea water and there was a salty tang all the way through her nose and down into her throat which wasn't helping her breathe. But the sea was becoming less choppy and it was clear that she was making progress, thanks in part now to the fact that the storm appeared to be easing and heading inland, and the current seemed to be in her favour.

Soon the rain stopped entirely and she was able to make out more detail on the coastline, although it was too dark now to see if Walter was still there on the cliff top, and she was too far away now for him to be able to hear her. Not that she could waste any energy on shouting. She was shivering badly now, not sure how long she could remain in the water, but hoping that by keeping moving she was helping keep her body temperature up. Her target was a little further east, where the River Cuckmere entered the sea, as she knew there was a beach there and it would be safe to come ashore.

As she swam her mind could not help flashing back to the moment she originally fell from the top of the cliff, when she was with Walter. They had been a little closer to the edge of the cliff than was probably advisable, and Walter had been playfully grabbing hold of her suddenly as people do when they think it would be amusing to give their loved ones a bit of a fright. Lillian thought a stern talking-to had put paid to that game as, along with most recipients of such pranks, she had not greatly appreciated this amusing jape. So as they had hurried back along the top of the cliff – the distant storm clouds that looked so dramatic on the horizon when they set off having charged towards them before they had a chance to escape – the sudden strength and noise of the waves below had prompted them, even though by now it had started raining, to take one last closer look at the dramatic exploding plumes of white spray.

It was at that moment that Walter, for reasons known only to himself, seemed to have decided to give Lillian one last scare by trying to playfully grab and hold on to her. However, as he did this she turned round and took a step towards him. Rather than grabbing her, the quick movement of his arms somehow turned into a push, she stumbled, lost her footing, fell backwards, and suddenly she was gone. That was it.

But as she considered this, she had to ask herself why on earth Walter would do this. He knew she didn't like it, and they were much closer to the cliff edge than they had been before so it was far more dangerous this time, and any close companion would surely have been extremely careful to ensure that there was no risk of their partner falling. The more she thought about it the less it made sense and the more angry she became at Walter's out-of-character stupidity, if that is what it was.

However, she did not have more time to think about this as she could now make out the dull grey of a chalky beach as the high cliffs plunged down to sea level at the mouth of the river. She had to use all her remaining energy to reach that beach.

Twenty minutes later, a bedraggled, injured, exhausted, and very cold Lillian Jones felt her hands touch the pebbles beneath the waves and used the motion of the breaking waves to help haul herself onto the beach and clear of the water.

Her elation at reaching land, surviving that fall, was tempered by how close she felt she was to just giving up. Drained of all energy, and with what was left of her dress clinging to her like cold seaweed, the amplified spasms of violent shivers that coursed through her body were making her teeth chatter as though they were being powered by a motor. What an irony it would be if, having done the hard bit, she died because she could not drag herself off a beach.

She lay just beyond the reach of the waves for a few minutes, recuperating, determined not to slip into unconsciousness, before managing to drag herself into a seated position. She knew she would not be able to put any weight on her left leg even though the pain had now eased a little, so she looked around the beach for any driftwood she could use as a makeshift walking stick. She couldn't see far in the gloom but it appeared to be all stones and small bushes, so it looked as though she would have no choice but to painfully drag herself to a port of safety. The moon suddenly appeared from behind the dispersing clouds, and the soft grey light was just enough to paint in the outline of a small building at the other end of the beach across the bay, with a faint light in the window.

Despite still feeling as though she just wanted to collapse into sleep there on the beach, she knew she could die of hyperthermia if she did that, so she summoned up her last reserves of energy and set off in a crawl across the pebbles and towards the direction of the light.

CHAPTER 9 : JED

Marlo's fingers were starting to ache so he paused to think. Almost without realising it, the flow of his story had taken him to a point where he felt he might be able to accommodate the story behind the unexplained death of the other man whose body was found on the cliffs at around the same time that Lillian had gone missing. His mind was racing with potential story lines now, so he ignored the dull ache in his fingers and continued writing.

Jed Whittleborough was a beachcomber now. He spent his days wandering up and down the coast looking for what he liked to call his 'little treasures'. He was remarkably successful in his searches, but that was unsurprising given his less than rigorous filtering process. An interestingly shaped stick was as likely to end up in his bag as a piece of cheap sea-worn jewellery or a potentially valuable trinket. The inside of his house, therefore, was less recognisably a home and more redolent of a pirate's junkyard. Every available space was either piled or filled with sea-smelling objects of mostly natural origin, almost all of them likely to remain there untouched until time and circumstance removed them or their owner.

Jed was a small man, scrawny but strong from a life of hard manual labouring on building projects that had kept him fed and watered (if beer can be described as water) until his late 40s. Given his lifestyle he had done well to reach 52 but with the added challenge of living by the sea – cold winds and sea spray not being noted for their moisturising properties - he looked a good 15 years older than that when judged by today's standards.

He had been married, to Mary, but after she died in childbirth some twenty years ago (the baby failing to survive her first week) his grief had pushed him into a solitary home life which, in the end, seemed to suit him. Yet a worsening back problem meant that he could no longer easily lift the heavy loads his foremen were demanding without finishing every day in so much pain that he found it hard to sleep, but if he was seen to be slacking there were others ready to take his place.

He lacked qualifications for any non-manual work so if things carried on as they were he could see himself ending up in the workhouse, and no-one wanted to end up there. Then fortune smiled on him for the first time, and at just the right time. His old Uncle Charles died. This in itself was not a cause for celebration, but the consequences were, as the elderly recluse had no immediate relatives and had made no will; some quick genealogical investigations established that Jed was the sole heir to his estate. Given that Jed had not even spoken to his uncle for the previous twenty three years and had all but forgotten about him, this was an unexpected but extremely timely surprise.

Uncle Charles had not been rich, but nor was he poor. When all expenses had been deducted, Jed received an amount sufficient to offer him a way out, but no more. He knew that if his health demanded he give up labouring and he could not find another steady job, he wouldn't be able to keep up rent payments. So he made some enquiries and discovered that even with his inherited money, if he wanted to buy his own place, there wasn't much he could afford if he was to keep some back for bread and water.

It was only when he bumped into Nathaniel, an old labourer colleague, a few weeks later, that a plausible option presented itself. Nathaniel had just done a job for a land owner who had mentioned that he was trying to offload one of his properties for a knock-down price to get him a quick sale. There was a reason that it was a knock-down price - it was on the other side of Seaford, more than twelve miles from Brighton, and it was old, semi-derelict, uninhabited and remote. Previously a fisherman's cottage, it was of thick stone construction to withstand the elements, but barely habitable. It was right next to the beach at the head of the Cuckmere river with only an overgrown track to provide access to it, and the land owner was having trouble finding anyone who would want to live there. Even for fishermen it was too remote now.

Jed was happy in Brighton and had friends there, but he had to weigh that against continuing to pay rent and ending up on the streets when his money ran out, so this seemed to be pretty much the only option he had. And he had always dreamed of living right by the sea so maybe this was the time to do it.

He could afford the cottage, and at least it was a roof over his head. He would have some money left over, and if he lived extremely frugally and maybe found odd jobs here and there, well, it could work. In fact it would have to work, he didn't really have any other options. Mind made up, he went ahead and bought the cottage, then spent the next three years repairing it as best he could whilst using it as a base for his exploration and foraging.

He was struggling, though. He was living mainly off the land but not eating well. He had become thinner and weaker than he was when working, and he was always hungry. With no family or work colleagues to fall back on he missed the building site banter, good conversation, and general interaction with other people, and as a result had become increasingly unhappy and withdrawn. Despite his underlying good nature and kind heart, he found himself cussing and shouting at things far more than he ever used to, accusing inanimate objects of tripping him up when he walked into them.

But in calmer moments he found that talking to himself and his collection of beach sourced objects to be a strangely fulfilling substitution. He had favourite pieces of rescued beach wood, stone or metal that now had personalities and voices of their own, provided by Jed of course.

A smoothly gnarled and whitewashed tree stump by the front door, for example, one of the first and certainly one of the largest pieces of beach furniture dragged back to Jed's abode, always received a greeting when he got home, and responded through Jed, in a rough voice that Jed guessed was how a tree stump would sound, with something along the lines of "all quiet here sir, nothing to report."

On the evening of September 22nd 1886 Jed had seen the storm coming and made sure he was indoors with the doors battened and windows fast. He wasn't taking any chances after what had happened the previous year, when a howler of a wind had taken his front door clean off and blown it half way down the beach. Now he had put on extra hinges and strengthened all the bolts and latches and was confident he would be safe to ride out all but the worst of storms. When this one struck he took an occasional glance outside but was not particularly concerned. "We'll be fine, Stumpy," he noted to his wooden companion before he closed the door, "we'll be fine.

"Aye aye skip," said the tree stump, standing guard.

Marlo hadn't realised he was hungry until he stopped writing. He didn't feel cold any more. It was 8:45pm and dark outside now so he put a ready meal in the microwave – he had stocked up on his way home. He drew the curtains and sat down to eat. Normally he would turn on the TV and watch something while he ate, but his mind was still racing.

He had saved Lillian - in his imagined world she had not drowned as the newspaper had reported all those years ago. But what now? He had been guided by history but now thanks to those messages he was branching away into a new fiction that didn't happen. Or did it? Who was to say that the newspaper didn't get it wrong? What if Lillian had actually survived in the way that he had described and started a new and different life under an assumed name? It seemed unlikely. That kind of thing didn't happen in those days did it?

He looked across at the diary. The diary held the key. Both messages were in there, it had opened itself; it must have more to reveal. Before he went to bed that night he made absolutely sure it was closed.

CHAPTER 10 : GETTING CLOSER

The next morning nothing had changed. The diary was still there, unopened. It was Friday, so once he had got this day's work out of the way he would have more time to focus on what he would do next.

The Help Desk Manager, Mike, was young but professionally mature beyond his years and had risen quickly up the chain for good reason. It had not escaped him that for the last couple of days Marlo was not his usual self and even accounting for any hangover effect on Thursday, his stats were suffering – he wasn't getting through the calls quickly enough and his resolution success rates were lower than they should be. Marlo was normally one of his best performers, so he called him in to his office. Marlo sat down warily.

"Everything ok Marlo? You seem to be in a different world this week."

"Sorry Mike, I'm fine, just had some difficult calls to deal with."

"No more than usual Marlo. There's more to it than that. Now if you're struggling so am I – my overall stats get dragged down. I need you to re-focus, yeah? Normally I can rely on you as one of my best guys. Anything you want to tell me?"

"No, no, it's all good, I've just got a few things going on at the moment outside work but I'll make sure they don't affect my work from now on."

"Ok my friend, I trust you to do that but I want to see the evidence going forward ok?"

Marlo emerged from Mike's office a little shocked – he hadn't realised that the Lillian story had affected his work but clearly he had been thinking about it too much.

So as he travelled home that evening he resolved that he would get everything clear in his head over the weekend. Maybe it had all been an amazing coincidence; perhaps the diary wasn't the magical oracle that he was subconsciously turning it into.

That thought immediately disappeared when he opened the door of his flat. The diary had disappeared.

Everything else was where it was before he left that morning, but the diary which he had left next to the computer was gone. With a fast-rising panic he rushed round the flat checking every surface, just in case he had inadvertently put it down somewhere else without remembering. But there was no sign of it. He then checked every shelf and cupboard in his lounge but still nothing. This was a disaster. That diary was everything to him now, it was the soul and guide he had relied on to complete his book, and who knew what messages it still had to reveal? This was so annoying – he must have put it somewhere different this morning and then instantly forgotten. What an idiot! Unbelievable! No wonder he was a loner. A loner and a loser, the perfect combination. Maybe that was why there was only one letter to differentiate them; in his case they were practically the same thing.

Angry and sad at the same time, he watched a film on TV that night without really taking it in, the computer remaining switched off. But he couldn't stop thinking about the diary - he couldn't continue the story without knowing where it was. Why was he such a numbskull, where had he left it?

He had a shower and went to bed. Before switching off the light he decided to read a chapter or two of the sci-fi thriller he had in his bedside table drawer to take his mind off things and help him get to sleep. He opened the drawer and pulled out the book. But it wasn't his book, it was the diary.

Now he was scared. Someone or something had moved it, had been in his flat - he knew for certain that he had not put it there himself, even he was not so stupid as to move it away from the computer for no reason and put it in a random drawer that he then immediately forgot about.

And this wasn't just a page opening, this was a physical transportation from one room to another, with a drawer being opened and closed. This was serious.

A sudden panic struck him. Perhaps someone had managed to get hold of the key to his flat? He immediately got up, turned all the lights on, took a screwdriver from his 'man-drawer' for self-defence, and with trepidation and extreme care checked every nook and cranny in his apartment. But there was no-one there. He checked the door was locked then quickly grabbed a chair from the lounge and wedged it up against the front door handle, just in case.

He realised he was breathing heavily. This had really shaken him. 'What now, Marlo, what now?' he asked himself. 'Should I call the police?'

No, that would be silly, no crime had been committed. Ok, the diary, the diary. So far, all the answers had been in the diary.

Slowly he edged back into his bedroom, sat gingerly back on the bed and picked up the diary that he had left there. He scanned through every page but without knowing what to look for he would find it difficult to pick out any more messages.

Finally, tired and defeated, he returned the diary to the drawer and turned off the light. His heightened state of anxiety meant that it was some time before he finally dropped off to sleep.

He awoke with a start. He had heard something - a voice, he thought. Eyes instantly wide open and heart racing, he slowly moved his hand under the covers towards the bedside light switch that dangled on the cable hanging down next to his bed. With a click it was on and despite squinting from the sudden light Marlo scanned the room with radar-like speed, tensed to fight off the assailant he felt sure was about to leap on him. But the room was empty.

He sat upright, holding his breath and listening acutely for any unusual noise. But he heard nothing. He glanced at his bedside cabinet. The alarm clock showed 2:21am. And the drawer was slightly ajar. Oh no, he thought, here we go. He knew he had closed it firmly before turning off the light.

His hand went to open the drawer, then hesitated. He felt sure something was going to happen now, but would that be a good thing or a bad thing? Well, he had to find out. He slowly opened the drawer, revealing the diary, now open, this time on March 18th. He quickly pulled it out and read the entry, which began:

Last week I went with Mama to visit Mr Dobson, who is
a purveyor of fine silks and materials and lives close to the
sea in Hove. Papa had heard that he was retiring and was keen
to clear his stock. So today we went back, this time with
Papa as well so we could carry back home all the materials
and other items that we had ordered. We have no horse so to
get home we had to push a cart loaded with boxes, taking turns
every few hundred yards. It was really hard work as
Mama is not well and could not help much, and the roads

are not smooth! But every part of the order did eventually
reach its destination safely and in good condition.
Lots of new material, so a good but tiring day although
oh how my feet ache!

This one was easy, first letters again, but his heart almost stopped when he got to the last five lines and spelled out his own name.... LASTPAGEMARLO. Last page, Marlo. This was the final proof if any was needed. The message was irrefutably directed to him. This was real.

With trembling fingers he turned to the last page. He knew that it was blank, it always had been. But as he reached it he could see through from the previous page that there was now some writing on the other side. He took a deep breath, turned over the page, and saw the words

Nearly there

And as he read those words, the light flickered, the air suddenly became cold, he felt a breeze around his neck, and from somewhere he heard a girl's voice, faint and echoing as though far away yet with noticeable excitement: "Marlo, it's me, Lillian! You're almost there, just....." before it suddenly faded and disappeared.

Then the breeze stopped, the chill went, and everything was quiet and still again. All Marlo could now hear was the pounding of his racing heart. "Lillian! Lillian! Just what?" he exclaimed urgently under his breath, not wanting to wake anyone up, "are you there? Hello? Lillian!" But there was only silence.

He looked at the diary again. The words were still there, in the same style and ink as the rest of the diary. He definitely wasn't still dreaming. It was Lillian, it had to be. He knew his life was about to change, and he was not scared any more. He was suddenly more excited than he had ever been.

CHAPTER 11 : WHAT NOW

Marlo did not go back to sleep. His heart was pounding like a piston engine and his thoughts whirling in multiple directions. He was still sitting upright in his bed, but was desperately tempted to rush outside in the middle of the night and find a poor unfortunate street dweller to whom he could breathlessly describe what had just happened to him. He wanted to tell someone!

But his rational head – which all his life had managed to overrule any rare impulsive tendencies – told him that that would be a pointless exercise as his hyper-excitement would probably come across as dementedness and lead to at best ridicule and at worst get him whisked off to a mental institution. In any case, since his parents had died he had never really had anyone to confide in. He was used to bottling it in, living in his own world. No, this was something he could not share yet, however much he wanted to.

So he started trying to think rationally. He was almost there, whatever that meant. How, and why suddenly now, why not before? What had triggered this breakthrough at 2:21am in the morning? More importantly, what should he do now? He desperately wanted to hear Lillian again, even talk to her, find out what this all meant. How could he get in touch with her again?

To spark this contact, he must have done things that no-one had done before. The diary was obviously key to this, the mere fact that he owned a physical representation of Lillian's thoughts was a good start. But then he had attempted to build on those thoughts and get into her mind.... Perhaps he had succeeded; perhaps he was so attuned to Lillian's state of mind that somehow, the two of them had connected through some unexplainable dimension because he was so aligned with her thoughts when she wrote the diary.

But why had the connection not come before? It had only happened after he had imagined what happened to her on Sept 22nd 1886. Was this because his description in his book of what had happened to her was accurate? The fact that the diary had been giving him clues as to what happened to Lillian did steer him to that conclusion.

However, he did not understand why the diary had given him those clues in the first place, how was that possible and why would it have happened? Too many questions, and too few answers.

Marlo got up, got dressed and turned on his computer. He was too awake to sleep now. He had to do something that would take things forward; Lillian was depending on him. Although what she was depending on him for was something he had not quite worked out yet.

CHAPTER 12 : WALTER AND JED

By the time the first whisper of dawn light began to colour the lower reaches of the night sky and start gently re-painting the city buildings beneath him, Marlo had thought things through. The connection with Lillian where he heard her voice was only fleeting, just long enough for her to say a few words. He did not know where she was or how she was communicating with him but that didn't matter at the moment. He had to not only reproduce the circumstances which enabled her to talk to him, but also make it last longer. Then she could perhaps tell him more, tell him what to do next.

It happened in the early hours of the morning, and at that time he had been asleep. He must have been dreaming, perhaps of Lillian, and although he could not remember the dream, he guessed it might have involved him thinking like her, maybe pretending he was her. Of course this was something he had done many times before while he was writing his book, it was just a natural part of writing a narrative. But the difference this time might have been that he had by chance dreamt something that had perhaps opened some sort of portal or something from the past that had allowed her to somehow move the diary and then write in it while he was dreaming, then briefly speak to him when he woke up and read what she had written.

He shook his head. This was just so far-fetched. For a moment he wondered if the whole episode had been a dream. He re-checked the last page of the diary, but the new words were still there. That was indisputable proof. None of this, though, explained how she had moved the diary earlier when he was at work.

What else, though? The diary itself. All the strange feelings he had experienced, the cold air, the unexplained breezes, the noises, happened while he was close to the diary. As soon as he left the flat and the diary behind, everything was normal again. Well, for him anyway. Back at the flat Lillian – he presumed it had to be her – had somehow moved the diary from his desk to his bedside table, so perhaps this was a sign that the solution was a combination of the physical and the ethereal, and she was trying to make him see how important the physical element – the diary – was.

Perhaps if he actually held the diary while thinking of Lillian, and again tried to imagine what she was doing and feeling at the point he had reached in his story, then the connection would be opened again.

He was at his desk now, his computer switched on. The diary was in front of him. He carefully picked it up, slightly apprehensive now, and thumbed through a few pages, watching the words as they turned from one page to the next, thinking of Lillian writing them all those years ago. Were there any more hidden messages? He tested out a few paragraphs but nothing stood out. It would take too long to go through every entry, so he turned to September 22nd and stopped, leaving the diary open on that blank page. In his story, Lillian was now on the beach, in need of help, trying to reach safety.

He started typing, but with his right hand only. In his left hand, he held tightly onto the diary. That was awkward, so after a while he put the diary on his lap and continued.

As Walter drew closer to the stone dwelling he noticed a light coming from one of the windows. Well that was good, as least there was someone in. He was by now completely wet through, slipping on the muddy path and sodden grass, struggling to see where he was going, and desperate for the rain to stop. With renewed vigour he slithered down the final slope and ran up to the house.

The sudden loud knocking on the door gave Jed such a shock that he almost dropped the cup of hot cocoa he had just brewed up. Who in God's name could be hammering on his door in the middle of a storm out here in the middle of nowhere? Even in good weather and during the day he was rarely troubled by visitors. He got to his feet and unlatched the window next to the door, shouting out of it "What do you want?" A bedraggled head appeared opposite him. "Please sir," shouted Walter back, "my fiancée has just fallen from the cliffs and I need your help!"

"What would you be doing up on the cliffs in this weather?" growled Jed suspiciously.

"We set off for a walk before the storm appeared and were caught in it on our way back, it came across very quickly."

"Where did she fall?"

"About half of the way back to Seaford."

"The cliffs there are not entirely sheer at the top, she may have broken her fall and still be there, have you looked down?" suggested Jed, still a little suspicious that this was a hoax and the man would suddenly try to force his way in.

"Of course I looked down, I saw her, but then she fell further down and out of sight. I tried to save her when she slipped but I was too slow. One minute she was there, the next she was... well, she wasn't." Walter shook his head sadly and drops of water fell from his hair.

Satisfied now that the man's story sounded genuine, Jed closed the window and unlatched the door. "Come in now, come on," he shouted. "Mind, there's not much room."

Walter stumbled in, bowing his head to duck under the door as he was well over half a foot taller than Jed. Jed closed the door against the rain and turned round, his small craggy bearded face now glistening in the flickering candlelight from the spray blown in when he opened the door.

"Now, if she fell from that lower level then there's not much hope for her. From there it is straight into the sea. And in this weather her chances would not be good, that's a rough sea out there."

Walter nodded, then wiped away the water dripping into his eyes. "I agree, I cannot see how Lillian could have survived such a fall. If a rescue attempt is now futile, I would like to ask your kindness sir in keeping an eye on the waves and seeing if her body is washed ashore. I will of course inform the police as to what has happened but I will also give you my name and the address and would be grateful if you could advise me immediately if you should find my fiancée's body."

Jed nodded, although he knew his first port of call would be the police, not Walter. He felt sorry for the man – who he admired for his composure in what must be a time of great personal stress - but was a little surprised at how well he was keeping his emotions in check after what sounded like such a traumatic experience.

But in any case he knew that he would have a job to do as soon as the sun rose tomorrow as there was every chance that the young lady's body could have been pulled by currents and washed onto his beach. It was best if he found the corpse before anyone else did.

He took Walter's details just to be polite, then opened the door to let him out. The rain had now almost stopped.

"Should be an easier walk back," advised Jed, "looks like the storm is heading north and the moon's coming out."

Walter glanced up and nodded. "Thank you again, sir," he said "I'll bid you good day." And he gathered himself to begin once more the slippery climb back up the cliff path to then head back into Seaford and find the police station. Then once they had found the body he would return to Brighton and inform Lillian's family in person. It had to be done.

For the next hour or so Jed sat mulling over the tragedy of a young lady losing her life so close by and prepared himself for what could be an unpleasant beachcombing exercise at first light. Eventually he felt tired enough to rest and so extinguished the light and went to bed.

CHAPTER 13 : LILLIAN AND JED

The building at the end of the beach was only a few hundred yards away but to Lillian it seemed like a hundred miles. Cold and wet, crawling over the pebbles with only one good leg to push on, and with lessening energy, she wasn't sure she could make it. She fixed her gaze on the small, dimly lit window ahead of her, using it as a homing point, making it pull her closer. The bigger it got, the closer she was. Then suddenly it was gone. The light had been extinguished. Momentary despair turned to hope as she realised that this meant someone was definitely there.

She cried out but her voice was weak and the wind against her so she would not be heard until much closer. She closed her eyes, took a deep breath, opened them again, and began once again to drag herself forward.

Jed was awoken by a dull thud, followed by another. He half rose and listened again. Another thud, not as loud but it was there. Quickly he got up. It was coming from the front door. How could this be? Two visitors in one night? And this time it was almost midnight. Perhaps Walter had returned with some news or, heaven forbid, found the body of the young lady.

He grabbed a metal pole that he kept by his bed in case of intruders, stood next to the door, and using a deep gruff voice that he hoped would make himself sound as frightening as possible, shouted "Who is it?" There was a pause, then another thud.

Jed moved quickly to the window, opened it and peered out. In the gloom of the night moon he could just about make out a large white-ish bundle of something on the ground by the front door. 'Strange...' he thought.

He paused momentarily before cautiously and slowly opening the door. The bundle in front of him suddenly moved, causing Jed to leap back and bang his head on a rescued lobster basket hanging from the ceiling.

"Aagh!" he cried.

The bundle replied weakly. "Help me," said a female voice.

Now Jed was not a stupid man. He may not have had an education and he may have spent his working life in a non-academic job but he had plenty of common sense. So he very quickly realised that this was probably the young lady who had been washed into the sea, and mercy of mercies, she was alive. He flung open the door and carefully pulled her inside and up onto a chair.

She was alive, yes, but only just, and it was clear from her half-closed eyes and complete lack of movement that further conversation was at this stage unlikely. She would need food and water and plenty of rest, then he could find out what had happened to her and if she had any other injuries. She was certainly in a bad state, covered in scratches and bruises, wet through, and with her clothes in tatters. He also noticed a very large bruise on her left knee that to the untrained eye did not look good at all.

There was no point in trying to get a message to Walter yet, he was long gone and Jed could not abandon the young lady. He also wanted to determine her side of the story first, as there was something odd about Walter that he just couldn't put his finger on.

He managed to get her to drink some water, then with almost involuntary motions she chewed and swallowed a few mouthfuls of bread before collapsing into sleep. Jed carried her to his bed – no easy job for a small man with a bad back - and fashioned a temporary resting place for himself on the floor.

Marlo realised that he had become lost in the story and been typing for nearly an hour. He looked at the diary. Nothing odd had happened and there had been no sign of a visitation, but then he had really been setting the scene around Lillian rather than describing her own situation, and had got diverted off into describing Walter and Jed's actions rather than those of his heroine. Even so, he noticed that once he had started writing this section the whole storyline just seemed to flow from his imagination without effort and far more easily than usual.

Maybe his current state of high excitement had charged his brain with increased powers of creativity. Or perhaps this is what he had dreamt last night and now his subconscious thoughts were re-living the dream and guiding him as he wrote. He didn't know, and it probably didn't matter as long as the words kept flowing.

It wasn't even time for breakfast yet but he was hungry so made some toast, then resumed his writing.

Lillian slept for 12 hours. When she woke it was slowly and with a pall of lethargy. Through half-open eyes she saw she was in a room with stone walls that were mostly obscured by a vast collection of driftwood and netting, stones, fishing tackle, and other assorted treasures from the sea. Where was she? Was this a dream? Then, with a shock that shook the sleep out of her, she remembered it all. The cliff top, the fall, the cold sea, the long and painful crawl across the pebble beach towards a house with a light. After that she remembered nothing.

So she had made it though, and she was alive. Someone must have found and rescued her. She still felt half dead – she smiled inwardly at the irony – but she was breathing and she was thinking, and after what she had been through she felt that this was a good start. Her leg ached but not with the intense pain of last night, and that apart her main feeling was one of exhaustion, even though she had only just woken up.

She heard footsteps outside. She tried to struggle into a seated position but was so weak that she gave up and resigned herself to waiting for the stranger to arrive. She heard the front door swing open and someone stride in and exclaim "a fine morning, stumpy!" followed by "oh!" as he no doubt remembered he had a visitor. Boots were stamped on the flagstones to loosen some shingle, and the door closed with a clatter. Then it was quiet for a minute or so before there was a gentle knock on the bedroom door as it swung slowly open. A scrawny face peered round, bringing with it a waft of sea air.

Jed wasn't sure what to expect and was somewhat shocked yet delighted to see the young lady looking clearly back at him, sizing him up no doubt. He straightened up and eased slowly into the room, not wanting to frighten her.

"My word, lass, I wasn't sure if you were ever going to re-surface there, in the end I had to go out and find breakfast as there was no sign of you joining me!"

Lillian tried to speak but nothing came out. "Hey now young lady, don't you be exertin' yourself, you rest there for a while until your body catches up with you, then you can talk as much as you like. I'll cook some rabbit and eggs to give you a bit of energy." And with that he disappeared round the corner into a small kitchen area from where the sounds of clinking pots and pans was soon followed by the smell of cooked food, prompting Lillian to suddenly realise how enormously hungry she was.

She had guessed that this was the man who owned the house with the light in the window that she was trying to get to last night, and by the looks of things had succeeded in reaching.

She reflected on the events of the previous evening and soon her mind was a whirl of emotions as she realised the position she was in and the implications of what had happened to her. The incident where Walter accidently pushed her off the cliff still troubled her; something about it wasn't right.

And what about her family? They must be worried sick, but what had Walter told them? As it was now morning and any search party, assuming there was one, would have determined that she was no longer clinging to the cliff side, the natural conclusion would be that she had fallen into the sea and drowned. Her mother and father must be distraught. She must get word to them that she is alive - she could not bear the thought of them suffering unnecessarily.

She slowly propped herself up on her elbows and tried to talk. "Excuse me sir?" Her voice was suddenly stronger than she thought it would be, and as a result within seconds Jed was scurrying back in and crouching down next to her. "Go on," he encouraged gruffly.

"Sir, I must get word to my family that I am alive, they must be frantic with grief."

"Indeed miss, we will do that," replied Jed. Then he thought about it. "Although I've no means of transport and I'm some way from neighbours, so it means a long walk." He looked her in the eyes. "And if I take a message anywhere I want to make sure I can safely leave you on your own, and you must be of a stronger constitution than you are now. Best way of course would be for you to come with me back over the cliff, assuming you live that way of course, so as you can walk in and surprise them yourself - that would be quite something."

Lillian smiled and nodded before pointing out "My family lives in Brighton though. Perhaps that's a little too far to walk in my condition."

"Ah, right then, I'd thought you were in Seaford. Yes, you'd need transport for that, sure enough." Jed scratched his matted beard thoughtfully. When this failed to result in any ideas, he used the edge of the bed to lever himself back up to a standing position and backed towards the door. "I think all this will depend on how you are feeling, you know? Let me just finish the breakfast, then we can talk it all through."

The smell of food was now over-riding her need to talk, so she nodded back at him. "Of course."

The bowl of boiled rabbit and scrambled eggs that Jed placed before her was probably the best food Lillian had ever eaten, this being not necessarily a compliment to the chef for his culinary flair, but more a reflection of her desperation to eat something together with the restorative effect that she knew it would have.

Jed watched her eating ravenously and inwardly smiled at the thought that this was probably the first time in her adult life that she had not cared or worried about the meat juices running down her chin.

"Well, miss," he said once she had finished, "can you now tell me what happened to you? Oh, by the way, my name's Jed, Jed Whittleborough. And although your man Walter mentioned your name I'm darned if I can remember in all the excitement of last night!"

"I'm Lillian Jones.... – wait! You said 'Walter'? When did you talk to Walter?" Lillian asked urgently.

"He came knocking just as the storm was dying last night, he was after help or at least to let us know to look out for your body if it got washed ashore. He didn't stay more than a couple of minutes then he was back off up the cliff path."

"Was he upset?" asked Lillian.

"Well, in a way, I suppose," considered Jed. "He wasn't crying or anything but he looked a bit shaken up. Well, more out of breath I suppose. Why do you ask?"

"I'm not sure....." Lillian hung her head.

"Anyway," resumed Jed, "it is one mighty adventure that you've had last night, are you up to giving me your account of proceedings?"

Although Lillian had never met Jed before, the way he had helped her persuaded her that she could trust him, and she saw no reason not to relay her account of what befell her. This she did from the point that she and Walter set off for their walk right up to where she lay on the beach, saw his light go out and then must have continued to drag herself on and up to his door.

When she had finished Jed blew out his cheeks. "Whew, that is quite a tale!" he exclaimed. "Even in my younger days I am not sure I would have been the equal of you – you are a special lady, that's for sure. There's not many fall from those cliffs and live to recount it, I can tell you. So tell me miss, what is it you would like to do now, shall I go and find a policeman to report the good news of your survival?"

Lillian thought for a moment. "No," she said, "not yet."

Marlo sat back. Why wasn't anything happening? He had already made the connection with Lillian, what did he have to do to get it back? Perhaps he just had to reproduce whatever it was he was dreaming about earlier but this time make it last longer. Then Lillian might be able to tell him exactly what he needed to do. He felt mentally energised, though, as though the writing wouldn't stop, so he continued.

Lillian lay in bed all morning. It was a sunny day and that helped lift her spirits and seemed to aid her recovery. By lunchtime she was ready to get up. Jed, being a gentleman, but also being a gentleman of less than average stature and so similar in size to his guest, felt obliged to loan Lillian a shirt, trousers and jacket, as her shredded dress was even less becoming of a lady than an old man's apparel. He did make her promise to return them when she could, though, as it was a long time since he had been able to afford any new clothes and he needed to keep all those that he had.

The clothes were not a perfect fit but Lillian didn't mind, she was grateful to have something different to wear and although Jed had no mirror, she imagined that she looked rather unusual and dapper in a working man's clothes, even though they were a little pungent. It was a good disguise too should she need it, although she was not sure why she would.

She sat on the bed and tested her weight on her left leg. It actually wasn't too bad. Perhaps it was just a severe bruise with nothing broken. "Mr Whittleborough!" she called, as she could hear him pottering about outside, "can I ask you something?"

"Of course, miss!" he shouted back as he added some more reclaimed firewood to the stack piled up under a shelter he had constructed from large flint stones, "but the name's Jed. What is it?"

"I want to tell someone that I'm alive."

Jed smiled. "You can tell me if you like," he replied.

Lillian laughed, for the first time since yesterday afternoon. "You know what I mean," she said. "I feel strong enough now, after lunch I'm ready to give it a try. I should be able to walk with a bit of help."

And so mid way through the afternoon, the two of them set off up the cliff path, Lillian leaning a little on Jed but managing surprisingly well now that she had some food inside her. She hoped that they would come across some afternoon strollers on this bright fresh afternoon, but as it was Thursday Jed knew that there were unlikely to be many people with the time to be out walking on the cliff top and any encounters were more likely to be with people not there for leisure. He told Lillian as much but she was sure that there would be people around, particularly if word had got out that someone had fallen off the cliff.

As they cleared the first ridge, Jed pointed forwards. "Look!" he said "there's someone, right enough, over on the crest of the next ridge, coming towards us."

Lillian looked up and let out a gasp. "I'm pretty certain that's Walter!" she exclaimed, "or if not it is someone very like him."

The figure was silhouetted against the sky but as it strode towards them and away from the sky down the grassy bank she became more certain. The figure looked up, saw the two of them, and paused. If it was Walter, then he would have been more likely to recognise Jed than Lillian, as the latter was now in men's clothes and not immediately recognisable as a woman.

The figure looked round, checking if there was anyone else close by, then looked back at Jed and Lillian. He set forth again, his stride quickening, possibly having in the same way recognised a resemblance that needed further investigation but unwilling to break into an unnecessary run should he be mistaken.

But Lillian was sure now. "Walter!" she cried, then immediately wished she hadn't. Now he ran, his legs juddering as he bounded down the hillside, his coat billowing behind him.

With 20 yards to go he shouted breathlessly "Lillian, you're alive! How? How in God's name?" He ran up to her and grabbed her, giving her a brief hug, then stood back to look at her.

"You look well, too, considering." He glanced at Jed. "Where did you find her?" he asked, a touch too aggressively.

"Wasn't that way round, sir," replied Jed, "she found me."

"I swam, Walter," Lillian answered his initial question, "I was sucked out in the swell and managed to swim to Cuckmere beach. I crawled to Jed's house." She looked at him carefully, deciding not to stand on ceremony. "Why did you push me off the cliff?"

Walter's eyes widened. "It was an accident," he replied immediately. "You stumbled and I tried to catch you, don't you remember?"

"No, I don't remember stumbling, I just remember turning round, then it felt like a push," she replied, almost as though she was searching for a reaction.

Walter noticed that Jed was looking at him suspiciously now. "Well I can assure you," he said angrily, "that there was no more to it than an accident. Let that be an end to it. Now, you can come with me my dear," and he grabbed Lillian by the arm.

The reply was not what Jed wanted to hear. There was something about Walter's behaviour and the way that he was talking that did not quite ring true, and he could see from Lillian's reaction that she was also taken aback and was not happy that he was manhandling her in a way she had not experienced before.

"Now hold on, sir!" said Jed, bristling slightly and readying himself to intervene, "let the lady be, she's had a real bad time of it and needs rest."

Walter turned to look disparagingly at the smaller man. "This has got nothing to do with you now. Lillian belongs to me, kindly return to your......" he searched for a suitably demeaning description ".... hovel, and leave us alone. Go on, be on your way!"

Jed did not take kindly to being insulted. He also saw the look of anxiety and discomfort on Lillian's face, and knew he could not stand back.

He stepped forward and grabbed Walter's arm. His wiry frame came with a strong grip. "I'm sorry, sir," he said firmly but with some trepidation too, "I can't allow you to do that. The young lady is coming back with me until she is fully recovered. Would that be better for you, miss?"

Lillian nodded wordlessly, fear rising in her breast.

Walter looked at Lillian, then back at Jed. Scanning the horizon he saw that they were alone. Letting go of Lillian, he stood back, pushing Jed's arm away. "Very well. I think I have a solution."

As Walter reached into his inner coat pocket, Jed's surprised realisation that the silver object being withdrawn was a knife came too late for him to make the necessary mental and physical leap from caution to self-preservation. A quick, hard lunge and the knife was embedded in Jed's stomach. Shock turned to fright, then pain, excruciating pain. He sunk to his knees and just managed to wheeze "Why did you.....?" as he fell backwards, convulsed, then lay still, his shirt and jacket rapidly turning crimson red.

Lillian screamed. She looked aghast at Walter, frozen momentarily by the awful enormity of what she had just seen. Then she tried to run. But even *had her left leg been uninjured, she would have struggled to make headway against a man so much taller and faster than she was.*

Within five strides he had grabbed her arm, pulled her roughly to the ground, and was sitting astride her, forcing his hand over her mouth to muffle her screams. "Quiet damn you!" he shouted, "otherwise you will get this too!" He brandished the bloodied knife over her face.

Lillian had no option. Her scream became a whimper. "Don't hurt me, please, don't hurt me!" she pleaded. "Why did you do that to Jed, Walter, why?"

A different Walter to the one she knew looked down at her. He was grinning, seeming to take pleasure in the horrific act he had just committed and the power that he had over his cowering girlfriend.

"I don't have to explain," he replied brusquely, "it just had to be done, the risks were too high. He won't be missed. Now, get up and come over here with me." And he pulled her roughly to her feet.

"But what about our love, Walter, did that mean nothing to you? I loved you!"

"It passed the time," he replied. "But it was a game, my dear Lillian, it was never real, not for me anyway. Now, come on, damn you!"

He started pulling her towards the cliff edge, then stopped, as though thinking. Abruptly, he changed direction and began heading along the path back the way he had come, pulling Lillian behind him. "Come on!"

Now uncertain as to what was going on, Lillian tripped and bumped behind him, keeping up because his grip on her was so tight she had no other option, and as long as they were heading in the right direction, towards Brighton, then there was a small glimmer of hope. "Where are we going?" she whimpered between sobs, "are we going home?"

Walter didn't answer. His face was grim, set like a man heading into battle. After a few minutes he stopped and looked around. Still there were no other people in sight. Lillian longed to see some heads bobbing over the horizon so she could attract their attention. If Walter was going to let her live then screaming now might make him change his mind. But he wouldn't kill her as well, surely? After all they had been through?

The answer wasn't long in coming. Walter seemed satisfied that they had gone far enough, took one last look around, and started dragging Lillian towards the cliff.

Now Lillian could see what was coming. She screamed "help! Somebody help me!" but nothing was going to stop him and there was no-one else within earshot. She was hitting him now with her free arm, as hard as she could, but to no avail. Then she deliberately fell down, so he grabbed her legs and dragged her backwards by the feet, looking over his shoulder as he went.

She grabbed frantically at clumps of grass but they came away in her hands – there was nothing she could do. "Why, Walter, why are you doing this?" she screamed, but Walter said nothing, his jaw clenched as he focused on the effort required to deal with her bucking legs and squirming body.

As he reached the edge he maintained his momentum and suddenly twirled round and flung her, hurling her off the edge. Lillian knew what was coming. She just had time to look down and this time the tide was out; hurtling towards her were rocks, not water.

As Marlo wrote the last word of this last paragraph, the diary on his lap moved a little. Suddenly he felt cold, the breeze was back, this time though it was accompanied by light, almost unnoticeable at first, then rising into a burning intensity so that he had to close his eyes. Then he heard the voice, Lillian's voice: "Marlo, Marlo, you've done it, this is it, it's time, hold on, hold the diary, keep thinking of me!"

He grabbed the diary. It was warm, still moving slightly. He couldn't open his eyes now, the light was so bright. Then he began to feel as though he was moving, and the breeze became stronger. Suddenly his stomach dropped and rose alarmingly as though going through a burst of turbulence on a plane. He no longer felt the chair beneath him. He could hear Lillian again, somewhere in the distance, calling "nearly there, Marlo, nearly there!"

Then there was a kind of a bang, a bit like a fuse blowing, and the blinding light was gone.

CHAPTER 14 : MARLO AND LILLIAN

Slowly Marlo opened his eyes, but wasn't sure that he had because he could see nothing. Everything was white and silent.

"Hello," said a voice behind him. He jumped, turned quickly and there in front of him was a smiling and bright-eyed young girl in a white dress. She had auburn hair, not quite as he had imagined but no less attractive.

"Lillian?" he ventured hesitantly.

"Yes," she said simply, a huge grin on her face. "Marlo, you beautiful person, you have done it. This hardly ever happens you know, but I am so lucky that you have found me, so lucky." And with that she grabbed him and gave him a hug.

Marlo's arms flapped uselessly, unaccustomed as he was to having a young lady hug him but highly appreciative of the experience and reeling slightly at the novelty of being described as a beautiful person. As she stood back he smiled happily at her.

"The pleasure is mine," he said, immediately berating himself for such a lame and formal reply. "I mean, to meet you at last after all this..... I'm just really happy that you are happy, and....." He stopped, realising that he was babbling, and tried unsuccessfully to compose himself. "Sorry. Wow. Oh jeez. You really are Lillian? What.... how did I get here? And where am I? What's..... happening?"

He looked around, relieved that his eyes were evidently still working but unable to pick out any detail in the bright whiteness that surrounded them. A thought suddenly occurred to him. "Am I.....dead?"

Lillian grinned at him. "No, you're definitely not dead. I'll answer your other questions, but let's get comfortable first. You've had a shock. Follow me."

She grabbed his hand. Holding a girl's hand was something Marlo also wasn't used to but he liked it. As he stumbled behind Lillian through the whiteness, unsure of his footing but sure that he was in safe hands, he briefly reflected that she had not seemed disappointed that he was not a chisel-jawed Adonis but had instead appeared genuinely thrilled to see him. He knew from bitter experience though that even encounters with initial promise soon reverted to type and so sternly told himself to forget the soft feminine hand he was holding and concentrate on something far more important - the bizarre situation he found himself in.

After a few minutes Lillian stopped. "Right, you can sit down now," she said.

Marlo looked around. Everything was still white. It looked like they hadn't gone anywhere. He looked beneath and behind him but couldn't see anything. He wasn't really sure why they had moved from where they first met. "What do I sit on?" he asked.

Lillian laughed. "Just sit down and you will find out!"

Expecting to land on his bottom and hear shrill laughter, Marlo cautiously sat down. To his surprise, he found himself seated, although what he was sitting on still wasn't clear as his hands couldn't feel anything. As far as he could tell he was sitting on air.

Lillian sat down opposite him, presumably also on some air. "Welcome to the Midrift," she said.

"The midriff?"

"The Midrift. With a 't'. So called because it is a rift in the fabric of time, and it exists mid-way between consciousness and unconsciousness, so it works in two dimensions. On one side, all the people on Earth who are alive, on the other side, death. So a rift in the middle, as in mid-rift. It sometimes has a bit more of an overlap with the living side than was intended, though; the edges can be slightly fluid, shall we say."

Marlo continued to look puzzled. "But why give it a name that sounds like your stomach? That's what I thought you said at first – midriff." He pointed at his belly in case Lillian was in any doubt about where the stomach area was. "Why not call it something that can't be confused with anything else. Like Limbo or something?"

Lillian shook her head in amusement. "The Midrift was here long before the English invented the current words for parts of the body or came up with their own words for what happens after death. Anyway, lots of words sound like other words so whatever name you give it runs that risk. Then there are the other languages on earth to worry about as well. You are never going to please everyone."

"Fair point," Marlo conceded. He looked around him at this 'midrift', hoping to see something to help him make sense of the situation he found himself in.

Lillian pre-empted his next question. "You won't be able to see anything except white light and nothingness. That is what people on earth assume they will see in this kind of place, so that is what they do see. Only people who have died can see what The Midrift actually looks like, Marlo. You will just have to trust me!"

"So what does it look like to you?"

"Well, it is not like Earth. It is very different. It has colours you have never seen before, and movements and light that is all around you yet inside you as well. It's....it's....." She paused and began to say something, then stopped. "Can we leave that one for now? Let's just say that you can't see what I see, that's all you need to know."

Marlo sighed. "Well this isn't going to be much fun for me then if all I can see is you." Immediately he rolled his eyes, furious with himself and grimacing apologetically. "No, sorry! I've done it again, that's not what I meant. I didn't mean that I didn't..... I do want to see you, it is just that I...well, as you can see, I always say the wrong thing. I'm an idiot when it comes to conversation. Just ignore most of what I say."

It was normally after a faux pas like this that a girl would look uncertain and then start making excuses to go and talk to someone else, but Lillian just said "Shhhh!" and put her finger on his lips, causing him to recoil slightly. Jeez, a girl touched his face, voluntarily, and in a nice way. That hadn't happened before.

"I know what you meant, don't make it worse," she said, and smiled knowingly at him, almost as though she was expecting him to embarrass himself like that. But how would she know?

"Thank you." Marlo half-smiled back, uncertain what to make of her yet still angry with himself and now feeling like a little boy for the way in which he had reacted both with his words and also to her touch. Still a child in an adult's world; he could not escape it. Realising that he needed to start again, he took a deep breath and calmed himself down.

"I have a million questions, or at least I will have when I've thought of them," he said.

"And I have a million answers, but they may not all be what you are expecting to hear." She paused and suddenly grinned at him again. "You would not believe how excited I am, I can't believe you are finally here!"

"Nor can I..." agreed Marlo, with slightly more muted but still cautiously optimistic enthusiasm.

He realised he was staring, but he just couldn't help looking at Lillian. She was less than average height, probably around 5ft 3", but then in Victorian times that might have been more than average. Her face was quite round, her mouth small but with slightly protruding front teeth that made her endearing rather than gawky. She had a medium sized nose rather than the small one he had imagined, but she did have the sunniest of large brown eyes, set quite far apart, that really took your attention. As far as Marlo was concerned, she was beautiful.

Her voice was soft and a little husky but quite high pitched and distinctive. He of all people knew that looks and first impressions weren't everything but boy, she really was incredibly enticing. Even with all that was going on, and with the inside of his head caught up in a sandstorm of bewilderment and confusion, he still felt magnetically drawn towards the girl in front of him.

But the cold sponge of realisation that the feeling would not be mutual almost immediately doused his hopes, as it always did, so he reluctantly but necessarily dragged his thoughts back to focus on the situation he found himself in.

"Ok, let's start off with how did this happen? How did I get here?" he asked, trying to shake off his brief moment of melancholy. "As the first of my million questions, that's quite a heavy one!"

"Heavy?" Lillian looked puzzled.

"Sorry, that's probably a modern colloquialism. Significant, large....."

"Ah right, yes, you could have started on something a little less broad, but to be honest I don't think there is an easy way of answering any of the questions I know you will be wanting to ask. So.... I think I should explain from the beginning, but there is a lot to take in, a lot of concentration required! You will probably end up asking the rest of your questions as I go through the explanation but I'll warn you, it is complicated. Are you ready?"

Marlo nodded at her as though in a trance. "You are beautiful, you know," he heard himself saying. Where did that come from? He would not normally dream of saying that to a girl he had only just met. But then he hadn't really only just met her, he felt he had known her for ages, and all he was doing was completing the jigsaw, stating a fact, wasn't he? That assumed all this was real of course, and even if it was, who was to say that this strange place wasn't just letting him see who he wanted to see, a constructed vision. Maybe the real Lillian on earth had been a beefy lass with a face like a trout. That would be just his luck. Momentary trepidation consumed him as he waited to be slapped down for being so forward.

But Lillian just giggled slightly and looked down. "Gosh, thank you," she said, "I wasn't expecting that. With compliments like that I expect you are quite the ladies' man back on Earth."

"Ha!" spluttered Marlo, "chance would be a fine thing. I think you could safely classify me as the exact opposite of that," then upon realising what he had just said "ah, no, that's not what I meant, I mean, I'm not gay or anything, just not very successful in the lady department unfortunately."

"Why are you not gay?" asked Lillian, "it is a good thing to be happy! Maybe that is why you are not so successful in love?"

"Yes but….ah, sorry, I see what you mean." Marlo started on an explanation. "Gay doesn't mean the same as it used to… the word was quite recently adapted to describe… well… two people of the same…er…." Aware of Victorian sensibilities and feeling that the conversation was going in a direction he did not need to progress, Marlo steered it back on course. "Anyway, it doesn't matter. You were going to tell me how I got here, sorry, I diverted you. I'm ready."

"Good." She briskly took hold of both of his hands and looked intently at him with those doe-like brown eyes. "First, you need to know about this place and why I ended up here. And this does immediately get…. er… 'heavy'. See, I'm learning already."

Marlo smiled, whilst underneath his multitasking brain wrestled with worrying about the situation he was in and simultaneously revelling in the experience of having an attractive girl holding his hands.

"It is hard to know where to start," Lillian began, "so I might jump around a little and miss out important bits so please bear with me. Let's start when people die and so what happened to me."

His attention total, she let go of his hands and placed her own neatly on her lap, as though readying herself to tell a story to a class of primary school children.

"You won't need me to tell you that most people on Earth have a belief or religion that tells them that they, their souls, will pass on to another level, either a good place or a bad place, for example heaven and hell. And guess what?"

Marlo looked expectant. He was about to learn the answer to questions mankind had been asking, and failing to answer, since it had the consciousness to do so. Here he was, the insignificant, puny non-entity that was Marlo Campbell, about to find out.

"They just die," continued Lillian somewhat too brightly, "and that's it. Pouff! It's as simple as that. There's no bothering with souls, spirits, angels, heaven and hell, all those things, they are just unnecessary complications made up by man. Number Five's view....."

"Who is Number Five?" interrupted Marlo.

"Sorry, yes, maybe I should have started with him! He created everything. Although he is not really a 'him' as he has no gender, that is just an Earth thing, something he decided to experiment with. In some places in his empire they don't have sexes at all. In other places he created multiple sexes – I'm not sure how that works, but I suppose he wanted to find out. But I will call him 'him' because the English language was constructed around the concept of there being males and females and also it is less confusing than referring to him as 'it' all the time."

"He could be a she?" pointed out Marlo.

Lillian cocked her head slightly to one side. "I hadn't thought of that. It wouldn't sound right though really, would it - how many of mankind's gods are female?"

"Aphrodite?" suggested Marlo. "There were lots of female Greek gods weren't there?"

Lillian forced a smile. "Alright, yes, there were some, but you get my point. Anyway, Number Five is actually more of a creator and overseer, not a god. Well, not in the sense that humans would think of it, anyway."

Marlo was already finding it hard to take in the enormity of what he was hearing, not least because it was strangely concerning to have it confirmed that someone or something really had designed and created him, along with everyone and everything else. He stayed quiet, but she sensed his unease and laughed.

"Don't look so disquieted! You are probably thinking that a creator must be a god of sorts, and I suppose you could theoretically describe Number Five as such dependent on your definition of the word, but it is all just a big game, Marlo, a big experiment! And when I say big, it is bigger than we could ever imagine, so much bigger. Our world is just one small, tiny speck in Number Five's experimental creations. There are so many other places."

"Other places....?" Marlo was hanging on every word.

"Other worlds, other dimensions. I am sure that science has evolved from when I died and you probably know a lot more about space and what is out there, but you can't know what I know now."

"Oh, I don't know about that," said Marlo slightly smugly, thinking of the astonishing advances in scientific knowledge since 1886 and the space explorations and calculations that had given the human race a rapidly increasing comprehension of the vastness of space.

Lillian gave him the kind of smile a mother gives to a child whose answer is amusingly wrong.

"Number Five is like an inventor, an experimenter. He has millions, billions of projects on the go simultaneously. Out there in his space experiment there are more worlds than you can count, with so many variants of life, all operating in completely different ways, all with their own rules and boundaries."

"So there is life out there – I knew it! I always thought there must be."

"Oh yes. Just too far away for us to know about. And also beyond space too."

"Beyond space?" interrupted Marlo, "what is beyond space?"

"Space as we humans know it is just one part of his domain. There are more 'spaces' elsewhere, lots of dimensions. You can think of it like a beach of sand." Marlo had heard the grain of sand analogy before, but only ever in a theoretical argument. Lillian continued. "Our universe is just one grain of sand, there are billions of others too that he is working on. Our human minds are too small to take it all in."

"What about the Big Bang?" Marlo said slowly, coincidentally not sure if he was taking this all in. "Isn't that how it all started?"

Lillian looked blankly at him. "What do you mean?"

"Sorry, Big Bang……it's what we now term the start of existence. Everything in space is moving outwards and expanding, so it must have originally begun with an explosion from nothing, to explain why everything is moving outwards." Marlo looked hopefully at Lillian, feeling now like a student on his first day at university trying to explain macro-economics to a professor.

"Ah right, well, yes, that is how this particular space experiment started, yes, because it had to start from somewhere. Number Five created that explosion to test a theory, then let it be for a while, then came back to it and started tinkering and creating. He wanted to try out new things, and the Earth and everything that lives on it was one of his experiments amongst all the others that he was working on in this universe and all his others."

"So this really is big…." mused Marlo, "it's kind of… beyond our comprehension to take in." He had a sudden thought. "So who or what created Number Five? And does this mean there are at least four other creators?"

Lillian nodded earnestly. "You are right, yes, Number Five is not alone – there are others like him, all with their own beaches full of sand. They all have free rein to create whatever they want within their own dimensions, probably competing to see who comes up with the most interesting life forms. And perhaps the whole process expands further, with bigger and more powerful creators who created Number Five and his like, so that his empire is just a grain of sand on their beach. But we are not told that when we enter The Midrift, the boundaries of the revelations offered to us are contained within the realm of Number Five's empire only. But that is enough! As you say, it is way beyond what we can take in or need to know. Humans are so, so insignificant Marlo, however important we like to think we are, we are so tiny in his world, if world is the right word. He keeps an eye on us to see how we are doing, makes sure we aren't destroying his work, but he is busy elsewhere as well. When you look outwards and scale everything up, the enormity of what we are a part of is just inconceivable."

"So the answer to what happened before Big Bang and how can something come out of nothing, is that there wasn't nothing there to start with."

"A very inelegant sentence, but yes, effectively."

"But surely even on a larger scale, wherever this Number Five came from before he triggered Big Bang, there must have been a state of 'nothing' originally. Philosophers have been wrestling with this for centuries haven't they?"

"Well, I don't know the answer to that. We aren't told. But why did there have to be 'nothing' in the beginning? Why shouldn't there just always have been 'something'?"

Marlo winced. "My brain hurts."

Lillian laughed. "Well I'm sorry but it is not going to get much rest in the next twenty minutes."

"You said earlier that it was just a big game? Why did you say that?"

"Because it is evolving, that is part of the experiment. If you just take The Earth as one example, Number Five has set it all up as a living entity to see what happens, with guiding rules and ways of doing things. But not everything is perfect, and he knows that. He wants to see what happens. I have to say...." and here she lowered her voice and looked around her as though eavesdroppers lurked in the mist "... he doesn't really care about us as individuals. We are just chess pieces on his board, albeit with a limited intelligence and a free will. So if thousands die in an earthquake, he is more interested in the earthquake and why the earth he created isn't as stable as he might have anticipated. But if humans...." she searched for an example "... sent a man in a balloon up to the moon, say, then he could be very interested in that, because horizons are being expanded and creatures that he created are trying to break out of the world he created for them."

"Oh, we've got a lot further than that," said Marlo almost proudly, even though it had nothing to do with him. It was nice to briefly be the tutor rather than the ignorant school child.

Lillian raised an eyebrow but continued on, seemingly keener at this stage to impart information than listen to tales of the future. "Number Five's game is in creating, watching, perhaps amending or improving, and also enjoying the output, seeing where it goes."

"When has he amended or improved though?" Marlo asked. "Wouldn't we as humans have noticed that? If we had seen that something had changed with no explanation, that would have proved that there must definitely be a superior power, wouldn't it? And that hasn't happened, as far as I know."

"Number Five wasn't happy with dinosaurs, you know, those big terrible lizards. They were impressive, yes, and fun for a while but after millions of years watching them lumbering about he realised that they weren't developing fast enough on their own, he wanted a change. They had become a bit boring. And part of the game was to find an interesting and challenging way to remove them which could then facilitate a re-generation of the planet. So he used an asteroid."

"I guess that was a fun way of doing it from his perspective. He doesn't mess about, does he?"

"Well no, why should he? In the early days he played around with the shapes of the land masses – Madagascar was a case in point as splitting it away from Africa gave him a chance to create a huge isolated island with the right climate for all kinds of experiments that he could set up and leave, then come back to thousands if not millions of years later to see how they were getting on. Humans won't have seen any evidence of Number Five's activities affecting them yet, they haven't been around long enough. And if they start destroying things to a greater degree than he is comfortable with, he might put a stop to it somehow or he might just let them do it to see what happens. He doesn't have to step in if he doesn't want to. That's up to Number Five. It might be interesting at some point though, think what effect that could have on religions!"

"Ah! Religions.....!" Marlo interjected. Being an atheist (except when he required a God to shout at for letting-off-steam purposes) this was a particular point of interest for him. "Most of them are convinced that a supreme being exists, so it turns out they have got that one right, but also that this being is watching their every move and if they follow the guidance of a holy book they will have their reward in the afterlife. But that is just a false comfort."

Lillian nodded. "I'm afraid so."

"So just to confirm then, does Number Five, the creator, if he doesn't care about us I guess he doesn't, well, .. love us?"

Lillian smiled and shook her head. "Think of it like this. If you spent ages making some toy soldiers, and you carefully painted them all and lined them up in a row on a table, you would be very proud of them, wouldn't you? You would look at them every day for a while, perhaps move them around a bit, then maybe create some different environments for them like a battlefield or a castle. Then after a while you would lose interest and go and do something else. You wouldn't love those soldiers, you wouldn't care about each one individually, they were just things that you made. You would still look at them now again and think 'I did that!' but love doesn't really come into it."

It was Marlo's turn to nod. "But humans are different from toy soldiers. We have brains, souls, emotions. We change, we evolve, we breed. We're more interesting than toy soldiers. Well, not all of us I suppose. But anyway, wouldn't a creator have a deeper relationship than that?"

"Well, I agree that my analogy isn't perfect, I was just using it to illustrate the basic point. Certainly Number Five has invested much more time and effort into creating The Earth and everything on it than would be the case for a few toy soldiers, so he's always going to be monitoring how it is getting on and keenly interested in what happens. But this whole thing about a supreme deity personally loving every human being is...well.... it's nonsense, unfortunately. Man wanted to believe that so he did. Number Five can do a lot of things but even he doesn't have the time or ability to be personally watching over millions of people twenty four hours a day. Think how much effort that would need. The more you think about it the more unbelievable it becomes."

"But so many people *do* believe it. And it is billions of people now, not just millions that he would have to be monitoring. But even if religions have got it wrong, this means that atheists were wrong too, doesn't it? There is a creator after all, just not a religious one, as in one who expects mankind to worship him, or listens to their prayers or watches over them individually. So when atheists say 'there is no God, or no proof of a God', then in that sense they are right, because he is not a God, as such, but they are wrong because....oh jeez, I'm confusing myself."

"It's not easy is it? It just shows that as humans we know nothing about things we cannot know about so there has never really been any point guessing. But we still do, and always have done because some innate force of curiosity and hubris compels us to. And we all got it wrong!"

"We don't know what we don't know, basically. But most religions pretend they do, all with different conclusions. It's a mess." Marlo exhaled slowly. "In a way I suppose it was the deists who were closest."

"What's a deist?"

"Someone who believes in a god but not one who looks after us, just one that created everything then went away and left us to get on with it.

Or something like that, anyway." He had recently read The God Delusion by Richard Dawkins and it was described there but he only vaguely remembered the exact definition.

"Well I suppose that's quite close to the truth. But it isn't quite right; Number Five does keep an eye on us, just not all the time."

"But he definitely doesn't love us or look after us individually."

"No."

"Right, ok. Well, that is quite a thing to know isn't it? But...." Marlo decided to play devil's advocate, which would normally be an unwise option when the subject was God but given what he had learned so far he hoped he was on safe ground now "...supposing a different God created Number Five? An even more powerful, loving one that you don't know about, who does actually have the ability to monitor every person on earth?"

"Oh gosh, what a thought! Once you start along that road you have to start thinking about whether there is another creator above that God, and maybe another. It becomes potentially infinite, doesn't it? Then your head might explode if you think too hard about it. All I am saying is that what we are told is that the creator of earth and all the stars we can see is Number Five and he does not behave like any God that humans want to believe in."

"So all those prophets in all those religions who over the years have claimed to be connected to a God?"

"Just men like anyone else. Well, not like anyone else as most were clearly exceptional people and were able to command followings, and for the most part taught good things. But anyone can claim they are connected to God, it's just that none of them can prove it. All those assurances about what God thinks, how he works and so on, it is all a product of their own imaginations. And the tales of miracles and so on are just that – tales. No-one can prove absolutely that they happened, and the documenting of them was usually many decades afterwards anyway."

"That's true," said Marlo, "the different religions can't all be right, therefore by definition most of them are wrong. Or all of them, as it turns out. It's a bit like... we have some countries now where the head of the country, the dictator, claims he has done miraculous things which clearly aren't true, but his followers believe it because they are brainwashed into believing it. If no-one believed him he wouldn't last long, but because he is all-powerful people in that country are brainwashed into accepting what he says as the truth."

"Well there you are," said Lillian. "People can turn into sheep if they follow a charismatic shepherd. Some believe in re-incarnation, for example, don't they, where good or even bad people come back to earth as animals or different people. But what would be the point when Number Five has already set up the process where new creatures are easily created whenever you need one. If you think about it, with the population continually expanding, there would never be enough re-incarnated souls to meet demand, so you would have to create new souls anyway, in which case you might as well not bother with the re-incarnations."

Marlo nodded at what seemed an entirely logical point. "So to summarise then, religions are a waste of time? All the worshipping and praying is redundant?"

"Yes and no. Praying and worshipping is pointless, yes – as I said, Number Five isn't interested in individuals. But religions can give people a code of ethics and a set of principles. Of course these are often enforced by a fear of what could happen to them if they don't adhere, so by believing there is a God watching them and monitoring their actions can make them behave better. That might be a good thing, assuming the author of the principles was himself principled. Beyond that, religions don't really have a point – most people can come up with the same definition of what is right and wrong without needing a religion to tell them. It's common sense that hurting someone is a bad thing, for example, you don't need a book to tell you that. Even people who do feel entitled or able to hurt others are intrinsically aware that what they are doing is not 'good', unless they have some kind of mental problem. All religions are created by man anyway so if the people who wrote the holy books had just listed a set of guidelines instead of all the God stuff that went with it, it would have made things a lot easier. But then that would not provide as much entertainment for Number Five. I imagine he is quite amused by how in this one sphere man has sacrificed logic for faith, and all the consequences that has."

Marlo chuckled knowingly. "You don't know the half of it in terms of how religions have affected the world in the 21st century," he said. That was a conversation for another time. A thought came to him. "Weren't you religious on Earth?"

"Oh yes," she laughed. "Everyone was. Well, most people. We went to church three times a week, said grace before eating, and followed all the traditions. Turns out we didn't need to! If I knew then what I know now...." she trailed off, the memories reminding her of her family and her life in Brighton.

"So you said there is definitely no heaven or hell?" Marlo picked up on her earlier comment, still keen to have this absolutely confirmed.

Lillian straightened herself and looked hard at Marlo to emphasise her sincerity. "Yes, Marlo, no heaven, no hell. Whether you were a good or a bad person on earth you end up in the same place, which is effectively...nowhere! You're just gone, not there any more. If some people want to create these concepts as a deterrent or enticement for their fellow citizens to behave in a certain way, there is no obligation on Number Five to then turn those beliefs into reality. It would be far too much work when you think of all the different afterlife solutions concocted by all the thousands of different religions. Whether there is any truth in their predictions is in any case irrelevant – it would make no difference to how religious people behave on earth because all that matters to them is what they believe, and they, along with everybody else, will never know the truth for as long as they are alive, however much they pretend they do. It is quite entertaining for Number Five though! I don't think he had predicted just how enthusiastically humans would embrace the idea of deities, and how many different ones they would come up with."

Marlo shifted in his seat, even though it wasn't really a seat. "How do you know all this stuff about Number Five?"

"Ah, yes, The Priming." She stood up suddenly and stretched her legs, tossing her hair like a pony flicking a fly. "I should have told you about that, otherwise much of this won't make sense."

For Marlo nothing that was happening to him was making sense anyway, so he just looked up at her and waited for the next revelation.

"It's the first thing that happens to us as transients when we enter the Midrift. It is knowledge, Marlo, full knowledge of how it all works, why we are here, where we go, what it is all about – all the things I have been explaining to you. As we enter this dimension, the restricted earth-view we have down there is discarded and we are infused with the knowledge of, well, everything I am telling you, but in an instant. It is an amazing feeling of enlightenment. And whatever happens to us from that point, except if we die for good of course, we keep that knowledge, as a sort of a reward for what we have been through....."

Lillian trailed off and Marlo saw that she had stopped now and was staring into the distance, as though recalling better times. He waited, then asked cautiously, "What about me? I didn't get primed, if that is the right term...."

"No, because you haven't died yet."

She sat back down again and re-focused her attention on him. "But I can tell you things, and it is up to me how much I tell you. It won't be like receiving the priming yourself because that is like a thunder flash of awakening where you learn everything instantly. All I can do is answer your questions and tell you fragments of what I now know."

"Wait, you said I haven't died *yet*?" Marlo hadn't really focused on what Lillian had said after that.

"Everybody dies, Marlo. I didn't mean anything sinister was going to happen to you in the near future."

Marlo relaxed, but Lillian couldn't resist. "But it might...." she added.

Seeing the smile that accompanied her words, Marlo didn't rise to the bait. "Ok, I guess anything could happen at the end of the day," he reasoned, "and if I die now at least I'm already in the right place."

"This isn't heaven, remember," cautioned Lillian. She brushed aside a loose hair. "Look, I really do need to start from the beginning, in terms of what happened to me personally. I keep getting diverted."

"Sorry, yes, I'll try to keep quiet," said Marlo, knowing full well that he wouldn't.

"You are probably asking yourself exactly why you are here? How can I be looking at you, talking to you... when I am dead? Well, I shall tell you. It's because, well..... a small number of people have a different rule applied to them, and I am one of them."

"Why?" Marlo was hoping his head could handle this.

"It was an experiment introduced by Number Five a few thousand years ago in order to right some wrongs, so to speak. To be honest I am not sure how much longer he will continue with it, but I hope he does at least for a little while! He wanted to see what would happen, but he also wanted to limit and contain it because it does play with time so gets a bit complicated; it introduces some risk to the order of things. It is probably easier if I just explain it, then you will see what I mean. To start with, I am known as a transient, and all transients are held here in the Midrift."

Marlo couldn't help looking around even though he assumed he wouldn't see anyone.

Lillian smiled. "Here, but not here," she said, emphasising the last word with a sweep of her hand. "You can't see them physically. The only reason you can see me like this is because you have made the connection and are seeing me as I was on Earth so that it makes sense to you, but I am not here as a human being, I have no physical needs - I just retain enough of myself to be able to re-enter and become a physical being should I get the opportunity."

Marlo could see that this was not going to be easy. But why would it be? On Earth, the phrase 'the devil is in the detail' might not be the ideal motto for describing how the afterlife worked, but if the two human guiding principles of 'good – go to a good place like heaven; bad – go to a bad place like hell' didn't exist, why should there not be others to take their place? And given that life on Earth was so inordinately complicated and unfathomable, why should the afterlife not reflect some of that complexity? It seemed illogical, now he thought about it, that any form of life after death would necessarily be as straightforward as most religions have painted it or as humans would like it to be. But then again, Lillian had also said that when we die, we just... die. That was pretty short and sweet. Yet although Lillian herself was also pretty short and sweet, what had happened to her clearly wasn't.

Lillian continued, "Anyway, the difference with a transient, compared to normal people, is quite simple really: they died in sudden and unexplained circumstances at the hands of somebody else, and the true cause of their death was never discovered or recorded. Basically, there was an injustice involved that remains unresolved and someone literally got away with murder. Because no-one else on earth knows what really happened, the perpetrator was never punished. That's an unfair anomaly; it is counter to the order and finality with which most human life is processed. You always want to know why someone died, especially if at the hand of another. If you don't, it is unfinished business. Number Five thought it would be interesting to give some of these victims the chance to put this right and restore what is known as Finality. So.....

when an unsolved murder occurs the victim does not die in the same way as other people. They become transients."

"But supposing the murder is then resolved fairly quickly afterwards and the murderer convicted?" asked Marlo. "What happens to the transient then?"

"Ah well, then they do die. We only stay here if our death meets three criteria: it is by the hand of another, the circumstances and motives surrounding the death are not accurately recorded, and the murderer has not been caught or punished. It has to be all three though. If the murder is solved and the killer is identified and dealt with and experiences the punishment they deserve, even if it is a year or two after the event, justice has been done so the transient is removed from the Midrift. Just like that. Dead. Pfoofhhhh!" Lillian broke her hands apart like an exploding puff of smoke.

Marlo looked at her slightly open mouthed. "So let me get this right. If you were murdered, find yourself here in the Midrift – I'm sorry but I still think that's a daft name - then see the murder get solved later and the murderer convicted and punished, you would be immediately vaporised?"

"Ha! Well, not quite that dramatic perhaps but in a sense, yes. That would be it, the end, just as though you had died normally. No more Midrift. So there are plenty of us who are only here briefly, just for the time that it takes for the reason for your murder to be unearthed and killer to be dealt with."

"But I don't understand why it is a good thing to be a transient then. It's just prolonging the agony isn't it? Either you eventually die anyway, if your murder is sorted out back on earth, or you are stuck here for eternity. Unless, oh, I get it, that's why I'm here isn't it?" As soon as he said it he realised that he didn't get it at all.

"Exactly. It all changes if the killer dies without getting discovered, if he gets away with it. No-one knew for certain what Walter did to me, why he did it, or even that it was actually him that did it. He was not brought to book for what he did. You found out, or at least worked it out, and now you are here to put that right, and if you do, we both benefit."

"We do?"

"Yes, shall I tell you how?"

Marlo wanted to just reel in a last strand of thought before moving on. Trying to manage all these ruminatory tangents firing off inside his head was not easy.

"Yes, of course, but just to clarify... in a way, then, it is better for the transient that the murderer is not caught and punished, as then they get to stay in the Midrift and hopefully see someone in the future solve the mystery of their murder? That's weird."

Lillian nodded emphatically. "Yes, it's what every transient prays for. Well, in a manner of speaking! It's the only way to put things right – which is what I am about to tell you about. But remember that for those transients who do stay in the Midrift, there is still only a very small chance of a happy ending. Not even 'very small' actually, more 'miniscule', as once the killer has died then a transient is relying on someone doing what you did for me and solving the mystery well after the event so that justice can be done. "

"Jeez, that's....." Marlo trailed off, muddled thoughts continuing to swamp his brain. Why would justice be done just because he had worked out who killed Lillian and how he did it? He shook his head as though faced with an exam paper for which he had done no revision. "Believe it or not, I'm having a bit of trouble following all this. Why is it so complicated?"

"Those are the rules. Don't worry, you'll soon understand. It's a bit like your first day at a place of work – nothing makes sense initially but after a week it is all second nature and you can't understand why you found it hard to start with."

"It's going to take a week?"

"No, no no. Less than a day, I promise! Although having said that, there's more to the rules, I'm afraid. For example, I forgot to mention, there's a cut-off. If you were over fifty years of age when you were murdered, that's it, I'm afraid, you just die like everyone else. That's what happened to poor old Mr Whittleborough, for example. You've had a decent lifespan. Under fifty, and you pass to the Midrift like I did. We are told it's because Number Five wanted to keep transient numbers down – it was only an experiment and he didn't want the Midrift clogged up with millions of unresolved murder cases, so he set some pretty stringent criteria. It may not seem fair I know but, well, life is like that and so is death."

"What if the killer dies naturally, and just a week later someone solves the case and works out who did it?"

"If the killer dies naturally without being punished or knowing he has been caught, then that is not justice, so if someone solves the crime a week later that would be good news for the transient. Very good actually - it would mean that all the three criteria have been met, and there is now a chance that the person who worked it all out could be in the same position as you are now, and the transient would not have had to spend years and years waiting in the Midrift like I have."

"Sorry...." ventured Marlo politely but knowing it wasn't his fault.

Lillian laughed. "Don't be! Years and years is still a finite amount, so much better than not at all. Anyway, I think it is time that I now told you what that position is that you are in."

CHAPTER 15 : TIM

Tim Jenkins sat back, stretched, and absent-mindedly scratched the back of his neck. His brain was starting to hurt. Why hadn't he thought this through before he started writing and getting sucked into the storyline that emerged as he wrote? How would he finish explaining the rules around transients without making it sound totally implausible? It was already getting really complicated and the reader's brain would probably be aching as much as his was.

The 'story within a story' concept using Marlo seemed to be working well, but he had written himself into a bit of a corner now. Perhaps he should have gone on one of those writing courses where they told you how to map out your storyline, flesh out all the characters, ensure you have a beginning, a middle and an end, all that stuff, and do that before you even start. But, somewhat surprisingly for him given the renown he had enjoyed at work for his obsession with studiously detailed planning, he couldn't be bothered with that. He just wanted to write, let it all flow as he went along, and maybe now he was coming a bit unstuck.

Rumpling his thinning hair distractedly, he tried to think how best to answer those million questions that he himself had engineered Marlo to start asking. He looked down at his large teak desk on which his old Amstrad word processor stood. A cold cup of tea stared back at him. Damn, he thought, forgot to drink it again.

Before getting up he adjusted his position in the chair to help ease the 'sitting still' aches he was suddenly aware of, then slowly raised himself up, cursing the spreading paunch that was slowing his progress, and the process of ageing that made everything harder than it used to be. As he stood up a soft crack suddenly came from one of his knees, accompanied by a quick shot of mild pain. "Ow!" he exclaimed loudly, before hobbling towards the kitchen holding the cold cup of tea.

"You all right, love?" he heard Liz call from upstairs.

"Just my knee again!" he called up wearily, "damned thing, always cracking these days. Badly designed piece of engineering if you ask me."

But no-one did, and the silence from upstairs as Liz continued with her dusting told Tim that that particular conversation would go no further. It was funny that as you aged, the threshold for eliciting partner sympathy seemed to rise as each party compared the ills of the other with their own in order to judge whether a kind word of consolation was merited.

He looked at the kettle and wondered if it was worth making another cup of tea, and if he did, whether he would remember to drink it. No, he sighed, probably not. So he poured the cold tea down the sink, rinsed the cup, and put it on the draining rack. The cup looked clean enough for re-use to him, as it always did. He knew that as soon as Liz saw it though, it would be quickly transferred to the dishwasher accompanied by a loud tut. One day she would fail to notice it and he would use it for his next cup of tea, then exclaim triumphantly that it hadn't killed him so his point was proved. It still wouldn't win him the argument though.

He shuffled back into his study, eased himself back down into his faithful Victorian writing chair, and stared at the screen in front of him.

He had looked forward to writing this book when he retired, as he never seemed to have time when he was managing his small government department. Always too much happening, too many people to please and too many emails, and with all those cutbacks and changes of political direction it never got any easier. Every time you thought you were getting somewhere, the rug was pulled from under your feet.

Thank goodness he got out when he did, he reflected. He certainly didn't envy his successor. What was his name now? James somebody, that was it. Can't remember his surname, not that it matters any more. He had been a nice enough chap, transferred in from a different portfolio as part of the reshuffle caused by Tim's retirement, but if only he knew what he was letting himself in for. He'd soon find out, he thought, then realised that as ten years had passed it was highly likely that James had already found out otherwise he really would have been in trouble, and equally likely that James had long ago been replaced by someone else anyway.

He wondered how his successors were coping with the latest round of drastic austerity measures and budget cutbacks that were sweeping through the corridors of power like a tsunami of iced water, no doubt sending chills of despair through all department heads as they realised the potential implications. But almost everyone who reached department head was savvy enough to pull some political levers and steer a course through whatever watery graves were placed all around them.

He liked to think that he had been just such a person, someone able to keep those above him convinced that he was implementing their vague yet politically eye-catching instructions to the letter, yet at the same time paying *enough attention to the details of reality to ensure that nothing that really mattered was affected by those orders.*

Look at me now, though, he thought, how things have changed. No-one left in my department would probably even remember me. All the work I did there has probably been superseded and replaced. Now, nothing in my in-tray. I haven't even got an in-tray. Just a word processor in front of me, bought all those years ago when they were just coming out but still perfectly serviceable for the purpose of processing words, which was what he was doing with it now.

Having spent much of his early working life dictating to typists and secretaries, the advent of word processors and computers, where he was suddenly supposed to write down everything that came out of his head himself, using a machine he didn't understand, and a skill – typing – that he did not have, seemed to him to be a backward step and a real waste of the money they were paying him to think important thoughts and make vital decisions.

But once he realised that even he was not going to stop the march of progress and technological innovation, he bought one of the earliest and bulkiest Amstrad word processors and resigned himself to learning at home how to type a bit faster than the 5 misspelled words a minute he had achieved when first confronted with a keyboard at work.

He smiled ruefully at the thought that even now he had barely doubled his typing speed since then, but writing this damned book might at least get him some payback on all that money he had wasted on this confounded contraption. And he had to admit, it was a lot easier to correct your mistakes than paper, given that the days of having a secretary or a typing pool to do that for you were long past.

He re-focused on the screen. Now, where was he? Oh yes, Lillian.....

CHAPTER 16 : THE EXPLANATION

"As you know, I was killed," said Lillian, "and that is not a sentence I thought I would ever be saying to anyone." She paused, unsure as to whether what she had just said was mildly amusing or overwhelmingly sad, or both.

"So now I am a transient. I said that we have a chance to put things right, to ensure that the true cause of my death becomes known and documented on Earth, and all consequences of that amendment are progressed to a conclusion that brings some justice. So, this is the thing. The incentive for me is that, if successful, I get another go. I get to go back to earth and finish my life. It's a big incentive."

Marlo's eyes widened and he blinked. "Wow. Really? You can come back to life? Jeez. You're right, that's a hell of an incentive. That's brilliant!" Then he had a thought.

"But how would that work? Ok, the true cause of your death might have been unknown, but you still did actually die, so if you went back you would either have to rise from the dead somehow or maybe alter time and go back to before you died, depending on when that was. Wouldn't you?"

"Not quite. You are close though. The Lillian Jones my friends and family knew died on Sept 23rd 1886, and that won't change. You can't bring justice to a murderer if he hasn't murdered anyone yet." Her voice became a little unsteady and there was a sudden moistness in her eyes. "Sorry."

She flapped her hands in front of her eyes in the way only women do, and Marlo wondered how long ago this affectation had actually started. He assumed the expression most men adopt in these situations in order to indicate their empathy and compassion: one of confused puzzlement, masking a sense of general uselessness.

After a pause, she continued. "If I complete my life, it will be somewhere else. It will be in a different time zone – that of the person who saves me. I would come back to Earth with you, Marlo. I would still be the same person inside, just living in a different time, outwardly as a different person. It is less disruptive to the fabric of order and consequence, and also, it sounds quite fun, like a reward for going through all of this, although....... of course..... I would not see my family again." She looked down, her hair falling forward, partly covering her face. "Anyway, those are the rules."

Marlo hardly registered that Lillian was now remembering the family she would never see again. Instead a surge of hope fuelled adrenalin was now rampaging through him; he couldn't believe his luck. Lillian could eventually be returning with him? Blimey.

He hoped his face was not betraying his feelings of sudden exaltation and so tried hard to make a muted 'well, what a pleasant surprise' expression instead of the all-out big giveaway grin of delight that he wanted to. All the questions about how they would explain the sudden appearance of someone in his world who had not been there before could be explored later. There were answers to everything, he was discovering – all in good time.

But he needed to at least say something. "That's, well, how good is that, that you could come back with me? It would be brilliant, actually. It would, wouldn't it, do you not think so? Or do you think.... Well, what do you think?"

As usual when faced with any subject that involved him and the possible proximity of a girl, his unstructured words had jumbled out of his mouth like a flurry of bats coming out of a cave.

Thankfully Lillian just looked up and smiled, rather serenely. "I would look forward to it very much," she reassured him, "but there is a lot to do first. Let's not get ahead of ourselves."

"No, right, yes. Fair point." Lillian's calm response had thrown a light but effective blanket over his emotions, and so he returned his focus to the present. "So what is it exactly we have to do, to get you to come home with me?"

"Well, let's start with how you got here, then it will all make more sense."

"Yeah, you're right, that was the first question I asked, wasn't it? We got kind of diverted."

"We did. So here we go. As a transient I have been waiting a long time, such a long time now, in the hope that I would be one of the lucky ones. Transients can only stay in the Midrift for a period of three hundred earth years after their killer dies, after which we are removed and cease to exist like everyone else who dies. If we have not made a connection before our remaining three hundred years is up, that's it. No going back, no resolution of our situation when we left Earth, and all that time waiting here would have been in vain."

"Now that would be a real bummer," mused Marlo.

"A what?"

"A bum.... er, sorry, I mean a real disappointment, really frustrating. In fact, worse than that."

"Yes, and I was already about half way through my time period when you found my diary. As a general rule, as time goes on it becomes increasingly likely that the descendants of the victim or anyone else for that matter would have moved on to other things and no longer be concerned about the mysterious death in their family that happened so long ago, and there would be no sign or likelihood of anyone ever speaking the deceased's name again. So I can see why it makes sense to set the time limit. Of course although every transient is desperate to make a connection to someone on the living Earth who can help them, they are not allowed to directly initiate that connection, it has to be done from Earth. I think that if you hadn't started researching me when you did, I probably did not have long left before that diary got lost or thrown in the rubbish and all records of me would have been lost."

Marlo had rarely felt so self-satisfied. "I am so, so pleased I found it."

Lillian nodded happily then continued. "It was lucky you did, because to get the full connection that you and I have just experienced, there are more rules – they are called the Transient Conditions - and they are not easy ones to match. The diary was part of them."

Marlo jumped in. "Why not, though? Why aren't they easy? When Number Five made the rules he didn't have to make them hard, did he? Surely if they were easier it would be beneficial for everyone?"

"Good question," replied Lillian. "I have asked myself the same thing. But when you think about it, how can every rule be perfect to everyone? Who says a rule is good or bad? Nothing in the way we exist is necessarily clear and straightforward and easy – Earth is just the same. Why do humans not all like the same food? That would be easier, wouldn't it?"

"Well I suppose it's because everyone has different tastes, because they all have different DNA....."

"Different what?"

"DNA. It's……it's…..deoxy….something. Well, perhaps I should go through that that another time, it's very complex." Marlo made a mental note not to refer to things he couldn't properly explain until he was back in the world of the internet.

Lillian raised one eyebrow but continued as though he hadn't interrupted. "Why do humans all have to live to different ages, why not just have a pre-determined lifespan so you can plan everything more easily? Why does the hair on our heads never stop growing so we have to waste so much time cutting it? Why have different weather all over the world, why not have the same climate everywhere? Why are there so many illnesses, can't everyone just be fit and healthy? Why do we need so many different types of animal? Why does….."

"Yes, but they are not rules, as such. Are they? They are just things that, well, happen. Aren't they?"

Lillian gave a hint of a smile. "You don't sound confident in your argument!"

"Well, I might be once you have tried to answer my question."

"Touché. Ok, I agree those are not examples of hard and fast rules, but they are boundaries, things we cannot change easily. The fact that man will not live much more than 115 years at most is a boundary, for example. Someone or something had to set those boundaries, correct?"

"I suppose……"

"And boundaries are set by rules that are a just a pre-defined way of doing things, with consequences if you don't. So man knows if he jumps off a tall building, he will hit the ground hard and probably die. The rule – don't do it or you will hurt yourself - defines the action and consequence of jumping off, the boundary is the height – which in this case is anything higher than is safe - and the consequence is that you probably die or at least get injured."

"So gravity is really the rule there, isn't it? But then gravity is a law, not a rule." Marlo scratched his ear in the way that footballers do when being interviewed. "Ok, not for the first time I'm officially confused."

"Well, mankind can call it a law if they want. As far as Number Five is concerned, it is a rule. Just with a bit of flexibility around it, whereas the rules he created for transients were more precise. Remember also that when he first created the earth it was like cooking a stew – he set out all the ingredients, mixed them together, then left to simmer, coming back periodically to see how it was all getting on and perhaps tinkering a little. So some of the natural rules just developed on their own accord through evolution, as Mr Darwin called it, and there's no reason why they shouldn't adapt and change again in the future. The transient thing is quite recent, and this time I think he wanted more control, to engineer the entertainment it would give him."

"How recent?"

"Just a few thousand years. Intelligent man hasn't been around for that long so it wouldn't have worked before that."

Marlo still wasn't convinced. "Well I think he's being harsh. Although I suppose tough rules mean a greater challenge, fewer successes and so more satisfaction all round when you prevail. More fun for Number Five. Yeah, I get that. I suppose it's not too different to some of the dumb rules that mankind comes up with. Like languages that define inanimate objects as male or female. Daft, just makes everything harder. But to someone it must have made sense at the time."

"Yes, and we are not here to challenge any rules that Number Five set in motion unless there is anything we can do about them or there is an obvious big flaw somewhere. All we know is that all of this is just part of a big game being played by an entity or entities of which Number Five is one, and those players, if you like, can make and change the rules in their own domains in whatever way they wish, whether they are logical and sensible or not. For us, the rules defining what constitutes a connection are made clear to all transients when they first arrive, and we are not expected to challenge them, although I suspect that if hardly anyone is making any connections they may be revised, or indeed the whole idea scrapped. But it does unfortunately make it very rare for a connection to succeed. Although there have been thousands and thousands of transients created over the years, we are told that only twenty three of them successfully made a connection, although we don't know how many actually ended up getting their lives back. That is why I am so lucky, and incredibly happy, that you made it through."

"Twenty three in thousands of years, that isn't many. So what were the criteria for a successful connection then?" asked Marlo, "I must have been close a few times before now, especially last night when I heard your voice but then you went again."

"Yes, that was a shame, you were so close, I almost pulled you in. You had vaguely dreamt the answer and so made a weak connection but because your thoughts were wandering I couldn't hold onto it, and anyway I wasn't really allowed to. Dreams don't count, they just help sometimes if you wake up remembering them. I was being a bit naughty. I was so devastated, I thought I... we... had done it but I was being premature. Anyway, enough of that."

She shook her head a little and Marlo watched the soft waves of her hair wriggle. It fascinated him. Here was a beautiful girl, right up close, staring at him, not looking to get away, in fact positively eager to talk to him. This was weird, but so nice. Surely it wasn't real, he must still be dreaming. He surreptitiously dug a fingernail hard into his leg and winced. Ow, that certainly did hurt. That would have woken him up but he was definitely still here. That's good.

Lillian interrupted his musings. "Why are you pulling faces, Marlo?"

"Was I? Oh, sorry, I'm just, er, well, no reason really." This was silly, why was he hiding the truth? Why not just tell her? Maintaining this damned Mask Of Sensibility all the time never seemed to do him any favours. "Actually I was pinching myself, just to check, you know, that I wasn't...."

"... dreaming." Lillian completed his sentence for him. "Yes, I can see why you might. But I can assure you that you are not. This is real." She opened her eyes wide for emphasis.

"Good, I'm glad. Sorry, you were saying...."

"Yes, I was going to clarify the two key criteria for making a connection. First, as I was intimating before, a living person has to work out the true cause of death of the transient, and who killed them. That isn't as easy as it sounds if it is an old unsolved crime. Usually it is historians, students, or relatives whose casual or determined research unwittingly draws them into the possibility of a connection, and when we are talking about a case that is many decades or generations old with no recorded evidence, often there is guesswork involved. What made you so special and this case so unusual is that not only were you looking at a case from so long ago, you also had no real evidence at all yet you still came to the right conclusion that I had been killed by Walter throwing me off the cliff a second time after surviving the first fall. When I first entered the Midrift I really did think that it was a waste of time as no-one would figure out my death in a thousand years, let alone a hundred, but you did it!"

Marlo tried hard to mask a little frisson of hubris.

"Secondly, and this is really why there are so few connections, there has to be a physical item which connects the transient and the living person, so that the living person can touch and hold something that the transient held or owned when they were alive, and which can act as a sort of portal, an enabler. In our case it was the diary. This is really important because it allows the transient to sense what is going on, and also gives them something to work with, to use to give clues, as I did for you. The closer you are to the physical item, the better the chances of a connection. The diary was perfect because it contains words and I worked out that I could use that to send messages, although I may have been pushing my luck a little. If it was just a hat or something it offers fewer opportunities. You also need that physical item later on, as I will explain later."

"That's amazing," mumbled Marlo, "but I'm still not sure how I managed to get your story right. I mean, it was either an extraordinary coincidence or I had some unseen guidance. Sometime I felt like the story was writing itself."

"Nonsense!" said Lillian hurriedly, "it was all your own doing, I just gave you a few signs that you were on the right track, that's all. And don't forget that although you probably can't remember dreaming that Walter killed me and Jed, that may still have been in your subconscious when you sat down to write." She looked away as though suddenly distracted by an interesting piece of white mist. "Let's not dwell on that."

Marlo nodded slowly. That kind of made sense, although he was starting to realise that the thoughts and ideas that Lillian had been somehow breathing into his dreams as he got closer to the connection had been more extensive than he had thought, and perhaps she was worried that a closer look from above at the assistance she had managed to give might not be welcome.

Her composure regained, Lillian continued: "As I said, that final piece of the jigsaw can happen in dreams, but that is not enough on its own. The dream sows the idea, then when you awake hopefully you will have the solution in your head and come to the right conscious decision. That's why I couldn't pull you in then, but I found I could get through to you, even if it was only for a few seconds. That was a mix of joy and frustration!"

Marlo remembered the range of emotions that experience had given him and considered that shock had probably been the overriding sensation for him.

"Well," he said, "those are two pretty tricky requirements, no wonder hardly any connections are made. So I guess it was you who moved the diary to my bedside cabinet so that it was closer to me when I was dreaming?" he asked, "how did you do that?"

"Soon after you started writing about me, Marlo, I started receiving little thoughts and messages via the diary – a transient can see and feel fragments of things that are happening in and around the physical objects that were connected to them in life. It's all part of the overlap between the Midrift and the living world through these items. I can't explain how excited I was when those first thoughts started coming through - to know that someone down there, after all this time, had found me, was looking for answers, it was the best feeling you can imagine. But as a transient you can't really see anything. I could not open up some window in the clouds and look down at what you were doing."

Marlo breathed a secret sigh of relief. There were certain things that he was very glad Lillian had not been able to see him doing.

"Initially all I could do was wait and hope. But as you got closer, as you discovered more and got closer to the truth, I could give you some signs that you were on the right track. I could start to use the diary as my gateway into your living world, just enough to push you on. You might have noticed the occasional physical thing like noises and the air getting colder but we are limited in what we can do – I was trying everything to make you realise that it was worth persevering, that something strange was going on, even if I may have been stretching the rules a little on occasions. The diary was the physical gateway I needed, the physical thing that is the connection and enables a transient to break into your environment, reach out and generate the signs of encouragement that could help. I was trying things that maybe I should not have been able to do, but I was desperate and if I could find a little loophole somewhere why wouldn't I try to use it? That's what most transients do. It's not my fault if Number Five hasn't thought of everything. Or maybe he has, and he is letting us use our initiatives a bit. Moving the diary was not easy, it took me a while to get the hang of that. Some transients are much better at that kind of thing."

"What, moving things? Like poltergeists, you mean?"

"Any time a living person witnesses something moving, flying across the room – anything that defies the laws of physics – it will be a transient who has a link to a physical item close by and is trying to trigger someone to look into the paranormal, perhaps discover an unexplained death, and then investigate it. So it is self-interest really."

Marlo's mouth was open once again. So this explained poltergeists. "All poltergeists are transients then, desperately trying to get someone to realise that there is someone 'on the other side' trying to contact them, so that with a bit of luck they will do what I did and....... right, I see that now. But it isn't a very smart way of persuading them, scaring them out of their wits, is it?"

"It's all we have!" laughed Lillian. "I didn't scare you too much did I? The fact that we are constrained in what we can do is all part of the game that Number Five constructed, just to make it more challenging. If we transients could just communicate directly with living people, as easily as you and I are talking now, while still here in the Midrift, it could cause chaos. Think of the implications. Talking is most definitely not allowed. So we have to somehow find the balance between scaring you and persuading you that something needs investigating."

"But you talked to me at the end, before I came here to the Midrift?"

"Only once you had solved the mystery of my murder and were about to be pulled out of your world and into mine. That is alright."

"But I thought I heard you before that as well. You know, when I saw the 'nearly there' message in the diary last night. I heard your voice, I'm sure I did. Only faintly, but.... or did I dream it?"

Lillian looked sheepish. "Ah, well, yes, that sort of, well, it shouldn't really have happened. I managed to get through before I should have done. You were 95% there and although strictly speaking you needed to be 100% there, I was so excited that I tried calling out to you, and somehow you must have heard me. I suppose I was a bit lucky with that. I might have ruined things, but it seems I got away with it. As you know, not every rule or law works perfectly and if it can be flexed, shall we say, then at some point the boundaries will be tested either deliberately or unwittingly, and small holes will be found. Seems I found one!"

"Naughty girl!" Marlo smiled, immediately wishing he hadn't said that, given the slightly raunchy connotations. "Sorry, I didn't mean to say that, it wasn't meant to be rude."

"No offence taken," Lillian grinned back, "and you are right, I was a bad girl and I got away with it."

Marlo liked it when she said that but knew he shouldn't. "So if transients can't talk directly to living humans and have to send signs instead, what about ghosts in general? When people on Earth think they have seen ghosts, that's different isn't it? Poltergeists you don't see, they just move things. Ghosts are usually in the image of a person, apparitions that appear silently in front of people. You know, white sheets and going 'wooo', although I think that is more cartoons than reality. Scooby-Do stuff."

"Scooby who?"

"Scooby-Do! Which...you....would....know nothing about. Sorry. He's a dog who helps to catch ghosts. Well, caretakers who dress up as ghosts, usually. But he's not real."

Lillian adopted a puzzled half smile. "A dog who isn't real who catches ghosts who are caretakers? Are you mad?"

"Probably, but this is a kid's TV programme."

He wasn't surprised to see Lillian's "... and this helps me?" expression, followed by "You might as well be talking a different language, I'm afraid. I didn't understand any of that."

Marlo grimaced slightly. "No, sorry, I suppose you wouldn't. Probably best explained another time. Anyway, these kinds of non-poltergeist ghosts can't be transients as well, surely?"

"You're right, transients can't usually come down to earth and present a physical representation of themselves like that. You can rule out most of the reported ghost experiences as they are just people either pretending, or faking, or genuinely mistaking something perfectly natural for a ghostly effect."

She paused, as though unsure as to whether she should carry on. "But, sometimes, just occasionally, the system has a bit of a hiccup and people see things they shouldn't. A face or something. That is where a transient has got through, found a loophole in the overlap. Number Five didn't design it that way; I suppose it is just like anything on earth, you can't do everything perfectly all the time. And transients are ex-people, and people are crafty, they'll look for advantage, especially if the stakes are high."

"Wow. That would explain a lot. So there are no ghosts, as such, but there are some ghostly happenings caused by transient souls trapped in a waiting game. Waiting to be rescued, effectively. But most people who claim to have seen ghosts usually won't have done, and there must be some other explanation. But if they do experience genuinely strange things happening, then it might be that they may have come into contact with a transient trying to get them to investigate the past. Right, I think I've got it." A thought suddenly struck him.

"What about a haunted house? There's usually a ghost there who won't leave and lots of people might experience supernatural phenomena there. How does that work?"

"There could be one or many personal possessions in the house which a transient has a connection to, so anyone who goes into that house could be a potential resolver. You could see why a transient would want to attract their attention."

A look of realisation spread across Marlo's face. "So that would explain why most haunted houses are old, often large too. Far more likely that there are still old things and possessions inside them, so the connection to the past is still there."

"Exactly!" agreed Lillian. "The older the house, the more chance of an old painting or piece of crockery, a diary hidden under the floorboards, or anything that was directly owned and used by the transient. And lots of evil deeds have probably happened in those big old houses with lots of secret killings."

"Ha, yes, you see it all the time in crime dramas. So the ghosts, sorry, transients, try to give signs to people, either by moving things, making noises, or changing the atmosphere with cold chills, that kind of thing..."

"Yes, I did some of those, didn't I?" An apologetic smirk played around her lips. "I do also wonder if some of my fellow transients go even further than I did and overdo it a bit with the moving things and frightening the living. Which they shouldn't of course. But if you were given the power to make objects move or create strange noises under certain conditions, wouldn't you perhaps sometimes try to bend the rules a little, just to see what happens? There are thousands and thousands of transients; I suppose not all of them were model citizens when they were alive. And as they retain their personalities, some of them retain their, well, abilities to make mischief. Particularly if they think there is no great chance of their murder being investigated, they think 'what have I got to lose?'"

"Aren't they punished?"

"I really don't know, and I never wanted to be the one to find out, but I think it is a test. This is just my theory, but I wouldn't be surprised if significant transgressions are punished. That's why I was so careful, and tried not to overstep any boundaries. Well, not too much."

"And the messages? When did you make sure that the first and last letters of those particular diary entries spelled out a message?"

"Just before you read them," said Lillian. "I wrote that diary, they were my words Marlo, so I couldn't see why I shouldn't be allowed to move a few words around such that you might not notice the changes but they now held a hidden message. I really didn't think you would spot them but you did."

"But how is that even physically possible? You can't rub out ink and rewrite it."

"Just like you can't be sucked out of your home and end up in the Midrift talking to me?"

Marlo acknowledged his defeat and scratched the back of his neck despite not needing to. "Well, yeah, just like that. Ok, so the laws of physics I'm used to are slightly different up here."

Lillian grinned. "Indeed they are. Then I chanced my luck last night by trying to add some more of my own words on the last page – I wasn't sure that this would work or I would be allowed to do it but, well, you saw the result. I was just getting so desperate and you were so close, so I asked if I could do that. I think I was allowed to at that stage because Number Five might have been trying to chivvy things on a little bit. He may neglect Earth a little occasionally but if he hears that something interesting is developing within his little transient experiment, he comes and has a look, and if he is enjoying what he is seeing then he might just agree to any request from FiveTwo to... assist a little bit, just to move things along. That's what I found anyway...."

"What?" interrupted Marlo. "FiveTwo? Who's he?" He looked around quickly, concerned that they might not be alone and a huge dark figure with a big stick could loom out of the mist at any moment. "That sounds like someone reading the time, not a name."

Lillian bit her lip. "Ah, yes, I should have mentioned him earlier, sorry, I didn't want to confuse things for you. He looks after things in here, he is Number Five's number two, if that doesn't sound too confusing. Hence FiveTwo. He administers The Midrift. He's the one who monitors the earth and plucks out all the unexplained deaths, all the candidates to be transients. Then he ensures they all get the Priming when they arrive, and then keeps an oversight of progress whenever there is any transient activity, as well as sometimes getting a bit involved as I mentioned. He is my conduit. Anything that needs clarifying, I ask him, then if necessary he checks it with Number Five. But don't worry, as a resolver you won't ever come into contact with him, in fact you won't physically be able to see him at all."

"A resolver? You mentioned that before. Is that, like, an official description?"

"Yes, that is the description used for any living person who makes the connection with a transient by solving the mystery of their death, and then begins on the journey to put things right. As you did. And will do."

Marlo quite liked the term. He could see himself in a big cape with 'Resolver' written on it, striding through the land putting things in order.

"Are there any other resolvers in here at the moment?" he asked.

"Apparently not. The last one was a little while ago, but I don't know whether he or she was successful or not. Perhaps none of the previous twenty three made it, we don't know."

Lillian paused, realising the impact of what she had just said. "But of course they may all have been successful, in fact I am sure they were!" She brightened as though her words had reinforced her sudden confidence. "Why wouldn't they be?"

"Well doesn't it depend on what they had to do?" asked Marlo.

"Yes, but...." Lillian trailed off. "Anyway, you can see why Number Five pricks up his ears whenever a resolver makes it to the Midrift, it is a rare event. Which makes you quite special!"

Marlo felt humbly smug, if that was possible, and could only think to jokingly flick some invisible specks off his shoulder in the 'look how important I am' fashion of the time before realising that this gesture would probably mean nothing to Lillian other than that he had dandruff.

"I'll take that!" he added.

"Take what?"

"The compliment."

"Oh, I see. Well, so you should, shouldn't you? Why wouldn't you?"

"Well, if someone..... ." Marlo paused, realising he would now have to start checking what he said before he said it. "Oh I don't know, it is just a saying."

He cleared his throat and decided he had better become more serious. "Ok, would you mind if I just summarise the main bits of what you've told me to make sure I have understood the basics?"

"Not at all."

"Thank you. So you will become a transient if you are less than fifty years old when you die and you've been killed by another human, but mystery surrounds your murder and the killer is not known and not punished, yes?"

Lillian nodded.

"But the transient will die if back on Earth their murder is then subsequently solved, and the perpetrator is punished before they die anyway of natural causes."

"Yes."

"However, the transient will stay in the Midrift if the killer dies unpunished, because at that point the crime was not solved and they have escaped justice. And that means that the transient now has to wait for someone like me to solve the crime after the event."

"Full marks!"

"Ok, good, I think I understand then! Please continue."

Lillian looked pleasingly impressed with Marlo's grasp of the rules, which in turn pleased Marlo. "Right, you and I, Marlo, have some work to do now. We need to put things right back in my world, back in 1886, and you are going to help me. Resolvers need to solve things, their job is to finish what they started."

Marlo laughed nervously as he put two and two together. "So I'm going to time-travel?" Then he realised that that was no less ridiculous than the situation he was in now.

Lillian hadn't laughed either so he knew. "Ok, I'm going to time-travel." Lillian nodded. "In a way you are, yes. Time works differently in here. You'll see."

CHAPTER 17 : A CONCERNING MOMENT

"Supper, Tim," Liz shouted from the kitchen, "can you do the table please?" Tim realised he had been so absorbed that two and a half hours had somehow passed since he had lowered himself into hsi writing chair.

"Right you are dear," he shouted back, wondering how long he would have before she repeated the request in the sure knowledge that he had not moved. He decided to surprise her, creaked himself up, and was pleased to find that this time his knee did not object.

The dining room was small but elegantly furnished in a style that Tim felt reflected his previous status as a senior civil servant. He had been used to a working environment of understated and often overstated opulence that the corridors and rooms of power had inherited from previous occupants, so it would have been unbecoming, he felt, to have returned home to a house filled with plywood and MDF from some bargain bucket always-a-sale-on furniture store. Also, Liz had been instrumental, indeed forceful, in pointing out that on his salary, there was no reason not to have nice furniture.

Looking at it now, though, it was so traditionally middle class, like something out of a BBC sitcom from the 1980s. The dark rosewood table and matching regency chairs were resting on an elegant light cream carpet, the walls papered with a light blue Laura Ashley design that Liz had liked more than he did, but he had to concede actually went quite well as a backdrop for the other dark wood dressers and cupboards that edged the room and corralled the table into the middle.

Far too many vases of flowers and ornaments completed the effect. Tim did not like clutter, but his wife did, and he had long ago realised the futility of venting his opinion on this subject.

Oh for the times when he gave the instructions and people did what he asked them to. Those days were long gone. If his subordinates could see him now they would marvel at how dramatically his powers had ebbed away.

He put out the table mats and arranged the cutlery as silently as he could. Then he crept to the kitchen door and waited next to it. Sure enough, he soon heard, louder than before, "Tim! Are you doing that table?"

He strode instantly in to the kitchen "All done dear!"

She jumped and looked round from the saucepan she was stirring. "Oh! Good. Right. Give me a minute then, just need to, er, finish heating this sauce."

Tim retired back to the study, comfortable with his small victory. He'd shown her he wasn't such an unresponsive old slowcoach after all. The downside was that he was now standing there doing nothing, waiting for her. He knew she had asked him five minutes before she needed to because he normally responded five minutes later, so when he tackled the job immediately that he was asked, this left him with five minutes to then wait for her. He couldn't win, he reflected, as his eyes were drawn back to the glowing monitor on his desk. Had he time for one more paragraph? He quietly eased himself back into his soft, buttery old leather chair and started typing.

How do dreams work? What does the inside of a dream look like? It still felt to Marlo as though he was in a dream, and even if he wasn't, this was undoubtedly the closest he would get. Was he really here with Lillian, a girl who lived and died over 130 years ago? Was his physical body no longer on Earth, no longer walking around down there, going to work, coming home again, eating his tea? Was he actually sitting on white mist having a conversation with someone who was dead? It did seem the stuff of dreams but he knew that it wasn't. It was real yet completely unreal.

"I don't understand why you don't just throw that thing away and write your literary masterpiece on the computer." Liz's sudden interruption behind his back jump-started his thoughts back to the present in a most disagreeable way.

"Do you have to do that Liz?" he cried, "I hadn't heard you creep up on me."

"Firstly, I did not creep," retorted Liz as she finished folding her apron in a businesslike fashion. "Secondly, remind yourself of just a few minutes ago when you did the same to me in the kitchen. And thirdly, supper is ready."

Tim grunted, realising he had no answer to the second point and so it would not be worth arguing the first one. The smell of chicken in white wine sauce was in any case far worthier of his attention, so he followed Liz out of the study to help take the plates from the kitchen to the dining room.

He had some very good reasons for not using the computer. The explanation he always wheeled out for Liz when she was in a mood to listen was that the computer was more complicated and he preferred something basic and simple now that his old brain was shedding cells faster than autumn leaves from a tree. He was an old dog who couldn't be bothered to learn a new trick.

He would also point out that if he was always on the computer then she wouldn't be able to use it, and this seemed to do the trick, until the next time she complained about the old green-screen machine taking up space or spoiling the ambience of the room. The real reason for his attachment to it was that he knew that the archaic start-up routine, which required inserting floppy disks and had taken him an age to get the hang of, would prevent her nosing around on it and no doubt breaking it when he wasn't there, as she had no interest in it other than to wish it wasn't there.

Not that he had anything to hide (yet), but given that she was far more adept with the modern computer than he was, it was nice to have a digital man-cave just to fall back on just in case. It was one of the few parts of the house that he could call his own, even though technically it wasn't a part of the house but a small thing within it.

After supper, the dishwasher was filled, a small brandy poured, and both of them would then settle into their electrically adjustable recliner armchairs to soak up a television drama and News At Ten.

Usually it took Liz about fifteen minutes to drift off and she would then occasionally jerk awake to ostensibly absorb another two minutes of the programme before closing her eyes again. This greatly irritated Tim as he could not see why she bothered to watch anything when in reality her eyes were closed. Not only that but her heavy rattly breathing when half asleep was quite distracting, and he was then unable to discuss anything interesting about the programme afterwards as she almost always didn't know what he was talking about.

He had contemplated suggesting that she brought in one of the more uncomfortable dining chairs and sat on that instead, but thought better of it having considered the likely reaction. But this routine was the one that they had played out every evening and indeed almost every day since he retired. Getting home late after a bad day at the office to find a cold dinner and an argument waiting for him was a thing of the past – now every evening was identical, predictable, and slightly dull if he was honest.

Despite having spent the previous ninety minutes mostly asleep, Liz would always somehow wake up for the weather, then once the weatherman had said goodnight the whine of the electric footrest would indicate that she was preparing to head upstairs to do some reading in bed.

"I'll carry on down here for a bit," said Tim tonight, "I'd like to finish off a section of my writing while I still have it structured in my head." In reality he had no idea what he was going to write but that small fib didn't matter, he thought, he wasn't tired yet so just wanted to get on with some more of the story.

"Mmm, ok, but don't be too long, I don't want to be woken up by you clomping upstairs at some ungodly hour," mumbled Liz as she shuffled out with a still-half-asleep gait.

Tim watched her go, knowing that although Inspector Morse repeatedly shouting at Lewis had failed to rouse her earlier, if the bed creaked even slightly as he got in, she would be instantly alert and complaining that he had woken her up.

He found the little button on the cord and pressed it to raise the back of the recliner and lower the footrest. Fortunately he was not yet decrepit enough to need to keep the button depressed long enough to get to the 'tip the old person out of the chair' angle, and so as soon as the footrest was back in position he stopped the motor and pushed himself up and out of the chair. He had long ago convinced himself that this counted as exercise.

Back in his writing chair, he sat and thought for a bit, then slowly began typing, his two forefingers prodding the keys like a pigeon pecking at some seed.

Marlo turned back to Lillian, the conversation on time travel prompting him to divert the conversation with another question. "Lillian, what has happened to me on Earth now?" he asked. "Have I just disappeared? Will everyone at Convestia be wondering why I don't turn up for work now?"

"I don't know what Convestia is, but no," she replied, "at your workplace they won't notice anything. All the time you spend here in the Midrift does not count towards time on Earth, so however long you spend here, if you return to Earth it will be from the same time and point as you left it to come here."

"But.... if time up here does not align with time on earth, how do you measure the three hundred years you are allowed in The Midrift? Surely if I am frozen in time down there, the time we are spending now does not count towards the three hundred years?"

Lillian looked up at him and sighed a little over-elaborately. "Oh my, you certainly are asking some hard questions, you are going to wear me out!"

She was still smiling though, as despite all Marlo's questioning she still couldn't disguise her excitement and happiness at finally meeting her resolver. Marlo could have asked her how many toes she had and she would still have given him a patient answer.

"Time on Earth and time in the Midrift work on different dimensions. Here it is flexible. It has to be, in order for us to go back to the time of our deaths. So while we track the three hundred years against Earth time, here we can reverse it, but only to help resolve the crime that killed us. Each transient can do that individually too. What I mean by that is that if I go back to 1886, that doesn't mean all the other transients do as well, they have control over their own timespan. You can have multiple threads of time so two transients can go back to different time periods at the same time. How that works is something you would need a particular type of brain to understand. One thing we can't do though, is go forward beyond the current Earth time. We do not see into the future."

Marlo nodded, despite being pretty sure he had not fully understood it all. It was like those films when people went back in time and did things which affected the future. That didn't make sense because the future had already happened, yet it was conveniently explained away with theories about a parallel time path where the old future and the new future happened at the same time, but separately. Or something like that. He had always dismissed this as nonsense but recently science had been starting to suggest it might not actually be that far-fetched.

He frowned suddenly as a thought occurred to him. "You said that a resolver might not succeed. If they do fail to bring finality and order to the death of the transient on earth, what happens to them?"

Lillian sighed and looked skywards even though there was no sky to look at. "I was wondering if you would ask me that." She paused long enough for Marlo to realise that the answer she was about to give might not be the one he wanted to hear.

"There has to be an incentive for you too. If you lost interest, or decided you really didn't like the transient once you had met them, you might decide you would rather just go back to your normal life. But that can't happen, it would make this whole experiment pointless. So there's another rule. If you do not solve the crime and bring the perpetrator to justice, you do not go back."

Tim glanced at his watch and realised with horror that it had gone half past midnight. He had got completely carried away. Liz would be fast asleep by now, which meant that however quietly he crept about, he would wake her up and be on the end of another admonishment, as though he was a child. He knew how Liz would respond to that: "well don't act like one then." He switched off the Amstrad and waited for the whirring to die and the screen to go black.

Liz was not asleep. She had done some reading, then at 11:00pm turned off the bedside lamp and lay back in the dark hoping that Tim wouldn't be long. Silly old duffer, she thought. Married 46 years now, and here they were still together, still in love with each other, but still getting on each other's nerves. Even more so since he had retired.

Having him getting in her way all the time, moping around the house looking for things to do, was probably not the end-game that either of them had envisaged when they did their financial planning all those years ago. Then, the vision was of a thatched cottage surrounded by roses and honeysuckle, with the two of them contentedly sipping mint tea on the terrace overlooking the pool and the striped lawn, planning their next exotic walking holiday or cruise and looking back on a life well lived.

Yes, they were well off with a good pension and a nice house, albeit without the thatch and the pool. But Liz's heart condition, which was diagnosed after the last of the three children had left home and shortly before Tim retired, had put paid to much of what they had planned. For years now she had been taking a cocktail of colourful drugs every day and putting as little strain on her heart as possible. She hated it. She wanted to be active, out there enjoying life, but she was under strict instructions to be careful and so spent most of her time in the house, pottering about, finding little things to do.

Flying was not allowed and travelling generally was felt to be not worth the risk. Worse still was the guilt she felt in obliging Tim to do the same. Bless him, he had always refused to go off on a walking holiday on his own – it just wouldn't be the same, he had said. But he worked so hard to earn that retirement, and in ten years they had hardly left the village.

She did drift off for a while but a brief but sharp pain in her chest woke her with a start. She sat up, frightened. "Tim?" she whispered. When there was no answer, she reached for the bedside light, then looked back to see an empty pillow. The alarm clock read 12:17. He must still be downstairs, either still writing, asleep in the chair, or..... no, he was bound to outlast her. He'll be up soon.

She turned off the light and lay back down but she was scared. It had been a while since she had felt a pain like that. But it had gone, so perhaps it was just a false alarm, perhaps she had dreamt it. But she lay there worrying.

It was 12:33 before she heard a noise on the stairs and then the door slowly opening, creaking in a way that it only does when you don't want it to. She sensed Tim squeezing himself through the gap, her senses now heightened so that every rustle of his clothes was amplified. Normally she would have made him creep about carefully and slowly then only confess she had been awake once he had got into bed, but this time she could not wait.

"Tim? I've just had a pain in my chest," she said more weakly than she had intended.

Tim started, then turned on the light quickly. "When? Just now? Was it bad?"

The worry in his voice re-assured Liz. "I don't think so," she said, scrunching her eyes against the light, "I was asleep so it was hard to tell. It happened about ten, maybe fifteen minutes ago....."

"You've taken all your pills today, haven't you?"

"Yes, yes, I always take them, you know I do."

"And it just happened once?"

"Yes, just once."

Tim was unsure what to do. He couldn't risk Liz's health but this might just have been heartburn or something. Maybe indigestion. "Ok love, let's go back to sleep and if it happens again I am taking you straight to A&E, ok?"

Liz nodded slowly. "Alright," she replied. Suddenly she was no longer in control, and Tim was there to look after her rather than her having to manage him all day. She supposed that is what marriages were for really, so both sides could support each other when they needed to. She eased herself back under the sheets, and both of them eventually went to sleep.

Liz was almost relieved when she woke up early the next morning; she had been worried that she wouldn't wake up at all.

When Tim's dreams were disturbed by her running the shower, this was one morning when he found himself breathing a sigh of relief rather than cursing her for interrupting his rest. It must have been heartburn or some other minor aberration, thank goodness.

After breakfast, and with Liz now back in house management mode, albeit just doing the shopping list, Tim retired to the study and headed for the Amstrad. When he had started this story, he was on firm territory with Marlo's life in London and his personal search for love.

Tim had always lived and worked in or around the capital, and as a young man, he had been similarly frustrated with his disappointing physical appearance and lack of success with the opposite sex, so he knew what he was talking about. Yes, he knew he had banged on about it at length in this book, maybe for too long on a subject that very few people reading his book would be able to relate to – or would they? Surely he hadn't been the only one? Or had everyone enjoyed multiple relationships and sexual encounters when they were young? That's how every book, magazine, newspaper, film and TV programme portrays it. Well he certainly didn't, and maybe there were others like him out there too, keeping quiet, just like he did.

He would describe his frustrations through Marlo, give readers a window into a different world, even if they did have to plough through pages of self-pity and angst. Let them see how the other half lived. Not that it was half, of course, more like a fraction of one per cent probably, if that. But he also wanted to show that there could still be hope. After all, for him it had turned out all right in the end, eventually.

When he met Liz he was in his late 20s and had thought he would never find love, but she arrived and changed his life. She wasn't a looker either but they just clicked and would later joke that the only reason they ended up with each other is that no-one else would have them. Desperation can have its benefits. However much she now occasionally irritated him, he would be eternally grateful to her. It was her support that had bolstered his confidence and helped him succeed at work.

But now he was about to take Marlo's story in a different direction. This would definitely not be firm territory, indeed he felt like a foreign invader whose confidence in successfully negotiating the open plains had persuaded him to charge into a canyon and thereby blunder into an ambush. He knew almost nothing about Victorian life, only what he had read in Dickens, which is what had carried him through so far. At some point he was going to have to do some serious research.

He might have to ask Liz for help as the computer would have to be utilised, although there was always the nearest library. Then he realised that he didn't even know where it was now – they were always closing them these days. Anyway, that could wait for now, he still had to get Marlo back in time to 1886.

CHAPTER 18 : PREPARATION

"If I don't succeed, I don't.... go back?" Marlo stuttered. "If I didn't go back to London, where would I go then?" He actually didn't really have much of a life to go back to, so if he ended up somewhere else that wouldn't necessarily be such a bad thing.

Lillian looked at him carefully to make sure he was taking it in. "You stay in the time zone and world of the transient until you have done what you were brought in to do."

"That could be until I die, then? If it is impossible to resolve... which it might be. That doesn't sound fair. In fact it's not fair." Marlo's voice rose. "How can it be right my life is potentially ruined because I was trying to help? Can't you do something, ask Number Five to change the rules?"

"That isn't going to happen," Lillian said, with a rueful shake of her head. "We have no influence over anything. I'm sorry. And not many people have got this far in recent times, I doubt he will want to change things yet anyway. Also, it does sort of make sense to have that huge incentive. Supposing once you had met me you thought I was not worth saving, what then?"

"I do!" Marlo replied instantly, "of course I do!" He hoped she could see that. "But you must see, I don't know what I'm going to have to do and what I'll encounter. I might fail through no fault of my own."

"I know, I know. But..... we both have no choice. We have to do this. Life's not fair, and it would appear life after death isn't always fair either."

She stood up suddenly, keen to move the subject on. "Right, so we now have to go back to 1886, the day that I died, and you need to embark on the second part of the process and put things in order by bringing Walter Threadwell to justice. In the same way that I was able to transport you through the diary into the Midrift, I can now use the diary to move you back in time to the time and place that I died."

"The diary!" Marlo suddenly realised, his heartbeat rising as he looked frantically around. "Where is it? I had it in my hands when the connection started, but now I haven't got it. Where is it?" He used his feet to feel around in the mist and checked his pockets but it wasn't there.

Amused at his reaction, Lillian waited for him to look back at her, then said softly "I've got it. It is temporarily back with its rightful owner." She smiled and reached down, pulling the blotchy old book from the bleary mist that swirled endlessly around them. "I made sure it was safe as soon as you arrived with it, you didn't even notice I'd taken it!"

Relief enveloped Marlo, garnished with mild annoyance. "Well thanks for making me panic there. But thank God it is still here. I really thought I had lost it."

"Well you hadn't, so all is well. Anyway, back to what we need to do - this is what is going to happen. I am going to transport you to Brighton, but I can only take you as far back as the point at which I died, so you will arrive on September 22nd 1886. Obviously I haven't done this before but apparently you should appear just after I have died, at the spot where it happened."

"Apparently....?" Marlo looked a little concerned.

"Well, it is what the Priming told me, I suppose I just said apparently to make it clear that if it doesn't happen quite like that it won't be my fault! So you won't be able to get there before I die and change anything that led to me becoming a transient. It all has to be addressed after I die." She paused thoughtfully. "That is the game."

"Hang on... " said Marlo, "presumably after your second fall wouldn't they have eventually found your body on the rocks, and that would have backed up Walter's story, so why wasn't that subsequently in the newspaper archives? The entry saying your cause of death was unknown and there was no body was the last reference to you that I could find."

"That's what you need to find out," advised Lillian. "When I died, that was the last I saw of Earth. Transients have no contact with Earth after that unless a resolver appears, and even then we can't see anything, only sense it. So I don't know why that would be the case. Maybe I wasn't important enough to warrant another paragraph advising that my body had been found!"

"Or perhaps the tide came in and washed you out to sea, then back ashore somewhere else?" realised Marlo. "You could be lying in some remote cove that no-one can see or get to."

"Yes, that could be the case. I know from my first fall that the sea comes right up over the rocks at high tide. You might even see that happening when you get down there, my body might still be down there about to get buried at sea."

"Well, if you can transport me to that cliff just after you died, I might be able to climb down and rescue your body before the tide comes in," suggested Marlo, "then you could have a proper burial."

"Burials don't matter to me any more," said Lillian simply. "In any case, it would be too difficult to get down there, and even worse coming back if you had me to carry too. And I don't want you injuring or even killing yourself as well, that wouldn't do either of us any good."

Marlo nodded. "No, I suppose not." He looked up suddenly. "Suppose I take a photo with my phone and show it to the police!" He grabbed his trouser pocket. "Except... I don't have my phone, it was on the desk beside me. Damn."

"And also I have no idea what you are talking about," said Lillian.

"So you don't get to see anything that has happened in the last 130 years, you don't know about mobile phones for example?"

"Is that like a telephone? I read that someone had invented such a thing a few years before I died, so you can talk to people a long way away over a wire."

"Yes, that sort of thing," said Marlo.

"Ok. Well all I know," said Lillian "is what I knew on the day I died. For me, it is still 1886 and if for some unfathomable reason it seems you are now taking photographs with telephones instead of cameras, and carrying them around with you.... although that wouldn't work as you would have nothing to plug them into. Oh, but that doesn't matter now, it is something I can learn about later. Any words or things which have appeared since then will mean nothing to me, I'm afraid, and once you start explaining them it could take a long time." She paused. "Anyway, that is just silly, telephones are for talking into, as far as I know."

Marlo smiled. "Are you sure you don't want me to tell you about them now, and how they are now little things that fit in your hand? You are right, I could spend at least the next week just telling you what happened since 1886 and you would be amazed."

"I'm sure I would, but there is another thing I haven't told you yet. I don't have long to get you back down to Earth. A resolver is only temporarily allowed in the Midrift, it is designed for transients only. So I have only a limited time from the moment you arrive to the moment where you transport back. We are alright at the moment, but I don't want to risk anything by you spending too much time here. You can tell me more when you are back in 1886. Then if you succeed, I will find out all about the future anyway when I come back in your time-zone to finish my life. So I need to use this remaining time to get you ready and then transport you back. Don't ask me why there's a time limit, there just is."

"Number Five....?"

"Yes, he made all the rules. I don't know if he is watching us now, none of us do. He might be busy in another dimension, or he may have heard from FiveTwo that another resolver has entered The Midrift from Earth and is keen to keep touch with what is happening as it is not a common event. I suppose that was part of the reason he created all this, as a form of entertainment." Lillian looked down. "It is odd describing my death as entertainment."

Marlo understood. If there was a clock running, having got this far the last thing he wanted to do now was prevent Lillian returning to life by talking for too long about a future she would then never see, however much he was enjoying her company in the Midrift.

"Ok, so I find myself on Earth just after your death. Walter might still be there somewhere, possibly trying to hide Jed's body, and if I can catch him doing that, then he would have some explaining to do. Incriminating him on that front will draw immediate suspicion over your death as well. Hang on though, that wouldn't work. It would be his word against mine. He could claim that I was the murderer. Or supposing he kills me too? Oh Jeez, this is not good. Maybe this isn't such a good idea after all."

Lillian grabbed his hands and stared hard at him. "Marlo, you have got to do this, but you must not, under any circumstances, get yourself killed, do you understand? You have got to be careful, not take any silly risks. If you die, then effectively I die too, for good this time. So don't run after Walter and confront him. He is much bigger than you and we have already seen what he is capable of. Also, he probably still has the knife."

She let go of his hands and sat back as Marlo nodded, the full seriousness of what he was about to embark on beginning to strike home. This was no game. He would have to have his wits about him. Knowing that another life depended on his life doubled his incentive to be careful, yet he still had to bring a dangerous man to justice, so this was really risky, especially as he had no idea how he was going to do it.

He addressed Lillian. "Ok, I'll be careful." A thought occurred to him. "If Walter has already gone, and hidden Jed's body, am I allowed to search for it even though no-one will be looking for him yet. Is that in the rules?"

"Marlo, once you are back on Earth you can do anything you want if it will assist in capturing my killer and making the truth known."

"Can I tell people about the future?"

"Theoretically yes but practically no. Think what would happen. If you start telling people on earth some of what you know, or saying that you have come from the future, you run the risk of being reported to the authorities and being locked up as a heretic or lunatic, which is the last thing we want. No-one will believe you. If you say that you can predict the future and managed to prove it somehow you could be seen as a threat to power or a dangerous mystic, and if you claim that you know what or who created the earth it will just sound like you have created another religion with its own theories and suppositions that you won't be able to prove. Why should they believe you? I think it is quite clever of Number Five actually, that he lets transients keep that knowledge. After all, what can they do with it? You really have to blend in. Otherwise, if you get locked up for life or something, the chances are you would never catch Walter before he dies of natural causes and then the game stops, and we both die."

"What?" Marlo was taken by surprise. "I die too? You never mentioned that! I thought I just had to live out my life as a Victorian."

Lillian fingered at her cuffs. "Sorry, yes, I was being a bit, er, duplicitous to start with, I didn't want to frighten you. But now I have. It just slipped out. Sorry. It's only if Walter dies naturally though."

"Why do I have to die too though?"

"Because you failed the task. Walter did not face justice. It is another incentive."

"More a threat than an incentive, surely. How would I....?" Marlo hesitated.

Lillian was straight in there. "You just instantly collapse and die, both in my time and in yours. I don't know how, but I don't suppose it matters. It is just the rules. If the transient dies, the resolver goes with them. The game is over. It all finishes."

"Holy moley..." exhaled Marlo, the enormity of the challenge ahead of him beginning to strike home. He thought for a moment. "Ok, so supposing I didn't actually openly tell anyone, but I did things that might, possibly, you know, perhaps be based on the fact that I had an idea of what was about to happen, that would be ok? Provided no-one realised I really had knowledge of the future?"

"If no-one guesses, then you are safe. And so am I. But you must not, under any circumstances, take any chances that might end up with someone reporting you. I really want to come and live in your world, Marlo. We've got this far, we can't let it go now. Agreed?"

Marlo nodded reluctantly. "That's a shame, I could have put some bets down on future events and made a lot of money."

Lillian's smile was forced. "Money is of no consequence in the situation we are in, Marlo, I'm sure you know that. You can't take it with you to the future. To achieve your task, you may need to be in my world down there for some time. As I said, the last thing you want is people suspecting you of sorcery and throwing you in the asylum where you can't finish your mission. But, there may be occasions, provided no-one suspects anything, where you might find your knowledge of more modern detective techniques, for example, assuming there are any, helpful. As long as no-one suspects anything."

"All I really know in that department is what I have seen on TV, you know, crime thrillers and the like." He saw Lillian's blank expression. "No, you don't know, do you. I suppose you have never heard of TV, television?"

Lillian shook her head.

"Ok, no problem, I'll explain later. I take your point though, I understand. I'll be very careful."

"Good," said Lillian. "I'll be with you in spirit though, I can still give you guidance so you won't be totally alone."

"Really? Excellent!" Marlo looked relieved, then puzzled. "How?"

"Through the diary. In the same way that I was communicating to you in your world, I'm still not able to see what is going on in the living world in my era, only sense it through the portal of the diary and hear what you hear. Of course I would really love to be down there with you, but it wouldn't make sense – I can't be seen returning from the dead! So if you keep the diary with you, on your person or close to you, and talk to me, I will hear you, and I can answer you so that only you will hear me in your head. No-one else will hear what I am saying to you."

Marlo looked at her with some astonishment. "You're kidding me! Your voice will be in my head? How does that work?"

"I don't know," shrugged Lillian, "it just does, apparently. Remember though, you will need to keep the diary with you at all times as that will continue to be my gateway. If you lose it, you lose your connection to me. You can still complete the task of course, it would just have to be without my help, and I think you are going to need that help."

"Too right," said Marlo, "I'll be talking to you all the time. But isn't that going to look odd to other people?"

Lillian grinned. "I suppose it will! People will think you are a candidate for the lunatic asylum if you aren't careful!" She stopped laughing suddenly. "Actually, you had better be careful there. Keep your voice down and don't talk to me in the company of other people if you can help it. I really don't want you to be branded a madman, it isn't going to help. Just whisper, I will still hear you provided you have the diary."

"OK. If I'm giving statements to the police or dealing with the authorities in any other way the last thing I want is for them to think I'm insane because I keep muttering to myself."

Out of nowhere, Lillian suddenly leaned forward and gave him a peck on the cheek. "That is to say thank you for what you are doing for me," she said. "Talking about the diary reminded me that I may not get another chance to do that."

Marlo's automatic reaction was as uncool as it always was. All he could think to do was smile gratefully and say "thank you," in a weak voice, before internally kicking himself once again for that feeble response and wishing he had been able to take it in his stride like all other men seemed to be able to do, as though being kissed by beautiful girls was a regular occurrence.

Thankfully Lillian hadn't seemed to notice his self-diagnosed inadequacies and was already resuming her instructions.

"Now, you are clear what you have to do, aren't you?" Before Marlo could answer, she added "remember, I will be there to answer any questions, as long as you have the diary."

"The diary is the gateway......" reflected Marlo. "But if I do lose it, and complete the task, how do I get back to you without the portal?"

"Once the resolver has 'resolved'", said Lillian simply, "the diary doesn't matter any more. As soon as justice is done and Walter is punished for his crime, you will instantly be returned to your world with me, diary or not – I have nothing to do with that. There are bigger forces at play. It would be a big thing, Marlo, a really incredible achievement, if you can resolve the case of a transient, so the rules allow you to return even without the diary. But from the point you lose it, I can hear nothing, or communicate with you, so I won't know what's going on or be able to help you, which will probably reduce your chances of success, and also drive me crazy with worry. Also, I would quite like to get it back. So don't lose it!"

"I won't." Marlo shook his head in confirmation and they were both silent for a moment, each reflecting on the task ahead. Then Marlo spoke.

"Right then!" he declared. "I know what I have to do. Let's do it!"

CHAPTER 19 : GOING BACK

The process of transporting Marlo back to 1886 did not involve a time machine or the appearance of a wizard clapping his hands and exclaiming "Shazam!"

Lillian instead handed Marlo the diary and asked him to close his eyes. About to do so, Marlo suddenly realised that this might be the last time he would ever see her if things did not go as they both hoped. "Wait! When will I see you again?" he asked, embarrassed to hear a slight crack in his voice and knowing as soon as he said it that he hadn't really needed to ask.

"While you are in 1886, and for as long as you have the diary, we will hear each other, we will be together. And if you succeed in the task, you will see me again. So you have to succeed," said Lillian, trying to accentuate the positive. She could see the badly hidden emotion in his face and attempted to reassure him.

"Marlo, you are already my hero. You have done what I didn't think anyone would do. I want you to come back to me as much as you do. But this is the only way to do it. You have to go."

Marlo sighed and nodded. He looked up and took one last lingering look at Lillian, her concerned face now also a little tearful despite them having had so little time together. Determined to remember her every feature, he scanned her in his mind, the mental photograph locked in as he closed his eyes and settled back.

"Right," he said, "I'm ready. Wait! What about my clothes?"

"Don't worry," she replied with a laugh "you will be suitably attired!"

"How.... oh, it doesn't matter, I'll find out soon enough. Ok, I'm ready now."

"Right, here we go. Hold tight."

He felt a squeeze of his hand, then the bright light came, so bright he could not have opened his eyes if he had wanted to. His stomach started churning as he rose then fell, then the light went, and he could hear the sea, and feel a fresh breeze on his back, the wet air heavily fragranced with seaweed and spray.

"You're there," said Lillian, "open your eyes."

Marlo did so immediately and saw in front of him a swathe of wet grass and heathery tufts leading gently down to more rolling South Down hills dotted with trees. A couple of rabbits bobbed up and down in the distance. Grey clouds blanketed the sky and a gusty wind ruffled his hair. He turned round to see the cliffs behind him.

He was on the coastal path, a safe distance from the drop, and he was on his own. Lillian was nowhere to be seen, and nor was anyone else. Marlo looked down quickly to find that he now had Victorian clothes. His brown trousers were rough and ill-fitting, a white linen collarless shirt was covered by a stout jacket, and his shoes were brown and heavy.

He felt something on his head and pulled off a sort of a 'poor boy' cap with a big peak to it. He could imagine a hipster wearing it with a jaunty waistcoat. For his situation though, he supposed he looked like an average joe, perhaps a labouring man. He stuffed the diary securely into an inside jacket pocket and put the cap back on.

"Lillian? Are you still there?" he found himself saying a little too urgently to appear as cool as he wanted to be.

It would be an understatement to say that he was relieved to hear her voice a second time. "Yes, yes, I'm here, I'm with you! Well, sort of," she laughed, "I will always be here, ready and waiting. As long as you have the diary of course."

He reckoned she had made that point sufficiently now but it didn't matter. Her voice, sounding as though she was standing right there next to him yet with the faintest touch of an echo, was in his head and it was quite disconcerting, as though he had someone occupying his body, a talking spirit guide.

"So you are. Weird. Not just weird, but *really* weird," he said, almost embarrassed to speak even though there was no-one else in sight. "You sound as though you are in a small cave, but the cave is in my head. Hey, you can't read my thoughts, can you?"

He heard a laugh. "It depends if you have any. No, I'm joking. Definitely not!" came Lillian's voice. "That would lead to all kinds of complications. The only contact I have with you is aurally. So you will need to explain what you are looking at if you want me to help with it. I can hear what you hear though."

Marlo relaxed slightly. "Well, I suppose I'll have to take your word for that. It's bad enough having a voice in my head let alone anything else." He immediately realised what he had just said. "Sorry, I did it again. I didn't mean that like it sounded. I am glad you are there, I really am, it's not bad I can hear you, it's great, it's just bad that, well, different rather than bad.... you know." He trailed off. He was so used to digging his own holes that he now knew when it was best to just stop.

"One other thing," he said, quickly changing the subject before she could reply and adopting a whisper that even he could only just hear over the background noise, "can you hear this?"

"Yes!" replied Lillian. "A soft voice or whisper is fine, I'll hear it. There's no noise where I am."

"That's good. Ok, I had better get started," he said, happy that no-one was within earshot. "There is no-one around and I am guessing that I have arrived here just after you have been thrown over the cliff. I'll have a look and see if I can see you."

Marlo edged carefully towards the drop, the noise of the waves increasing as he got closer, the fresh salty smell assaulting his senses. Lying down on the damp grass, he peered over the edge. The sea was choppy but the waves not yet breaking over the larger rocks. He scanned the crumbling landscape below him and almost immediately spotted a human-like shape jumbled into the crevice between two boulders. He looked away, then forced himself to look back. He could see legs. It was definitely a body, but from this distance it looked like a man. Not a third murder, surely?

The sea was coming in, and it would not be long before it would wash over those rocks and presumably sweep the corpse back out to sea. "I can see a body, but it doesn't look like yours," he said, "it has trousers, and a black jacket. I can't see the head."

Lillian responded with a sigh. "No, that's me. Well, my body anyway. I was wearing Jed's clothes, remember."

There was the hint of a waver in her voice, perhaps from the shock of hearing her own lifeless corpse being described.

"I'm sorry," said Marlo, without thinking.

"Thank you, but nothing to be sorry about." She was firmer now. "That's all in the past. Now let's get after Walter."

Marlo inched backwards on his stomach then scrambled to his feet, wiping his hands on his trousers.

"I might catch Walter trying to dispose of Jed's body if I head in the right direction. Which way do I go?"

"If you are standing looking out to sea, you need to turn left and head east towards the river entrance on the other side of the cliffs. Don't do anything rash though."

Marlo looked up at the cloudy sky. "I won't."

The sun was up there somewhere but it gave no clues as to the time of day. It felt as though it was late morning. He turned east along the undulating coast path, nervous of what he might see over the next ridge. Walter could be there heaving Jed's body across The Downs, perhaps attempting to launch it over the cliff edge at this very moment.

Marlo thought quickly as he walked. If Walter wanted to hide or get rid of the body, tipping it over the cliff edge would be risky, as it might get stuck on the rocks as had happened (for the moment) to Lillian, or even a cliff ledge. Or perhaps the body would be washed out to sea, but arrive back on shore at the next tide. Throwing the body over the cliff would also link it almost directly to the remarkable coincidence that Lillian went over the cliff at the same time and the same place, bringing Walter under immediate suspicion. And when they found the stab wound, then he would be looking at two counts of murder, not just one, as he would be hard pushed to explain why Lillian slipped off the cliff and Jed didn't. Unless Jed has stumbled over the cliff having been stabbed, but that was unlikely.

And if Walter dragged Jed into a bush or tried to bury him, that would only delay the discovery before a walker or perhaps a dog sniffed it out.

Actually all this supposition was academic anyway, as, thinking about it, the local newspaper had reported on Jed's body being found fairly quickly, although it hadn't said exactly where his body was discovered. So perhaps Walter had just left the body where it was, even though that could have left him with less time to get away. He wasn't going anywhere, because he must have given the police much of the detail reported in the paper, and it said he was still helping them with their enquiries. So he was trying to bluff it out.

Provided they couldn't find the murder weapon and link it to Walter, there was no concrete evidence that he killed Jed, so why bother trying to hide him? He might as well just leave him there and pretend that after Lillian fell from the cliff, he headed back west and didn't even see Jed. Then, the police or another walker would have found the body later. That made more sense. And it would also explain why Walter pulled Lillian further along the cliff before throwing her off, otherwise he would not have been able to claim he had not seen Jed if Lillian had fallen off the cliff at the exact same spot that Jed's body was found.

But one thing Walter would definitely need to do would be to go back and double-check that Jed really was dead; if anyone was able to help Jed to recover so that the old man could identify Walter then the game would be up. Then he would also need to retrieve the knife from Jed's body, and possibly dispose of the murder weapon in case he was searched by police.

Marlo set off again, more quickly this time. If he could see what Walter did with the knife, he could direct the police to the knife's hiding place after he had pretended to stumble across it. Then they might be able to link the knife to Walter. Then he realised that he had no real idea how advanced police techniques were in Victorian times. Obviously they didn't have DNA profiling, and fingerprint dusting must have been barely invented, so perhaps Walter didn't need to get rid of the knife after all. How precise were autopsies in the 1880s? Could they match a knife wound to the type and size of the knife? He didn't know.

"Lillian, how likely is it that the police could tell if it was Walter's knife that killed Jed?"

"Um, I don't really know," came the answer he didn't want to hear. Then, after some thought, "I suppose they can work out how wide the blade was and how deep it went and get a good idea from that?"

Marlo nodded to himself. Yes, that made sense, although it was clear that Lillian knew as little about the subject as he did. Still worth searching for an abandoned weapon then. "Thanks," he said.

The top of the ridge was approaching. Marlo slowed slightly and kept his eyes fixed on the horizon ahead. As the hollow beyond revealed itself, Marlo could see no sign of Walter. "He's not there," he said to himself. He started as he heard Lillian's voice say "where?", reminding him that talking to himself – something he had started to do quite a lot in his flat recently – was something he was going to have to knock on the head.

"The next hollow. No sign of Jed's body either."

"We walked – if you can call it that – for about 5 minutes," advised Lillian, "so that should be the gap between my body and Jed's."

"Ok," replied Marlo, "I'll carry on, sounds like it might be over the next ridge."

Before he could progress more than a few yards, a bobbing head suddenly appeared in the distance about 300 yards ahead of him, heading in his direction. As the rest of the figure revealed itself and came over the ridge, Marlo's heart shot into his mouth and he almost stopped walking.

Under his breath he muttered urgently "there's a man coming over the ridge. He is tall but stocky, must be over six foot, dark hair, wearing a white shirt, brown jacket, black trousers. Is that him?"

"Yes, yes!" replied Lillian, "that's him! You'll have to just act normal now, like someone going for a walk over the cliffs. He has no reason to hurt you so don't give him one."

"Right, yes, ok," mumbled Marlo, sounding even less confident than he felt. He walked on towards the figure.

Walter was on his own – he wasn't dragging a body. So as far as Walter was concerned Marlo was just a stranger who knew nothing. The best thing to do was stay calm and act as though there was nothing out of the ordinary, just walk past Walter with a cheery 'good morning' and see what was over the ridge. But what if the body was still there, just lying on the ground? Marlo would be able to give a good description of a man who had come from that very direction; surely Walter would realise this? A cold shiver of fear swept through him.

The last thing the killer would want is a witness who could testify that he was in the area. And this man was a murderer, and could still have the knife on him. He could use it again! He would have to have eyes in the back of his head.

All these thoughts flashed through Marlo's brain in an instant. But events overtook him. Walter, spotting Marlo far ahead of him, suddenly turned round and headed back the way he had come, quickening his pace, his head disappearing from view again beneath the hilltop.

"He's turned round and run off," Marlo informed Lillian, not unhappy at this turn of events. Against his better judgement though he found himself walking faster towards the ridge and soon he was breathing heavily. "Careful!" said Lillian, rather unnecessarily Marlo thought – he certainly wasn't going to charge over the summit waving his fists and shouting a war cry. Indeed, he was petrified. "I know," he re-assured her, "I'm going to stop at the top here when I can see a bit more."

As he slowed down and edged closer, more of the vista ahead came into view. He could see the footpath, winding down towards Cuckmere Haven. But there was no sign of Walter.

"Where is he?" Marlo mused, relieved more than disappointed that he couldn't see him. Then, in the far distance to his left and away from the cliffs, almost lost in the scrub that soon became forest, Marlo saw movement and just caught the same tall figure merging into the trees. He must have run like the clappers; he definitely had something to hide. But where was Jed, and indeed where was the weapon? He might have taken the knife with him, but he hadn't taken Jed.

Feeling a little safer, Marlo relaxed slightly as Walter disappeared, not having realised how tense he had become. His 'fight or flight' instincts had automatically kicked in as he approached the ridge, a feeling not often experienced when fielding calls on the Help Desk.

"He's gone, Lillian, ran into the forest when he saw me."

"Oh!" said Lillian, sounding slightly surprised. "Well, there's no point chasing after him, and in a way that is a good thing he has gone as it means you are safe. Now, is there any sign of Jed?"

Marlo scoured the landscape. The grass was short near to the cliffs, a body there would have been obvious. But further inland it got longer, long enough that a distant observer wouldn't have noticed a body lying there. Walter could have dragged it there before he returned and spotted Marlo. After all, the further away it was from where Lillian died, the less suspicion there would be that the two events were linked. He looked to his right, back along the coast path. Another undulation meant that there was another hollow – perhaps the body was there, still lying on the grass.

"No sign yet," he replied "I'm going to have a look further down the coast, then come back here if I don't find anything and work my way inland."

He did not have far to go. Directly over the next rise, he saw what he was looking for. A crumpled brown lump, clearly a man's body, was lying, unmoving, about 150 yards away, close to the worn grass trail that guided people along the cliff top.

"I've found him," he muttered softly, keeping Lillian appraised. He slowly approached Jed's lifeless form.

CHAPTER 20 : LIZ

Tim stopped poking at his keyboard, his aching fingers matched by an aching brain, all telling him that he needed a rest. He had written far more than he intended, and had become so absorbed in his own storyline that he had lost all track of time. He glanced up at the solid old grandmother wall clock ticking solemnly away just to the right of his desk and was astonished to see that it was almost midday. No wonder he was feeling a bit peckish. Normally Liz would have suggested a cup of tea by now.

"Liz!" he called as he stretched out in his chair. "Do you need me to do anything?" This was always a good question when he sensed he might need to ward off an accusation of not helping or forgetting he wasn't the only one in the house.

Liz didn't answer. He levered himself up and walked stiffly into the kitchen. There was no-one there. "Liz, where are you?" Maybe she was upstairs.

Slightly concerned now, he made his way to the landing and poked his head into each bedroom in turn. Their own bedroom was at the end, and as he entered it he saw Liz, lying peacefully on the bed. He relaxed. She was asleep, probably catching up on missed sleep from last night.

But something wasn't right. She looked too still. He rushed to the bedside. "Liz? Liz, wake up, dear." He gently jostled her shoulder and her head lolled to one side. "No, no, no, it can't be, no, Liz! Liz! Come on Liz, wake up! Please!"

Tim grabbed her head with both hands and held it straight, kissing her forehead as though she was Sleeping Beauty and would now spring to life. "Come on Liz, you can't do this, you can't leave me! Wake up, please, wake up!" There was no response. He could feel no breath coming from her mouth. He felt for a pulse but there was nothing. Liz did not wake up. His cries turned to sobs, then an uncontrollable wail of anguish.

The funeral was at St Michael's parish church. They had talked about death and what arrangements should be made; Liz's diagnosis all those years ago had given them the incentive to do so, even though like most people they did not like thinking about it. It would be a low key service, and a small headstone with a simple inscription: just her name, her age, and when she died.

After the service and the burial, and with sympathetic friends heading for the church hall for refreshments, Tim stood silently by the freshly dug earth and looked at his three grown-up children standing moist-eyed beside him. "I took her for granted, you know," he said quietly, "even though we knew her heart could give up at any time, you just assume she will always be there. I'd long ago stopped telling her how much I loved her, and now it's too late." He got out a handkerchief and wiped his nose. "Mind you, it is quite hard to do that when she's chastising you for not washing the windows or something...."

Laura looked up at him with a wan smile smeared by tears. "She knew, Daddy, she knew. You didn't need to tell her."

"If anything, it's us who should feel guilty. We haven't visited enough. I hadn't seen you for at least 3 months." Edward's jaw was set firm, determined to keep it together but struggling to do so. "And now...." There was no need to finish the sentence.

David said nothing. He was always the quiet one. As the youngest he had probably been closest to his mother and Tim could see tears streaming down his face. Knowing your mother is now in a box beneath your feet, never to see you again, is not something you can ever fully prepare for.

The three families of the siblings stood back awkwardly near the church, conscious that the original family unit should have a moment of togetherness. All three children had married, and there were 4 grandchildren between them.

"What are you going to do, Daddy?" asked Laura. "Will you sell the house, buy somewhere smaller?"

"Not yet, love," Tim smiled. "Not while I still have my memories. Maybe once I start getting too creaky and can't manage the stairs any more."

"Mum always said you were creaky already," ventured Edward, "or was that cranky? Probably both, actually." They all needed to lighten the mood a little, he thought, life has to go on whether we like it or not. It did the trick, everyone smiled.

"Right!" Tim announced, straightening himself and pulling his coat together, "let's say goodbye to Mum and head to the reception – the others will be waiting for us." They all said their internal goodbyes and turned to face a new world without Liz.

CHAPTER 21 : BACK TO IT

It was another week before Tim felt able to sit down in front of his Amstrad again. The children had been great, fussing over him and taking time off work to help him in the house and prepare him for a life of looking after himself. He wasn't incapable, he thought, he could manage, but he did appreciate them all getting stuck in and offering help even when it wasn't needed. A bit like old times, having them around so much, with roles reversed so he was the one having things done for him.

Laura lived the closest and having always been Daddy's Little Girl it was she who spent the most time at the house, cleaning, organising, shopping, showing him how to cook for himself, explaining the things Liz used to do on the computer, and generally keeping him company.

Edward and David each now lived many hours' drive away so had shared 'keeping an eye on Dad' duties even though they could only be with him for half a day at a time. He didn't mind, he was just grateful that they made the effort at all. And with Laura just 45 minutes drive away he knew he always had someone to call on. He'd be ok, he'd lived on his own for long enough before Liz came along. He'd manage.

He'd completely forgotten where he had got to in his story. As he sat waiting for the machine to power up, he wondered what the point was. Why finish it? Even if he got it published, he'd be dead soon as well, assuming he didn't hang on until he was 105. Why was he going to all this effort?

But as the words appeared on the screen and he began reading back what he had written on that fateful morning, he knew why he had to finish it. It gave him purpose, something to keep his thoughts away from reality and steer them into a world where the personal pain he was going through now did not exist. He took a sip from his coffee and began the next chapter.

As Marlo got closer he could see Jed's white shirt was soaked in crimson. He was lying on his back, exactly where he fell, and Marlo supposed that gravity was helping to stem the blood flow a little, but it still looked horrific. Walter would not long ago have pulled the knife back out, releasing more blood, so it looked worse because it was fresh. He knew Jed was dead as this was what the newspaper had reported, so there was no sense checking for vital signs.

Also, he really did look very dead – he was completely still and his greying face stared sightlessly at the sky, mouth half open. Marlo had not seen a real dead body before but repeated binge watching of crime dramas over the years gave him the strange misleading feeling that this was not a new experience even though it very much was. It did not make it any easier to look at though. He shivered, not enjoying the situation he was now in and wanting to get out of it as soon as he could.

"Ok, Jed's here and it is not a pretty sight. I can't see a knife anywhere, although that's not really surprising. What shall I do now?"

"Poor man," he heard Lillian say, "he was so nice to me, and in the end he only died because he was trying to save me from Walter. It's so unfair." She paused, and Marlo tried frantically to think of something appropriate to say but could only nod and say "mmmm", which as creative answers went ranked quite low. Before he could muster some words, Lillian had resumed.

"Sorry, you were asking what to do now. Well, it is up to you but we can either go to the police and report that you've found a body, or you can go after Walter and see if maybe he hid the knife in the forest. Given enough time, I'd assume that Walter won't be creeping around in the forest as he will want to get back to Brighton, especially as he knows now that you have found Jed's body. He wouldn't want the police to know that he was up on the cliffs again on his own at the time that a man was stabbed. Then again, I suppose he could argue that he was still searching for me, on the off chance that my body had been washed back to shore, but didn't go as far as where Jed's body was found. Actually, that's unlikely, thinking about it. Why would he stop half way along? So my guess is that he will claim he wasn't on the cliff this afternoon, and so he'll need an alibi that he was somewhere else, therefore he won't hang around." She paused for breath. "Sorry, I'm talking too much."

"No, no, all good thoughts," Marlo assured her. "I was also thinking that when Walter left Jed's cottage yesterday afternoon after he first pushed you off the cliff, he would have gone back to Seaford and presumably reported what happened to the police there. If he didn't do that until the next day, that would look very odd. So the police would presumably then have wanted to go and see if they could save you or find you, so I am guessing they took Walter back up to the cliff top. He would have pointed out where you fell, but of course they couldn't see you because you had been carried out to sea."

"I swam!" interrupted Lillian, "It was hard work, give me some credit!"

"Sorry, yes," chuckled Marlo. "The sea had nothing to do with it! Anyway, it would have been pretty dark by then as well, so that wouldn't have helped. Now, if I was the police, I would tell Walter that there was nothing more they could do that night, but suggest they all come back first thing in the morning and see if you had been washed ashore. They would want Walter there for identification purposes ideally, so maybe he took a room in Seaford rather than going back to Brighton, then they all went up the cliff path early this morning and did a search, which of course yielded nothing. That would not have taken up the whole morning, so if you and Jed then bumped into him earlier this afternoon, he must have come back up on his own, possibly to be absolutely certain that you hadn't miraculously survived, which of course you did. So he was right to be thorough, unfortunately."

"If only Jed and I had set out for Seaford in the morning, we might have encountered the police searching for me and none of this would have happened," sighed Lillian.

"And I would never have met you," pointed out Marlo, "so every cloud, eh?"

"Every cloud what?"

"Has a silver lining! Do you not say that?"

"Ah! No, not quite, we say it the other way around, as in 'there's a silver lining to every cloud'. If you had said 'there's a silver lining' I would have known what you meant."

"I'll bear that in mind," said Marlo, although both of them knew he wouldn't. He considered his options. "I'm thinking that if I go to the police, they are going to be asking me a lot of questions. Not least, what I am doing up on the cliffs on my own. I'll be a prime suspect. I haven't got a back story either, where I live, what my job is and so on." His ruminations prompted a sudden realisation. "Hang on, so where am I going to sleep tonight? What am I going to eat? Lillian, has this all been arranged as part of this task?"

There was a brief silence in his head. "Well... not really," came the answer he didn't want to hear. "You have to find somewhere."

"Great! What do you suggest? I'm new in town."

He heard a short, quiet laugh. "Yes, I suppose this is where I need to give you some assistance. Ok, suppose you leave Jed's body and allow someone else to find it. Then tonight, go down to Jed's cottage and stay there for the night. There's food there as well. Hopefully no-one will immediately work out that is where Jed lives even if they find him. I saw him put the key in his trouser pocket; you'll need to take it off him."

"I really don't want to do this," said Marlo as he crouched down next to Jed. He had to stop himself saying 'excuse me' as he slid his hand into Jed's right hand trouser pocket. The leg still felt warm. Marlo shivered. He had to rummage to the bottom edge of the inside of the pocket before his fingers touched cold metal and he could extract the key, which was about the size of half a pencil and slightly rusty.

He immediately stood up and stepped back. "Got it," he said, placing the key in his own pocket and hoping no-one ever had to perform the same exercise on him.

"Good, well done," said Lillian. "Tomorrow you'll have to find lodgings. Oh, by the way, there is a wallet still in your back pocket, but the money in it is now from 1886."

"Oh, right!" Marlo pulled out a wallet that wasn't his own and was relieved to see it stuffed full of very large and very ornate £5 and £1 notes, with a little pocket inside it full of crowns and shillings. "Hey, this must be a lot of money."

"Yes, it should be," said Lillian, "it means you should not need to worry about affording food and lodgings for some time yet. But it also means that you have to be very careful for pickpockets or thieves. You might want to put a spare note or two in your jacket pocket as well just in case."

"Ok, I'll do that. In the meantime, as we've decided that I won't go to the police, I had better get away from here sharpish. If anyone sees me running away from the body then I really will be in the dock. I'll quickly check no-one is around, but if they are I'll just have to go with Plan B and tell them I've just found a body, then work out what I tell the police. If not, I'll head for those woods."

Leaving Jed, Marlo ran up to the top of the ridge closest to him, the way he had come. No-one was approaching. He charged back down again and his momentum helped carry him up the ridge on the other side. From here he could see a fair way down towards the river. A burst of adrenalin surged through him as he could just see two figures in the far distance, looking as though they were starting to head up the coast path towards him.

"Oh, shoot!" he exclaimed, ducking down. Marlo always tried not to swear when other people were around, or in his head as it had turned out.

"What?" gasped Lillian, concerned that Walter might have emerged from the woods, knife in hand, and started heading towards Marlo.

"People coming. I don't think they could have seen me though, my head on its own would just be a speck on the horizon. I need to make tracks."

Lillian knew not to start questioning modern colloquialisms now and instead focus on helping get Marlo out of danger. "Ok, you should have enough time to get to the trees before they appear, those people won't be running. Be careful though, just in case Walter is still skulking around in there."

That certainly didn't help Marlo's tightening chest, but he turned and strode forcefully towards the woods. If Walter was still watching him, he guessed he would be far more likely just to turn tail and head off rather than complicate things with another murder, especially if Marlo was striding confidently rather than edging timidly towards him.

It only took him three or four minutes to push through the lengthening grass and reach the first trees. They were mainly oak, with some beech, and without the sun to light it the gloom and foreboding silence of the forest floor gave Marlo the shivers. For all he knew Walter was hiding behind a tree, bloodied knife awaiting. But he could not stay exposed in the open.

He pushed aside some low hanging branches and crouched as he walked tentatively into the musty darkness. Screened by the leaves behind him, he stopped and waited for his eyes to adjust, listening hard and watching every tree trunk for signs of movement, his heart beating so loudly he was sure Lillian could hear it.

A twig snapped to the right of him and he wheeled round, ready to fight off his assailant. A squirrel bounded up a tree trunk, presumably the source of the noise. In the distance he heard some crows cawing. Then there was silence apart from the rustle of the leaves as the wind occasionally huffed through them.

He stood there, his back to the first tree trunk, for about five minutes, watching alertly, his eyes darting left and right, detecting movements even when there weren't any. He really wasn't enjoying this.

"What's happening?' whispered Lillian eventually, conscious of the tension and not wanting to make him jump.

"Thankfully, nothing," Marlo muttered under his breath "everything seems quiet. I don't think he's here."

"That's good. Can you see any footprints or sign of someone walking there? Broken twigs, that kind of thing."

Marlo looked down at the rough carpet of mud and leaves, broken twigs everywhere. He guessed Lillian realised that she was clutching at straws. "Unless he left a shred of trousers on a sticky-out branch, I don't think I'll have much luck in seeing where he might have gone. The ground is mostly covered in leaves. Anyway, I'm less worried about him now, more about finding the knife."

"I thought that if you could work out the route he took you could narrow down where he might have thrown or hidden the knife."

Marlo felt like a schoolboy again. "Ah yes, good point. I should have thought of that." His best chance of success was to find an area where there were fewer leaves, where a footprint might be retained in the earth. He had entered the wood in pretty much the same place as he had seen Walter disappear, so he only needed to find one sign of his presence to know whether he went left, right, or straight on.

He set out in an arc around his entry point, starting small then widening the arc as he moved deeper, scanning the ground for signs of human disturbance, but also for the glint of metal. He focused on the central and left side sectors, as turning right would have taken Walter in the wrong direction for Brighton. Seeing nothing unusual after ten minutes, he moved further into the forest to widen his arc and cover more ground.

About seventy yards into the forest, as he stepped over a fallen tree trunk, he spotted a foot-sized indentation in the earth just to the side of it. It was quite deep, as though a heavy step, perhaps as a final move before leaping over the log. He compared it with his own shoe – it was a good 2 or 3 sizes larger.

"I think I've found his footprint!" he announced proudly but with slight trepidation. "I'm going to follow the direction he must have taken from here and see if I can spot anything."

"Alright, good luck!"

Before he could move on he heard a distant shout, coming from the cliffs. Initial panic was replaced by a realisation that the two figures he had seen earlier had probably found Jed's body. He crept carefully back to the edge of the trees and peered out from between some low branches, taking care not to make any sudden movements and attract attention.

Jed was lying about four hundred yards from where he was now and he could see two men crouching over his body. One of them stood up, his hands clutching his head as though uncertain what to do. He was looking round, so even though Marlo knew he couldn't easily be seen at that distance and hidden in the undergrowth, he took a slow step back. Then the other man stood up and the two of them were clearly having an urgent conversation, with each of them gesturing and occasionally pointing. He could hear raised voices carrying on the wind but not what they were saying.

Eventually one of them nodded his head and turned back onto the path before setting off at a canter down to Seaford, pausing once to retrieve his cap which had bounced off his head as he ran. The other man stayed where he was, hands on hips, still looking round desperately as though someone who could help might suddenly materialise. He had presumably agreed to stay by the body until help arrived in order to preserve the crime scene.

Marlo slid very slowly back into the forest, conscious of every snapping twig even though the man by the body could not possibly hear them. Once far enough in, he whispered to Lillian "They've found the body. I'm going to have to find a different route down to Jed's cottage, I can't go back to the cliffs. I'll continue following Walter's path for a while but if I can't see a knife anywhere I'll head right, parallel to the coast, and hopefully I'll end up at the river."

"Yes, that should work. I was thinking, if Walter did dispose of the knife in there, he would have thrown it into the thickest part of impenetrable forest that he could find, ideally brambles. Also, the further he hides it from the murder scene, the less chance that a police search will find it. So I'd be amazed if you find anything."

"Thanks," said Marlo, "That's a great motivational speech." He knew Lillian would sense the humour in his voice. He liked that they seemed to be on the same wavelength already. Having Lillian in his head wasn't such a bad thing after all.

CHAPTER 22 : WALTER'S RETURN

Tim eased back in his chair and flexed his arms. That was a good session. And writing was successfully diverting him away from a world he really didn't want to be in at the moment. It was going to help, it really was. And so, over the next few weeks, he continued to write.

Walter was running, but no faster than he needed to. No point in slipping on these leaves and breaking his leg, that would ruin everything. He knew no-one would be chasing him anyway. If that fellow who he had seen on the cliff top and who he had watched discover the drifter's body had any brains he would realise that chasing after a murderer with a weapon, who might very well turn round and start chasing him instead, wasn't really a great idea. And by the look of the man he would be no match for Walter even if weapons weren't involved.

He was breathing heavily but not excessively as he loped along, and it helped that there was a very slight downward slope. His route through the trees wasn't too hard as there was plenty of open ground beneath the large overhanging branches of the oak trees, although the occasional clump of bramble sometimes forced him to briefly stop and retrace his steps to find a clearer way through.

He was confident though. He knew where he was going, as he had grown up in Seaford and had spent many hours as a child exploring the countryside and making dens in the woods, usually on his own as he was not the kind of child you made friends with unless you wanted to keep on the right side of him.

If he wanted help moving a log or something then he would call on Clarence, a pathetically obsequious child who tagged on to him at school and was happy to assist, knowing that other boys would be less likely to pick on him if they knew that he could call on Walter. And this was no idle threat as Walter had made a point of singling out every child, one by one, often outside school, and asserting his physical authority over them with an arm behind the back, or a headlock, or a bear hug, and all taken from behind so there was no chance of them making it hard for him. Only once they had begged for mercy would he release them, and this gave him a status, a reputation. He was someone not to be messed with, he had menace.

With Clarence it had been a case of wrestling him to the ground – not difficult given the size differential – and sitting on his back until he squealed that he couldn't breathe and would do anything Walter wanted if he would let him go. The difference was that Clarence meant it. He may have been a pathetic child but he was sensible enough to realise that aligning with the strong protected the weak. Walter didn't care about that, but he found the arrangement satisfactory as although he despised Clarence he was able to treat him as his own personal servant, which bolstered his growing feelings of self-importance.

He wondered what had happened to Clarence, not that it mattered. His own future had taken a new turn when he was twelve. His continually arguing parents had given up on trying to run the tavern through the strategic use of shouting, due to the unsurprising effect it was having on repeat business. They had at least agreed on something though, which was to up sticks and all head off to Brighton, where they could find jobs that did not involve working together.

So Walter lost touch with everyone and everything in Seaford. Not that he cared that much, he didn't really like it anyway. Brighton was bigger, busier, more vibrant. There were more opportunities to get his own back, compensate for the lack of interest or affection that his parents showed in him by making his mark in other ways of his own choosing. Then they would take notice.

But then his mother, a tall, rakish woman with long jet black hair and a sharp intelligence that could not overcome frosted emotions, died of diphtheria at the age of 43, and with his father now working as a blacksmith's apprentice, she wasn't greatly missed by either of them. "She'll be arguing with the devil now," his father used to say. Walter just remembered a mother who couldn't love, and thought bringing up a child was an obligation to be suffered, not a privilege.

At least his father had ruffled his hair now and again, but Walter felt he was doing it because he felt he ought to rather than because he wanted to, and to be honest Walter didn't like his hair being messed up like that anyway. Did anyone? It was as though neither of them had really wanted him and he was more of an inconvenience than a blessing.

Mr Threadwell Senior was at heart a taciturn, morose, introverted man who had regrettably found the perfect way to amplify these traits by marrying a woman who, in the very act of metamorphosising from girlfriend to wife, turned devotion into supervision and spent all but the first few months of their married life haranguing him and finding fault in everything he did.

The death of Mrs Threadwell should have released him from much of his misery but if anything it cemented his attitude that the Good Lord had got it in for him and had mapped out a series of misfortunes over his life that nothing could prevent. Walter was given the impression that he, Walter, was one of them.

The only real use that his father seemed to find for him was to treat him as an unwilling sounding board for a daily diet of depressing thoughts and exclamations, which Walter could only listen to meekly when younger, but as he grew older and larger and started answering back, this became the source of constant arguments between them, only just avoiding violence. It was no surprise, then, that he'd left his father's small two bedroom terraced house in Cobden Road as soon as he could afford to take lodgings himself, and rarely went back to visit.

He shook himself from his reminiscences as his mind returned to his current situation. He was certainly happier in the present than in the past. He was in control now and his plan was working, although it not been without surprises this time.

The fact that yesterday evening Lillian had turned round suddenly on the cliff edge and walked into him just as he put his hands out to push her meant that she bounced back from his outstretched arms, stumbled, then fell, without him having to exert any significant force. That probably explained why she was not certain whether or not he had deliberately pushed her when she suddenly appeared to have risen from the dead earlier this afternoon. But he had dealt with that unexpected situation confidently and this time knew with absolute certainty that she was dispatched.

His meticulous approach had paid dividends. He shouldn't have needed to go back up the cliff path in the afternoon after the police had disappeared, but he wanted to be absolutely sure and check the shoreline further up the coast. And what a good job for him that he did. He smiled smugly, pleased with his own foresight.

Then a tinge of regret struck him, an emotion he was not used to. He had not really disliked Lillian enough to want to kill her however much she irritated him. He had been seeing her as a means to an end and so had put up with her being all sickly sweet and angelic most of the time, not wanting to hurt a mouse. Everything with her had to be good, and correct, and done properly. That wasn't Walter's modus operandi at all - in fact it drove him to distraction. He liked his women with a bit of fire and spice in them, a rebellious edge, a similar disregard for rules and regulations, and a willingness to take risks, all things you could never say of Lillian.

She hadn't deserved what happened to her though. It was the one part of this whole plan that Walter felt was unsatisfactory. Lillian had been a casualty of war, the war that someone else had started when he made Walter look a fool, but she was blameless. A little gullible, granted, to fall for a bad boy like him so quickly, but definitely blameless.

She had even swallowed his story that he was a trainee accountant, when in fact he was a debt collector, a job much more suited to his talents. It was just that accountancy sounded a lot less threatening and also more likely to impress. He doubted that many accountancy firms had their own horse and trap so that was a bit of a risk, but for debt collections you had to be out and about all day so needed your own transport. In a way though, the fact that she was so nice would make the loss even more keenly felt by the person he wanted to feel it, so there were compensations.

And as for that old fool who was with her, he shouldn't have got involved, grabbing Walter's arm like that. Who did he think he was? Walter didn't like anyone grabbing his arm, let alone anyone trying to take his girl off him. That was disrespectful, and had consequences, as the witless old vagrant had found out. Walter had made a snap decision to take the man's life, partly because of the enjoyment and brief thrill that it gave him, but mainly because he couldn't afford for there to be anyone who the police could talk to who might have suspicions. If Walter had marched off with Lillian, and then Lillian had 'gone missing' again, there would be a key witness who would be pointing his finger very squarely at Walter. And there was no way that was going to happen.

Had he covered his tracks though? He thought so. He had dragged Lillian far enough away from the man's body so that it could not be assumed that the two deaths were definitely connected if someone happened to see her on the rocks. Meanwhile the tide was coming in fast and with a bit of luck should wash Lillian's body back out to sea. Even if it did get swept back to shore, there would be no evidence to suggest that she had been thrown from the cliff as opposed to stumbled off, as Walter had described to the police.

As far as the dead man was concerned, he had removed the knife from his stomach, cleaned most of the blood from it on some moss once he was safely in the forest, and it was now back in his inside jacket pocket. He might need it again, although perhaps it would be sensible to swap it for a different one just in case. He liked it though, it was a nice knife, and it had served him well so far. He would clean it thoroughly when he got home and then consider what to do with it.

Before escaping through the woods, he had watched from afar as the man who he had seen coming towards him on the cliff path had found the body, so he knew it would be reported soon, which meant he needed to get back to Seaford town. It would help that the police had been with him that morning, as he had been careful to make a show of saying goodbye after the fruitless search and heading in the opposite direction to the cliffs. So Sergeant Hillcroft would have no reason to think that later that day he had turned round and gone back up again, as surely there would be no point in him doing so.

Feeling his breath becoming more forced, he slowed to a walk. The woods were quiet, and the afternoon sun was breaking through the clouds now and piercing the leafy canopy with javelins of gold light. Walter came to a small hollow, thick with fallen leaves. He couldn't resist shuffling through them just as he used to do when he was a child playing in these woods, then kicking them violently so that they exploded into the air. It still gave him pleasure. Perhaps we all have a playful child inside us, he thought, even people who kill people.

Having caught his breath, he quickened his pace again, realising that the sooner he got back to the inn the sounder his alibi would be. He knew that he would soon emerge down onto some cornfields which backed on to the town. Harvesting was still a week or two away so the crops would provide excellent cover; as it was important that no-one saw him until he was in the town.

Coming to the last of the trees, he turned his jacket collar up, pulled down his cap, walked out of the forest and merged quickly into the rows of corn. His horse and trap were still at the Ship Inn, which fortunately abutted the fields on this side of town. He had taken a room for the night here when it became clear that heading straight back to Brighton last night was not the best option.

It was awkward walking on the lumpy earth and being assailed by the scratchy corn stems and leaves, but he moved through them parallel to the town until he had lined himself up with the roof and chimneys of the inn, which was just visible though the top of the corn stalks when viewed straight between the north/south rows. Then he turned to follow the planted row, walking in the gap between the stalks and brushing through the papery leaves as quietly as he could.

As he approached the edge of the field, he stopped to look up, checking the back windows of the inn that overlooked the field. There were no faces staring back at him and no sign of movement, other than a dirty looking net curtain flapping aimlessly from an open window on the third floor. He could hear the shouts of some children playing in a yard a few houses down, and in the distance workmen were hammering and banging, presumably working on that big new convalescent home down on the High Street.

Not far away a horse whinnied and stomped its feet. It sounded as though it could be Gertie, who he had secured in the stables to the side of the inn yesterday. He had checked her before he set off to meet the police first thing this morning, and he'd soon be hitching her up to the trap again for the return to Brighton. Because he had had to stay overnight in Seaford the police should have taken care of notifying Lillian's family so he wouldn't have to worry about that encounter for now, although he wasn't particularly concerned as he had his story in place, and he considered himself a good actor. But before he left he had to secure his alibi.

In front of him was a chest height wooden fence which marked the boundary between the fields and the back yard of the inn. Thankfully it was in such poor condition that parts of it had blown over in one of the many gales that swept in off the sea, and so he was able to crouch along to a damaged section and step through, then quickly move to the back wall of the inn at the far edge of the building so that he would not be seen.

Earlier this morning, after coming back from his police-escorted walk up Seaford Head, he had returned to the inn and made sure he bumped into Henry Wilkinson, the genial, mutton-chopped innkeeper, in order to ensure that he knew Walter was back. Then after lunch, he had crept quietly out of the inn when Mr Wilkinson was having his afternoon nap, which Walter knew from previous visits that he always took at around 2 o'clock. He supposed it was because Mr Wilkinson had to get up early in the morning to prepare the breakfasts, as he can't have been much past fifty and so hardly ready for one of those convalescent homes where sleeping after lunch was the norm. Walter hadn't wanted anyone associated with him to know that he was heading back up to the cliffs, in case the police started asking questions, and so now if he could sneak back into the building and get back into his room unseen, he could give the innkeeper the impression that he had been there all afternoon.

The north-facing yard was muddy from the recent rain. Balding tufts of grass, struggling with the lack of any direct sunlight, provided a few dots of colour amongst the puddles and dried up corn leaves that had been hustled through the damaged fence panels every now and then by a playful gust of wind.

Although kept generally tidy the yard was also used as a storage area for the kind of detritus and odds and ends that accumulate from maintaining a large building, most of which would probably never be used again but would be immediately required if thrown away. So planks of wood, pots, small sheets and lumps of metal, a spare window frame, a tarpaulin, a pile of bricks, and numerous other odds and ends were stacked neatly up against the back of the building. Henry might be a hoarder, but he was a tidy hoarder.

Walter skirted past them, ducking underneath the windows, and softly tried the back door handle. The door was bolted from the inside. This was hardly surprising as no guests would be wanting to take the morning air in that dirty grim yard when the beach was just down the road, so the door was only opened when it needed to be. He looked at all the windows. He had left his own room's window slightly ajar, which was good, but it was on the first floor, which was bad, as there was no easy way to get up to it. The open window he had seen earlier was on the top floor.

When he had left this morning he had spent more time working out how he would leave without being seen, and much less time planning how he would effect an equally stealthy return. That was an uncharacteristic oversight; he wouldn't make that mistake again. There was no easy way for him to climb up to the first floor so if it did prove that the front entrance was busy he might have to find his way in through a window on the ground floor and take his chances.

As he approached the first sash window, he heard a muffled cough, then some baritone humming, coming from the kitchen window a bit further down. If that was Mr Wilkinson, his luck might be in.

He crept further along the wall of the building towards the noise, careful to duck under the other windows as he went. Now he could hear clanking and scraping, and then a faint whiff of cooked meat. Very carefully he eased his head towards the window and with almost imperceptible movement peered round and into the room. The portly innkeeper was there, with his back to the window, attending to something being fried on the hob of his range cooker.

This was Walter's chance. He ducked back under the window and strode quickly to the other corner, down the side path, and around to the front of the building. There were a few people in the street but he didn't know them and he doubted they would remember seeing him. He was quickly through the front door and into the porch area, then a set of wood-framed glass double doors led to the entrance hall where the reception desk faced the visitors.

As he expected, he could see that there was no-one there. As he carefully opened the glass doors they rattled loudly, the thin wooden frames of the inner doors amplifying the sound. Walter cursed under his breath. Then he heard Mr Wilkinson's voice from the kitchen shouting "I'll be with you in a minute!" Damn. Probably a default response from the old duffer, after all it could be a new guest. But it meant he would be bustling into the hall within seconds, so Walter threw caution to the wind and sprinted up the stairs, acutely conscious of the loud creaks that his planned slow-and-cautious approach would have avoided.

His room was at the end of the landing, and he fumbled for his key as he moved swiftly down the corridor, hearing behind him the weighty footsteps of the owner slapping onto the black and white square tiling of the entrance hall floor. "Anybody there?" Mr Wilkinson now started up the stairs, presumably having heard noises upstairs as well and wanting to check that it was not an intruder.

Walter had to think quickly now. He had reached his door but the damned key was caught up on some thread in his pocket and he was struggling to get it out. The creaks on the stairs grew louder. If Mr Wilkinson reached the top step in time to see Walter's door closing behind him, the game would be up – his alibi could be compromised. He made a snap decision, stopped trying to extract the key and turned round, slowly walking back along the corridor towards the stairs he had just ascended. "Mr Wilkinson?" he exclaimed as the man reached the top of the stairs, slightly out of breath, "did you hear something just then?"

Hand clutching the top balustrade for support, Mr Wilkinson jumped slightly then relaxed as he saw who it was. He raised an eyebrow. "Wasn't it you, Mr Threadwell?"

"No, no, I've been in my room this afternoon. I thought I heard someone in the corridor so I came out to check, especially as you said that there was no-one in the room opposite me."

"Well that's very strange," said Mr Wilkinson, "I know my other guests have all gone out for the day and the first of them isn't due back for another hour or so. I was just preparing their evening meals. Would you mind coming with me and just checking upstairs?"

"Of course!" replied Walter, thinking that this had turned out rather better than he had anticipated. The more he fed the line that he had heard the same noises, the less suspicion there would be on him. "I'll go first. You know, just in case..." He left the words hanging.

Mr Wilkinson swallowed hard, a bead of sweat now appearing on his brow. "Wait. Do you think we had better get something to defend ourselves with?"

"No, don't worry, I can handle myself," replied Walter entirely truthfully this time, but also aware that there was nothing he would need to defend himself from anyway. Mr Wilkinson looked up at the imposing young man ascending the stairs in front of him and believed him. He nonetheless followed at a distance that he judged would allow him sufficient leeway to turn tail and escape if he had to.

Walter pretended to be cautious, reaching the top of the stairs to the second floor with an exaggerated stealth and peering around the corner as though prepared for a masked assailant to leap on him. When that didn't happen, he checked both ways, up and down the landing, then took the last step up and turned to face the innkeeper.

"Nothing!" he announced. "Perhaps it was the wind, or the noise of the builders down the road. Or perhaps one of the other guests came back early after all and are in their room up here."

Mr Wilkinson looked thoughtful. "Yes, well, that could be it I suppose," he said, "if so, no need to disturb them." He paused. "Can't be too careful, you know, can't be letting any old ruffian in off the street." Then, realising he was still holding the slightly stooped position he had inadvertently adopted while creeping up the stairs, he quickly straightened himself up and, with a brief shake of his head to indicate that only a fool would have thought that there was anything to worry about, announced "that's that, then!", turned on his heel and made his way back down the stairs, calling up "oh, and thank you for your help, sir," as an afterthought.

"The pleasure's mine," called back Walter flatly, satisfied that his alibi was now secure. He followed down the stairs, headed back to his room, and was not surprised to find that now that he was not in a hurry the key came out of his pocket without hindrance.

CHAPTER 23 : THE FIRST NIGHT

Lillian was right, there was no sign of any knife. To be honest, Marlo knew there wouldn't be, but you had to hope you might strike lucky. At least if he knew where it was, he could go to the police at any time, once he had his own back story worked out, and claim that he had stumbled across it after a walk in the woods and wondered if it might be connected with the terrible murders he had read about.

But Walter had probably kept hold of it, either to hide somewhere from which he could retrieve it and use it again, or in a place so far from the cliffs that there would be no obvious link should it be found. That's what Marlo would do, anyway, and he had to start thinking like this, trying to get into Walter's head, if he was to second-guess him and bring him to justice.

He checked his watch, only to find it wasn't there. "Lillian, my watch has gone! How will I know the time? And why has it gone?"

"What type of watch was it?"

"It was there on my wrist, it was a digital......oh, I see."

"What?"

"Well, if a Victorian person saw it would give the game away. That Number Five thinks of everything. Damn."

"Check in your jacket pocket, the front. The same way your money was converted, you should find a pocket watch in there."

Marlo patted the front of his jacket and sure enough, felt a small round lump behind a pocket next to his heart. He pulled the watch out. It was silver in colour with a plain white face and roman numerals for numbers, smooth on the back, and with a small knurled ring for winding it up. It read ten past four, which seemed about right.

"You were right, I've got it. It's quite neat actually. I'll miss not having it on my wrist though."

"Why would you strap a pocket watch to your....oh, never mind. I'll find out all these things later I'm sure. You had better start heading for the cottage now."

The search abandoned, he made his way with guidance from Lillian, through the forest and down to the river valley, turning right once he had found the partially overgrown track that led to Jed's hideaway cottage.

The home was very much as he had visualised it, although he had to admit it was not quite in the place he had expected. Instead of facing the beach with sea spray lashing it daily, it was actually a little further back up the track that led down the side of the river. It was set into a hill, its rear flank protected from the elements but the front door facing south east with an unrestricted view across the river mouth, the stony beach it flowed through, and directly out to sea. It was quite a vista.

Marlo could imagine that this would be a wonderful place to live in the summer, but in the winter, a real test of endurance. He didn't envy Jed his lifestyle - not that he had a lifestyle any more, of course.

The cottage was also a little larger than he had envisaged. The once whitewashed walls were now dirty and stained, the slate tiled roof greener than it was grey as moss spread itself from every crevice and across each tile. A couple of small buddleias clung to the edges of the roof, growing out of nothing. Spray and salt had turned the window panes semi-opaque and the wooden frames that held them were peeling and disintegrating.

The weather-bleached solid wood front door looked strong and sturdy though, with large rust coloured metal hinge plates and a hefty black handle that must have been forged to withstand the elements. A thick sawn-off tree stump that looked as though it had a face – the small stub of a broken branch made a fetching nose – was positioned against the wall to the left of the door, as though guarding it. That was uncanny.

"Stumpy!" he exclaimed. "How can that be possible?"

"Who is Stumpy?" Lillian sounded worried.

"Don't worry, it is only a tree stump. But I described it in my book, and now it is here, where I thought it would be. This is weird. There's more to it all than meets the eye, Lillian, there must be. How could I have predicted this?"

There was a short silence, then "Well.... I do remember the tree stump by the door, I nearly kicked it as I left the house with Jed that morning. But as for you writing about it, I don't know. I suppose it must either have been chance, which seems unlikely, or maybe my thoughts and memories were somehow getting through to you as I was trying to nudge you towards coming up with the reason for my death. Maybe there are things about this process that I still don't know, and Number Five keeps back some secrets for himself."

"Keeping our brains on their toes, perhaps." Marlo immediately realised what he had just said and laughed. "Not that brains have toes, of course, unless they missed that bit out at school. Could be that it was a glitch and your thoughts got through to me but shouldn't have done. I did feel at that point that my writing had a mind of its own, it just flowed so easily. Maybe that was it then, you were helping me more than you thought."

"Best not dwell on that, Marlo." Lillian now seemed keen to close the conversation. "What else can you see?"

To the side of the house was an improvised chicken coop, all random pieces of wood and wire but with enough little 'buk-aargh' noises for Marlo to realise it was still well stocked with chickens. That was probably how Jed survived out here on his own, together with trapping rabbits and some fishing, perhaps.

He approached the front door with unnecessary caution, as though Jed was going to burst out and challenge him, but there was no noise from within. It was clearly empty, a lonely house now. But it was where Marlo was going to experience Jed's old life for one night, even if it was only September and so hardly an epic trial.

He extracted the pitted key from his jacket pocket and opened the door. It required a bit of a shove and creaked open to reveal a cluttered, chaotic collection of beachcombing treasures, stacked up in every corner, hanging from rafters, and adorning the tops of every cupboard and unit.

"Wow," he said.

"Have you just walked in?" asked Lillian. "It's not like your average family home is it?"

"You can say that again. There's bits of wood, pebbles, wooden barrels, fish nets, all kinds of stuff, and it's everywhere!" He checked himself. "But why I am telling you this, you already know."

"Yes, I do, but I'm glad you have the same reaction as I did. Jed must have brought back almost anything he found on the beach, but hardly any of it was worth keeping."

"Well, at least he was helping to keep the beaches clean," supposed Marlo, "maybe it's better in here than out there."

It was around 4:30pm now, and the late afternoon sun was painting shafts of golden light onto the floor through the one west-facing window. Motes of dust hung in the air, moving to avoid him whenever he came near, and the smell of saltiness and seaweed was overpowering. A wooden beam festooned with bushels of seaweed might have had something to do with it. But the room also felt strangely heavy, sad with the knowledge that the person who had occupied it and tended to it for so long would never return.

Marlo closed the door behind him and did a quick tour of the place. First was a small lounge with a fireplace, above which was a grey stone mantelpiece weighed down by a thicket of carefully balanced sticks and small branches. They were all interestingly shaped, smoothed and bleached by the sea and piled up in a way that resembled a game of impossible Jenga. Marlo could imagine Jed returning home with his latest sea-carved stick and trying to balance it on top of all the others without the whole lot coming tumbling down.

Their stability was aided a little by the support of a heavy black clock which occupied the centre space and peaked through the mini forest around it like an owl emerging from a hide. The clock was working, a key for winding it placed on the ledge in front. Marlo opened the glass front and gave the key a few turns to keep the clock going for while he was there.

Facing the fireplace were two crumbling wooden chairs and in one corner of the room was a decrepit old armchair with what remained of the upholstery clinging on for dear life. Across from it was a small wooden dresser, naturally covered in reclaimed sea rubbish. A thin door, basically some planks of wood screwed together, led to a rough bedroom that was slightly larger than he had expected, which might explain why the tin bath was in here, propped up against the wall in the corner. Marlo wondered how often Jed actually used it.

Unlike the rest of the house with its heavy set stone slab flooring, this room had floorboards, making it feel a little more homely. A rusty tin commode lay beside a metal framed single bed with what looked like a horse hair mattress and some stained blankets.

"Did you sleep in this bed?" Marlo asked Lillian with a degree of horror, "it must be filthy!"

"Yes, I did, and to be honest I was in no state to worry about how hygienic it was," Lillian reminded him. "I probably made it worse if anything."

Marlo chuckled. "Yes, but now it's my turn. I supposed I'm going to have to adjust myself to a different level of cleanliness in this era, and what better place to start than in a manky bed."

"Manky?"

"Dirty, a bit smelly, you know. The kind of bed you would rather not sleep in, basically. Like this one."

Next to the tin bath was a chest of drawers, upon which sat a dark wood framed dressing mirror, the kind that that swivels half way up so you could point it to the ceiling if you wanted to, although it would be hard to see what purpose that could serve. The mirror sported a distracting crack all down one side, but this was Marlo's first chance to see what he looked like now, and as he got closer one thing immediately struck him.

"My glasses! They aren't my glasses." There was an implied injustice in his tone, as though someone had stolen them. The ones now adorning his face were wire-rimmed and round, as though borrowed from Harry Potter.

"Anything that could incite suspicion is changed when you are transported," Lillian reminded him. "Presumably your glasses were too obviously not from this age."

"Well, I suppose...." muttered Marlo, now more interested in tilting his head back and forth in order to decide whether or not the new style suited him. "Do you know what, they don't look too bad actually." Then, remembering what lay behind the glasses, qualified his comment, "well, not bad in a comparative way of course. It's only re-arranging the deckchairs on the Titanic really."

"It's only what?"

"Re-arranging the deckchairs..... oh, right. Sorry, yes, that will mean nothing to you. I'll explain later."

"Ok, add that to the list!"

Marlo continued his exploration. He had already noticed that an outside privy adjoined the bedroom and that was another thing he wasn't particularly looking forward to trying out. Back on the other side of the lounge was a rudimentary kitchen area with a soot-blackened fireplace in which a battered metal pot hung from a cast iron rack that straddled the charred wood beneath. There was no range cooker so everything was cooked at the hearth.

Opposite stood a stout table with thick knobbled legs, two of them with little squares of decaying wood propping them up to compensate for the uneven flagstones. A couple of plain wooden chairs were pushed under it. To the side of that was an open doorway through which was a utility area with a sink and a pantry. He was pleased to see some food on the pantry shelves, although how safe it was to eat was anybody's guess.

"The food," he asked Lillian, "do you know if I can eat it? I can see a bowl of uncooked meat, some eggs, what looks like a jar of sugar, some potatoes, carrots, and an apple that looks as though it has fought a war. Oh, and here's a salt pot, and what's in this tin..... some small dried leaves." He sniffed it. "Tea! Where did he get this?"

"Seaford I expect," said Lillian sensibly. "There are shops in Victorian times you know, we don't have to send out hunting parties and rummage in the bushes for berries."

"That's not what they taught us at school," Marlo countered with a grin, astonished to find that he was occasionally able to keep up with Lillian when it came to banter, even though he said so himself. And she was a girl too. Maybe it helped that he knew she did not have to look at him, so he could relax a little, let his brain focus on the conversation a little more.

Lillian laughed. "It was so long ago, eh? Anyway, the meat should be rabbit, which I had this morning and was fine. The eggs should be alright as I would assume Jed collects, sorry collected, them most days, and the fruit and veg you can work out for yourself." She sighed. "I did just say I ate the rabbit this morning, didn't I? It is very odd saying that, as to me the day that you are in now was over 130 years ago now. So much time has passed, and yet here we are, back there again."

"It may be again for you, but it's the first time for me!"

"Oh yes! That's very true. Sorry."

"Not a problem," replied Marlo without thinking, being occupied now with sniffing the eggs and prodding the vegetables. "Food seems ok, so that's good, I won't starve. I can maybe make a stew or something. I just need something to cook it in. Ah, there's an old frying pan on the windowsill here."

He picked it up carefully. "And it is old, too. Jeez. It's filthy. Well, burnt anyway, completely black. Not ideal for a stew really, either."

"Maybe you could do a kind of soup," suggested Lillian. "Cut up the rabbit, and add crushed vegetables and water."

"In a frying pan? I've not tried fried soup before."

Lillian laughed. "I meant fry the rabbit first, then add the rest and simmer the soup in the frying pan. Not fry the soup. Actually it would probably be too lumpy for a soup anyway, it would be more like a...... well, alright, you win, it would be a kind of stew I suppose."

Marlo, who could only ever have been called a cook if that had been his surname, politely tried to downplay this unexpected validation of his hitherto undiscovered culinary vision.

"And I thought all I was good for was cooking baked beans. Turns out I'm Gordon Ramsey."

"Gordon who? Why would you be..... well that makes no sense at all, why would you be someone else?"

Just as Marlo drew breath to answer though, Lillian cut across excitedly like a child relaying to their mother a fact they had suddenly remembered from school. "Baked beans, though, let me tell you something I read about in an advertisement in a national newspaper, just before I.... well, you know. Did you know that Fortnum and Mason have started selling them in tin cans? In a sauce too, actually in the can. Isn't that peculiar?"

Marlo, having already only narrowly avoided a smug reply over the stew, found himself struggling to avoid falling into that trap again.

"I suppose it is, yes, when you think about it, but....."

He heard an over-emphasised sigh from Lillian. "Oh, alright, don't tell me, everyone eats baked beans from a can in the 21st century. Am I right?"

"Yes. I'm afraid so. Millions of cans of them, every day, probably."

"Gosh. Imagine that. They must eat nothing else then?"

"But there are so many more people now. Over seven billion now."

There was a short pause, no doubt as Lillian reacted to and processed the implications of that number.

"Seven billion? *Billion*? Are you sure? Where do they all live? They must be falling into the sea! How can there suddenly be so many?"

"Just maths I suppose. The more people there are, the more children they have. Plus they are mostly all living longer now so they don't die off so quickly. And health too, there are fewer diseases that kill people now. It all adds up. It's a big problem though as it will get to the point where the Earth can't support so many people. Some say we are already there."

"I'm not surprised."

"So how many people are there now? In 1886, I mean?"

Lillian did a little snort-laugh. "Ah, well, good question. I don't know. Maybe there are more than I thought. I assumed it would be in the millions, but when you add up everyone from all around the whole world, maybe... well I suppose we could be over a billion. But that just seems such a huge number."

Marlo had been looking round as she spoke. "Well, let's not worry about that now. Far more important is that I have found a cooking pot in the fireplace. I think that's a better bet than the frying pan."

"I agree, and who could dispute that deciding between a cooking pot and a frying pan is more important than the overpopulation of our planet."

"Exactly!" Marlo was only half listening now as he had his mind on the pot, which he had picked up and was examining as though it was a rare coin. "Yep, looks about as good as the frying pan, although 'good' may have been the wrong word to use there. I just have to hope that all the burnt on bits stay burnt on and don't migrate into the soup, or stew, or whatever I end up with." He looked across to the little tin again. "And I can drink tea, too, that's a bonus."

A thought occurred to him. "Don't you eat or drink when you're in the Midrift, how does that work?"

"No, no need for food and water here. That would be too complicated. We exist without the need for any of the bodily functions we had on earth, and yes, before you ask, that includes going to the lavatory."

"Well I suppose if there is nothing inside you that needs to come out, then....."

"Yes, well, no need to dwell on that really."

"I wasn't planning to."

"Good!"

163

The conversation had come to an end. Initial explorations completed and before it got too dark, Marlo went for a quick walk down the track to the edge of the stony beach, observing the way the river Cuckmere carved lazily through it like a big fat watery snake and emptied itself into the sea. He knew from his research that in the time that he came from, it remained the only undeveloped river mouth in Sussex, and here it was all those years earlier, not looking very different.

The track to Jed's house had been periodically used over the last 50 years or so to transport shingle for banking further up the river, in order to prevent flooding. Who knows, perhaps Jed had assisted with those exercises and earned himself a few pennies.

He could see where the bedraggled Lillian would have hauled herself across the stones after her remarkable ordeal in the sea, then somehow made it up onto the track and to Jed's front door. What a girl.

As dusk quickly ushered in the cool dank air, made heavier by the close proximity of the river, Marlo turned and headed back up the track, thinking deep thoughts. "We still don't know why Walter killed you," he said suddenly to Lillian, just before he caught his foot in a rut and stumbled slightly. "Aargh!"

"What was that? Are you ok?"

"Yes, sorry, can't see very well now, it's getting dark quickly. Stubbed my toe."

"There are no street lights in the country!"

"Are there street lights in Brighton?" Marlo was embarrassed to realise that his research on life in Victorian Brighton for his novel wasn't quite as extensive as he had thought.

"Not very good ones, yes. They are gas lights and only just manage to light up what is directly beneath them. But the new electric ones they have installed in London, they are coming down here too now. There are some at the Royal Pavilion but I haven't seen them yet. They are much brighter, apparently." A pause. "I said 'yet', didn't I? I have to stop doing that."

Marlo wasn't sure what to say. "It must be hard..." was all he could think of. Then he brightened. "But if this all works out, you'll be coming back with me and you'll see street lights that will blow your mind!"

"They'll do what? That doesn't sound good at all."

"Sorry, what I meant was, they'll amaze you."

"Ah, right. I tell you what, once you have had your supper, let's talk about your world and what it is like. I have been so curious to hear but obviously we have had other things to focus on first. In the meantime, yes, I'm still desperate to know why Walter turned from being the perfect beau into a monster who could do something like that. And to Jed too. He must be deranged, yet I never had an inkling. My family aren't rich so there's no motive there, even if I could think of how that would have been a factor."

Marlo reached the front door and pushed it open. "Did Walter know anyone else in your family, someone he might have had a grudge with? He could have killed you just to get back at them."

"Well, possibly. But everyone knew I was going out with him so if they had had any concerns they would have mentioned it. It would be worth double-checking with my parents though. They might...."

She stopped, and Marlo could hear sniffling. "Hey, come on now, you'll get to hear their voices through me soon, won't you?" he consoled, "that's more than most dead people get to do, isn't it?"

"But I won't be able to let them know about me, or communicate with them. Neither of us can, under any circumstances, reveal what is happening or the fact that I can hear them. You can't even pass on any messages from me, although I really, really want you to. If that happens, the experiment ends and I die for good. And you... well, you know. You are going to have to be so careful, Marlo, so careful."

"Oh boy," sighed Marlo, "talk about an emotionally charged situation. That's going to be difficult. I suppose I will definitely have to meet your parents won't I? There's no getting round it. And they'll be grieving too, so you are going to hear their grief. Did Number Five realise this when he created these rules? Did he understand how transients might have to hear their relatives mourning them? It's cruel."

It was a while before Lillian responded. She had been crying quietly. "I don't know," she said eventually through some sniffs, "I suppose it is all part of the game for him, part of the challenge. Then if you succeed, the reward really has been earned. I don't want to hear my family grieving for me though, not when I can't let them know that I can hear them, and can't tell them what happened. I really don't want to go through that. To be so close to them, after all this time, even though for them I only disappeared yesterday, it is just going to be awful."

"Can you switch off? Do you have to be in my head all the time?"

"I can't stop hearing things, no. I'm in your head until we finish it. I will have to listen."

"Oh, right, ok."

They both fell silent. Marlo didn't really have anything useful to add, and he wasn't sure what Lillian would have wanted him to say either. He wasn't used to dealing with other people's emotions, especially girls. He was bound to say the wrong thing at some point, he always did. Best stop now.

He was in the house now, but he was standing in virtual darkness. It was a good reason to change the subject. "How do I get light in this place?" he asked, realising that if he had to do anything fiddly like rub sticks over some tinder he wouldn't be able to see what he was doing - a bit of a Catch-22 situation.

"Candles," replied Lillian simply. "Oh, and he might have an oil or kerosene lamp. To be honest, I was so exhausted when I got to his house I just blacked out and didn't see how the house was lit. When I woke up it was daylight. Actually, the light I saw from the beach which guided me to the house was quite bright so there's a good chance there's an oil lamp there somewhere."

There was. Marlo could now see it hanging from the ceiling in the centre of the room. "It's here. How do I light it?"

"With a candle."

"How do I...."

"I know, light the candle. If you are really lucky, he will have some matches."

"You had matches? Ok, that's good. All I have to do is find them in the dark. Oh boy. I'm so used to just turning the light on with a switch. Hang on, what's this...."

Marlo had previously noticed a half melted candle on a shelf on the dresser, and now he had spotted a small box next to it. Fumbling to open it, Marlo could just make out a number of small wooden sticks with coatings at each end. "These look like matches, but why have they got the heads at both ends?"

"What you have to do is break one in half, then rub the two ends together. Be careful though."

"Weird. Ok." He snapped a stick in two, and gently rubbed the ends against each other. Suddenly the phosphorous end flared up and there was a flame. Quickly he lit the candle, and then the oil lamp. The room flickered in the golden light.

"I can see!" he announced. "Thank God for that. Not that I do, of course, it was all my own work."

He was pleased to hear Lillian laugh. "You should be thanking Number Five anyway, not God," she reminded him.

"Oh, right, yeah. Trouble is, it is such a figure of speech now, and also Number Five is a bit of a mouthful isn't it? Much easier to say God."

"I don't think it matters really does it. You say what you want."

"Be careful what you ask for!"

"Oh Mr Campbell!" Lillian swooned exaggeratedly, "you mustn't get a lady excited like that."

"Chance would be a fine thing," Marlo rejoined, loving this exchange even though he had lost the thread of what they were actually talking about now. This was almost flirting, wasn't it? Or was it still banter? How were you supposed to know when bantering (was that a word?) with a girl crossed over into flirting? Having no visual element to it didn't give him any clues, and whether verbal or visual it was something he had not experienced before. He'd seen countless girls flirt with men around him and watched silently with a furious jealousy, but the thought of anyone doing it to him for real had, over the years, become ridiculous in its improbability, so if it were actually to happen the chances are that in the flush of hope he would mis-read the signs when in fact they were just being generously friendly or were naturally gregarious.

He'd almost made that mistake before. No, his only experience of flirting would be to watch other people doing it while he was supposed to smile and feel pleased for them. Initiating flirting himself would be interpreted as creepy, possibly harassment, so he had to wait for someone to do it to him first, then maybe that gave him license to do it back. It was recognising it which was the problem though. He was determined not to get it wrong with Lillian; he would bide his time, as he always did, rather than ruin everything with a comment which was taken the wrong way.

"No-one knows what the future will bring, remember!" replied Lillian with a sigh, bringing everything bumping back down to earth. "Look at what happened to me."

That was it then. A glimpse of excitement, quickly ended, no doubt deliberately. Marlo couldn't come back with a jovial and witty retort after that even if he had wanted to.

"Mmm, yes, you're right. I'm going to look for some more candles now," he said slowly, realising that there was no point trying to keep the conversation going but secretly contented that it had happened rather than not at all, even if it meant nothing. It was a start.

He found some more candles in the other rooms and lit them all. Who cared now if they melted down, it was only for one night.

With light to see now, he looked for things to do. He tidied up the bed, tried out all the chairs to see which was the least uncomfortable and started looking in all the nooks and crannies and furniture drawers in case he could find anything worth keeping, holding a candle to help him see. It wasn't just Walter who had a knife. Jed had some too, but they were for practical purposes in keeping a human alive, not killing one.

He found a small folding penknife that felt a bit flimsy, but then came across a whittling knife with a nice fat handle. The knife was about the length of his hand, well worn but still nice and sharp, with some traces of wood shavings stuck to it that led Marlo to assume that Jed would have kept it in good nick. It fitted nicely in his inside jacket pocket and the thickness of the material would ensure that he didn't stab himself inadvertently. Well, you never know, he thought, and left it there. Given that he was chasing a murderer, a bit of thought towards his own self-defence was a sensible precaution.

On one shelf, under some decaying string and a cracked vase, Marlo was surprised to find a small pile of books. He had assumed Jed couldn't read as he must have been born in the 1830s when literacy rates were very low.

"Do you think Jed could read?" he asked Lillian.

She replied immediately. Always there, in his head, always attentive. You would think she might be doing something else and have to say "Oh, pardon? Hang on.... right, now what was it you said?" but no, she was straight back at him every time, even after a long break from speaking. It was quite disconcerting. She was always listening to him, but it felt as though she was watching him too.

"I would be surprised. You never know though, he might have gone to a ragged school."

"A what?"

"Ragged school. It's because the children are usually in rags. They're for poor children, although that's a statement of the obvious isn't it?" She laughed. "Imagine well-to-do parents dressing their children in rags to go to school. Anyway, maybe he had acquired the books to try and improve his reading. He wouldn't have much else to do in the evenings."

"I can empathise with that! It's boredom city here, there's nothing to do."

"Boredom city? What are you talking about?"

Marlo realised he would be spending a lot of time explaining what he had just said to Lillian. Languages constantly evolved and there were so many words and phrases that he used automatically without thinking that Lillian might never have heard of them before.

"It means very boring. If you put city at the end of a noun it emphasises the meaning sometimes." He considered what he had just said. "But why we say that now, I have no idea."

"It does seem a very odd thing to be saying. So if I have a nice cake, I can say, 'this is delicious city'?"

Marlo laughed. "Ha! No, that sounds daft!"

"And you think boredom city doesn't?"

"Ok, I know, you win. Let's leave that one for now. I guess there are words and sayings you use now which I'll never have heard of either so you might get your own back soon."

"I'll look forward to it. What books has he got?"

There were five small volumes on the shelf in conditions varying from stained and yellowing to falling to bits. A dry 'Compendium and History of Greek Statues' and 'Tales of the Grotesque and Arabesque' by Edgar Allen Poe were thankfully unreadable, with missing or stuck-together pages and possibly with a provenance of having been preserved in seawater for some time until rescued and dried out. The other three were more promising: the pages turned and were legible, even if they did sometimes start to slip out when you turned them. A collection of poems by Victor Hugo wasn't something Marlo would curl up in bed with, but he was pleased to see Dickens' Oliver Twist and a well thumbed Robinson Crusoe, both eminently readable.

"Excellent!" he announced, "that's my evenings sorted now, I have something to read!"

"Don't forget to take them with you then, you'll only be here for one night," Lillian reminded him.

"Good point." He put the Dickens volume on the floor in front of the front door to jog his memory in the morning and kept the Robinson Crusoe to read first. "Right, now I had better turn my attention to food. I might need some help - I'm more used to ready meals in the microwave."

"I don't know what you just said," observed Lillian, "please translate?"

Marlo was liking Lillian more and more; her sense of humour was cute. "Well, I'll start your education of the 21st century here. Ready meals are meals in a sealed plastic tray. They..."

"What's plastic?" interrupted Lillian gently.

"Hey, right, yes, you wouldn't know that either would you? Jeez. I can't imagine a world without plastic. It's everywhere, which is more of a bad thing now actually. Basically, it is a material that can be moulded into whatever shape you want, like metal only supple and pliable and light. But it can be rigid and hard too. There are lots of different types, so you can have plastic to hold your meal in, then more very thin transparent plastic to seal it over the top. When you think about it, it's an amazing product. It has transformed human life on earth."

"When was it invented then?"

"Do you know what, I have no idea. I should know, but... well, some time in the 20th century I suppose."

"Ok, it doesn't really matter, I was just interested. So then you have this meal that you have put in a plastic tray, what do you do with it then?"

"Well, just to clarify, you buy it from the shop already in the tray, then you put it in the fridge to stay cool or the freezer to stay frozen, then when you are ready to eat it you...... ah. Do you want me to explain fridge and freezer?"

And so the evening continued in this vein. Lillian contributed instructions and assistance on how to prepare and cook the rabbit and vegetables over the open fire and turn them into a form of stew, but it was mostly Marlo trying his best not to go off on explanatory tangents as he described aspects of his old life in the new world that Lillian had never known and was struggling to comprehend. At one point though,

Marlo took a break from revealing the future to raise an issue that had been bugging him.

"Lillian, can I ask you something – that message you sent me in the diary, saying 'I live'. You didn't did you? Live, that is. I eventually killed you off in my story, which turned out to be the accurate thing to do. Actually I don't know why I didn't let you live, but my narrative just seemed to flow in that direction. I wasn't really conscious of what I was writing but I turned out to be right - you didn't get washed out still alive to sea, captured by pirates and forced into an alternative life, for example. You did actually die. So although I ignored your message I was right, but presumably how I described your death was just my imagination. How did you really die, and why did your message to me say that you lived? Sorry, I could have said that a lot more succinctly."

He took a deep breath, his mind now spinning a little with the complications of what he had just said.

Lillian was silent for a moment, perhaps thinking through how to answer. When she spoke her voice had become serious.

"Marlo, what you wrote was to all intents and purposes what actually happened. I was able to give you some clues because I took advantage of that fluidity at the edge of the Midrift I was telling you about, where we sometimes overlap with conscious earth. I managed to go further than is normal because you were on the right track and the closer you get the more I am allowed to 'encourage' you, shall we say, with a few signs, like jumbling a few of my words around in the diary to lay some hidden clues. It had to be surreptitious; I wasn't allowed to do anything that meant you didn't have to do most of the work but I could help steer you in the right direction when it looked as though you were almost there. So the reason you made the connection was because you got it near enough right. Whether by luck or judgement, you got it right. Even that Jed was killed by Walter. And yes, the message was that 'I live' but that was when I first fell from the cliff the first time, it did not mean that I lived for ever!" She laughed. "Although being here in the Midrift has felt that way to be honest."

"Ok, that makes sense. One other thing that has been nagging me, though. Walter didn't throw you a rope from the top of the cliff, did he? Was I right to take that out?"

"You were. He didn't. Once I was half way down the cliff on that ledge, I didn't see a rope but I could hear Walter calling for a while, and of course I called back as best I could, but now I realise he was calling in the hope that there would be no answer."

"Nice."

Lillian looked puzzled. "No, it wasn't, at all, actually."

Marlo smiled. "Sorry, we say things ironically these days sometimes. So nice, in the sense that it clearly wasn't."

"Well just say that it wasn't, then? It would be a lot less confusing."

"You're right, it probably would." He steered the conversation back on course. "So I did well to take out the rope!"

Lillian tilted her head to one side a little. "Well, yes, but having said that, even if you had left that in, although it wouldn't have made a lot of sense, I don't think it would have mattered. You can't be expected to get every little last detail correct in your account of my death, and whether there was a rope or not, Walter still killed me in the way you described - that's the main thing."

"Right. That still leaves us with the biggest puzzle about this whole thing, what his motivation was. Why on earth would he want to kill someone as lovely as you? It just doesn't make sense."

"You're right," said Lillian. "On two fronts. Not only does it not make sense, but I am indeed lovely. And thank you for the flattery."

Marlo liked her sense of humour the more he heard it. He was glad he had risked the surreptitious compliment. That was twice now, and neither had spectacularly backfired like they usually did. Careful though, don't blow it. No more for now.

She seemed to be quick-witted as well as attractive, and he realised he was already starting to fall for her. But then he fell for lots of girls, because if you know you are not allowed the finest foods at the buffet, your hunger steers you to the dishes that others are avoiding.

It was just a little depressing knowing that it was almost certain that she would not be falling for him. Experience told him that it never worked like that, so he'd continue to keep his emotions under wraps in order to avoid potential embarrassment.

Lillian continued. "But I really have to find out why he killed me. What did I die for, why did he turn on me like that?" Her voice wavered. "It doesn't make sense. I had everything to live for. He was a monster!"

She paused to control her sudden anger, taking a deep breath, and Marlo could hear her exhaling slowly before resuming. "But as you say the connection works if you have found out how I died, not necessarily why. The 'why' is something that needs to be resolved, it is partly why you are here. To be a resolver."

"Yeah," agreed Marlo, "easier said than done though."

"Yes, but…. very rarely are things easier done than said."

Marlo smiled. "That's a good point actually. As pretty much everything is easier said than done then there is not much point saying so, is there?"

They shared a chuckle and went back to talking about the future. Then at 11:00pm Marlo had to call a halt. Lillian now knew about cars, televisions, mobile phones, aeroplanes, space exploration, and numerous other major advances that he could not help mentioning and then having to explain in more detail. Well, she didn't necessarily know, she just had a vague understanding. He could appreciate how hard it would be to visualise all these things. She would probably have envisaged a flying machine as having big feathered wings without him trying to explain thrust, airflow and lift, and their effect on a metal wing. But even then, what did it look like in her head? Probably very different to the real thing. He also knew that if she was anything like him she would forget much of what he had told her as there was so much to take in. It would be so much easier if he could just show her. He so desperately wanted to show her.

But in the meantime not only was his voice starting to feel strained, but it had been a very long day and the excitement and adrenalin that had kept him going until now had finally run out. He suddenly felt shattered. He was grateful that there was enough moonlight to allow him to use the outside privy without needing a candle, but less grateful that Lillian could hear exactly what he was doing in there.

"I have brothers," she pointed out, "I have heard those noises before, you know."

"Yes but these are my noises, and normally no-one listens to them. It's somehow intrusive, but I'm not quite sure why."

"Well it's something you're going to have to get used to I'm afraid!"

Marlo felt initial discomfort at this thought, but then a sudden feeling of release and hope. Normally only people who were very close got to hear each other's toilet noises, and already he was this close to Lillian.

He liked that. Maybe he could live with it. Not that he had any choice of course. And those kinds of noises were not likely to make her think any the better of him either.

"Just don't listen too hard, ok?" It was a daft thing to say but she knew what he meant even though they both knew it made no sense. "Of course not!" she replied, laughing, "why would I want to? But don't be too noisy, will you."

Even the pleasures and smells of the manky bed couldn't stop him drifting off almost immediately, and in his dreams he was suddenly at work, but not at his desk. Instead he had been called away to assist in an important task that required the assistance of a girl who was to work with him, and the two of them, despite having not met before, seemed to click immediately, and so quickly. Within minutes they were looking at each other knowingly, and now she was now somehow there in a bed and he was snuggling up to her, confident that she would want him. They kissed, and it was the best feeling ever. She was beautiful, with big eyes, long dark hair, and a mouth that just sucked him towards her. He felt so good, so powerful, so in command of the moment. Their lips touched, and now he at last knew what it was like to be passionately entwined with someone who wanted him as much as he wanted her. This was what he had been waiting for. It was desire, in every sense, and he wanted it to last for ever.

It didn't, as his dreaming mind soon realised the absurdity of the situation before anything could happen, and stupidly woke him up, like a bar man calling time just as you begin your first pint. But the dream was so potent that it took a long time before the gradual realisation of reality washed over him and cleansed all traces of the theatre of sleep from his mind. He clung onto that warm feeling though. He didn't want to lose that brief yet brilliant experience of a woman actually talking to him, wanting him. Was that what it felt like in real life? Could he be about to find out?

CHAPTER 24 : THE MOTIVE

Walter waited until it was half past four. He only had the saddle bag he had brought with him when he brought Lillian out here, and all it contained was a small flask of brandy as he was never originally intending to stay the night. When he had pushed Lillian off the cliff that first time he had not expected her to disappear. He thought he would be able to go and get the police, show them her body, answer some questions, then head back to Brighton that evening. He knew there were rocks down there, but was taken by surprise by the particularly high tides which meant that the sea would sweep over them and provide Lillian with a route out to sea. So when he couldn't see her, and then when the police wanted to search in daylight as well, he had to amend his plans.

He was in the same clothes he had on yesterday, between his mutton-chop sideburns he was unshaven and his hair was unkempt, but it didn't matter. He had just lost his girlfriend; no-one would expect him to look smooth and handsome right now.

He grabbed his bag from the bed – there was nothing in it but he hadn't wanted to leave it with the trap. He hadn't told the innkeeper the reason for his overnight stay; he didn't want unnecessary and tiresome questioning from anyone, however well-intentioned. When the police questioned the man, as they surely would, the main thing was to ensure that Walter was not reported as being jovial or in good spirits. Not that he often was of course. It would not require an award winning acting performance from him to remain morose and moody.

He left the room, walked heavily down the creaking stairs, this time wanting the innkeeper to hear him, and rang the little gold bell on the lobby desk. He heard a muffled shout from a back room, then after a minute or so Mr Wilkinson emerged, wiping his hands on a towel.

"Sorry Mr Threadwell, just doing some washing. Are you leaving?"

"Yes I am. How much will it be?"

"Normally half a crown but two shillings for you because of the assistance you gave me earlier."

Walter might have been a murderer but that didn't mean he wasn't averse to saving money. "Thank you sir," he smiled thinly, "very kind."

"Back off to Brighton then, sir?" The older man felt he had to engage in some small talk, but he was at the same time updating his ledger, tongue slightly out as he concentrated on keeping the writing neat.

"Yes, that's right." Walter was saying no more than he had to. Wilkinson had served his purpose, he was the alibi. Now he just wanted to get out of there and return home.

Walter put the two shillings on the desk to move things along. "Thank you very much," he said, and turned to go.

He was halfway to the glass doors when he heard: "Mr Threadwell?"

He turned to look back, concerned something was amiss. "Yes?"

"Is everything alright, sir? You just look a little, shall we say, jaded."

The man was probing - why would he be interested in Walter's health. Probably just a nosey parker. "I've had a difficult couple of days," Walter conceded. "But I do need to go. Good day to you."

"Good day sir."

Henry Wilkinson watched Walter bump his way through the glass doors and heard the front door slam. He wasn't sure what it was about that fellow, but there was something odd about him; he didn't know what it was. Why did he not want to talk? He went to the window and peered out, watching the young man hitch up his trap to his horse, climb up and give the reins a shake. The horse trotted off obediently, eager to get active after its enforced rest, the large spoked wheels of the trap bouncing over the kerb as it turned right towards Brighton.

It was not a quick journey, two hours if there were no hold ups, but it gave Walter time to think as he passed through Newhaven and headed out onto the coast road.

He had killed two more people. Each death had given him a thrill, a pleasure that no life ever could. It showed that he had power, he had control. It was he alone who had decided when these people should die, and he had executed them with ease. Other people weren't strong enough to take these decisions, but he was. He had proved it before. Two other people had already died at his hands, and his careful planning and perfect execution – he smiled at the unintended pun – had illustrated just how good he was at this. He had left no trace, and he had not been caught. He wasn't like your average criminal, who looked suspicious before they had even opened their mouths and became even more so as they talked. No, Walter was like a tiger, stalking his prey with stealth and majesty, concealed in the long grasses and only emerging for the kill before quickly disappearing again. He was camouflaged by his outward respectability, his superior intelligence, and his ability to talk his way out of trouble if he needed to. He had bided his time, thought ahead, created his opportunities. Now his time had come.

He knew he had to be careful though. This whole business with Lillian and the old fellow with her had not gone according to plan at all. One slip-up, one stupid mistake, and he could be heading to the gallows, he knew that. But look at how he had turned it round and adapted to the situation he found himself in. Here he was, heading back to Brighton, with everyone going to think that he was merely a grieving suitor, devastated at the unfortunate accident that had resulted in such tragedy.

He had covered his tracks beautifully, and no-one would ever know the truth. That would show them, all those teachers at school who called him a wastrel who would never do anything with his life. Well it wouldn't show them because they would never know, but he knew. He knew. He knew that he had probably already done more than they would ever do in their entire pathetic little lifetimes. He always considered himself different from the other children, special even. And when he felt like it, he might go back and find some of those teachers and teach *them* something for a change. He felt a shiver of pleasure at the thought of what he could do.

A sudden jolt nearly unseated him. The padded seat gave little protection from the yaws and pitches of the hard wheels of the trap as they seemed to seek out every rut and ridge, and both he and Gertie needed to be alert and concentrating on the road ahead to avoid potholes and any large puddles which may disguise a deep hole. Sunset was around seven o'clock, so the road ahead was not too difficult to see even though the light was fading.

The occasional carriage passed in the opposite direction, and both he and the other driver would give a nod and half a wave, nothing too friendly. He passed the Portobello Coastguard Station, the marker which told him he was half way.

Walter turned his thoughts to Lillian's family. He did feel some fleeting sympathy for Thomas and Mary, the parents. It wasn't their fault that they had a stupid son. No-one crossed Walter Threadwell and got away with it, as the old man with Lillian had found out. Frederick Jones had also got what was coming to him, but in a way that would hurt him so much more than a physical injury. He would be distraught at his sister's death, he would never stop grieving, he would never forget. Yet he would never be able to prove it was Walter, and that was the clever part of it. Walter knew that Frederick didn't even know Walter's name from the time that they had clashed, otherwise he would long ago have said something to his sister, and Walter had been careful never to encounter the fellow while accompanying Lillian in case he was recognised.

But Walter was really looking forward to being recognised now. Frederick would be so convinced that Walter had killed his sister, but he wouldn't be able to prove it. Some subtle taunting, a sprinkling of seeds of suspicion, would rub salt in the wound. He couldn't wait.

Walter well remembered that fateful encounter with Frederick. They had both been drinking in different sections of the same tavern, the Blue Boar. It was late in the evening and the merriment and general noise had reached a crescendo. Walter was with a conveniently attentive lady of dubious repute who had attached herself to him after his drinking companion, a business acquaintance - if a supplier of illicit gin for private use can be called such a thing - had cried off early. A man carrying drinks and obviously slightly the worse for wear had stumbled past on his way back from the bar, and caught Walter's elbow. Copious amounts of ale had jumped from the tankards and landed on Walter's head. "Sorry," the man had said casually, as though it was but a trifling inconvenience.

But this was embarrassing. Walter had beer dripping through his hair and down his face, and he was entertaining a lady. This had to be sorted. Unfortunately he had not realised quite how inebriated he was at this point so as he jumped up to confront the man and teach him a lesson, he found that his legs were no longer capable of fully supporting him, and he instead fell directly into the man.

Both of them collapsed in a heap on the floor, ale spilling everywhere as the glasses smashed and the pub crowd fell silent. Walter was already furious so despite still being on the floor took the opportunity to land a couple of wayward body punches, advising his adversary in no uncertain terms that he would be setting about killing him now, and in a variety of ways, which of course is, when you think about it, not actually possible.

But it soon became clear that Frederick, for it was he, had consumed considerably less alcohol than Walter. He jumped to his feet and stepped back. "Sir, I'm sorry!" he shouted, "I didn't mean to spill the drink. It was an accident. Forgive me."

Walter didn't want to know. It was too late for apologies now. Still on the ground, he swung his legs against Frederick's, causing the younger man to come crashing back to the ground. But as he manoeuvred himself up to deliver the punches that the man deserved, he realised that the other man was quicker. Frederick was already on his knees, and perhaps sensing that apologies were not going to win the day and aware that Walter was lining up another attack, delivered one haymaker punch to Walter's jaw that sent him spinning back unconscious to the stone floor.

When Walter came to, he was propped up in a stall, blood dribbling from his mouth. The lady he had been entertaining with a view to closer union later, had disappeared. People were looking at him with distaste as though he deserved everything he got. And the man who had done this to him had left. He knew the barman though. He got the man's name. And he began to plot his revenge.

Now, as he rode back to Brighton, his revenge was enacted. It was beautiful. Frederick Jones was dealt with. Now who was the better man?

As he finally saw the first of the outer streets of Brighton coming into view, Walter checked his pocket watch. It was half past six. Dark in thirty minutes or so. He flicked the reins and Gertie picked up the pace. They headed into town.

CHAPTER 25 : THE REALISATION

Marlo opened his eyes slowly. Would he see opposite him a framed print of the Athena B shipwrecked on Brighton beach – a memento from his dad's house - on the wall at the end of his bed, next to a photo of himself aged fourteen frozen in mid-air leaping off a sand dune? Or would he see a bare grey, lumpy wall? Before he had even fully focused he knew. He could smell, very strongly, that this was not his bed. And his back hurt from lying on a mattress that had all the firm support of a rice pudding.

Yes, he really was here in 1886. It had not been one incredible dream, it was definitely real. Really, really real. He lay there for a few seconds.

"Lillian?" he ventured croakily, fearing suddenly that she would be gone.

"Good morning!" came back that enticing voice inside his head, immediately and brightly.

"Hi. I'm so glad to hear you. You don't sleep up there, do you?"

"No! We don't need to. How are you feeling, did you sleep alright?"

"Yes, thanks, I think so. Although the bed did its best to prevent me."

"You realise that the last person to sleep on it before you was me?"

He wasn't sure whether Lillian was being a little suggestive or just factual. He hoped the former but as usual he couldn't tell so he played it safe.

"Oh yeah, so it was. So you know what I'm talking about."

"I might not have been too mentally alert when I woke up but I did realise that I wasn't in a hotel," remembered Lillian. "The bed gave it away pretty quickly."

"It stinks," agreed Marlo, "and I don't think either of us caused it. Right, I'm getting up."

He got to his feet and eyed the tin bath warily. "I need a wash, but there's no hot water here is there?"

"You would have to heat some on the fire," advised Lillian.

"That will take forever! Oh, I can't be asked. I'll just have to whiff a bit today."

"Can't be asked? What does that mean, man of the future?"

"Ha! All it means is that I can't be bothered to do it. Which takes longer to say hence why I couldn't be bothered to say it." Marlo smiled at the unplanned wittiness of his reply and hoped Lillian would admire it.

He heard a laugh. "Very good," she said. "Thanks for bothering to explain that to me, or should I say thanks for asking to explain it to me. No wait, I thought I was being clever but that doesn't make sense now."

"I'll never understand how foreigners learn English," sighed Marlo, "it's going to be hard enough just to bring you up to speed from where you are now, and as far as I know you already speak the language fluently."

"I'm not bad. People sometimes understand me."

Same sense of humour. Still on his wavelength. This was so nice, even if he couldn't see her face. Just having a relaxed humorous chat with a lovely girl who was not checking her phone or trying to find an excuse to leave was something completely new to him; it was what he had always dreamed of. He had her complete attention. Yes, Marlo Campbell had a pretty girl entirely focused on him. This was something he couldn't afford to throw away. It was his biggest incentive for completing the task in front of him. He wondered how motivated he would be if his transient was some hairy old bloke with a pot belly – but then he remembered what would happen to him if he failed. Number Five had this all worked out. He had just been extraordinarily lucky that the diary had belonged to Lillian.

He washed his armpits in the sink, then realised he had no deodorant. But then it was 1886, it hadn't been invented yet. Well if everyone else had body odour, so would he. He put yesterday's clothes back on, went to the pantry and eyed the two remaining eggs.

It took a while but the fire was lit, the eggs cracked into the pan, and together with the last potato and a cup of strong tea, Marlo ended up with a perfectly serviceable breakfast, after which he tidied up and made sure there was nothing that could associate him with having been there or make it obvious that someone other than Jed had stayed in the cottage that night. It probably didn't matter but better safe than sorry.

"Right," he said to Lillian, "I think I ought to go now. I need to get to Brighton, don't I."

"You do. The challenge is getting there without arousing suspicion. You can't really go over the cliff path in case the police are up there doing a search for clues to Jed's death. They'll pounce on anyone walking past and start questioning them."

"Right, good point. So round the back then, through the forest again, the way I came?"

"Yes, then once you are out the other side and heading into Seaford it doesn't matter so much, as no-one knows you. You'll need to get transport from there; there should be a carriage service I can direct you to, or you could take the train of course but you would need to change at Lewes."

"You have a train? Well, yes of course you do. It just seems strange that you have no cars but you do have trains. Excellent, I have a choice!" He thought for a moment. "I think I'd like to try the train if that is ok. Hopefully a bit less uncomfortable and I'd love to ride on an old steam train as well."

"It is not old," protested Lillian, then, on reflection "well, about 20 years old I suppose. The same age as me! I don't count the time I have spent up here of course. And yes it is steam, what else would it be?"

"Well, it could be electric, or diesel, or these days it could be magnetic! Well, I say 'these days', but.... well, you know what I mean."

"You still have trains then?"

"Yes, of course! Although they probably cause more problems for people and run less efficiently than they did in 1886. That's progress for you."

"Don't you all travel in those flying tubes you were taking about last night? The air vessels, what were they called?"

"Aeroplanes. Yes, them too. But trains are still a massive part of our transport systems."

"Interesting. Well, by all means take the train to Brighton then!"

"Right, I shall. My planning is complete. I'll head off now then."

Marlo picked up the Dickens book by the front door and slipped it into one of his front jacket pockets, with the Defoe in the other one. His pockets were becoming quite congested, what with the diary in his inside pocket as well; he would have to buy a bag of some kind once he got to Brighton. He placed his Victorian cap on his head – a routine that would take some time to get used to as his head had never previously hosted headwear as far as he could remember - and closed and locked the door behind him. It was a sunny morning and squawking seagulls were wheeling high overhead, each shrieking like a child who has spotted their first rainbow. A fresh, brisk wind from the sea buffeted him and jostled the trees further up the track, making them roar like a fluctuating threshing machine.

"What shall I do with the key? Might be best not to keep it."

"I agree," said Lillian. "Can you hide it somewhere near the house, just in case you do ever have to come back here?"

Marlo looked round. "Under the tree stump by the door? At least then I won't forget where it is or which stone I put it under."

"Sounds sensible to me."

The tree stump was heavier than he thought, and Marlo ended up having to put the key on the ground, then tip the stump over using both hands and slide the key under it with his foot.

He stood back, satisfied that the hiding place was secure. "Well, that should keep it safe from old ladies. That stump is made from solid wood, you know, it's heavier than a heavy thing."

Lillian giggled. "Haha! I like that, very clever."

Marlo realised that it was not just Blackadder word play that Lillian would not have heard, he had a whole lexicon of recent comedy to choose from in order to impress her with jokes that he could pass off as his own. All he had to do was remember them, then filter out the ones that would not make sense to a Victorian. He decided he would see if he could dredge any up as he walked back to Seaford, which he could then somehow crowbar into a conversation.

The chalky track was pitted and stony, with a central ridge that provided an opportunity for grass, dandelions and other weeds to flourish despite the lack of good quality soil. Marlo had to watch his footing but at least he could see where he was going this time.

He had barely gone a hundred yards when a question he had never got round to asking Lillian yesterday suddenly popped back into his head.

"Lillian?" he asked "You know how yesterday you said that my story had a few things in it that I got wrong, and didn't actually happen? The rope being one of them?"

"Yes, I did."

"What were the other things?"

"Ah, well." She paused, as though she didn't want to tell him. "They were only little things, you know, before I died, when you embellished what I had written in the diary and described me doing things I didn't do. But that didn't matter! The only bit that mattered was the description of what caused me to die and who killed me."

"Oh, ok. So, for example, when I wrote that after Walter first pushed you off the cliff he came down to Jed's house rather than go the other way into Seaford, was that correct? I always felt that was a little bit unlikely but it helped with the drama of the story."

"Yes, you mean that it would have more sense just to go straight to the police to report I was missing? I actually don't know. Whatever Walter did on that cliff top, I wouldn't have known about as I was trying not to drown at the time. So he might have gone to the nearest house for help, but then he wouldn't really want help would he? If I was him I would have just walked slowly back to Seaford and then gone to the police."

"He probably ran the last hundred yards so he could appear out of breath and desperate. Yes, you're right, he probably never met Jed until he ran into you both the next day. Well, at least that wasn't a crucial part of the 'who killed Lillian' story."

"You got away with that one!" Lillian agreed with a smile that Marlo couldn't see but heard in her voice.

It made more sense that he hadn't got everything right about Lillian's life, and in a way he was glad, as this whole adventure had to make sense somehow. It was so fantastical that anything bringing it closer to logic would help him process what was on earth was happening to him.

He was soon back at the point where he had emerged from the forest yesterday. The bright blue of the cloud-dotted sky was replaced by the greens and browns of a high latticework of leaves and branches, filtering out the light and the wind and giving him some quiet seclusion as he walked. He reached the location where he had searched for Walter's knife and crept carefully to the edge of the forest. Peering out onto the grass above the cliffs, he half expected to see a police cordon with tents and forensics teams scouring every inch of grassland. But there was nothing. The body was gone, and so were all signs that anything had ever happened there. But there could still be a policeman over the next ridge, so best to play safe. Marlo slunk back into the trees.

As he walked on, he and Lillian took the chance to discuss and agree his back story. Who was he, this stranger who would shortly appear in town? What was his job? What was he doing in this area? Where had he come from?

They agreed first of all that there was no need for him to adopt a pseudonym. There were lots of strange and unusual Christian names in Victorian times, and the name Marlo wasn't obviously too modern, so to make things simpler they would stick with it. He would be a writer, which suited Marlo just fine because in a way that is what he actually was, albeit an unpublished one who happened to have a full time job doing something else.

If anyone asked he could say that he had previously been a journalist writing for a local paper who was now working on a novel, and after coming into some money from a small inheritance he had taken a sabbatical to come to the seaside to concentrate on his book, the content of which he was keeping to himself. It was all sufficiently vague to make it hard for people to get into a detailed conversation, and better than having to explain about the intricacies of some other invented job that he knew nothing about.

They decided that he wouldn't have come from London. Everyone knows of London and people would always be interested to hear about what it is like up there in the Big Smoke (as it had recently been termed) if they hadn't been themselves. If Marlo absent-mindedly started describing skyscrapers, tube trains, and the London Eye that would not be a good thing. It couldn't be a made-up town (even though Marlo had wanted to go with Barchester, from The Archers radio programme, because he would remember it) because that could be checked, particularly if he ended up being questioned by the police.

So they settled on Salisbury, which was far enough away for most people not to have been there, but close enough to explain why he didn't have a different regional accent. He would make sure he said as little as possible about it if anyone asked, and if they did he would divert attention onto the cathedral, which he had visited once and could vaguely remember.

He walked slowly as they chatted, thankful that no-one could see him apparently walking along talking to himself with great animation and intensity. Long conversations like this could not be explained away as easily as a single sentence or question which he could, albeit dubiously, claim was just his way of thinking out loud.

It took him ten minutes to reach the edge of the forest, and he emerged a short distance from where Walter had previously slipped into the corn field. He could see to his right that the footpath that ran between the trees and the field and led to the main connecting road between Seaford and Eastbourne. In theory he could head that way and go backwards in order to go forwards. But it would be much quicker to turn left and take the more direct route. Marlo had no reason to hide, so he wasn't going to plough into the cornfield.

Instead he turned to face the sun, and walked the short distance along the muddy path until he reached a rough gate. Through that he could see an open weed-strewn area that housed a small barn. Some farm machinery was poking out from amongst straw bales in an adjoining stable. Beyond the barn was a larger gate to the road, and further to his right he could see a small block of grey-brick houses next to a larger building with the words 'Ship Inn' stencilled in large black letters on the side wall.

"Here we go then," he muttered under his breath, readying himself for his first encounter with a Victorian stranger. It wouldn't be long now.

He could hear noises inside the barn so he closed the gate quietly behind him and walked quickly but carefully across the open space, hoping no-one would come jumping out of the barn waving a pitchfork and shouting. They didn't. He reached the large wooden gate and was pleased to see that it had limited purpose given that there was a missing fence panel right next to it that he could easily step through. He found himself on Sutton Road – a road sign was helpfully right next to him.

It was a Friday, and it was 10:40am. Marlo couldn't help just standing and staring at what was around him. This really was Victorian England. The rough surfaced street, the ramshackle half wooden houses - some looking as though they would fall down if you opened the front door - interspersed with small clusters of the newer and more recognisable traditional Victorian townhouses; the lady in the distance bustling away from him along the pavement in a voluminous dress and hat - this was what he had seen in history books. But now he was seeing it in 3D. Well, 4D really; he was surrounded by it.

Up on the cliffs and in the forest it hadn't been that different, but here..... this was where it got real, where the full magnitude of what had happened to him was assailing his senses. This was not a film set, it wasn't a dream. Marlo Campbell was in 1886. It was just so bizarre. He wanted to get his mobile out, phone someone from work and say "guess where I am?", then astonish them with his story. But he had no phone and no-one to tell. He had Lillian though.

"It's amazing," he said quietly, still slightly in shock.

"What is?"

"What I'm looking at. Victorian England. I'm in it. I just....can't believe it."

"Well, yes, I suppose it is, for you. For me it is normal of course. But you are a time traveller, Marlo, which definitely isn't normal."

"It's mad, just mad. Jeez."

"Why do you keep saying this 'jees' word?"

Marlo smiled. "It's an abbreviation of Jesus, as in when you see something amazing and exclaim 'Jesus Christ!'. Just sounds less blasphemous I suppose. Will I cause offence if I say that here?"

"I don't think anyone will know what you are talking about. They'll just think you have a speech impediment or something. Actually, that's a good point. If you do say any words from your era that no-one understands, you will need to have an explanation ready. Maybe you can say that before you moved to Salisbury you grew up in some remote community far away and anything nonsensical that you say is just dialect, words you picked up from your old grandmother before she died, that kind of thing."

"Would they believe that?"

"Well, maybe not, but feel free to think of something better!"

"I will! Feel free to think of something, that is. But I probably won't be able to. You know, it doesn't half whiff here."

"Pardon?"

"It smells. Horse shi.... I mean, manure. It's a bit rank." Marlo wrinkled his nose disapprovingly.

"I suppose it takes a bit of getting used to. It didn't really bother me."

"Well, maybe if that is all you've ever known you don't notice it. For me, it stinks and I don't like it. It's probably better than exhaust fumes, though, so there is that."

Conscious that he was in the open now, and constantly looking round, Marlo realised that he now was inadvertently talking more like a ventriloquist, trying not to move his lips, although unlike a ventriloquist he was keeping his voice very low. He decided to try raising his hand to his mouth so that he would look as though he was rubbing his mouth or coughing lightly, so that it would be even harder to tell that he was talking. Even when you can see no-one looking at you, that doesn't mean that someone isn't.

"How many people live here Lillian?" he mumbled through his hand.

"I'm not sure, I think about 1,500. It is not a huge town."

Marlo tried to remember from his research what the population of Seaford was now. Somewhere between 25,000 and 30,000, he thought. Could that be right? He had never actually been to Seaford so had nothing to compare against, but looking around him, there was open land everywhere between the clusters of houses, big square patches of grass and earth, some being used for crops, some for animals, others just bits of waste land with chalky white paths through them where people had taken short cuts. A 21st century corporate developer's dream, he thought; too bad they weren't here to wheel their bulldozers in.

There really wasn't much sign of life either. There were no cars on the poorly maintained crushed stone road, and so no engines revving, no horns sounding. He could hear some distant shouting and hammering as though something was being worked on by a gang of men. Probably a new house or building; Marlo was very aware of the enormous industry of the Victorians in creating places to live and work. But apart from that it was remarkably quiet.

He crossed the road onto the pavement on the other side, as the side he had come from had only a grassy verge. Beside him was a fairly new terrace of four townhouses, in the familiar Victorian style he was so used to from London. The front gardens were small and neat, bordered by a low brick wall with waist high cast iron railings above. He was almost surprised not to see any wheelie bins.

As he passed the second house the door opened and he looked round in alarm. A balding middle aged man with a big bushy brown beard was coming out of his house. He was wearing an ill-fitting suit and carrying his hat and a small leather briefcase, presumably containing papers. The man glanced at Marlo and nodded before turning to call back inside the house "I will see you again next Tuesday then, Mr Gurford."

Marlo barely had time to nod back but as he hastened along the road, not wanting to get into conversation with the man, he realised that he had passed his first test. The gentleman had not looked shocked to see him or reacted as though Marlo was a man from the future wearing a jetpack. He had just nodded and turned away. Excellent. The biggest test to come though would be when he first opened his mouth.

CHAPTER 26 : COPING

It was three weeks now since Liz had disappeared from his life. Tim wondered how long it would be before he forgot how many weeks it was, or whether he ever would. Everything had been interrupted, the path of life diverted instantly, shockingly. The house was so quiet now, so Liz-less. Their lifelong cruise ship journey together had ended – the ship had docked briefly, he had remained aboard but somehow she had got off without even telling him, or saying goodbye. Now the ship, and he with it, had resumed its passage towards the soft horizon, and he was left looking at an empty deckchair and wondering what just happened.

He had got by, as he knew he would. People he knew had been nice to him, very thoughtful. Almost everyone had used the word 'condolences' when they spoke to him - a miserable word that only enters the vocabulary when someone has died - then been unsure what else to say.

Time had moved on, and in due course so would he. But for the moment it was hard, and he really missed her. He could talk to his children on the phone, and Laura rang him every evening for a chat and to keep his spirits up, but it wasn't the same. There were things you said to your partner that you wouldn't say to your children. He wanted his Liz back.

The story of Marlo and Lillian was going well though, and it was helping him cope. He could lose himself in the world that he had created for Marlo, manoeuvre his brain's thoughts away from his own despondency and self-pity and towards a creative imagination that was flourishing after being squashed for so many years by the pressures of work and the demands of modern life.

Now at least he had no distractions. He didn't have to watch Coronation Street if he didn't want to. He could lay the table whenever he wanted, and it didn't take as long either now. He could let the grass grow and no-one would nag him to cut it. Nor would anyone be disrupting his train of thought, and he could take as long as he wanted perfecting a paragraph, knowing that the dusting could always be done tomorrow because it really didn't matter any more.

Tim was finding it harder now though. Marlo was now in Victorian England, and while Tim had plenty of experience to draw on when it came to life in modern London and the soul-destroying misery of being unable to form relationships through your formative years, he had absolutely none when it came to wandering about in Seaford in 1886, particularly as he had never even been there.

He had ended up layering his own imagination over a thin base of reality, and he rather wished now that he had chosen a town that he had at least visited. It was just that it seemed a good option once he had settled on Brighton as Lillian's home. At least he had been to Brighton a few times, although even that was going to be of little use when it came to describing it in Victorian times.

He had explained away Marlo's ability to write the 'story of Lillian' in 1886 Brighton by describing how Marlo had extensively researched what it was like to live there in Victorian times, but now he, Tim, was finding himself in the same position as his character, which was a little annoying as it meant he would actually have to do the research that he had got Marlo to do just by writing one explanatory sentence. If only it was that easy.

As far as Seaford was concerned, he knew it highly unlikely that there was a field of corn where he said it was, and even the forest he described was nowhere to be seen on the old maps he had subsequently found online, albeit that they were from a different decade. Even if he made the awkward journey down to Seaford to have a look at it, he would no doubt find that he had got it so wrong that if he wanted to be wholly accurate he would need to rewrite the whole story.

But this was not a biography or historical record, he thought, it's a novel, it is fiction! It shouldn't matter, should it? And so reassured, he crafted an introductory foreword to the book that served mainly as a get-out clause that would hopefully ward off the battle cries of knowledgeable locals.

He had found himself starting to rely on the computer rather more than he had anticipated. The internet was significantly quicker to get to than the local library, and researching how Victorians lived was proving to be more interesting than he anticipated. Who knew that so many roads were made out of wood? Wood block paved roads were all the rage back then. And some streets of houses had just one or two outside toilets to share between them – that would have been fun in the middle of winter. It was easy to get distracted but he needed to educate himself on the historical context that would affect the characters of his story, something he was finding more difficult than he was expecting.

Trying to find old maps of East Sussex from the 1880s, for example, led him down a number of blind alleys, which is not what maps are supposed to do. He found promising websites that then offered only one line references or requests for payment, and even then what they produced was usually from the wrong era. He wondered whether perhaps the library was a good backup plan after all, but then a brief visit confirmed that he wouldn't find what he wanted there either.

So his output slowed at the same rate as his need to balance imagination with historical accuracy grew.

His son Edward had finally convinced him to move his writing onto the computer, and consign the Amstrad to its place in history. It took Edward a while to migrate the data from one machine to the other, but fortunately he was a secret nerd and relished the challenge. Not only did Tim now have the computer to himself, but he understood Edward's point that it was safer on the computer, easier to do backups, and would allow him to print or upload his story much more easily when he needed to.

Tim didn't pack the Amstrad away though. It continued to sit stoically on his desk, its rubber foot pads half-stuck to the wood from years of gentle pressure, so that it could bequeath him an affectionate reminder of his little ding-dongs with Liz.

And so Tim filled his days with writing and researching. Most of his research ended up being of no use to his story, but of great interest to him. Some afternoons he realised he had written one sentence and probably read a few thousand as he hyperlinked his way from site to site and found himself absorbed in the development of the cotton mills in Manchester, or some similar subject that had no relevance to Marlo and Lillian. He could almost hear them calling him back, telling him to get on with it and sort out where their fictional lives were heading.

He was still making it up as he went along. He had a rough ending in his head, but how he would get there, and all the twists and turns that would be needed to reach that endpoint, were not in his thoughts. He wanted to improvise this, just write and see what happened, what sprung from his imagination. He knew you weren't supposed to do it like this but it seemed to be working so far (albeit this was his own critique, which was likely to lean slightly in his favour). He'd let his family read it when it was ready though, not before. He hadn't been called Mr Red Pen for nothing in the old days – it had to be perfect.

And so the weeks and months rolled on, and Tim continued to spend his days hunched over his monitor, reading and typing, but mostly reading.

CHAPTER 27 : HEADING TO BRIGHTON

As Marlo walked as casually as he could down Sutton Road towards the centre of the town, the bitter smell of ground-in horse manure residue intensified a little, and more signs of life started to appear.

The odd carriage or cart was parked at the side of the road, some with a waiting horse or two attached, one of whom had passed the time by gifting a fresh deposit underneath it which would no doubt be transferred to a vegetable patch in due course.

A straggly-bearded man in his mid-thirties with a bowler hat rode past on a very uncomfortable-looking penny farthing bicycle, a slight grimace of endurance etched on his face as the hard rimmed wheels bounced and crunched on the uneven surface. It made Marlo feel as though he had briefly wandered into a circus. A cluster of ladies stood gossiping on one corner, one of them carrying a cloth bag with what looked like the tops of cauliflowers poking out of it, another grasping the handle of a rudimentary pram with three wheels, a baby asleep inside it.

As he got closer to the town centre, the gaps between the houses got smaller and the buildings larger. The newer ones looked magnificent, the bricks still clean and untainted by exhaust fumes or paint, all the ornate detailing and architraves sharp and freshly sculpted. It was nice to see the original windows and doors as well, and not a double glazing salesman in sight.

A couple of small scraggy dogs trotted down the road towards him, tongues out and tails up, neither of them having to worry about being run over unless they paid absolutely no attention to an occasional carriage or horse coming towards them. People too were traversing the road with just a cursory glance, knowing that if a horse-propelled vehicle was approaching it was easy to hear and step to one side. The dirty surface of the road itself was trammelled with the imprints of lots of overlapping thin lines, marking the passage of wheels that were but a fraction of the width of the car tyres of today.

Marlo put his hand to his mouth and pretended to slowly scratch his upper lip. He was surrounded by buildings now. "I'm reaching a crossroads," he said softly, "it's a T-junction, do I turn right?"

"Not yet," replied Lillian confidently, "that will take you back out of the town. Go straight across, then it should be first on the right after that." Lillian's apparently comprehensive knowledge of Seaford even though she did not live there was probably explained by the fact that there was hardly any town to remember. Just a few key roads in the centre, then some streets that headed into the countryside. You only need to have gone there a couple of times to be able to give directions.

There was a lamp post on a small round concrete plinth in the middle of the crossing, but that and a red post box just down the road were virtually the only street furniture. Marlo found it slightly strange that he here he was negotiating a crossroads in a town, yet there were no traffic lights, no road markings, and no pedestrian crossings. But that was because they weren't needed. A horse and cart were trotting towards him about a hundred yards further down to his right, but other than that it was completely clear of anything moving that could strike him down in a cloud of dust.

He strolled across the road in the same causal way that everyone else seemed to. As he stepped up onto the pavement on the other side he realised he could hear birds singing in the trees above him. He wasn't sure he had ever heard that sound on his way to work in modern day London. Then again, he was struggling to remember whether there were any actually trees available for the birds to sing from on the route that he took. There must be, he had just never noticed once in commuter mode. No doubt in Berkeley Square and similar London havens away from the main roads, birds in trees were more audible, but here in the centre of Seaford it sounded slightly incongruous to him.

"I feel like I've gone abroad, like I'm in a different country," he muttered quietly. "It's just so....weird. Oh, hold up, what does this guy want...."

He had spotted a man of about his own age, with a thick beard and unruly dark brown hair poking from under a large cap, approaching him with a worryingly quizzical look. "Excuse me," he called to Marlo, who immediately started to fear that he would be asked who he was and what he was doing there.

Marlo looked at the man expectantly but nervously as he drew closer. He was wearing rough hewn trousers that looked as though they were made out of recycled door mats, but the white shirt under his jacket was teamed with a waistcoat that smartened his appearance considerably.

He carried a rolled-up newspaper in one hand and a paper bag in the other, as though he was returning from an errand. "I don't suppose you could tell me the time, sir? My timepiece has broken."

Marlo's initial relief was tempered by an ingrained London mentality which led him to assume that the man was readying himself to steal his watch or consider some other form of thievery. "Of course," he said, because that was all he could really say. He checked his wrist then quickly realised his mistake and hurriedly withdrew his pocket watch, holding it tightly enough to ensure that it would take a deft thief to prise it from him.

"It is just coming up to eleven o'clock."

"Thank you," said the man with a brief smile, and continued on his way. Marlo's heart rate stopped rising and he breathed out slowly. Maybe this wouldn't be so hard after all.

"Already making friends with the natives?" he heard Lillian tease.

He put his hand over his mouth, pretending this time to scratch his nose and realising that if he continued with this voice concealment tactic he could soon gain a reputation for having the world's itchiest face. "Looks that way, doesn't it? Seems I have already managed to blend in. My disguise works!"

He was less confident than he sounded. But he continued on, passing St Leonards Church on his left and then reaching a junction where a right turn took him into the road that headed to the railway station. Looking to his left he could see that this led to the centre of the town, where most of the shops were, but even here on the outskirts there were small independent shops all around him now, possibly taking advantage of the footfall from railway passengers. Most had large windows proudly displaying ranges of goods in perfect alignment.

On one corner there was a draper, a large hand painted sign on the wall between the first floor windows above, black letters on a whitewashed background detailing all the key services provided. Next to it was a greengrocer, noticeable only for what seemed to Marlo to be a very limited range when it came to fruit. As far as he could see it was mostly apples, perhaps a lemon or two if the flash of yellow he could see wasn't some form of gourd. They were outnumbered though by huge piles of carrots, onions, turnips and other earth-born vegetables, all being perused and scrutinised by a disparate clutch of ladies planning their meals and weighing up what they could afford. The third of the row of shops was an ironmonger, its window display filled with an assortment of unrelated items including a fireplace and a row of cooking pots, and finding itself untroubled by the level of custom generated by the greengrocer next to it.

Marlo noticed the lovely ornate iron railed balconies adorning the first floors of the terraces above the shops on both sides of the road and wondered whether they had survived the passage of time. Somehow he doubted it. On his side of the road was a funeral parlour with a striped awning over the window and shading most of the pavement. Next door was a butcher - he hoped the two were not connected in any way. Then private housing resumed.

There were more people around now, all going about their daily business. He half expected a film director with a peaked cap to step out of a side road and shout through a megaphone "Cut! That's a wrap, folks!", at which point the film extras Marlo was looking at would immediately stop what they were doing, get out their mobile phones, and head off for a tea break. But that didn't happen, and life continued to roll on around him, no one paying any particular attention to the gawping man standing on the corner looking at them all.

It suddenly occurred to him that almost all the men sported beards or other forms of face thatch, but much bushier than the modern hipster of today – these were generally of bird nest proportions. This worried him.

"Lillian!" he hissed. "Everyone has beards. Well, maybe not the women. But all the men, they all look like those old photos of important Victorian statesmen and politicians with half their waistcoats smothered by a beard. Why is no-one clean-shaven?"

Lillian laughed. "Well, some men are, but I agree not many. It is the fashion now. When the soldiers came back from abroad with beards it sort of became a manly thing to do, so now it is just normal really."

"Ah, well that could be a problem then." He didn't want to say it but felt he had to. "I'm not sure I can grow a beard. Not a proper one anyway. Maybe a moustache. But I've never tried. What should I do? I don't want to stand out like a sore thumb."

"Oh, don't worry, it's not as though no-one has seen a male face before. A few decades ago the fashion was the exact opposite and no-one had beards. Some other men can't grow them either, or don't choose to, so you are not alone. But if you can force out a moustache that might not be a bad thing, just to help with the blending in."

"Right, ok, I'll just have to try that." He felt deflated. He had only been here five minutes and already he was being made to feel inferior by everyone else walking around with look-at-my-impressive-beard nonchalance, and had had to admit to Lillian that he wasn't man enough to cultivate a bit of facial foliage. How not to impress a lady, exhibit A: Marlo Campbell.

With a familiar knot of frustration in his stomach he turned his attention back to his surroundings and realised that he could now see the station further down the road. It was not as he expected: he had assumed that the Victorians always built huge, grand stations, imposing buildings with large arches and architectural flourishes as he was used to in London. But this was smaller, no more than a large house really, but with a large overhanging lead-roofed porch above the entrance. All the windows were arch shaped, as was the entrance door. The sign on its front wall simply stated 'Railway Station', which hardly came as a surprise given that this is what it was.

Three evidently well-to-do ladies of a mature disposition had just come out of the station and were crossing the road diagonally towards him. Long ruffled skirts flounced merrily in the breeze, boosted in size by hidden bustles that gave their owners the overall shape of a formidably thick-handled hand bell. Only the tips of the shoes could be seen beneath them, and their tight fitting jackets sported voluminous sleeves. All wore hats of varying artistry, secured to their heads by means of a bow under their chin. One held a parasol even though the sun was only fleeting.

They were deep in conversation and as they drew nearer Marlo could hear the one in the middle saying "... whatever his intentions the whole affair is very unsatisfactory. I did tell him, you know, I told him fair and square, if he ever set foot on my doorstep again he would have me to deal with, so we knew where we stood and that's that. But he's gone too far this time. He has crossed a boundary, is what I say. If Mr Higgins won't do anything, then I shall have no option but to....."

And with that they were past him and he couldn't hear any more. He was tempted to turn round and follow them so that he could learn what the fearsome lady was going to do, but decided against it.

A few more steps and he had reached the station. "How much will this train journey cost, Lillian?" he mumbled under his breath.

"It should be about tuppence for standard class, I think."

Marlo smiled. He would have to get used to these prices. He found a shilling in his wallet and walked through the entrance and into the lobby. To his left was a wood panelled ticket office in which a young man with short slicked down hair sat looking at him expressionlessly yet expectantly. Ahead of him was the gate to the platform, manned by a whiskered old ticket guard in a smart buttoned-up uniform with gold watch chain and peaked cap, rocking on his heels and toes to keep the blood circulating and his mind alert should it ever need to be.

The three ladies he had seen coming out of the station must have been the last passengers from an incoming train as he was now the only traveller there and therefore the centre of attention, which he didn't really want. He walked quickly across to the ticket clerk.

"Hello, could I have a single ticket to Brighton, standard class? Oh, and when is the next train please?"

The young man glanced down at the timetable on his desk although they both knew he probably didn't need to. His voice was deeper than Marlo was expecting. "It's thruppence, sir, and you're just in time for the next train. It leaves at a quarter past the hour. Change at Lewes."

"Good, thank you." He slid his shilling under the glass and received his ticket and change in return. The ticket was small and made from thick card, not the thin paper he was used to. The pennies were large though, two or three times the size of modern ones. Quite good condition too, he thought, probably worth something. Except they weren't of course, they were worth one penny.

He was glad to see a couple more people walking into the station as he headed for the gate, so at least the station staff would have other people to attend to as well now.

The ticket guard waited expectantly, his impressive moustache bristling. "Thank you sir," he said, holding out his hand to take the ticket. Marlo found it odd that someone needed to check his ticket even though he had only just bought it, and the man had seen him buy it, but he handed it over while the guard clipped it with great authority and passed it back to him.

"Have a good journey, sir." He held open the gate.

"Thank you." Marlo smiled and stepped onto the platform. There were two trains waiting, one either side of the platform. The end of the train that the engine was attached to was the biggest clue as to which one was his, but before heading for the right hand side he stopped to admire the majesty of the steam locomotive that had just arrived.

It was cooling down like a horse that had just completed the Grand National, wisps of grey steam rising and colliding with the platform canopy, and with heat still emanating from its metal flanks. The three large spoked wheels on the platform side were connected along the side by a long piece of metal which went up and down as the wheels rotated. Marlo knew very little about trains but he did wonder why you needed to connect them all like that – surely if one wheel jammed then being connected would stop the other two as well? Or maybe the combined force of the other two would get the other one working again. But then the metal bar didn't look strong enough to.... well, anyway, it was not his concern.

He passed the driver's cab and looking back he could see the still glowing coals through the little metal hatch, which was slightly ajar. The sweat soaked driver was tidying up and wiping his hands with a rag, talking to the train guard who had climbed up to join him. He did not look quite as clean, or as rested, as the well paid train drivers Marlo was used to seeing sitting comfortably at the front of the train controlling the whole train with a knob on a stick and a few buttons, and no doubt being paid considerably more even accounting for inflation. He wondered who had the greatest job satisfaction though.

Behind the engine was a carriage just for the coal, then behind that another four quite compact carriages, this time for people. His train on the other side of the platform was the same. There were doors between every row of seats, like the trains he used to remember from his childhood and which were no doubt still running in other parts of the country where budgets were more important than the welfare and durability of the customer's nether regions.

There were a few people already on the train but it wasn't busy. Marlo got into the second carriage in an area where no-one was sitting and flopped himself down by the window, away from the sun. He immediately wished he had been a little more cautious in lowering himself down, as the seats were squashy and unsupportive and he could feel the frame underneath, not like the rock hard equivalents on some modern trains and buses, where the fabric was there to give you a mental illusion of softness which soon dissipated when your rear portions came into contact with what felt like a block of wood. He still preferred them though, as he could see he would have backache by the end of this journey, which was worse than backside ache in his opinion.

He tried the seat opposite and it was no different, which wasn't surprising as he could see permanent dents in almost every seat. These carriages must have been in service for some years, and well utilised too. Never mind, he would just enjoy the experience of riding in a steam train and seeing the countryside as it looked, or looks, all those years ago.

He saw the people who had come into the station just after him, a couple, who were now approaching on the platform. They looked to be just a few years older than Marlo, possibly mid-thirties, the rather attractive lady holding the man's arm. He looked contented, as well he might given that, in Marlo's opinion, he was only marginally better looking than Marlo himself.

This gave Marlo hope, as he wondered whether Victorian girls were more impressed by manners and intelligence than the girls he had always failed to lure. Then he remembered, he didn't need to worry about that, he had Lillian! Well, he didn't have her, not yet anyway. But it was clear to him now that she was definitely the one he wanted and it was all in his hands now. Thank goodness she couldn't tell what he was thinking. Or had she just said that to re-assure him? Perhaps she was delving around inside his mind now. But then, if she could do that she wouldn't have needed him to explain modern life in so much detail and have no understanding whatever of anything beyond 1886. He relaxed again, although a tiny part of him wanted to see if he could catch her out.

The couple walked past and on to another carriage. He double-checked around him. The nearest person was a silver haired man sitting about five rows in front of him, reading a newspaper. Provided no-one else got on, he should be ok to talk softly and not be heard, particularly once the train was moving.

"Lillian," he whispered, "can we talk about what I'm going to do once I get to Brighton? I'll need to get lodgings, so how do I do that? Where do I go?"

"Well," replied Lillian thoughtfully, "what you don't want is to end up in a doss-house, sharing a room with who knows who. So.... I do have an idea. Two weeks before I died – and I don't think I shall ever get used to saying that - I had to deliver a hat to Mrs Chomsy in Arbuthnot Street, one of our regular customers. She's a really nice old lady, bit of a dizzy age now, probably well past seventy, and quite frail. I think she has trouble with her lungs as she takes lots of short breaths and can't move fast. We got talking and she said that since her husband died a few years back she had wondered what to do about her house and whether it was now too big for her. Her husband Albert, well you should have seen him, he was a huge fat fellow. I'd never seen anyone that size before when I first set eyes on him or even half his size for that matter. He was so overweight he had to go down the stairs backwards, because he couldn't see where his legs were. It was a wonder he lasted as long as he did. But Mrs Chomsy was telling me that he snored like a billy goat, so she had to put him in his own room at night so she could get some sleep. That room is empty now and she was thinking that enough time had passed now for her to consider using the room for renting out for lodgings. She wasn't sure though, I think she was a bit trepidatious about letting a stranger in her house, even though the money would come in useful as it is a large house for one person. It would be a safe haven for you though, and I doubt she would charge too much."

"Sounds perfect," said Marlo, but if she isn't advertising it how will I approach her?"

"Ah, yes, good point," conceded Lillian. She thought a while. "Alright, supposing you say that you bought your cap at our shop last week and were served by me, and you mentioned in passing that you were looking for lodgings, and I mentioned that I knew someone who might be interested in renting a room."

"Yep, that's plausible. Although you couldn't really vet me in that short time, for all you knew I could be a ruffian or a thief, and Mrs Chomsy might be wary. It might be better if we make out that you knew me already somehow and could vouch for me. That should put her mind at rest."

"Yes, true…"

There was silence for a while as they both tried to come up with a back story that would not require too much explaining.

"Hang on," said Marlo suddenly, "Will Mrs Chomsy know that you've died? If I turn up announcing that you're dead but can vouch for me, that would look suspicious - and logically impossible too, of course."

"Another good point. This is harder than it ought to be, isn't it. It would be best if she doesn't know, then when she finds out you will already be established in the room. But if she does already know, and has read it in the newspaper..." she trailed off.

"Yes, that could be, because the report I saw in the local paper announced your death on the Friday edition, which is today. Does she read a newspaper every day?"

"You'll be surprised to hear that I never asked her that. So I've no idea. Let's hope she doesn't."

Marlo berated himself for the stupid question and tried to move things along quickly by adopting an impressively decisive tone.

"Ok then, how about this. If I turn up, mention your name, and she immediately says 'oh, isn't it terrible news' or something, I can pretend I haven't heard and look equally shocked. Then I'll encourage some reminiscing about you, mention the lodgings idea, but if she says no I walk away. If she says 'oh yes, lovely girl' or something and obviously doesn't know, then I still pretend I don't know anything either, and use the back story that we are about to come up with to persuade her to rent me the room."

"Yes, that's good. So all we need is a back story. It has to fit in with your new identity as a writer as well, recently arrived from Salisbury. You can't be a friend of the family because my parents could confirm that you are not. You can't say you went to school with me because I went to a girl's school and anyway I'm guessing firstly that you are not a girl and secondly that you're a little bit older than me?"

"Possibly," hesitated Marlo, before quickly realising that it was obvious that he would know Lillian's age, and admitting "make that probably. In other words, yes, I am."

He was thankful she did not linger on that point, but continued "so we need to have already known each other. Or...." she suddenly sounded excited "how about, you knew me because you first saw me being assaulted in the street by a thief who grabbed a package I was delivering, and you bravely came to my aid, chasing after the thief, retrieving my package and returning it to me. I was so grateful I said you could have a discount on a new hat so the next day you came back to the shop. How does that sound?"

"Brilliant. That makes me sound like someone who anyone would be pleased to have lodging with them. I'm not going to come up with anything better than that!"

Marlo had already noticed, with some delight, that compared with other Victorian men he had seen so far in the town, he was not as short and feeble as he felt in modern London, in fact he was positively lanky. So to believe that he had got the better of a thief didn't perhaps require quite the same stretch of imagination as it would do normally, as there would be a good chance that the thief would be no taller than him, albeit almost certainly stockier.

At that point Marlo heard two loud whistles from the front of the train. That was a proper steam whistle, he thought, and a burst of nostalgia reminded him of holidays of his youth, riding on enthusiast-restored steam trains all around Britain thanks to his parents' penchant for holidaying in the UK. "All this on your doorstep, why would you go anywhere else?" his father used to say when Marlo hinted that to go abroad for a change might be nice.

It wasn't the same after Mum died, Dad couldn't enjoy himself on a holiday in the same way as it just served to remind him that he no longer had a partner. So holidays after that became less frequent and more about day trips and weekend breaks in Belgium than full holidays.

Yet here he was, back on a steam train, actually living the nostalgia that preceded his own nostalgia. He heard the rush of steam as valves were opened and levers released, then after what seemed like an age the carriage slowly started moving, more slowly than a modern train as it struggled to overcome the initial inertia. The chug-chug of the engine, each exertion puffing out great clouds of steam that rushed past as though they were on a factory production line, increasing in frequency as they got faster.

Soon the world was rattling by and he was experiencing glorious, proper, clean, pollution-free, beautiful, as-it-should-be rail travel. He slid the window down and stuck out his head like he used to do on those childhood holidays and took in a big breath of clean country air, only to be battered by a big puff of greasy steam that made him quickly withdraw and close the window again. It didn't matter though. He thought of the train that would be running on this line in his modern parallel world – a functional, unromantic, dull-looking metal tube with a diesel engine. It might be a bit quieter, faster, and smoother, but it just wasn't as fun.

On his left was the sea, on his right open countryside with the odd house or barn, some in ruins, dotted around like lego bricks on a patchwork quilt. He could see a man leading a horse with a plough in one field, tilling the earth in the same laborious way that man had done for centuries, not knowing that it wouldn't be long before the tractor arrived and changed everything.

Then the train started to slow and before he knew it they were already drawing into Newhaven, the steam slower to blow past the carriages, then wrapping them in a blanket of shifting vapours as the train came to a halt.

"I'm at Newhaven now," he informed Lillian quietly. "The station looks nice, very clean."

"Well, it should be, it only opened a few months ago," advised Lillian. "That should be the Harbour Station, as opposed to the Wharf station that it replaced. It was in all the local papers when it opened."

There were quite a few people on the platform – perhaps mid-morning was a popular time to travel. He heard a few doors opening and shutting and three people got onto his carriage a little further down, thankfully not close enough to hear him whispering.

The station was adjacent to the harbour that formed the sea entrance for the River Ouse, and now that most of the steam had cleared Marlo had a clear view across the water. He could see even then that Newhaven had become an important maritime town. There were boat houses, landing docks, wharfs, loading cranes and a lifeboat house. Further back where the water channelled out into the sea, lighthouses marked danger points.

On the far side he could just make out a tram making its way to the West Pier promenade, like a beetle crawling steadily along a window ledge. Nearest to him were moored a number of large engine-powered boats, the funnels standing proud above the deck cabins like extended top hats, whilst amongst the fishing boats, smaller sailboats went about their business in the water, tacking to and fro to catch the wind as they headed out to sea or back to port.

Working men in crumpled trousers and jackets looked busy as they scurried around along the harbour edge, some leading disinterested horses slowly pulling wagons loaded with piles of large sacks or wooden crates. As the train moved off again and smeared the quayside buildings with steam, he could see what looked like a ferry moored further up, just before a swing bridge that led to the main town. But then the track moved away from the river, past some gas works on his right, and on out of town, and his view back to the harbour became ever more distant. From here on into Lewes the river accompanied the railway though, guiding it steadily through the fields and open spaces, never leaving its side.

Soon Marlo could see ahead the outline of Lewes Castle on top of the hill, and to his right the flat landscape suddenly reared up into more South Downs hills, sheer chalky cliff faces towering up as though to deflect the train to the left as they neared the outskirts of the town. The track duly veered away, crossed the river, and looped round past a goods depot into the railway station at the southern end of town.

As the engine sighed to a halt and the steam, tired of being bellowed past the carriages, instead rested and settled upon them in a slowly disintegrating shroud, Marlo heard a whistle from the platform and the sound of a station attendant shouting "all change please, all change ladies and gentlemen!"

"You're at Lewes now then?" said Lillian, hearing what he was hearing.

"Yes, just getting off now, then I'll need to find the Brighton train."

"It's probably coming down from East Grinstead. You might be in a siding."

Marlo opened the door and stepped down onto a platform partially obscured by the slowly dispersing wisps of white cloud, like something out of The Railway Children. He looked up and down. "Yes, looks like I am in a siding now. There's a track on the other side of this platform though."

Most of the disembarked travellers were heading for the footbridge that took them over the tracks and out of the station, but as this was the only line heading south west he couldn't be far wrong if he waited here. He wasn't alone, there were about half a dozen others.

He was just debating whether or not to summon up the courage to ask someone whether he was definitely in the right place for the Brighton train when the platform attendant, now visible in his smart black uniform with a double row of shiny silver buttons down the front of his jacket, called out "Brighton train this platform, Brighton train in five minutes!."

Marlo relaxed. "Looks like I'm ok," he whispered. Who needs digital signs when you can rely on communication via a good old fashioned shouting human.

He could hear the train before he saw it. The shriek of the steam whistle as it emerged from the tunnel under the town announced its arrival, and as it eased majestically into the platform Marlo still couldn't help feeling the same delight that he had felt waiting to get on the Ffestiniog railway in North Wales, his favourite steam train journey, all those years ago when he was ten. Although the journey this time wasn't up a mountain, it was no less exciting watching the steam engine arrive.

A lot of people got off the train, but a fair number remained on it as well.

"I might not be able to talk easily on this train," said Marlo quickly under his breath, "there are more passengers."

"Alright, that's fine. I'll just listen and wait."

CHAPTER 28 : GEORGE

Marlo found a door with no heads in the windows adjacent to it and got on. There was a young man sitting on the other side of the aisle, open book in hand but looking out of his window. Marlo looked around but it seemed that most seat rows had at least one person so he sat down where he was and settled in for a contemplative and internally silent trip to Brighton.

But it wasn't silent. Barely two minutes had passed since the train had hauled itself out of Lewes station and past the ruins of the old priory before Marlo's gaze was diverted from the window. He heard something drop to the floor and then roll and scuttle across the aisle and under his feet. He looked down and saw a silver fountain pen, which he picked up. It was an impressive implement, engraved with a swirly pattern that felt good to the grip.

The young man on the other side of the aisle was looking at him nervously. "I'm so sorry," he said loudly over the noise of the train, "I dropped my pen. It was in the same pocket as my pencil, and as I pulled the pencil out the pen came too."

Marlo reached across and handed it back. "No problem. Nice pen," he said.

The man smiled. One of his side teeth was missing at the bottom.

"I use it for work, I spend most of the day writing things down, so I need something good to write with. Can't use it without ink of course, so I was just about to pencil something into this book actually." He waved the book, although Marlo couldn't tell what it was and wasn't sure whether he really needed all the explanations.

"I do a fair bit of writing too actually," said Marlo before he could stop himself, feeling he now had to say a bit more than 'nice pen', but already well out of his comfort zone. Talking to strangers wasn't his thing.

"Really? Do you have a favourite pen too?"

That wasn't the reply he was expecting and the awkward 'did I just say that?' look that flitted across on the young man's face perhaps indicated that as small talk went that wasn't the best rejoinder he had ever come up with.

Marlo was about to say "no, actually," and explain that he used a keyboard but stopped himself just in time. He wasn't even sure when typewriters were invented so decided not to go down that avenue either. "Er...yes." His mind raced. "It's a black one, not as nice as yours though." He rescued the situation: "But I haven't got it on me."

"I carry mine everywhere," advised the man solemnly as though this was information of great importance. "I do ledgers and books, for a solicitor. Always writing! May I ask what is your occupation?"

This chap was certainly eager to talk. Marlo decided that this was as good an opportunity as any to try out the back story that he and Lillian had come up with, as this fellow seemed the friendly sort. "I'm an author. Well, not a published one yet, but I'm writing my first novel."

"How exciting," said the man politely, his face struggling to reflect this excitement. Perhaps he didn't read many novels, which would be helpful as it would indicate that Marlo may not have to answer too many questions on the subject.

The man was about Marlo's age, perhaps a few years younger. His black hair was greased down and parted not in the centre, and not at the side, but half way between, in a style that Marlo thought very unbecoming but was a not uncommon look of the times. He had the wide mouth that Marlo always envied, and had topped it with a cultivated and tidy moustache with the hint of a twirly bit at each end, presumably fashioned with some wax. He was otherwise clean shaven, and this reminded Marlo that he himself hadn't shaved this morning. Not that it mattered really. As he had already explained to Lillian, he was no Desperate Dan when it came to stubble. Even when a token selection of hairs decided to timidly emerge from random places on the lower half of his face, they were so wispy and spaced out that you couldn't see them unless the light was at a certain angle, at which point someone might be tempted to try to brush them off, not realising they were attached. It was yet another example of his terrible luck when it came to trying to look manly in order to attract women.

The man was wearing a jacket that looked like a coat, or perhaps vice versa. It was frayed at the edges as though he had favoured it for some years or more likely, could not afford a new one. His trousers were rumpled and he had thick legs. Not fat, just thick, very thick, as though he so favoured trousers that he wore a lot of them, all at the same time. Although he was shorter than Marlo, his legs were probably twice as chunky as Marlo's spindly limbs, which would have annoyed Marlo were it not for the fact that they did look just a little too large, as though he had baby elephantiasis. His shoes were quite considerably worn away at the heels, perhaps not helped by the weight of his legs, to such a degree that when standing up he was probably a good inch shorter than when he had first tried the shoes on. It appeared that doing ledgers was not a path to great wealth and fortune.

"Are you going to Brighton?" Marlo changed the subject then realised his haste to do so had resulted in him blurting out a rather foolish question, given that they were both on the train to Brighton.

"Yes," said the man without hint of a smirk, "I've been visiting my aunt in Chailey – she has been celebrating her fiftieth year, so my employer was good enough to let me take an afternoon's unpaid leave yesterday to go and see her."

"That was nice of him," said Marlo, not sure whether or not he had been ironic in his tone as he well knew that many employers would relish the chance to save a bit of money.

Clearly the man was more talkative than he was, but it might be useful to make an acquaintance, particularly as he would probably know people in Brighton who Lillian would not, so he continued the conversation. "Do you not have to work today either then?"

"Well, yes, I do," the man seemed happy to explain, "but I convinced Mr Gradforth – he is my employer, you understand, and a bit of a rummy old cove, if truth be told – that I would catch up on the workload by working extra hours if necessary. I wanted to stay overnight as my aunt and uncle had invited me to stay for a special evening meal they were cooking and they were keen for some company. Then I regret to say I overslept a little this morning. But hey-ho. I will be alright. Mr Gradforth knows he would have trouble finding anyone else as good and conscientious as I am." He paused and smiled before adding the word "... normally."

Marlo laughed. This was someone he already quite liked. He decided to be bolder than he ever would have been in his previous life. He reached over and held out his hand. "My name is Marlo Campbell, by the way. How do you do."

The man eagerly grasped Marlo's hand and shook it firmly. "I'm George Smith. Pleased to make your acquaintance." He sat back contentedly as though having just finished lunch, then, feeling as though he couldn't really leave it at that and was obliged to continue the conversation now, turned again to Marlo and looked at him curiously. "Forgive me for asking, Mr Campbell, but if you are writing your first novel, do you not have some other means of earning an income while you are pursuing this objective? Man cannot live on bread alone, as they say."

Seeing a look of mild surprise on Marlo's face at the directness of the question, George held up his hand and apologised. "I'm sorry, I didn't mean to be so impertinent. It is nothing to do with me. Please forget I asked."

"Ooh, what a naughty man!" Lillian's unguarded comment in Marlo's head was quickly followed by "oops, sorry, couldn't help it." Marlo couldn't help smiling and cleared his throat to indicate to Lillian he had heard her. The fact that George was still looking at him cautiously confirmed that Marlo was definitely the only person who could hear what Lillian said.

"Well," said Marlo, enjoying the fact that the power dynamic had swung his way, "there is no harm in telling you I suppose that I did benefit from a small inheritance, so I am using that to live on while I write the book." Then, in case George had any ideas, "it was not a lot of money so I do have to live frugally."

"I know the feeling," returned George, glad to steer the conversation back to firmer ground, "almost all of my wage goes on board and lodgings and food. My aunt and uncle were good enough to pay for my train fare to Chailey as with the missing day's wages yesterday I'd be in a right pickle otherwise. There's one rule for the likes of us and another for those that pays us!"

Marlo couldn't argue with that. It was no better all those years later, with his senior managers' salary and bonus packages looming over his own pay scheme like an elephant standing over an ant. Yet every year they pleaded poverty when it came to announcing the general pay rise, saying the company was trading in a very competitive market, tough conditions, stormy waters around us, firm hand on the tiller required, and so on until they ran out of sailing metaphors. Then the staff (or 'colleagues' to give them their newly designated collective noun), upon receiving their 0.5% pay rise, were encouraged to consider themselves delighted by the benevolence and largesse of their kind employers given the trading conditions. It was only when the company accounts were published and it was shown that the board of directors had not only reluctantly accepted a 10% salary rise in order to prevent them all leaving for greener grass being grown in the same way by executives in other companies, but they had also raked in shovelfuls of gold bars in share options schemes, bonuses and pension contributions, that it became clear how hypocritical they had been. The wealth gap was growing, and Marlo wondered whether it was now worse than in Victorian times.

"Couldn't agree more," he nodded. "That's partly why I decided to write this book, to see if it could make my fortune. Not that that is likely, of course."

George held up the book in his hand. "You never know! This might only be a reference book for my job but someone wrote it, and someone bought it, so money changed hands. It just depends how popular your book is. What is it about, if you don't mind me asking?"

There was no reason not to tell the truth, he just wouldn't mention the diary. "It's about the life of a girl growing up in Brighton and all the adventures she gets into." He reflected on that description, then added "It's better than it sounds."

George may not have been convinced by that re-assurance but he didn't let it show. "If it's about Brighton then it can only be good. You know Brighton well then?"

"Ah, well, no actually. That's why I am going there now."

"Would it not have been easier to set the story in your home town?"

"Er, well, yes, it would but.... well, I wanted somewhere by the sea, and part of the story involves the Royal Pavilion." Marlo hoped he had come up with something believable. "Well done," he heard Lillian whisper, "a good recovery!" She sounded like she was enjoying eavesdropping on the conversation.

George nodded, seemingly buying the deception. "It certainly is a remarkable structure; I can see why you might want to write about it. Did you know it is about 40 years since the Queen last visited? Despite its royal history she stopped coming. Rumour has it that she went for an incognito walk with Prince Albert on the pier and some young scamps spotted her and were so rude she never came back."

"Really? I didn't know that."

"There's a lot I know about the town actually. I'm a bit of a secret history scholar and Brighton has a lot of history so in my spare time, not that I get much of it mind, I sometimes find myself down at the library just poring through big old books from the past. You learn so much!"

Marlo couldn't help smiling at George's enthusiasm. Before stumbling across Lillian's diary he had always found history to be a dry, boring subject, which perhaps stemmed from the fact that his history teacher all through secondary school, Mr Webb, was a dry, boring old man. Lessons would consist of him standing at the front of the class reading aloud from some dusty historical text book, reciting at length the reasons for the spread of the Ottoman Empire in the 14th century, in a drawling, monotone voice that could have made a lottery win sound regrettable.

One friend had once commented that he had once stared at some dishwater for ten minutes and could confirm that it was more interesting that one of Mr Webb's lessons. Pupils were expected to listen to and memorise the salient facts, but most of the class spent the time writing notes to each other, doodling, or staring out of the window, none of which Mr Webb noticed due to his dogged persistence in wanting to get through his pre-determined forty seven pages of dusty words before the bell went.

But the diary had changed all that. History had become real, not a text book. And now, of course, he was part of history, not to be recorded by it but to be absorbed in it. It had become fascinating in a way that no-one else could possibly imagine.

"As you know Brighton so well," said Marlo hopefully, "do you know a good place I might be able to rent a room? I have a possibility lined up but if that falls through I'll have to find somewhere else."

George thought for a second. "It depends how much you want to pay, of course, but if as you said you have a budget to keep to then there is a lodging house not far from where I am that is well run and not too dear. But you have to share the common areas with other people, it is only your bedroom that is private, and that can be more like a cell to be honest. But it is cheap, about thruppence a night, and clean."

Marlo winced. "Hmm, not too keen on that. I'd rather keep myself to myself really. Also I need somewhere quiet where I can sit and write. Just so that I have no distractions, you understand."

It was a lie of course, but he couldn't think of anything worse than sharing his private space with strangers – the comparatively luxurious living conditions he enjoyed in 21st century London would be hard to let go, but privacy was probably the most important aspect as he had to be able to talk at length to Lillian without anyone watching him.

"Of course, of course. Those boarding houses are much better regulated than they used to be but they are still not the most delightful of places to reside, I will admit."

"Where are your lodgings?" Marlo asked.

George sighed. "I still live at home, believe it or not. My father is ill and has trouble working so my income helps my mother and sister look after him. You see, now that I am earning I pay board and lodgings as though I was, well, a lodger. We live in Sillwood Road – it is not too far a walk from the station. I do at least have my own room, so that compensates for the lack of independence."

Marlo was not as surprised as he might once have been. In his world he knew lots of young people who could no longer afford a deposit for their first home and rather than renting, were making use of the family home so that they could save their earnings. How little things changed sometimes.

"I'm sorry to hear about your father. Is he seriously ill?"

"He has trouble breathing and just can't get enough air into his lungs. Some days he has difficulty walking from one room to the next. We are not sure what it is. He survived pneumonia a few years ago and the doctors think his lungs never recovered properly. He used to be so healthy and active too."

"I'm sorry to hear that." Marlo guessed that whatever it was that Mr Smith Snr was suffering from, and it sounded a bit like emphysema to him, in the 21st century he would be diagnosed almost immediately and possibly given treatments or guidance that could bring him back to full health, but medicine in 1886 still had a lot to learn.

"What did he do before he was ill?"

George had diverted his eyes to the hills and trees flowing past the train window, possibly remembering the old days, but he quickly looked back at Marlo and replied "He was an architect. A good one too, and we had a good lifestyle once; my sister, little brother and I had a happy childhood. But now he can't easily get to the office, and visiting sites and directing builders is virtually impossible. It's so sad. He just sits in a chair at home most of the time. He gives advice from time to time, but mostly people travel to him now rather than the other way around."

Marlo needed to get the conversation back on track. "I think we should lighten the mood, or at least return to where we were. If I want to rent a nice room and not encounter hoards of people sharing my space every day, where should I go?"

George was happy to shake off the melancholy that had enveloped him. "Yes, you're right. Well, then you are into private landlord lodgings really, assuming you don't want the expense of a hotel?"

"Correct." Marlo did not know how long he would be here or how long his money would last so he could not be extravagant.

"Well, I would have to ask around. I have friends and working colleagues who rent rooms, I can see if any of them know of a vacancy that they could recommend then let you know. If I give you my address you could call round tomorrow evening."

"That is really kind of you, thank you." Marlo rummaged in his jacket pocket and brought out Robinson Crusoe – he could write on the inside cover. Except, he realised, he didn't have a pencil, or any writing implement come to that. "I don't suppose I....."

But George was already proffering the pencil. "It is 7 Sillwood Road. It's just off Western Road. It's not too far from the seafront actually, just a road or so back."

Marlo took the pencil and wrote the address down inside his book. He only just stopped himself from saying 'and the postcode?'

"Thanks," he said, handing the pencil back. "If my initial suggested option doesn't work out, then all I will have to do now is find somewhere to stay tonight!"

"You didn't plan ahead much then?" asked George, curious that someone would just arrive on a whim.

Marlo hesitated but heard Lillian whisper quickly "say you were going to stay with my family – friends of your parents – but then my death changed everything."

"I had family friends I was going to stay with but then their daughter died this week and obviously that has... well, you know. I had to make alternative plans." Marlo looked down, feigning a modicum of grief.

"Oh, gosh. I see. I'm so sorry. That's awful. How old was she?"

"Twenty. In the prime of life. A beautiful girl. One of a kind." Marlo shook his head sorrowfully, at the same time wondering if Lillian would say anything.

She did. "Thank you, sir. Four unarguable truths," followed by a giggle.

Marlo had to use every ounce of control to maintain his solemn countenance when all he wanted to do was to burst out laughing, which would not have been appropriate at all. He stifled a laugh with a cough and decided to quickly move the conversation on.

"So I just have to hope the lady suggested to me will rent out her spare room. Otherwise I may be on the streets!"

George was silent for a while. The train chuffed on, the rhythmic noise of the engine borne on the breeze blowing through the carriage from an open window further ahead.

"Well," George said finally, "if you can't find anywhere, come to my house and we will see what we can do."

He said this with the air of a man not remotely confident that he could actually do anything, and Marlo realised he may have just said it because he felt he had to.

"Oh, I didn't mean.... look, thank you, but I wasn't expecting you to step in – after all, you've only just met me. I'm really grateful, but this is my problem, and I'll find a solution. Please don't worry about me. But thank you, I do appreciate it."

George gave a half-smile of barely disguised relief in return, perhaps realising he had been more gregarious than he ought to have been, given that this was a stranger he didn't know and here he was almost offering him a place for the night five minutes after saying hello.

"I'm sure you'll find somewhere," he offered, still not being sure at all.

Marlo nodded. Maybe he would just have to put up with a backstreet lodging house just for the one night at least; it couldn't be that bad.

It took less than half an hour to reach Brighton from Lewes. As they approached the town and passed by Moulsecoomb and Preston Barracks, Marlo could not believe how few buildings there were. He had driven this way so many times on the way to his Dad's house, but he hardly recognised it. This was country, not town. The site of the university was just a field. Where were all the housing estates? Even as they drew close to the station terminus it was just open land around them.

This was a backwards comparison: rather than seeing how things had changed over time, Marlo was seeing how things had reverted over time. Not that time had run backwards of course, it just felt like it. One thing that hadn't changed much though, whether you looked backwards or forwards, was the station. As they coasted in under its magnificent sweeping double-spanned curved glass and iron roof, glass panels shedding light into the grateful gloom below, Marlo concluded that it was no less impressive from whichever era you viewed it.

The train eased to a halt, contributing a touch more obscurity to the general fog that hung damp within the terminus. Marlo looked across at George.

"Are you going straight to work from here, Mr Smith?" he asked, remembering to avoid engaging the 21st century habit of addressing everyone by their forenames however briefly you had known them.

"Yes I am, and I am hoping that Mr Gradforth is in a good mood!" said George, standing up and adjusting his coat. "He probably won't be letting me have another afternoon off in a hurry."

Marlo smiled and opened the train door. "After you!"

"Thank you." George stepped past him, and it did not escape Marlo's notice that the young man was an inch or too shorter than him. Marlo joined him on the platform and they headed towards the barrier in that uncertain way that friends who have only just met each other do.

George glanced down beside him. "You travel light, don't you? Do you not have a suitcase?"

Marlo wished he had prepared for that question rather than having to quickly make something up on the spot. "Well, yes, but that is because..... I sent the case on ahead of me. To the family of the girl. I'll collect it later."

"Oh, right." George appeared to accept this as perfectly plausible, which was a relief to Marlo, who had been expecting George to look at him as though he had just taken his trousers off.

As they approached the barrier George pulled out his ticket from the depths of a large pocket. "Do you know where you're going now?"

"Well, not really." Then, remembering he had Lillian to guide him, "but I have a pretty good idea. I just need to know where I'm starting from."

"Which street does this lady live on? I can point you in the right direction once we are outside."

"Thanks, it's, now let me think...." Marlo waited for Lillian to interject.

"Just off Edward Street," she advised, right on cue.

"Ah, yes, just off Edward Street."

"Oh right," said George, handing his ticket to the guard at the gate, "I know it. Easy to get to from here as well."

"He's right you know," he heard Lillian say. "Good!" he replied, responding to them both at the same time.

Marlo followed George through the platform gate, which resembled a wide picket fence, but in cast iron, and taller and thinner. A big sign saying 'Main and East Coast Lines' arched over the gas lamps that were positioned either side of the entrance.

The departure area was still busy with people even if peak travel time had finished. Most of them, it had to be said, were men in hats, and most of the men in hats were wearing some form of suit, even if it was the slightly more down-at-heel versions that he and George were sporting - although the mystery of whether George's jacket was a coat or not perhaps disqualified him from that categorisation.

The hats were varied, but primarily of the bowler or cloth cap variety, with a few top hats for good measure, giving added height to the wearers which perhaps helped to bolster their sense of superiority. It was strange how some of the working men wore bowler hats like the city gents, albeit a lot less cared for, yet despite the sartorial advantages only a few wore the top hat, presumably because that did actually look a bit silly when teamed with filthy, rumpled clothes. It would also be more likely to give the owner back ache from having to constantly pick it up in the course of any non-upright manual labour.

He followed George out into the sunlight, through the large entrance arches and onto the plaza, giving Marlo his first view of a large Victorian town in Victorian times.

He could see that beyond a protective wall in front of him, stretching away towards the sea, was a long wide thoroughfare, Queens Road. He knew the road even though he had always driven into Brighton rather than taken the train, as it dissects the town from north to south and is hard to avoid if you are out shopping. It runs right down to the seafront, if you discount the fact that it becomes West Street for the last section. But it looked (and smelled!) nothing like it does now.

In fact the station didn't either, despite being the same building, because it was so fresh and uncluttered. He looked back to see a beautiful Italianate frontage, a row of columns framing the arches, and on the first floor fifteen – he counted them – identical architraved sash windows, rectangular and solid, eyes to the town below. The ornate wrought iron canopy above them, looking as clean and pristine as its recent installation warranted, stretched the length of the building to provide shelter for passengers coming and going in carriages and coaches, the taxis of the day. In front of them a chest high light brick wall prevented you falling onto the road beneath.

Instead of concrete frontages and 1970s office blocks that valued function over form and squeezed the road between them, looking down Queens Road he saw substantial terraces of classic Victorian splendour, brickwork sharp and bright amongst the older, more shambling buildings, and the whole road seeming to have more space, air and light.

Instead of buses, taxis and cars competing to push their way along a dull grey tarmac thoroughfare, he saw horses, carriages, carts and people, far more of them than in Seaford, weaving haphazardly past each other on a dark beige macadamised crushed stone road. If you ignored the horse droppings, he knew which vista he preferred.

"You look like you have never seen a town before," grinned George. Marlo started, forgetting his fellow traveller was still there.

"Oh, sorry, yes, well, I...." He struggled to explain his apparent open-eyed wonder at a normal street scene. "I am just impressed by the architecture of this area."

George accepted his compliment on the town's behalf. "Thank you. Anyway, look, I do have to hurry now I'm afraid. So, to get to Edward Street, do you see that road down below us that goes under that bridge? That's Trafalgar Street. Go that way, then when you get to the end you will see a church in front of you. Turn right along a big wide boulevard that leads to the Pavilion, then when you reach it turn left and that is Edward Street. Told you it was easy!"

"Excellent, that does sound straightforward, thank you."

"Not at all. Anyway, it was very nice to meet you, and remember that if you do need somewhere to lodge, come round to my house tomorrow evening after eight o'clock and I might have found a vacancy somewhere. I can't promise though, and even if I could I wouldn't." He smiled while Marlo tried to work out what that meant then pretended he had.

"Of course! Listen, I'm not expecting anything – if you have no luck then that's fine, I will just have to take my chance with something temporary. And I might secure more permanent lodgings this afternoon anyway of course. I do really appreciate your efforts though." He clasped George's hand. "Many thanks, Mr Smith."

"Call me George, please."

"Thanks, likewise call me Marlo."

"I will. An unusual name! No time to explain it, though, my employer will be tapping his pocket watch and getting angrier." He turned sharply, narrowly avoiding bumping into a man carrying a large box on his shoulder. "Whoops, sorry! Alright, I shall say goodbye. Perhaps see you tomorrow!"

And with that he trotted off, his loose fitting jackoat (Marlo had decided to christen it as such) bouncing up and down on his shoulders a little as he ran.

"Goodbye!" Marlo shouted after him, "thanks again!"

He walked to the wall to look down into the road below and become further accustomed to his surroundings.

"He's gone then?" Lillian suddenly asked.

Marlo jumped. "I wonder if I'll ever get used to having you in my head, you gave me a start there. Yes, he's gone."

"Sorry, can't help it! Anyway, the sooner you bring Walter to justice the sooner I'll be out of your head! Meantime, shall we head off to Mrs Chomsy?"

Marlo felt confident enough in Lillian's sense of humour to mock her a little. "What's this with the 'we'? I'm the one doing all the walking remember."

"And I'm the one in your head doing the thinking and directing now, so that makes us a team, which means we are a 'we'. Does that not suit you, Mr Campbell?"

He could tell she was ribbing him. Or was she? This is where he kept getting things wrong, misjudging other people's feelings towards him, assuming they thought like he did. He rowed back.

"Yeah, of course it does, it's great. I suppose it means I've turned into The Man With Two Brains. Except one of them isn't mine. That's just so weird." He brightened as a thought occurred. "Does that mean I am effectively twice as intelligent now? "

Lillian didn't miss a beat. "Well, half of you is."

Marlo smiled. "Your half, no doubt? Hang on though, if half of me is twice as intelligent then overall I am still more intelligent as the other half would not be less intelligent. Although I'm beginning to wonder as I'm not sure I've fully understood what I've just said."

"Point proved!"

They both shared a laugh. She was on his wavelength; this was so good. If only it could stay like this.

During this exchange he had been practising his novice ventriloquist's voice and finding it unsurprisingly impossible to say words beginning with 'p' or 'm' without moving his lips. Even 'moving your lips' begins with 'm', in the same perverse way that the word dyslexia is so hard to spell. He doubted anyone was looking at him though so when out in the street he was probably safe enough with the odd lip tremor.

"Anyway, enough banter," he announced, realising his 'b's were no easier, "I'm going to head down Trafalgar Street now."

"Alright. Shout when you need me."

Marlo turned to his right to gain access to the road which sloped down in front of the station, and set off into the unknown.

CHAPTER 29 : MR THREADWELL AND MR CARBERRY

Walter stretched and yawned. He had slept well, too well, as the knocker-upper had disturbed his dreams when he rapped on the window with his long bamboo stick, as he did every day at 7:00am. Walter wondered whether the time had come to try out one of those new alarm clocks that had recently appeared on the market so he could be more flexible with when he was woken, but he had heard they were not very accurate. He'd stick with what he knew for now.

Now, today. How would he structure his tasks. He had to go to the office first. Mr Carberry, his partner, would be wondering what had happened to him after his non-appearance yesterday, as the telegram Walter had sent from Seaford before he joined the police on that search just said 'NOT BACK TIL FRI WILL EXPLAIN LATER'. He wasn't going to waste money on a lengthy description of events, not when you are charged by the letter, even though that was two days he had taken off, not just the one they had pre-agreed.

Mr Carberry controlled the debt collection schedule amongst other things, so would no doubt be expecting him to catch up on missed appointments yesterday as well as today's list. He doubted that would be a problem even if some slipped over into next week. Mr Carberry knew he could only push Walter so far, so if Walter decided to leave some visits until Monday, there was very little Mr Carberry could say that would prevent that happening. Even though he owned half the business, it was a slightly smaller half. Mr Carberry knew his place.

Then he would have to squeeze in a visit to the Jones's, ideally as soon as possible. He wasn't looking forward to that, but not to do so would raise immediate suspicion. He had to play the part of grieving suitor for a while, but having only known her for a few months, it would be no surprise to them if he moved on with his life and left them to their mourning. Also, of course, he would have to provide them with his version of events so that they would know it was an accident and not be swayed by anything her brother Frederick might suspect.

He would string out the revenge with Frederick, at first claiming not to recognise him and having no knowledge of any fight in a tavern should Frederick bring it up, then a few months later, once the dust had settled, start coincidentally bumping into him, perhaps physically as well as literally, and dropping hints so that Frederick would realise what might have happened but be unable to prove it. That would be fun.

He got up and quickly got dressed – the early mornings were getting colder now and he could feel the chill of the floorboards through the small mat by his bed, which was no surprise as the upper sash window had been pulled down a little all night to keep the air fresh and prevent disease from stale air.

He had taken a stand-up wash last night so felt clean enough, and after a shave and some bread, beer and cold ham for breakfast felt ready to face the day.

He had already thoroughly cleaned the knife he stabbed Jed with, and it was back in his jacket pocket. Even if he wasn't using it in anger, just a glimpse of it could be quite an effective influencer when persuading debtors that he would not take no for an answer, so he wasn't going to hide it or throw it away unless it was going to incriminate him. But how could it? The hole in Jed's stomach could have been made by any knife with a similar blade, and if the police ever searched him he would just say he kept it for self-defence, or for whittling sticks or something. They couldn't prove otherwise.

He hadn't had time to make himself anything for lunch so he'd just have to grab a pie or some oysters from a street stall. He looked round his living room, making sure he hadn't forgotten anything. The room was gloomy, but he always kept the curtains half closed to ensure privacy despite the tired looking net curtains arguably already performing that function.

The room was much bigger than his last place, which was a pokey attic room with one small window that looked directly out to a disused cemetery. Now, the success of the business had allowed him to upgrade to a whole top floor of a house in Southover Road. Being on a corner it had a small sunless yard accessed from the side road which the landlord had accommodated to accept a horse or two, although how happy the horse was with this arrangement was another question.

Walter had to leave his trap in the road but he had secured the wheels with a chain. It wasn't ideal which is why he sometimes walked home and left Gertie and the cart at Burvey's stables two roads down from the office, but that cost money. It was extremely useful to have the option of taking the horse home, so this facility helped make his decision to move easier. At least it meant he would be at work in good time this morning.

Mr Carberry looked up as the bell above the door tinkled and Walter entered the office. "Nice to see you, Mr Threadwell," he pronounced, his tone even yet the sarcasm not hard to detect.

"It always is, Mr Carberry," replied Walter gruffly, wiping his boots on the mat and rubbing his hands together, "it always is." Addressing each other by surname had become something of an amusing habit and as a by product, they felt, lent an appropriate gravitas to their conversations.

His boots reverberated on the polished floorboards as he walked with heavy strides across to his side of the desk. It was, appropriately enough, a partners' desk, large and solid, hewn from mahogany and with eight lockable drawers on both sides, though one side was considerably less exercised than the other.

Walter pulled out the chair and sat down on his side, opposite Mr Carberry, eyeing his partner for signs of emotion, a clue as to what he was thinking. But Mr Carberry rarely did signs of emotion; that was not his thing. He was calm, level headed, and in Walter's view, would give a dead fish a run for its money when it came to his work persona. But teamed with Walter, it worked. He was the water to Walter's fire.

"I received your telegram," said Mr Carberry, sitting back in his chair and placing his palms together to make a steeple. "It didn't tell me much."

He was older than Walter by about ten years, and his unruly wavy hair, crawling randomly over his head like a clump of seaweed would if you threw it there, was receding slightly now at the front. This combined with the worry lines appearing on his forehead made him look older than he was. He had a firm jaw, set hard from years of frowning and grimacing at documents and parchments.

"It wasn't meant to," replied Walter. "My lady friend, you know the one I told you about?"

"Yes, Lily wasn't it?"

"Lillian. Anyway, she had an accident. She died."

Mr Carberry sat bolt upright, eyes and mouth open. "She what?? Died? Surely this can't be true? Why didn't you say so? Oh, my good heavens, I'm so sorry."

For once, Walter thought, he could see emotion in the man opposite, and as emotions go shock is quite a good one. He thought he had better start emoting a bit himself as the last thing he needed was his partner starting to smell a rat.

He looked down at his lap, as though now struggling to keep it together. "She fell. We were out walking on Seaford Head. She was too close to the edge, slipped, and..... she was gone. Washed out to sea. There was nothing I could do."

"Oh my goodness. Oh my. Oh my. How.. well... um....." Mr Carberry, normally so measured in his responses and in control of everything he said, was now jumbling his words. He ran his fingers distractedly through his hair, the resulting arrangement no worse than it looked before, before taking time to shake his head sadly in order to restore his composure. "What a terrible thing. I don't know what to say. Are you alright? No, of course you aren't. No wonder you didn't come in yesterday. When did this happen?"

Walter sniffed ostentatiously. "Late on Wednesday. There was a storm coming in and we were rushing back but she wanted to see the waves below. I had to stay in Seaford yesterday to help police with the search. Just in case, you understand."

"Did they find the body of the poor girl?"

"No, nothing."

"Oh dear. How awful, and for her family too."

"Ah, yes, that is the other thing," said Walter, looking up and trying to look earnest, "I'll need to go and see them today, explain what happened, you know. I didn't get a chance yesterday, I got back here quite late."

"Of course, of course my dear fellow." Mr Carberry had started to regain his professional shield. He adjusted his tie and pulled at his cuffs before opening the big leather bound book in front of him. "Well, I had already amended the schedule but I may have to do it again. When are you looking to visit the family and how long will that take?" He made it sound like a routine appointment.

Walter tightened his mouth as though thinking, even though he already knew what he was going to say. "Well....I'd rather get it over and done with, go there now. The police will have told them yesterday so I doubt the shop will be open today but they are bound to be in residence."

"Probably haven't slept much, I shouldn't wonder," noted Mr Carberry. "Where do they live?"

"Challenor Street."

"About 15 minutes walk from here. Do you think an hour will be enough? It is eight thirty now, and I've got Mr Debbard down for nine thirty but I suppose we will need to postpone that one again, then I'll give you, er..., give you...." He ran his eyes over the list of clients and their addresses, trying to find an efficient route between them all. "How about Mrs Whitlam in Regency Square at ten o'clock? Big house, big debt owed to her doctor. She's made a lot of promises apparently but he's lost patience with her now and wants what he's owed." He looked up expectantly, eyebrows raised.

Walter nodded, pushed back his chair, and stood up firmly in a way that showed he had pulled himself together and fully overcome his momentary exhibition of suppressed grief. "Yes, that should work. I had best get this out of the way now. I'll take the trap."

"Wait," said Mr Carberry, "let me give you the rest of the morning's itinerary to save you coming back here." He took a piece of paper from one of his drawers, licked the nib of his pen, dipped it in ink, and wrote down a list of names and addresses with amounts owed, then carefully applied the blotting paper, blew on it ceremoniously and handed it to Walter. "Right, that should do it. All look alright to you?"

Walter glanced at it, not really caring. His mind was only on his first appointment; he would worry about the rest afterwards. "Yes, fine. I'll be fine."

"Of course you will." Mr Carberry watched Walter turn on his heels and march back out into the street, impressed at his resolute fortitude under such trying circumstances. He knew not to question Mr Threadwell's methods. The man was an enigma, always kept himself to himself. But as a debt collector he was in his element. He exuded menace, helped in no small part by his considerable stature and saturnine looks, and Mr Carberry knew that people who owed money quite often responded to light intimidation far more readily than to polite requests, which was probably why the business was doing so well.

He himself was more than happy to deal with the administration side of things. As long as he left Mr Threadwell to his own devices and could not be held accountable for any of his methods, he felt secure in himself. He sighed, shook his head at the magnitude of this unexpected turn of events, then re-applied himself to the task of once again re-arranging all the remaining outstanding visits.

CHAPTER 30 : THE JONES FAMILY

Walter was usually confident in his own abilities and rarely troubled by self-doubt, but as he turned Gertie into Challenor Street and eased her up outside the shop, his heart was beginning to beat faster. This is where it could all go wrong unless he was careful. He would have to act the part, get into character and convince them all that he had no part at all in Lillian's demise other than in his attempts to save her. Then the job would be complete, the lid screwed tight on his deception.

He knew this place well; he had often collected Lillian from here when they went for walks. The street was slightly off the beaten track but peppered with small independent traders, some of whom relied on word of mouth and a good reputation to entice potential customers away from the main shopping streets nearby, but most who just needed some cheap office space for administration.

What passing trade there was could also be in no doubt that if looking for a hat, this was the place to come. The front window was festooned with hats of all varieties, shapes and sizes, many suspended by invisible wire, seemingly in mid-air like fleets of flying saucers. A good proportion were festooned with feathers from ostriches, herons and peacocks; some even had whole birds attached, although thankfully for the wearer they were of the smaller variety such as blackbirds and swallows.

Above the window the shop sign simply said 'Thomas Jones – Hatter' in gold lettering on a shiny black background. On the glass of the shop door to the right of the main window there was a sign saying 'closed'. Written on a piece of card underneath was 'due to a death in the family', an explanation that any annoyed customer would find it hard to argue with.

Walter tied Gertie to a lamp post next to the shop. He tried the door but not surprisingly it was locked, so he pulled the door bell handle and heard the clang inside, then stood back so someone looking down could see him. There was some movement in the net curtains and a minute or so later he saw Thomas Jones emerging from the gloom through the shop to open the door. He was a slim man and a good six inches shorter than Walter, but then a lot of people were. As usual he was well tailored, as befits a man used to presenting customers with a professional appearance no matter what the situation. He sported greying mutton-chop whiskers that clung to the sides of his face like swift's nests to a wall and were bridged by a substantial moustache that spilled like a frozen waterfall over his mouth. Every time he looked at him Walter had envisaged Mr Jones trying to drink milk or a pint of beer and having to constantly wipe his bristles. His hair was neatly parted to one side, although tufts stuck out this morning where he may well have been rubbing his head in distress.

He did not look directly at Walter but came slowly to the door and unhurriedly took a large key out of his pocket, only giving him a mournful glance once he had unlocked and then opened the door.

"Walter, come in. We've been expecting you. Perhaps sooner."

His tone was weary rather than angry and there was a slight crack in his voice that was not normally evident in the loud, exuberant greeting that Walter was used to.

Mr Jones considered himself the undisputed authority within his household and acted the role with relish, constantly scrutinising and correcting his children's behaviours, and very often those of Mrs Jones too. Being no taller than his wife did not prevent him metaphorically trying to look down on her when he felt this was warranted, which was most of the time, and especially whenever there was a conversation to be had. Mrs Jones tolerated this because most wives did, and because she knew that he needed to feel important whereas she did not. The reality was that he couldn't do anything without her and they both knew it. This time, though, there was no false bravado. Walter noticed his tired red eyes as he squeezed past him then waited for him to lock the door again.

Mr Jones stepped back past him and headed for the back of the shop. "Come on up."

Walter followed him through the small shop and up the stairs. Mr Jones ushered him into the living room on the first floor without a word. Walter entered to a reception of five tearful faces, all looking at him intently.

Mrs Jones, normally an efficient, brisque lady bustling around the shop, was slumped in a chair, handkerchief in hand as she wiped tears and blew her nose. She looked broken, but glanced up and then fixed Walter with a fierce stare as he walked in. The occasional shop assistant, Maisy, was knelt beside her, holding her arm. The children William and

Alice were sitting on the floor in a corner, looking bewildered and still disbelieving that they would never see their big sister again.

And there was Frederick, standing by the fireplace with a look of grief now tinged with surprise. Had he recognised Walter? It looked as though he wasn't sure and was trying to place the face. Walter decided to make the first move. He stepped forward and held out his hand.

"You must be Frederick? Lillian often mentioned you."

"Yes, yes, I am," said Frederick, shaking Walter's hand but only perfunctorily. He was a good looking man – dark brown wavy hair curled over a strong forehead, a narrow face framed by neat sideburns, piercing blue eyes, a tidy moustache, and a slightly jutting jaw. He eyed Walter suspiciously. "Have we not met before?"

"No, I don't think so," said Walter, quickly closing the subject by turning to face the rest of the group. "I must apologise for not coming to see you yesterday. I was detained in Seaford and did not get back until late last night. I assume that the police have told you what happened?"

Mrs Jones looked up at her husband, who was standing by the door, indicating that she would rather he responded.

"They came round yesterday," said Mr Jones quietly, "around mid morning. We already knew she was missing of course. When you and she did not come back on Wednesday evening, we were sick with worry. We went to the police station and they said they would let us know if they.... if they heard anything. We hardly slept but we thought perhaps a wheel had broken on your trap or something so you were having to make arrangements. It was the not knowing though, that was the worst part."

"*Why* couldn't you have sent us a telegram that evening?" Mrs Jones could not stay silent and shot the question at Walter like a valve opening on a pressure cooker. She looked pleadingly at him, desperation only just masking the anger. "You could have at least told us what had happened rather than leaving us completely in the dark."

Walter shuffled on his feet. He had to remain calm and not react to any understandably emotional outbursts. "I didn't know what to do," he said quietly. "I was upset, I had just witnessed the death of the girl I loved, and I thought the police would have contacted you. Once I had spoken to them....." he trailed off and looked down at the floor.

"Well perhaps they should, but they had to find us first. At least you knew us."

"I gave them your names," replied Walter as though that settled the argument. "What did they tell you about the accident?"

"Only what you had told them." Frederick had interjected. "But we need to hear it from you. We need to know exactly what happened." He looked at Walter with a strange mix of expectation and accusation.

"Can I sit down?" asked Walter, pulling up a spare chair.

"Of course," said Mr Jones even though it was academic by then.

Walter looked round the room, took a deep breath, then began explaining the story he had rehearsed in his mind so many times, adding little embellishments that he might not have told the police but would mean something to the Jones family, reflecting Lillian's character. Questions were interjected, and he answered them as convincingly as he could given that most of his answers were deliberately economical with the truth.

When he had finished there was silence in the room apart from the sound of sobbing. Mrs Jones's face was buried in her handkerchief, her shoulders rocking, Maisy stroking her arm but with her head bowed and her forehead resting on the edge of the chair. She had been friends with Lillian; the two of them had occasionally had tea together.

Tears streamed down ten year old Alice's face and older brother William had his arm around her but Walter could see he was crying too. He wanted to look up at Frederick, who was still standing stiffly by the fireplace, and sneer 'see what you've done? Not such a big man now, are you?', but he knew his time would come.

He turned to Mr Jones, who was staring vacantly and rheumy-eyed into space as though he was waiting to wake up from a terrible nightmare. "Have the police found her body?"

Mr Jones started slightly and reverted his attention to Walter. "No, they haven't." He took a deep breath before continuing. "They assume she was washed out to sea so we just have to wait now and see if she.... if her... her...body comes ashore somewhere. Then we can have a proper funeral."

At the words 'body' and 'funeral' Mrs Jones let out little cries. "No-one should have to bury their own full grown children," she sobbed, "no-one. Least of all such a beautiful soul as my Lillian. Thomas, why did you ever let her go out on her own like that, all that way? They were not even engaged! This was not just a ten minute stroll down to the nearest park, now, was it?"

It was an argument they had had yesterday but she raised it again because she wanted Walter to hear it. This man had taken her Lillian out of the house and not returned her. Her beautiful daughter had been entrusted to his care, and whether her death was an accident or not, he had assured her husband that he would look after her, and he hadn't.

"It was a mistake, as I said yesterday," replied Mr Jones solemnly, conscious of but not caring about Walter's discomfort at hearing this. "If I could turn back the clock..... I am sure Walter feels the same."

Walter detected his cue and quickly agreed. "Yes, of course." He would ordinarily have argued the point with Mrs Jones but had wisely decided not to defend his honour on this occasion, given that he didn't really have any honour to defend.

Mr Jones nodded and straightened himself up. He had heard nothing that made the grief any easier. "Well, thank you Walter. We realise this has not been easy for you either, don't we dear?"

His wife did not respond, instead staring at her shoes, her silence speaking volumes. By her side Maisy gave Walter a defensive stare, the intensity of which could not have been heightened if he had just suggested that à propos of nothing she take off her clothes for his own entertainment.

Mr Jones cleared his throat and turned back to Walter. "Well, I suppose there is nothing more to be said."

It was the sign Walter had been waiting for and he stood up smartly. "Very well, I shall take my leave. Is there anything else you would like to know? Or that I can help with?"

It sounded too flippant but he just wanted to close things out and get out of there before he said the wrong thing.

Mr Jones shook his head silently. Walter had presumed the answer would be 'no' on both counts and that this would be the cue for him to leave. So far, everything had gone to plan, although he didn't like emotional weakness and people crying incessantly. It annoyed him, despite an underlying understanding for why they were doing it. He didn't cry when his mother died, and he doubted his father's passing, when it came, would have him in tears either. Yet these people had been crying for two days now. Well, a day and a bit. It was too much; he had to get out of there.

As he took a step to the door Frederick suddenly spoke. "There is one thing, sir," he said firmly.

Walter froze, then turned to him. "Yes?"

"We will need your address in case we need to contact you."

"Why would you need to contact me?" Walter realised as soon as he had said this that the defensive tone was a mistake, but the question had taken him by surprise and his reaction had been instinctive.

"The funeral?"

Of course. The answer was simple yet unarguable. He would have to attend as to not do so would bring the spotlight back onto him, and they would have to be able to let him know the details. Yet he really didn't want to be giving Frederick, or anyone else for that matter, his address. He could give a false address but that would quickly backfire as they would find out and start asking why. He had no time to concoct anything, so all he could do was to stumble out a reply. "Ah, mmm, yes, very well. It is thirty four, Southover Road, Brighton."

"Thank you." Frederick picked up a pencil from a small table next to him, and Walter noticed his hand shaking as he wrote the address on the masthead of yesterday's newspaper which lay beside it. He was obviously putting on a brave front but feeling it as much as the rest of them. Walter smiled inwardly. The more that man suffered the better.

He turned to address the room. "I shall take my leave. My condolences to you all. Good day to you."

The family all nodded and mumbled a reply, and with that Walter stepped past Mr Jones, who escorted him out of the shop and made sure the door was locked behind him.

As Walter untied Gertie from the lamp post and set off for Regency Square, his mood brightened. Another successful operation. It seemed that once again he would be literally getting away with murder, and it gave him a thrill that literally nothing else did. He could out-fox anybody. He wondered what incident would trigger his next exercise of ultimate power and control over someone whose mistake was to get on the bad side of Walter Threadwell.

CHAPTER 31 : MRS CHOMSY

When Marlo reached the end of Trafalgar Street, he could scarcely believe his eyes. In front of him was the main road into Brighton and down to the seafront past the Pavilion. He had driven down it many times, and it was one of his least favourite places to be. Always clogged with far too many cars and buses, he was used to noisy dual carriageways straddling isolated islands of grass and trees, and interweaving lanes that in places resulted in six parallel lines of traffic with every opportunity to get in the wrong lane and find yourself being steered in completely the wrong direction. Traffic fumes, traffic lights, traffic signs, just traffic.

Yet here he was looking upon an elegant, open space. Refined regency and Victorian houses kept watch either side, overlooking wide boulevards populated by meandering horse drawn vehicles. In the centre, well dressed ladies with elaborate hats pushed prams in the gated gardens and enjoyed the fountains and colourful flower beds.

The roads were wide and almost empty compared to the frenzied chaos he was familiar with, and it was quiet, so quiet: the roar and constant background noise of tyres and engines was replaced by the sound of young children playing in the park and the gentle clip-clop of horses' hooves and crunch of turning carriage wheels, together with the odd 'whoa!' or 'giddy-up!' from a driver.

St Peter's Church stood before and just to the left of him, unsurprisingly looking very much as he remembered, albeit in a much nicer, greener setting and now standing like a big rock in the middle of a gently trickling brook rather than a relentlessly roaring river.

As if on cue the church bells began to strike midday, and it felt for all the world as though he had just strolled into a London park on a Sunday morning.

"I hear bells?" Lillian interrupted Marlo's reverie.

"Yes, I'm next to the church. I just can't believe the difference in this road; how it all looks compared with how it is now."

"But now is now!" Lillian chided him, "the past is the present, and your present is the future."

234

"That's not confusing at all."

"Sorry. I almost confused myself there. But you know what I mean."

"Well, yes, you're right, I do have a new 'now' now, which to be honest doesn't sound like a proper sentence does it. Let's change the subject."

"Agreed. You were saying about the bells?"

"Yes. Well no actually - you were asking me about them. Anyway, what it means though is that presumably I turn right here, down to the Pavilion, don't I?"

"You certainly do. I wish I could see as well as hear what you are experiencing. I feel like a blind person."

"Number Five probably reckoned it would be too easy if you could see as well. Actually, it's a good job you can't - I would have to close my eyes in the toilet and that could lead to unwanted consequences."

"Well, there is that, yes. A young girl's eyes may not be ready for that kind of thing I suppose, and that situation alone clinches the argument. Very well, I shall continue sightless, not that I have any say in the matter. Onward, good soldier."

"Yes ma'am! I'll cross to the other side and just keep checking the road names on the left until I get to Edward Street."

A rough looking man in a cloth cap pushing a trolley with a wooden cabinet on it gave him a funny look as he trundled by and Marlo realised that because he was enjoying the conversation with Lillian he had begun to forget to disguise his mouth movements. He mentally rapped himself on the knuckles. Must concentrate, too much at stake.

He strolled round the edge of the first park across to the far side of the avenue and made his way down towards the sea, along Richmond Place, then Grand Parade, taking in the splendour of the four and five storey bay windowed Georgian buildings that, by not having to face off against a daily barrage of noise and pollution, seemed so much more at ease and relaxed in their setting. Cleaner, too, the white paint actually bright white rather than gauzed in exhaust soot. With barely anyone giving him a second glance he now felt very much the Victorian man in the street as he blended in with the world around him.

Ahead of him the unmistakeable white roofline of Brighton Pavilion appeared between the trees, its onion shaped domes and pointy minarets seemingly completely out of character with its surroundings yet providing a magnificent focal point for the traveller coming into Brighton along the wide, green-centred boulevard.

Just as he was about to draw level with the Pavilion, a road branched off to his left and he saw the sign 'Edward Street'. Smaller houses here looked over a long, straight incline, both sides of which were intersected with threads of smaller roads leading off, leaving lots of gaps between the houses that gave the road a much more open and less enclosed feel.

"Right, I've reached Edward Street," announced Marlo under his breath, feeling like an explorer giving updates to a support crew on the radio, "where do I go now?"

"Arbuthnot Street is on the right about half way up the hill. It's a small road, but it leads through to St James's Street. There is one slight snag though." Lillian sounded apologetic. "I can't remember the house number. When I delivered that hat to Mrs Chomsy all I can recall is that it was one of the smaller terraced houses about half way along on the left."

"Ok," replied Marlo slowly as he made his way up Edward Street, "so..... is there anything you remember about the house, any distinguishing features?"

"Not really. Oh! Apart from the door, it had a door knocker shaped like a sort of a goblin's head. I remember thinking it looked a bit scary."

"Well that's good enough for me," said Marlo confidently, "and I've reached Arbuthnot Street. Right, let's have a look. I'll head for the middle."

He was surprised to see that the houses here in this smaller road were larger than on Edward Street, three and four storey Georgian blocks overlooking a small park behind the houses fronting the next road down.

"What colour was the house Lillian?"

"White, yes, it was white. Not sure about the door though."

"Ok, there's a block of four or five smaller white houses ahead of me... hang on...."

Marlo reached the first white house in the row and peered at the door knocker.

"Aha! It looks like a goblin – result!" He mounted the stone steps, mentally preparing his opening line and the reactions he would have to give depending on whether or not Mrs Chomsy had heard about Lillian's death. As he did so he glanced at the house next door. Different colour door, but – oh. The same door knocker; another goblin. Damn.

He quickly reversed back down the steps and walked further down the pavement.

"Lillian?"

"Yes?"

"There are five goblins."

"Five? What do you mean?"

"Every house in this row has the same door knocker."

"Ah. Dash my wig, that's not very helpful. The builder must have bought them in bulk to get a discount."

"Dash your wig? What does *that* mean?"

"Ha! You don't know? Finally I've got my own back. It just means 'damn and blast it'. It is an exclamation of annoyance." She pronounced the last three words precisely, for emphasis.

"Well, there's me told. But.... as you will have guessed we don't say that any more, probably because it sounds daft."

"Excuse me, but what was that one you told me last night about taking a cold pill or something?"

"A chill pill. Well ok, one-all. Anyway, listen, I need to stop looking as though I am talking to myself and get this done. I have two blue doors, two black, and one red. I suppose I will just have to knock on one of them and ask if they are Mrs Chomsy and if they aren't, do they know who is. Hold on tight."

"Wait! It was blue, I'm sure now that it was blue! Dark blue, matte finish. Could that be right?"

"Yes, although both the blue doors are matte, so I'll just choose one of them and go for it."

Just because it was less effort Marlo selected the blue door nearest to him, number seventeen.

The door was answered almost immediately by a lady who was older than Marlo, but not old enough to be Mrs Chomsy. Her dark hair was plumped up but tied back under a white cap, and a bright white apron covered most of the black dress she was wearing. In one hand she held a feather duster, which gave Marlo a fairly good clue as to her occupation.

"Hello, can I help you?" she asked in a slightly brusque and suspicious manner.

"I was looking for Mrs Chomsy?" asked Marlo, sounding more nervous than he would have liked.

The cleaning lady, assuming that was who she was, eyed him up and down as though debating whether or not he was any better than she was, then pursed her lips and said "hold on please."

The door was closed slightly and she turned and disappeared into the house. Well, at least he had chosen the right door. About a minute later Marlo heard a slow click-click of small approaching footsteps. The door opened again to reveal a small, kindly looking elderly lady looking up at him inquisitively. Her hair was bright white, parted in the middle and tied behind, and she had pale blue watery eyes that were like little pools of water in a dried mud bed – her face was caked in wrinkles. She was breathing quickly as though she had run all the way to the door, although clearly she hadn't.

"Mrs Chomsy?" asked Marlo before she had a chance to say anything.

"Yes, I am," she smiled in return, a fan of deep crinkles spreading from the corner of each eye. "How can I be of assistance?"

Her voice was a little wavery but the gaze was, in contrast, unwavering.

"Well," Marlo plunged in, "I was told by a mutual acquaintance that you might be considering offering lodgings, and I was wondering if I could put myself forward as a.....er... candidate. I'm very quiet and helpful, and would make sure I am no trouble at all. And I would also be happy to help around the house if there is anything you needed assistance with."

Mrs Chomsy tilted her head and surveyed him carefully, as though this would verify what he had just told her, then took a deep and deliberate breath, slowly re-charging her air supply. "And who is our mutual acquaintance, my dear?"

Well, here goes, thought Marlo. Either she knows or she doesn't. "Lillian Jones, the young lady from the milliners."

"Oh, you know Lillian do you?" Her face crinkled even more as she indicated her pleasure at hearing Lillian's name. "Very nice girl, she was here not so long ago, very kindly delivered a new hat for me. I can't travel far now, you know, not with my breathing."

As if to make the point she stopped and took another little gulp of air.

"Are you her friend?"

Well, she doesn't know, thought Marlo, that's good.

"In a way," he replied slightly disingenuously, "I helped her recently. A thief stole something from her in the street, I saw it happen and retrieved the item for her. She was very grateful, we got to know each other, and when she heard I was looking for somewhere to move to she hoped she could help me in return by suggesting I speak to you. She thought it might help you too, save you the trouble of advertising and that kind of thing."

Mrs Chomsy had listened carefully. "Well, I suppose that's true," she said. "So you tackled the thief then? That sounds quite brave?"

"Oh it was nothing," said Marlo, being quite truthful this time. "I'm quite a good runner, you see."

"Yes, there's not much of you, is there? Not like my Albert, did she tell you about him? Three times your size around the waist he was, at least. It was always a relief when he sat down and the chair didn't break."

Marlo couldn't help laughing, an image now in his head of a surprised fat man on the floor with broken wood all around him. "Yes, she did mention him, as the background for why you had a spare room now." Realising this could be insensitive, he quickly added "Sorry, I didn't mean to, you know, imply it was a good thing that he.... you know... passed...."

"Died, you mean? Oh, don't worry dear," she interrupted, "he's long gone now. Lillian was right, I have been thinking about the room, but I just haven't seemed to have the energy to do anything about it, even though I know I should. So perhaps now is the time to do something about that. Come in, come in."

She stepped back so that Marlo could come past her, and closed the door. "This is Edith," she said, glancing at the cleaning lady who was carefully positioned within earshot, re-dusting a table in the hallway. Marlo nodded at her and she replied with a brief half-smile, perhaps now regretting her earlier mild hostility, although Marlo understood she was probably just being protective.

"She cleans for me twice a week, helps me with the shopping too. Couldn't do without her, especially once Bert had gone and I couldn't afford my other helpers."

Edith smiled more openly this time, no doubt pleased to be working for a good employer and presumably thankful to have been the chosen one who was retained. Then she turned and headed into the dining room to resume what she had been doing before she answered the door.

"Right, come into the lounge, dear, and take a seat. That's it, just there on the chair by the window will be fine. Would you like anything to drink?"

Marlo suddenly realised he was actually quite thirsty; he'd not drunk anything since leaving Jed's house this morning. "A glass of water would be lovely, thank you."

"I think I can manage that, I'm very good at making glasses of water," she said as she disappeared out of the room. It seemed as though she had a good sense of humour too. If he did end up here, she would be a good landlady to have.

The lounge was large, high ceilinged and probably twenty feet in length, with a rather magnificent fireplace as its centrepiece, the egg-shaped mirror above it built into the carved wood design which stretched almost to the ceiling. Marlo was amused to see a stuffed fish that looked like a trout, in a nice bow fronted glass case, proudly occupying the centre of the mantelpiece. He wasn't really sure why anyone would think it was worthy of display, but these were different times.

The coving was decadent, multiple rows of plaster ridges supporting wide strips of intricate mouldings and complemented by an enormous ceiling rose from which hung a chandelier that probably gave Edith nightmares when it came to cleaning it.

In the gaps between the furniture the walls were covered in prints and paintings in a mix of landscape and portrait format appropriately depicting mainly landscapes and portraits, all of seemingly random styles and subjects. It was as though the objective was not to display beautiful things to look at, but to obscure as much of the wallpaper as possible. Given that this was a rather garish brown and yellow fleur-de-lys design, perhaps that was not such a bad idea.

Together with a deep red and brown patterned rug over dark wood floorboards, the dark wood dresser and sideboard, and the heavy draped curtains that covered half the windows, it felt remarkably gloomy in a room that should have been bathed in light through the large French windows to the garden. But Marlo knew that this was the style, it was how Victorians liked things.

One thing that was clear was that Mrs Chomsy and her husband had been well off. This was one of those houses that was deceptive from the outside, being bigger and more opulent than he had imagined. He wasn't sure how pensions and other financial matters worked in this era and it was not his place to ask Mrs Chomsy, but he was sure the money from his lodging there would help. He would ask Lillian later. Ah, Lillian, he could have whispered to her while the old lady was out of the room, but it was too late now - he could hear her returning, breathing heavily.

"Here you are, dear," she announced as she slowly appeared, holding out a nice big glass of water with a slightly shaky hand. Marlo took it gratefully and drunk half of it in one quick movement. "Thank you, that's better!"

She eased herself down into the velvety padded armchair opposite him, her many layers of skirts riding up either side of her, and her head resting against what looked like a flowery white tea towel laid across the top of it. "Now," she said, "tell me a bit about you. I don't even know your name."

"Oh right, yes, I'm so sorry, I didn't say who I was, did I? My name is Marlo Campbell."

CHAPTER 32 : SETTLING IN

And so it came to pass that half an hour later, Marlo found himself acquainting himself with his new residence – a large room on the second floor of Mrs Chomsy's house. It was full of the requisite dark wood furniture, and a big wrought iron black fireplace in the centre of the right hand wall framed a grate filled with coals, but at least the walls were a textured white wallpaper and the waxed floorboards supported a thin rug with a much lighter cream and brown pattern, so with his large window overlooking the small garden and letting plenty of light in, it was a more welcoming place to be than that oppressive lounge of gloom downstairs.

He checked inside the wardrobe – no such thing as clothes hangers yet, just wooden pegs. To the side of it a low cupboard with a sideboard top provided additional storage, and adjacent to the window was a small table sporting a vase of ancient dried flowers whose colours were merging into a uniform grey.

He had cleverly, he thought, warned Mrs Chomsy that she might hear him talking in his room, but not to worry because as an author he often found himself talking out loud when constructing conversations for his characters – it helped him formulate things in his head. Lillian had even felt obliged to give him a 'nicely done!' when he said that. It was good cover should the landlady or Edith the cleaning lady hear voices from his room and doubt his sanity. The door to his room was at the end of the landing, so it is not as though they would be passing by, but you never know. He would listen out for creaking floorboards, though, in case Edith turned curiosity into eavesdropping.

He had also had to think quickly when Mrs Chomsy asked where his suitcase was. "I've left it at a friend's," he had said, thinking of George for some reason, even though George didn't have his suitcase because the suitcase did not exist. "I'll go out this afternoon and get it." What this actually meant was some emergency shopping, which would now have to include a suitcase.

"Well," he said softly to Lillian, "so far so good, it is going to plan. There's a slight problem though."

"What's happened?" Lillian sounded concerned.

"I'm really, really hungry. It has gone one o'clock and I need food."

"Is that all? I thought it was something important."

"It is!" protested Marlo. "I'm surprised Mrs Chomsy didn't mention it actually, I wonder what time she eats."

"Maybe she assumed you had already eaten. I heard you agreeing the weekly rate and how that would include breakfast and supper so maybe because lunch isn't included she felt no need to mention it."

"Well I had better go and find something. What would you suggest?"

"There's a good tavern in St James Street – I can't remember its name but they serve decent lunches. Go to the end of Arbuthnot Street, turn left and it is about fifty yards along on the left."

"Excellent, then when I've eaten I can buy some clothes, toiletries, a notebook and pencil, the suitcase, and whatever else comes to mind. I've a busy afternoon ahead of me."

He had two keys now, one for his room, one for the front door. He locked his room even though he didn't need to, just to get into the habit, then headed along the landing, and down the wide staircase with its centre strip of Axminister carpet bordered by polished floorboards and held tight with shiny brass carpet runners. No light green polyester carpet from Floors R Us here.

Mrs Chomsy was in the kitchen at the back of the house, busying herself with preparing a light meal. Hearing Marlo approach, she looked up.

"Oh, I'm sorry dear, I forgot to ask you what you were doing for lunch." She put down a knife and steadied herself against a cupboard. "Ooh, there we go, another one of my dizzy moments. That happens sometimes when I am least expecting it. There, that's better. Have you already eaten?"

Slightly concerned for his host's health, Marlo hesitated, wondering if he could help, but as he clearly couldn't, ventured "No, but don't worry, it's not a problem. I hear there's a tavern around the corner so I thought I would try it out."

"Oh, The Boar's Head, yes that's right. They do a nice steak pie, or at least they did when I last went there but that was many years ago." She smiled wistfully. "Bert used to escort me, well drag me really, round there for a meal, but what he was really after was a few flagons of ale to wash his food down with. Of course he went on his own a lot as well, although he could only just manage the walk in his later years, and even if he wasn't drunk it took him five times as long to get home as in his younger days. It was about the only exercise he got, though, and he used that as a reason for going. Mind, I always said to him it was like putting one pea in your stew and saying you have eaten all your vegetables."

Marlo smiled. "Well, if The Boar's Head comes recommended I shall definitely try it out, thank you. Then this afternoon I need to go back into town to collect my things so I won't be back until late afternoon."

"That's fine dear, I normally do supper at around seven."

"Cool! That is to say, great! Thank you. I will see you later then." And with a hurried wave he was off down the hall, out into the street, and straight into the tavern, where they did indeed serve a steak pie which proved to be just as good as Mrs Chomsy had suggested.

He spent the afternoon shopping, following Lillian's directions to the shops he needed. It was a very different experience to modern shopping. Everything was individual, presented to him, no self-service allowed. Marlo felt remarkably self-conscious and awkward having to specify what he wanted in great detail to every store owner, your choices duly noted and judged by whoever was in the queue behind you, rather than just casually browsing around on his own and selecting it off a shelf.

Ironically this was more like online shopping, where you chose the items you wanted without moving, then waited for someone else to deliver them to you. How times hadn't changed. But in any event he ended up with a small suitcase, which, having already bought everything else on his list, he used as an over-sized shopping bag, stuffing everything into it and feeling like a tourist as he headed back to his new temporary home.

Back in his room, he hung up his new clothes in the creaky old wardrobe, placed his new notebook and pencil on the small table in the corner, and stood looking out of the window at the now slightly overgrown garden that was a mix of stone paths and untidy lawn surrounded by borders. He suspected keeping it maintained might have become more of a chore for Mrs Chomsy, or perhaps she used to have a gardener who she now couldn't afford. But he needed to focus on more important things.

"Lillian?"

"Yes?"

"What do I do now?"

CHAPTER 33 : SETTING IT UP

It was April 12th, 1884, two years before he would meet Lillian, and Walter had just turned twenty three. Things had been going well. He'd left school at twelve, as most children did who were lucky enough to have parents able to fund them to that point, and after a couple of years helping his father, it was agreed that he should take a job with a building firm as a labourer, as this would bring in a little more money.

He was not academically deficient, in fact quite the opposite. He found learning quite easy and it bored him. He just couldn't be bothered with school so didn't try very hard – he was better than that. Why should he let other people judge him? He would find his way through the adult world the way he wanted to, and he was happy to start that off with a man's job, something physical.

He was already big for his age and the four and a half years he spent on building sites during his adolescence bulked him up into an impressive figure as he grew taller. Even at sixteen he was looking down at most of the men he worked with – the average Victorian man was only 5ft 5, although this was rising due to more attention from successive governments on tackling the inequities of poverty and malnutrition that produced so many small children.

His size and often arrogant demeanour, together with how he once handled himself in a scuffle with a labourer who insulted him, led to a passing comment from one of the men on the site that he should talk to his brother, who worked for a bank, as he knew they were looking for people to help with the 'persuasion' side of things when it came to customers who had got themselves into debt.

Walter used that contact to get an interview and was taken on as a trainee, spending a little time in the office but mainly in the field assisting Mr Gorringe, a senior debt collector who was to train him in all of the techniques and legalities of retrieving the bank's money.

While Walter felt he was doing more watching than working when it came to the actual interactions with the 'clients', his mere presence lurking behind Mr Gorringe when the front door was opened probably did as much to alert the debtor to the seriousness of the situation as anything that subsequently came out of Mr Gorringe's mouth.

It was during this period, shadowing Mr Gorringe, that he realised that it would be to his advantage not to use the language of the building site if he wished to progress – he was in a world where a bit of verbal dexterity and eloquence, and an accent not clogged with gutter words and phrases and rough vowels or missing consonants, increased the sense of self-importance and superiority that came with the role. So he worked hard on his speech and gradually it became more normal to talk in the rarefied way of the upper-middle classes. It made him less conspicuous too, able to blend in, and ready to take advantage when opportunity came.

In time it was felt that he was ready to take visits on his own and he became one of the bank's most successful collectors. He had realised that his size and grim, masculine features gave him a significant advantage over his peers, and so he honed his technique to focus on subtle intimidation over the more 'courteous but firm' approach favoured by Mr Gorringe.

His manager occasionally had to have words with him when clients reported being threatened, but Walter always put this down to a misunderstanding on the debtor's behalf, and in any case his manager knew that his own success was built on the success of the people who worked underneath him, so provided no regulations were broken, Walter was on safe ground as long as the money kept coming in.

Three years passed, during which time Walter left his father's house and found his own lodgings, was rewarded with successive pay rises, and realised that this was a job he really was suited to. So much so that although he didn't realise it at first, he just needed a trigger to set up his own debt collection business, and that trigger came when he encountered Mr Carberry.

Ironically, given what was to happen, Mr Carberry was a debtor. It was especially ironic because he had trained in law, then progressed to working in the courts as a court roller, in charge of rolls and records. After a spell working as an administrator settling the estates of deceased people who died intestate, he had worked himself up from barrister's clerk to copying clerk to articled clerk, with which title came a degree of respect and an enhanced salary that was just sufficient to enable him to rent a small house rather than a small room in someone else's house.

Then, for reasons that hindsight depressed him with every time he thought about it, he took a gamble that didn't pay off. This is not something that William Carberry would ordinarily have done, being a meticulous and careful man who liked everything to be in order and order to be in everything he did. But, much as a well educated rich man can fall for a floozy from the streets, Mr Carberry was lured to his doom by a cleverly presented yet hugely over-ambitious share scheme that promised great wealth but failed to deliver. Mr Carberry was well aware that the market can stay irrational for longer than an investor can remain solvent, but there is something in the psyche of an intelligent man that tells him that he will never be the dope to whom the snake oil salesman sells oil, even as the barrels of oil are being wheeled into his house.

So having convinced himself, through research motivated by the carrot of easy money dangling from a metaphorical stick tied to his head, that great wealth could be his, Mr Carberry had, still against his better judgement, taken out the largest loan he could secure from the bank to maximise his investment. Initially the returns were good and Mr Carberry congratulated himself on his wisdom and sound judgement. Then to his horror the share scheme suddenly collapsed with the loss of all invested funds. The fund manager conveniently disappeared, and Mr Carberry was unable to pay back the loan. His world of financial probity collapsed. He was thankful that the concept of debtor's gaols had ceased the practice of indefinite imprisonment for non-payment of debt back in the late sixties – once you were in one of those places your chances for getting out quickly were as slim as a stick. But there were still consequences.

And so, on April 12th, Walter Threadwell had paid a visit.

What struck Walter when Mr Carberry first opened the door to him was that he showed no signs whatsoever of being intimidated. Indeed, his first words were "Why, you're a large fellow aren't you? Do come in, sir, and join me in a glass of something recuperative." And with that he had retreated back into his hallway before Walter even had time to reply.

Caught off guard, Walter followed him into his lounge where two small glasses of whisky were ready on the sideboard. Mr Carberry handed him one of them with the words "and to whom do I have the pleasure?"

Walter took the glass with a mixture of reluctance and gratitude. He shouldn't drink it while he was working, but he knew it wouldn't affect his judgement, so he took a small sip, then downed the fiery liquid in one, placing the glass back on the sideboard and carefully licking his lips.

"Walter Threadwell, from the bank. But you knew I was coming, hence the reception."

Mr Carberry smiled thinly back at him, giving his large jaw line additional prominence and drawing some attention away from the slightly wild hair. He was no small man himself, being only a few inches shorter than Walter, but he was slender and Walter guessed had never lifted anything heavier than a pen.

"Yes, I knew to expect someone, I just didn't know who."

He picked up his own glass and took a brief swig. "Glen Albyn, 1872, a fine Scottish malt. Before you ask, I've had this bottle since long before I got into debt. Now it just helps drown the sorrows rather than toast the occasional celebration."

"And am I a sorrow then, Mr Carberry?" Walter leaned forward slightly and furrowed his brow in manufactured displeasure. Two darkly sinister caterpillar eyebrows slowly merged into one. It was a look that he had found quite effective previously in establishing his authority. It seemed to have no effect on Mr Carberry though.

"Ha! No, sir, although your reason for coming could be classed as one. No, I just felt it would be an appropriate way to begin our dealings. Come, please sit down. Over here, these chairs are the most comfortable."

He pointed to a couple of stout upholstered brown chairs positioned opposite each other, either side of a small table by the window. Walter was mildly impressed – this man had certainly planned ahead. Most of his clients either tried to feign ignorance about the debt, or argue its validity, or plead poverty, and that was before he had even entered the house. They certainly were not prone to handing him glasses of whisky and arranging the furniture to accommodate him.

"So, you have the details of my misfortune," said Mr Carberry once Walter was seated.

"Indeed I do. I have all the information on your outstanding debt. That's not a compliment, by the way." This was a little witticism that Walter often used in these situations, more as a perceived aide to bolstering his intellectual superiority rather than any wish to lighten the mood. Mr Carberry felt obliged to offer a thin and very brief smile to acknowledge the quip, but his eyes did not join in. Walter, maintaining a stern expression, pulled some papers out of his case and pretended to study them, even though he already knew the details. "Mr Carberry, you owe the bank one hundred and fifteen pounds. That is a not inconsiderable amount of money. Please explain to me how you are going to pay this back."

Mr Carberry's slow smile again lacked conviction but gave him a moment to prepare his rehearsed answer. "At the rate I earn currently, I cannot repay the debt to meet your requirements. My re-payments to the bank would take years to be fulfilled, many, many years. You are probably aware of that. That is not satisfactory, not satisfactory at all. So I am proposing to do something about that. I am going to do something I have been meaning to do for some time but this unfortunate situation has forced my hand. I have thought this through at length, at great length actually. It might surprise you."

"Care to tell me then?" interrupted Walter, becoming impatient.

"Of course, sir, of course, I was just setting the scene. Firstly I am going to sell everything I own that I do not need," here he waved his arm around the room as though the furniture within it comprised all his worldly unwanted possessions, "then I will lease an office on the outskirts of town, with a room and facilities to enable me to bed down there as well. From there I will set up a business offering administrative services, focused on legal aspects, as that is my background and where my expertise lies. I have calculated a much improved income, based on custom I can be assured of from all the contacts I have built up over the years. This will enable me to greatly increase the repayments I make to your bank. I have all the figures, look."

He reached for a mottled grey and blue hard bound notebook and turned a page or two then handed it, open, to Walter. "There – see what you think."

Walter took the notebook and scanned through the figures. He was used to numbers by now and had regularly sat down with debtors to go through their income situation, so it didn't take him long to see that Mr Carberry's figures made some sense, assuming that they were based on sound foundations and estimates.

He looked up. "This is all very well, but it is entirely dependent on you being able to generate the business that you say you will. What assurances does the bank have that you can do this? Do you have statements of intent from your prospective customers?"

"I have verbal assurances from the majority of our long-standing clients. In my current role they see themselves as dealing with me rather than my employer, and they appreciate and value the service I personally provide them, rather than anything my firm supplies."

"Are there not rules that prevent you from poaching customers from your employer when you leave?"

"A good question. Not if I am not seen to approach them, and they switch to me of their own accord. Which they will, you understand. I have been careful not to directly request that they move their business to me, and have instead merely informed them of my intentions and then gauged their reactions. Overwhelmingly those reactions have been in my favour."

Walter considered the situation carefully. It was interesting listening to Mr Carberry because he had harboured almost identical ambitions himself, and he knew that setting up on your own was not a business to be taken lightly. But Walter wanted control, power over his own destiny. Mr Carberry was only doing it because he had few options left – he was doubtful that the man had been 'meaning to do it for some time' in the same way that Walter had.

He sat back, folded his arms, and surveyed Mr Carberry's expectant face, enjoying the power dynamic that this situation gave him. That was half the reason he enjoyed this job, he was always the one with the final say. He was minded to dismiss the man's plan as a distraction, short on certainty and certainly risky. But then a germ of an idea popped into his head, and the reader may well know what that idea was. He wasn't going to come out with it there and then, though – he would have to think about it.

"Well...." he announced quietly but sonorously, drawing the word out as though it was being hauled from a very deep hole (perhaps, appropriately, a well), "I will have to consider this. Possibly discuss it with my superiors. It is not the usual approach to a settlement, you see, and may require additional authorisation."

Mr Carberry's face fell slightly as he realised that this was not a positive endorsement but then brightened a little at the thought that at least it was not an outright rejection either.

"I understand, sir, yes, I do realise that this is not how you would normally deal with such a debt, and I do appreciate your diligence in taking time to assess this. I can assure you though that I really am very good at my job and this is why I am so confident in being able to entice my clients across, which will result in a better outcome for all of us, your bank included."

And with that he was on his feet before Walter had time to take the initiative himself, with his hand outstretched to thank him for his decision, even though it was neither a positive nor a negative one. Walter slowly rose to his feet and shook the man's hand firmly enough to re-assert his authority.

"I will be in touch, Mr Carberry. Will you be in this Saturday?"

"Only after five o'clock I'm afraid. I have to catch up on workload after, well, you know, today."

"Very well. I shall return at half past five on Saturday."

And with that Walter turned on his heels and strode out of the room with a brusque 'good day sir' over his shoulder. As he walked swiftly back towards the bank, his head was whirling. If he was going to set up his own debt collection firm, he needed someone to do all his paperwork and deal with all the legalities, liaising with clients and so on, and this man, being eminently qualified, seemed perfect for the job. He was going to set up an office – perfect. He was clearly a capable and articulate individual willing to work hard – perfect. But best of all he was in debt himself and so would not be in a position to make demands, and by that token be obliged to accept a sixty/forty ownership split in the new business, in Walter's favour of course. All in all, this seemed an opportunity too good to miss. And so it was.

Walter returned on the Saturday, having cleared with his superiors the principle that one of their debtors could defer some of the payback until his new business was established then ramp up the repayment schedule as earnings increased, the total to include a meaty penalty charge for late repayment. What he didn't tell his superiors was his own part in the plan. That would happen when Walter was ready to tell them.

Mr Carberry listened carefully to Walter's proposal, which suggested an even greater reward for his potential partner should he limit his legal workload to favoured clients only and at the same time handle all the administrative aspects of Walter's work.

Walter knew that even when he resigned from the bank, his offer to continue to provide the same collection service, yet take a lower commission on the work that they were paying him in salary, would be favourably received, and for him any deficit would be offset by the income from Mr Carberry's legal work, which Walter had insisted would be part of the deal. Then as he expanded the business and perhaps recruited additional collectors, the legal stuff could be gradually wound down and his prices increased in direct proportion to how dependent the bank had become on his services.

Mr Carberry realised his arm was being twisted but at the same time could see the logic behind the proposition, particularly given that he would now have the debt collector working with him rather than haranguing him. He accepted.

So the business was born, and in the end it took only a year and a half to clear Mr Carberry's debt, in part because he worked twice the hours that Walter did in order to keep pace with all the legal work he had carried over. Their enterprise became an established business venture that was all that both men had hoped, and after the debt was cleared Mr Carberry was able to gradually reduce his legal work in order to focus more on the debt collection administration, which involved a lot of liaison with both the clients who owed the money, and the clients whose money it was.

It was all going very well. Well enough to allow Walter to diversify into a new field – murder.

CHAPTER 34 : THE FIRST TIME

There are some debtors you can deal with, reason with, persuade. There are some for whom a little more vigour is necessary, a trifle more coercion. Walter quite liked these ones, as it enabled him to hone his intimidation techniques, exact a bit of duress, and watch the weaker person crumble under his thumb. He found that gave him pleasure. It was a bit like when he used to scare Clarence in those Seaford woods by forcing him to help pull the legs off live beetles he had caught, then telling the petrified child that he would be next unless he did as he was told. That was very effective as a persuasion technique. Walter had noticed that Clarence never, ever stood up to him, the little wimp.

Other debtors were compliant, but with varying degrees of respect. Those that presented Walter with the least job satisfaction paid up on time - so he could not take any persuasive action against them - but did it in such an ungracious and ill mannered way that Walter felt he was being personally insulted. This was something he really didn't like.

Outside of the work environment, he would have taken measures to ensure they never did it again. But in this scenario, it was more difficult. If he went too far, word would get back and he could lose his contract with the bank and his other clients. So he bit his tongue and seethed.

Yet the anger he had stored up could not stay simmering forever, and the unfortunate man who stupidly turned up the heat and caused Walter to boil over was called Henry Turner.

Turner was a shoemaker. He was also a drinker, which is no doubt where much of his money went and a contributory factor to his indebtedness. Walter wondered how durable the shoes he made were too; he imagined the stitching might be less than straight.

Turner was only about thirty five years old, but he had not taken a wife, and Walter had the impression that the drinking was a factor in that rather than the lack of a wife being the cause.

Every time Walter visited him, he answered the door in a state of mild inebriation, swaying slightly and presenting a veneer of courage not warranted by his position or stature. Walter didn't appreciate this; he expected and required respect and deference, and people who were tight as a boiled owl rarely exhibited those behaviours.

"Come for yer money, ave yer?" was often the opening gambit as the small, grimy door, accessed down some steps at the front of his rarely open shop, was opened and the unshaven and sunken eyed face of Henry Turner confronted him from his living quarters. It was a stupid question of course, what else would he have come for? But usually Turner would stumble back into the house muttering insults under his breath, then one of two things would happen.

Either he would reappear with a few coins which he then slapped into the hand of the larger man with unnecessary momentum. Then instead of a polite 'good day', the door would slam shut to a departing voice muttering "hope it chokes yer," or similar. Alternatively, he would shuffle back to the door, shrug his shoulders and grumble "haven't got it, yer'll have to come back tommorah." However many times Walter told him, sometimes with a strong hand clutching his lapels, that this was not good enough and he was just adding interest to his debt so had better find that money immediately, Turner would just ignore him and repeat "haven't got it."

So Walter would then have to waste valuable time returning the next day and go through the same routine, by which time Turner would somehow have found the necessary payment. Walter was convinced that Turner was doing this deliberately and had the money all along and was just trying to get his own back, even though the cause of his debt was nobody's fault but his own.

To say that all of this annoyed Walter would be like saying that a man walking up to a boxing champion in the street and punching him hard in the face for no reason would cause a curious irritation. Walter hated the man. Having a door repeatedly slammed in your face was like always being unable to have the last word in an argument, and being consistently insulted by a poorly educated drunkard, who was clearly his inferior, could no longer be tolerated.

Walter had roughed people up a bit in the past but this was different. This man had not just insulted him once, but continuously, and it had awoken a semi-dormant evil intent within Walter that could not now be restrained. But how best to deal with him? How far should he take it? Could he literally get away with murder?

The more he thought about it, the more that excited him. Here was an opportunity to see if he really had the guts to do what he had always dreamed of doing when he was younger, and the brains to make sure he got away with it. So yes, he decided, he would take another man's life, and he would experience the heady surge of power that he had always imagined it would give him. His victim had been fool enough to present himself on a plate. All that needed to be concluded was the method, and then he just needed the opportunity.

The anticipation was almost the best part; it gave him an entirely different kind of thrill. Planning was key, of course, because he could not afford to get caught. It had to be foolproof, with no chance of detection. Careful execution of the planning would be followed by careful execution of the victim.

He knew Turner had a dog. He had heard it whimpering in the house, although if it was supposed to be a guard dog then it hadn't been very effective, remaining remarkably docile, and, indeed, invisible. The appearance of a drunken and always aggressive cobbler at the door, though, was probably enough to deter any casual aggressor even if the dog was cowering in the back room, so perhaps the attributes of the owner compensated for the dog's timidity. Walter didn't like dogs anyway, always yapping and barking about nothing and defecating in the streets. He would happily dispatch a dog if it was necessary, and on this occasion it might be.

Walter's lucky break came early one morning at around 8:30am, when he was paying an early visit to a habitual defaulter in Pevensey Road on the north eastern edges of the town - where Turner also lived and worked – and he had spotted the shoemaker taking his dog for a walk, heading up the Lewes Road then turning right towards the Brighton Cemetery. The dog was a small, elderly looking Jack Russell which limped slightly, which might explain why it had opted to allow its master to deal with whoever was at the door.

Walter had hung back and watched as Turner disappeared out of view, shouting at the dog to keep up. Catching up and peering round the corner, Walter could see the two of them disappearing up the lane and through the open gates that led into the more recently added parochial section of the cemetery. He checked his pocket-watch. He was early, so he had a little bit of time to spare. He hung back then started to follow.

It was hard to keep Turner in sight because of the trees and the occasional traces of early morning mist, but he still kept him at least a hundred yards ahead, ready to bend down to tie a shoelace or study a grave should the man turn round. But Turner shuffled onwards without looking back. He was keeping an eye on the dog, which was now in front of him and appeared a little livelier, trying out the odd plaintive yap while it waited for its master.

They did a short and clearly well established circuit within the cemetery, which at more than forty acres in size provided plenty of room to allow both dog and owner to be sufficiently exercised. Then they passed by the small chapel and exited through the main tree lined avenue providing the official access from Lewes Road, Turner calling angrily at the dog as it veered off to the wrong side of the road.

This was perfect, Walter thought, planning ahead. At this time of morning there was likely to be no-one else about, and where better to dispose of a body than in a cemetery? And he knew exactly how to hide it. It was almost poetic in its synchronicity.

With Turner and the dog now gone, he looked round for a surface grave, a marble or stone affair rather than just a headstone on an earth plot which would involve any form of excavation, as though he were just some common grave robber. It had to be overgrown, or one hidden behind a bush, or in such a state that it was obvious that the occupant's presence inside it served no further purpose other than to provide evidence for future genealogy searches. This was not that straightforward as the cemetery had only been in existence for thirty or forty years and so most of the graves were well tended and still squeezing in new entrants as further family members died.

There were also still large areas of open space to account for future demand, which limited his choice. Close to the pathways though, there were row after row of headstones and grey marble tombs with elaborate descriptions offering generous praise of the deceased as though they were saints of the highest order when alive.

Walter looked for one of the older, larger graves which did not seem to have been attended to. It needed to have a stone lid, though, one he could lever off. Fortunately there were quite a few of them, some larger than others and reflecting more the status and wealth of the incumbent than their physical size when alive. The larger the tombs were, though, the heavier the lids, with a thickness of stone that was designed to stay where it was. He'd bring a crowbar of course but no sense making it harder than it needed to be, so he would need to find something a little more appropriate.

He walked closer to the chapel and came across a corner which had clearly been the scene of much digging and burying over the years, as there was barely a square foot that was not occupied by a tomb of some description. Judging by the dates there were some of the first tombs to have been installed. All of them presumably contained slightly more affluent owners, being proper carved stone caskets rather than plain rectangular boxes.

Having said that, they were hemmed in together as though assembled in a crowd to hear a speaker, who in this instance could look forward to very little applause. Towards the back, he could see what looked like a cheaper tribute to the unfortunate occupant: a grave of very plain construction with a thin slab of overhanging stone on top as opposed to the fitted casket lid of the others. That should be much easier to lever open and slide shut again. It would do.

Perhaps he should check though, give it a bit of a shove to see how easily it moved. He looked around and was annoyed to see an elderly woman with some flowers in her hand had suddenly appeared on a parallel path and was looking at him with mild curiosity as she headed for a grave at the far end of the cemetery. Oh well, another time. He did not want to attract attention, and being seen levering open a grave would require an excuse that would win awards for ingenuity if accepted at face value.

He checked his pocket watch. Blazes, look at the time – now he was five minutes late. He turned smartly on his heels and walked quickly past the chapel and out onto the main street, feeling a lot more positive than he ought to have done.

His only slight concern was that the cemetery had not been as deserted as he had hoped, but he assumed that the old woman with the flowers probably wouldn't be there every day. If she or anyone else did return at that time, he would just have to come back and deal with Turner on another day. It would be a nuisance, yes, but it would also prolong the anticipation, in the same way that a Christmas present often provided more excitement before it was opened than afterwards, especially if it turned out to be socks.

Later that week he returned at the same time to check that Turner took his dog out every day at the same time. It seemed that he did. Walter smiled and eased back into the doorway he was using as cover, until the man and his dog had disappeared round the corner. He didn't have time to go back into the cemetery and try moving that thin slab, but convinced himself that would not be an issue as it had not looked too heavy or difficult, and he was confident in his own strength. A few good kicks would be sure to loosen it.

Then he waited. He waited for an early morning mist, a fog that would help shield his activities, give him a little cover, help him move without being seen. And a few weeks later, he awoke to find that that day had come. A heavy blanket of white fog had enveloped the town, obscuring even the frontages of the houses opposite his room.

He dressed and readied himself quickly, and thankful that his first appointment wasn't until ten o'clock, left the house at eight and headed for the cemetery, taking a route that did not pass Turner's shop. Not that the cobbler could have seen him on the other side of the street with such poor visibility, but better safe than sorry.

He liked the fact that his heart was racing, every sense was alert and tingling with a surge of incredible anticipation but also with a heightened anxiety that pulled on the reins a little and told him that he could not afford to be complacent. This could go wrong, and that was part of the thrill. That morning, despite the chill damp in the air, he felt more alive than he had done for years.

The one big unknown was whether Turner would still take his dog for its morning walk when it would be hard to see where the dog was, but Walter guessed that an old limping dog would be unlikely to stray far from its owner in these conditions so that wouldn't be an issue.

He entered the gates of the cemetery and was slightly unnerved by the weighty silence of the heavy fog which had settled over the gravestones and given them a much more sinister aspect, revealing themselves suddenly as he got closer and walked by, as though they were the ones easing darkly towards him rather than the other way around.

He positioned himself behind a tree on the path that Turner had previously taken, very close to his pre-selected tomb, and waited. The air was so still, so silent, so muggy, that Walter felt as though his ears were not working. Small sounds, rustles and hums, could well have been coming from his own imagination.

But then he heard something. If this was Turner then he had timed it well. Sure enough, as the distant crunch of footsteps grew closer he heard Turner's voice growling 'Here boy! Where are you, you damned dog. Here! Bleedin' mutt. This way, come on!" The dog made an apologetic dog noise and presumably made itself visible, as shortly afterwards Walter could hear Turner getting closer.

He readied himself, heart racing, also suddenly realising that the dog might well find him first and give the game away. He hadn't even thought of that. But it seemed that the dog's nose was about as useful as its bad leg and it padded past on the grass opposite, completely ignoring the hidden threat behind the tree. Turner followed, shambling past the tree with his hands in his pockets. Almost silently Walter stepped out, took four long strides and grabbed him in a headlock before he had time to react.

"Wha....eumphhhhh!" was the only noise Turner managed as Walter squeezed as hard as he could, his powerful forearm pulling the man's neck backwards and pressing it hard against his assailant's chest. As Turner's airway was compressed, his arms started flailing wildly and his legs kicking, striking Walter painfully in the shins. He certainly was a feisty opponent.

Walter winced angrily but instinctively reacted by widening his legs, leaning forward and using his left arm to heave Turner underneath him so that he fell face first on the floor. Walter went down with him, landing heavily on the man's back as he continued to hold his neck but now with his whole considerable weight bearing down on Turner, restricting his breathing even further. Turner had no way of escape; all he could do was squirm helplessly and make almost imperceptible muffled whimpering noises, his limbs now twitching and shuddering rather than flailing.

The only thing preventing his face being buried in the gravel of the path was Walter's arm under his neck, and Walter could see the colour rising and the veins bulging on his forehead. Despite a rush of greasy body odour assailing his nostrils, he placed his mouth close up against Turner's left ear and hissed "I don't like people who mess me around, have no respect. I really don't like them. So I'm going to teach you some manners, Mr Turner. This is what happens to people who cross Walter Threadwell."

He wanted Turner to know who it was, to realise who he was dealing with, and make that the last thought that he took to his maker. "People like you," he growled with as much menace as he could muster, "don't deserve to live. So I'm doing the world a favour, and I intend to enjoy it. Do you understand me, Mr Turner?"

With that he released the pressure slightly, allowing Turner to take one last, desperate and noisy gulp of breath. Then he immediately clamped hard again, before the man could indicate whether he had understood or not. Walter didn't care really. As long as Turner had heard him, that was enough.

"You pathetic little squit. You're a drunkard and a lowlife," he whispered into Turner's ear, "get ready to go to hell." And with that he squeezed even tighter, as hard as he could, feeling the man's neck compress and crack as parts of it collapsed.

The squirming was briefly more frantic, then suddenly stopped. Walter held the grip for thirty seconds or so to ensure no air could get through, then slowly released it. Turner's head flopped forwards into the path with a small thud.

Walter quickly got to his feet and brushed the loose stones from his coat. Well, he had enjoyed that. It was every bit as good as he had imagined. The surge of power had been invigorating. But now he had to act fast. He looked around. The mist still swirled around him but it would not give him cover for long.

Then he realised – where was the dog? Why wasn't it fighting to save its master, raising the alarm with frantic barking? He looked behind him and there was the little Jack Russell standing ten feet away, head cocked, just staring at him with a puzzled expression, tail slowly sweeping to and fro. It was as though he was trying to work out whether or not what had just happened was a good thing or a bad thing.

"Good boy," said Walter almost without thinking, hoping without evidence that this would at least keep the dog quiet until he had dealt with the body. The dog continued to stare at him thoughtfully.

So Walter got on with the job. He grabbed Turner's legs and dragged him roughly between the tombs, head thumping on the uneven surface and banging against the sides of the graves, until he got to the one with the thinner lid.

Letting the legs drop with a thud, he turned and clasped both edges of the shorter end of the stone cap and, using all his arm strength, heaved to one side. He nearly tore a disc in his lower back but the lid did not move. Damn, it was heavier than he thought.

Quickly he placed his feet against a neighbouring tomb and his back against the stone lid. Using his legs as levers, he pressed with all his might, the stone biting into his back. Still it wouldn't budge. This was ridiculous. He looked round again, starting to panic. Someone could come along at any minute, and in this fog he might not hear or see them until it was too late.

The dog – the only witness to the murder - hadn't moved but was now letting out a few strangulated barks, presumably trying to ask Walter what was going on. At least that wouldn't attract attention, not unless it lost patience and started barking furiously, assuming it possessed the energy to do so.

Walter had left the crowbar he had brought by the tree. This was his last chance. He retrieved it and looked underneath the overhang, hoping to find a gap he could place one end of the crowbar in. Perhaps time and decay had naturally welded the stone, and one sharp movement would crack it open. Thankfully he found an imperfection on one edge which had created a gap just large enough for him to lever in the end of his crowbar. He wiped a bead of sweat from his brow, then put all his weight on the other end of the crowbar. Just as he was about to give up, there was a sudden split as the lid came free and rose slightly.

Walter dropped the crowbar and once more used his legs and back to try to lever the lid ajar. This time it slid an inch or two. Thank the Lord for that, he thought, although on reflection it was probably unlikely that God was actively helping him in this endeavour.

He stopped suddenly. He had heard a noise, a whistling sound, muffled behind the fog. Ears straining to pierce the fog, he listened intently. There it was again. Someone aimlessly whistling, and it was getting nearer. Damn, damn, damn, this was not what he needed.

Quickly he bent down and grabbed Turner's body under the arms and started pulling it behind the grave. As he pushed backwards, his legs, still recovering from their previous exertions, buckled beneath him and his backside hit the ground with a soft but painful thump. He cursed under his breath, and remaining on his backside, pushed his legs against the ground as with rising panic he levered and dragged the body backwards.

But the tuneless whistle was getting close now, too close. He froze, now not wanting to make a sound, then lay back quickly, Turner's torso between his legs, with the greasy haired head resting against his inner thigh. By lying flat against the ground he hoped to remain unseen but was fully prepared, if he had to, to leap up and deal with whoever it was approaching. His heavy breathing wasn't helping him to focus on the noise or indeed remain undetected, but the mist was still thick and he might still be safe.

The whistling suddenly stopped. Had he been spotted? Walter kept very still and listened, his ears almost painful with the effort. A short period of silence, then a cough and a clear of the throat and someone spitting, but a little further off. With a bit of luck they were on the other path, the one that ran parallel to his. Then the whistling started again, and gradually weakened into the distance as the owner of the noise headed away, perhaps taking a shortcut through the cemetery to get to work.

A huge sense of relief swept over Walter and after another minute or so of waiting in order to make absolutely sure the man – Walter hoped and assumed those noises would not have come from a woman unless she had abandoned all decorum – had gone, he got to his feet, stepped back over the corpse, and got back to work.

Once again he placed his back against the adjacent tomb and his feet against the lid, and pushed hard with all his might. The stone slab slid a few inches such that its overhanging edge was now flush with the side of the tomb. Now his feet were too big for the task so he turned round, put the palms of his hands against the edge of the lid, and used his legs, braced against the stone, to push forward again.

It was hurting his hands, but the stone moved and a gap appeared, giving him more purchase on the lid and allowing him to vary the position of his hands and lift slightly as he pushed. Gradually the movement became easier and with additional help from the crowbar the gap widened. Walter peered in. He couldn't see much in the gloom but there only appeared to be dirt at the bottom, mostly green and black in colour and with no sign of any bones.

Another push, and another, and Walter was exhausted, his legs feeling like those of a newborn giraffe. But, even though it was at an angle, the gap was enough now, it had to be. He quickly checked Turner's pockets and found a house key and a few coins. So he did have money after all, albeit not very much.

He placed the items on top of the adjacent tomb, then crouched down and put his arms under the shoulders of the body, dragging it back into place and then lifting Turner up so that his head faced the tomb before hefting him face first into the gap.

The top half of the torso went in, but Walter realised now that because he couldn't pull but could only push, pushing the legs was not the best approach as they just buckled. Now starting to sweat profusely, Walter dragged the body back out again, turned it round, and put the legs in first, before using the torso to force the legs further into the other end of the casket. Finally it was far enough in for him to be able to twist the head round so it could also drop in with a crack, like the final piece in a macabre puzzle.

Although desperate for a rest and with muscles aching, Walter rushed to the other side and once again used his legs braced against an adjacent tomb to heave the lid closed. This seemed marginally easier this time, presumably because any residual resistance had been overcome when it was opened, and so a few good hefty shoves and the lid was back in place.

He slid to the ground and sat there for a few minutes, breathing heavily and waiting for his muscles and lungs to recover.

The fog was lifting slightly now, and he could see across to the nearest path. The dog had trotted over and was now standing on a low grave, still watching him with a slightly bemused expression. This presented another problem. Walter had originally thought that he might dispatch the dog and put him in the same place as his owner, but he had been so focused on what he would do to Turner that the dog had become secondary in his thoughts and of little importance. He now realised that was a mistake.

If he left the dog here, wandering about the graveyard, it might well lead someone to the opened tomb and start pawing at it. If he took the dog with him, someone might recognise it as Turner's dog and he would be implicated. If he killed it, he would have to dispose of the body, and he wasn't about to try opening that lid again. He also wasn't sure of the best way to kill a dog when it would probably just run off if you raised a crowbar at it in an open space. He might end up chasing a dog around cemetery all day. Even a three legged dog was probably more nimble than he was.

It was the lesser of three evils: despite not liking dogs, he would have to take it with him, assuming it would follow him, then deal with it later. He just had to hope that it would actually follow him.

He couldn't use the main entrance now. Anyone could see him emerging with this blasted dog. He would have to climb over the wall at the northern boundary and head back on Bearhill Road. He grabbed Turner's house key and coins from the top of the other tomb where he had left them, then looked across at the dog, which was maintaining its "what just happened there?" expression. "Come on boy," he said unenthusiastically as he walked briskly back onto the path and up towards the Bearhill Road boundary.

The dog looked at him but did not move. Walter decided to call his bluff. He disappeared into the mist, called again, and after a couple of hundred yards stopped and listened. Sure enough, scuffled steps and panting breath preceded the appearance out of the mist of the limping dog as it realised that standing alone in a foggy graveyard was perhaps less appealing than following this stranger who appeared to have replaced his master.

"Come on," said Walter again, realising he didn't know the dog's name. He was sure it wasn't Bleedin' Mutt, as Turner had called it. Well, hopefully he wouldn't need to give it a name as he would be rid of it shortly.

He strode across the grass and under the trees until he reached the five foot high flint and brick wall border that defined the edges of the cemetery. No problem for him but how would he get the dog over? He would have trouble picking it up as the dog was keeping its distance, being rightly cautious of Walter's intentions. Then he noticed a gap in the wall further up, which turned out to be barred by a thin cast iron gate. The gate was locked but there was room for the dog to squeeze underneath, so Walter vaulted over the wall into the empty road, and sure enough the dog decided not to stand on ceremony and scurried under the gate once Walter was at a safe distance.

The two of them then made their way down Bearhill Road to the junction by the water works. It was a fair distance, and by the time they reached the crossroads the dog had given up worrying about Walter's motives and was trotting just a few feet behind him. Walter thought he had better give the area around Turner's shop a wide berth as the dog would be more likely to be recognised and might itself head back to its house, so instead of turning left he went straight across the crossroads, planning to cut back into town using Ditchling Road further along.

It was as he approached Ditchling Road that good fortune struck. He heard distant barking and remembered that there was a kennels just before Warleigh Lodge. As they approached, the barking and whining grew louder. The limping Jack Russell, who was by now flagging badly after such an extended and unexpected period of exercise, started making little yappy noises too in response, perhaps hoping for some canine company so that he could tell some other dogs all about the adventure he had just had.

Walter had no idea who ran Hollingdean Kennels – all he knew was that the establishment was quite isolated, being surrounded by open land that bordered the railway track. A small house looked over an assortment of wooden and wire mesh structures that housed the dogs, and the whole ensemble was surrounded by a five foot high brick wall, just high enough to deter the average dog from leaping over it should they escape their pen.

He looked at the Jack Russell, who, having only three fully functioning legs attached to an aging body, had by now almost slowed to a halt, its tongue hanging out. Taking advantage of this, he crouched down and held out his fingers. The dog, too exhausted to do much else, cautiously approached and sniffed them, as dogs are wont to do. Finding nothing objectionable, and grateful to have a rest, it allowed itself to be picked up.

Walter checked the coast was clear, then lifted the dog up and swiftly but carefully dropped it over the brick wall into the grounds of the kennels. Despite its surprise at suddenly being mid-air, the dog landed in a heap but without mishap, and, scrambling to its feet, looked up only to see Walter's arms disappearing back over the wall. Another owner gone – this was quite a day.

Well that was easy, thought Walter as he walked swiftly on. A perfect solution. The kennels wouldn't know who owned the dog that had suddenly appeared in their yard, and even if for some reason the police found out that Turner's dog had ended up there, what use would that information be to them? He was sure no-one had noticed him on the trip from the cemetery as the fog had been thicker further down the hill, but even if they had, and in the unlikely event that he was identified and tracked down by the police, he could just claim that the dog suddenly appeared and started following him and he had no idea whose dog it was, so left it at the kennels.

He turned left at Warleigh Lodge and headed back into town. It had been an interesting morning.

CHAPTER 35 : WHAT TO DO

"It's the only way."

"You're right." Marlo fingered at the flowery curtains as he stared out of his bedroom window, looking but not seeing. His mind was focused entirely on the conversation with Lillian.

"I don't like it of course, to be honest it scares me, a lot. But it's hard to see any other way to do this."

"I'm scared too," admitted Lillian, "for both of us. If anything happens to you, it happens to me too. That's why we have got to plan this from every angle and expect the unexpected."

They both knew that even if they found Walter's knife, and could prove that it might have been the right size and shape to match Jed's stab wound, this was not on its own enough to put him behind bars. They needed more than that. It really had to be a confession, an admission of some kind, witnessed by an authority. And for Lillian the confession had to include why he did it, not just the fact that he did.

It would require two key elements: engineering a situation where Walter would for some reason admit to the murders, and being able to convince someone in authority, ideally a policeman or a respected person of authority, or failing that a number of witnesses, to lurk nearby and overhear the confession.

Marlo repeatedly wished he had some of the technologies he had left behind in the 21st century that would have made this so much easier: a smartphone with voice recorder, a hidden camera in his lapel, anything that could record and play back what happened. Asking Walter to hang on while he set up the wax cylinder wasn't quite the same. Those Victorian police certainly had their work cut out.

So over the course of the evening he and Lillian worked on the details of their plan, interrupted only by a very pleasant stew served up by Mrs Chomsy.

By the time his light went out, they had worked out how to catch Walter Threadwell. Well, in theory, anyway. But they both admitted that it was not a good plan, it was just the best they could come up with in the circumstances. The fact that it involved using Marlo as bait emphasised just how bad this plan was. If it went wrong, as in 'Marlo gets killed' wrong, that was it, game over. Neither of them would be returning.

"But if Walter did eventually go to jail thanks to an overheard confession just before he killed me, would that not be at least enough for you to escape from the Midrift?" Marlo had asked, slightly fearful of whatever answer came. "Surely the conditions have been met?"

"No, did I not mention? In the same way that you have an incentive to complete the task, there has to be an incentive for the transient to keep the resolver alive too. Otherwise I could be manipulating you into some madcap scheme to save my skin while sacrificing you, and that is not the objective. After all, if we succeed, you have to introduce me to your modern world. It is supposed to be a team effort. You die, I die."

"I had better not die then."

"That would be my advice too."

Marlo struggled to get to sleep that night. His dreams, when they came, were dark and disturbing. A garden of flowers was being crushed underfoot by cackling demons while he uselessly tried to ward them off with a rolled up newspaper, his efforts largely unnoticed by the black creatures as they went about their business. But then when they had finished crushing all the flowers, they turned their attention to him.

CHAPTER 36 : THE SECOND ONE

They never found Henry Turner. The mystery of his disappearance quite literally went with him to the grave. Consequently, the police had no idea what happened to him, and no fingers of suspicion could be pointed at Walter.

He returned to Turner's shoe shop a few days after the report of the cobbler's unexplained vanishing act had appeared in the local paper, knowing that if challenged he would just say he had come to collect that week's debt money, not realising what had happened. But there was no one there and the shop looked no different than it did before other than that the lock had been forced and there was now a thick linked chain and padlock around the handle and a hasp that had been secured to the frame. Presumably the police had forced access in case there was a body in there.

The door from the living space down the steps was untouched, though. As Walter stood before it, fingering the key in his pocket, he hesitated. He had been planning to avail himself of that enticing opportunity that comes to anyone who acquires a key to someone else's house and knows they won't be there. Just a quick look inside could do no harm, could it? It was partly out of curiosity but also to see if he could acquire anything of value.

But, a little like a snooker player deciding whether or not to go for the difficult long pot or play safe, caution suddenly tugged at him. Even if the financially troubled Turner had highly improbably left a bag of sovereigns on a table, and the blundering police had not spotted them, was it worth the risk? Someone could see him entering or leaving and he would have very few good reasons for explaining what he was doing and why he had a key. Also, what was the point? When the estate was processed, creditors would be paid off, so in fact they could get the debt repaid more quickly than if the weekly instalments had continued.

He took the key out of his pocket and placed it under a flowerpot on the ground, then made his way back up the steps. It just wasn't worth it.

The police did then briefly interview him a couple of weeks later as someone who had previously had contact with the victim and might have a tenuous motive through being owed money, but as Walter pointed out, that applied to all his clients, and in any case he was in bed at the time of the murder and no-one could prove he wasn't. This successful conclusion infused Walter with feelings he liked. He felt quite proud, almost smug, and most definitely satisfied. He'd done it – he had taken a life and got away with it. He would rather like to do it again when the opportunity arose.

And that opportunity to kill again wasn't long in coming. It was almost as though Walter had set a wheel in motion and now it was gathering momentum, more frequently presenting him with suggestions as he encountered people who displeased or irritated him. Now that he knew he could do it and get away with it, his selection threshold was lowered - he did not have to be so choosy about who he picked.

Anyone who upset him was fair game, it did not have to be sustained provocation as was the case with Henry Turner. And it was a game. A game of chance as well as a game of skill but if you were someone who made your own luck then chance could be manoeuvred in your direction whilst still heightening the thrill. Walter was the player in control, he held the cards, and he was going to win each game. Walter enjoyed winning much more when the stakes were high.

And so before long he had decided on his next victim.

Tim wondered where this writing was coming from. Here he was, good old Tim, a mild mannered getting-on-a-bit ex-civil servant sitting comfortably in a pleasant house, stumbling down a metaphorical dark alleyway to douse himself in a world of savagery and evil, despite being completely unqualified to do so.

He knew nothing about murder, or wanted to, and yet, rather worryingly, he was quite enjoying the frisson of excitement drawn from the creative process of describing it. He supposed it was the same for people who made horror films, even people who watched them.

It seems that everyone has a dark cloud that lurks in the recesses of their soul – some, and he counted himself among them, can control it. Others, and Walter Threadwell was one of them, couldn't. That dark cloud periodically became a storm, and storms had consequences.

Yet in creating Walter and writing about Walter, he was having to think like Walter. Was that blurring the lines? Did that make him a worse person for being able to think like this? No, he was still in control. It was always ever thinking, not acting, and that was the difference. He wondered what his children would say when they read what he had written, assuming he ever finished it. They might be shocked, amused, perhaps even secretly proud of him. They would certainly never look at their wouldn't-hurt-a-fly father in the same light again. Not that he really cared any more what other people thought about him, he was too old now to worry. As long as the kids didn't disown him.

Be that as it may, the last few weeks had been almost cathartic as his focus on the world he was creating helped to blot out the pain of his own life situation. He had become totally absorbed in the words that were flowing from his brain; presumably this is what happened to most writers, otherwise how did they manage to churn out enormous novels one after the other.

He took a sip of the lemon tea that he had made earlier. It was cold. It was a routine he was used to: decide to make lovely cup of tea – make tea – bring tea to desk – allow tea to cool while writing another paragraph – drink tea – discover tea is cold – realise you have written ten paragraphs instead of one.

Anyway, all this work and it seemed as though he was no more than half way through the book. Marlo and Lillian hadn't even begun to trap Walter, and now he had become sidetracked onto Walter's back story and who he had murdered previously. Would the reader really want to know all this? Was it useful background or just padding? It was fun to write but was it interesting to read?

He sat back and looked out of the window, re-focusing his tired eyes on some distant trees. If only Liz was still here, so he could ask her.... no, actually, that wouldn't have helped, she could never seem to care less about his writing. To her it was just one of his pointless hobbies. He would make a decision. He would skip past Walter's second murder, as it wasn't really essential to the plot. It was obvious now that the man was a nasty piece of work, a psychopath with issues from childhood that were coming home to roost. A lengthy description of another killing wouldn't add any insights. Also, he would have to think one up, and that wasn't easy when all you knew about Victorian life was what you could find on the internet. He was skating on thin ice as it was.

The meat of the story would be the coming together of Marlo and Walter, the big denouement. That's what people wanted to read about, didn't they? All the expert advice he had read was to keep your book as punchy as possible, and by that they meant, not so long that you would only finish it if you were stranded on a desert island with nothing else to read. Already his word count told him that he had passed Treasure Island and was almost up to The Hobbit. That sounded bad but he wasn't even half way yet to Jane Eyre or Moby Dick, so he still had some leeway. Nevertheless, he could not afford to witter on for pages and pages about things that might bore the pants off a reader. But would a murder description do that? He supposed not.

Oh hell, he didn't know what to do. Ok, a decision. He would only briefly describe the second murder, then if the book ended up being shorter than he thought or, on reading back, appeared to have a gap in the story, he would come back to it and flesh out the detail. Yes, that seemed the best approach.

He absent-mindedly took another sip of cold tea, wished he hadn't, then turned his attention once more to the screen in front of him.

Part of the excitement Walter felt from his forays into darkness was the fact that only he knew. No-one else, not even Mr Carberry, had the slightest inkling of what he had done. Normally when you have done something significant, you want to tell people about it, perhaps boast a little, bask in their admiration. But for people who kill people in the way that he did, it is a whole different game. It is done for personal gratification, and part of that self-satisfaction is the very fact that no-one else can know. It is a secret that you must keep for ever, which in a strange way helps to prolong the excitement.

First Henry Turner, then, less than three months later, Alfred Godwin. It helped that they both had no close relatives to get in the way, and Godwin was an old fellow who, like Turner, lived on his own but in this case whose financial downfall had been gambling. His face peered from behind a big white scruffy beard and a lazy eye that made it look as though he was always looking over your shoulder. He was half deaf and had a scratchy high-pitched voice that he tended to shout with, to compensate for his poor hearing. This made him remarkably irritating to listen to even before you had taken in what he was saying.

Unlike Turner, Godwin didn't even have a dog for company, but seemed content to potter around on his own. To begin with, he had been tolerably civil. Not happy about handing over his money, but not too rude either.

That changed when the debt increased after he missed some payments, no doubt after backing a few lame horses. He became flustered whenever Walter appeared, then confused and grumpy, and after a while faintly aggressive. Nothing like the abuse that he got from Turner, but now Walter's threshold for retribution had decreased.

He had so enjoyed the tremendous rush of adrenaline that dispatching Turner had given him that he needed less of a reason to undertake a similar exercise with someone else, and he became tired with Godwin's shenanigans. The man was old and appeared to have no purpose in life other than to exist. If anything, Walter convinced himself, putting him out of his misery could be doing him a favour. It was time for him to go. At least then, again, the debt would be repaid more quickly.

This time, Walter made it easier for himself. He knew he could not attack Godwin while on company business, as Mr Carberry's schedule would direct the police straight to him, but there was no reason why on this occasion he could not to do the deed in the man's home, at a time of his own choosing. As long as he wasn't spotted and left no clues, why would he be caught?

Godwin always invited him to stand in the hallway while he fetched what he owed, so on the next occasion he visited he took the opportunity to quietly unlatch a side window that opened out into a narrow alleyway next to the house that gave access to the open land behind. That was all it took.

And so that evening after dark, at around half past nine, he returned. There were no street lights and it was a cloudy night, so it was dark enough to give him the necessary cloak of anonymity he needed. Waiting a little down the road until the coast was clear, he walked slowly along the road and checked that there was light coming from Godwin's lounge. There was.

He quickly nipped sideways into the alleyway. It was so dark here that he couldn't see what he was walking on, but he quickly found the unlatched window and slowly and quietly prised it open from the outside. Thankful that his height enabled him to shift himself up into the opening quite easily, but less thankful that this meant he had to bend double to squeeze himself through, he emerged on the inside and dropped carefully to the floor in the hallway. There was a slight thud as he landed and he froze, clenching his fist just in case. He could see flickering coming from under the lounge door and hear the spit and crackle from the fireplace. If Godwin was in there he probably wouldn't have heard anything unless his good ear was facing the door. The door remained closed, so, following his plan, Walter crept into the kitchen and found a large kitchen knife in a drawer. The blade was sharp and thick with no bend in it – just what he was after.

Back at the lounge door, he slowly eased it open, and through the gap could see the back of Godwin's head, not moving, poking above the back seat of an armchair facing the fireplace. Was he asleep? Already dead, perhaps, died of natural causes – that would be ironic but also extremely annoying. Or maybe he was just sitting there, watching the fire or reading a book. It didn't matter. All that mattered was that Walter was in control now.

This pitiful man's destiny was in his hands, and the feeling of power was intoxicating. He wanted to savour it, so despite the risk he stood there silently behind the open door for a few minutes, staring at the wispy hairs on the top of man's shiny head as they occasionally moved slightly in the waft of the warm draughts given off by the coal fire. Walter knew what was coming, Godwin did not.

It was time. Walter gripped the knife handle a little more tightly, squeezed through the door, and crept up to the back of the chair.

His final step elicited a loud creak from the floorboard beneath him, and immediately the head in front of him stirred and began to turn. But before Godwin could even rise from his seat, Walter's left arm was pinning his neck to the chair as the right arm swung round and plunged the knife deep into his chest with a satisfying thump.

Quickly he let go of the neck so that he could use both hands to force the blade all the way in. He had aimed to the left so it would puncture the heart, but he wasn't prepared for the blood that came pumping out, and so had to immediately release his grip on the knife, standing back quickly to prevent his sleeves getting spattered.

Godwin had let out a surprised but muffled high-pitched cry when the knife went in, but shock and adrenalin only gave him enough impetus to lean forward and topple from the chair, the hilt of the knife still protruding from his chest. He collapsed sideways in a wretched heap and lay moaning and twitching as a dark pool of blood formed around him. A few spasms, then the gasps for air turned to one long faint sigh, and suddenly he was still. Now nothing moved except the ever expanding lake of blood, spreading inexorably despite much of it being lost down through the cracks in the floorboards.

Walter savoured the moment for a minute. He felt nothing for the man he had just killed. Why should he? He didn't really know him as a person. All he felt was a strange inner calm and a sense of immense power, driven by the fact that once again he, and not any god, had determined when death should come to a human being.

Then he moved quickly. Carefully avoiding the blood on the floor, he stepped round behind Godwin, reached over, and wrapped both of the dead man's bony white hands over the hilt of the knife, squeezing the fingers into a tight interlocking grasp. It was awkward to do, and he felt surprisingly squeamish doing it, but it had to be done. He had to make it look like suicide.

Then he pulled out a scrap of paper he had brought with him and looked around for something to write with. He had brought a small pencil with him but if he could use something from Godwin's house it would look more authentic. Not that he knew how sophisticated the police's forensic techniques were, but if they were able to match writing to one of Godwin's writing implements, that could only help his cause.

A bureau in the corner contained a rudimentary quill pen and a bottle of ink, which was dried up and empty. But there were also two pencils, so he grabbed one and, leaning on a side table, scrawled 'Goodbye' on the paper using his right hand so that it looked nothing like his normal left-handed writing, and left the pencil resting on top of the paper. Even if it wasn't in Godwin's handwriting, it wouldn't matter; he could have been out drinking earlier for all the police knew and only just able to scrawl a word when he got back home. And if he couldn't write, he could have got someone else to write it for him earlier. The main thing was not to provide any possible connection to Walter Threadwell.

He looked around the room. The fire would burn itself out, that was ok. He wouldn't take anything, otherwise that would confirm someone else was involved, rather than the old man taking his own life.

He quickly exited the room, closing the door behind him, and clambered out of the hallway side window, dropping quietly back down into the alleyway, which was so dark that he couldn't see the ground he was lowering himself onto. He turned and pushed the window closed. Even if the police noticed it was unlatched, that wouldn't prove anything; it could have been Godwin himself who had forgotten to secure it. The alleyway was not overlooked as there were no houses opposite, so he lurked for a minute or two in the shadows, checking that the street was absolutely clear, while wrapping a scarf around the lower part of his head - even with no street lights it was always sensible to take precautions. Then he stepped back onto the street and walked back down the road, feeling euphoric yet strangely calm.

The local newspaper a few days later reported the death of Alfred Godwin with a little more prominence than would normally be the case, but only because he had committed a grisly suicide. The police seemed convinced, as they were reported as saying that they were not looking for anyone else in relation to his death, and they didn't even bother interviewing Walter this time. Presumably they felt they could do all their detective work just by gathering evidence from within the house.

Walter smiled contentedly. They were all fools, and he was playing them like puppets. One day he might taunt the police as they would by that time be unable to prove his involvement even if they wanted to. He would bide his time though, no need to rush. The next one could not be a customer though. It would be too much of a coincidence if three people visited by Walter as a result of owing a debt all mysteriously died unnatural deaths. The next one would have to be different.

Tim smiled weakly to himself as he saved his work and reflected on what he had just written. So much for skipping over the second murder. It was very difficult though – once started he couldn't stop himself explaining what happened in far more detail than he had planned. Hopefully the readers, if there proved to be any, wouldn't mind. The book would just have to be too long, although he consoled himself with the thought that you can never have too much of a good thing; he just hoped his 'thing' was good.

CHAPTER 37 : FIRST STEP IN THE PLAN

Marlo should have slept well after such an eventful and physically active day yesterday, but he still felt tired when he woke, and half-remembered waking fitfully and trying to get comfortable in a bed that was much softer and less even than he was used to. No pocket springs, memory foam, or any kind of mattress technologies in Victorian times, just some lumpy stuffing.

He lay looking at the ceiling, wondering if it was worth trying to go to sleep again. But his brain had already started recalling the plan he and Lillian had concocted last night and he knew he wasn't going to drift off now.

"Morning Lillian," he said quietly after mulling over a few things.

"Good morning!" The reply was bright and far too awake for this time of the morning.

The more he heard it though, the more he liked her voice. There was always positivity in it, despite what she had been through, while he himself always struggled not to sound miserable, because usually he was, despite not having been thrown off a cliff like she had. There was a lesson there.

"I've just had a thought. Maybe I dreamt it. Why don't I just, well.... kill Walter? Not that I want to of course," he added hurriedly, "but surely if I did do it somehow, wouldn't justice still have been done and I would have resolved the unfinished business? It might be easier than going through our elaborate plan to trap him." He rubbed his feet together, trying to warm them up a bit. "Also, if our plan fails, I might have no option if he comes after me."

"Well, I did think about that, but it wouldn't work. Think about what would happen." Lillian cleared her throat and adopted a slightly more school-ma'am tone that Marlo decided he wasn't so keen on. "First of all, you couldn't do that before Walter had confessed and the cause of my death was explained, as that is the first condition of the success of your task. But even if you somehow managed to kill him after that, things might appear fine because Walter had got his just desserts and so you would immediately disappear back to the 21st century and be a successful resolver. That's what I was thinking too at first. However, and this is the problem, Walter's murder would be either be unsolved, if no-one saw you do it, or even if they did, they wouldn't be able to catch you as you would have disappeared in a puff of smoke and so the police couldn't accuse or prosecute someone who wasn't there any more, and so couldn't bring anyone to justice for Walter's murder."

Marlo looked puzzled, even though Lillian couldn't see him assume this expression. "Well that's a good thing isn't it?"

"Not really. Under the rules, Walter would then become a transient and end up where I am now, because his death – killed by a mystery man who has disappeared – could not be explained or avenged. Meanwhile you, back in your 21st century world, already know how Walter was killed and are likely to be the only person who could ever know, so if you, for example, were ever to stumble across something owned by Walter in his lifetime – that knife for example – the transient conditions would automatically be triggered and you would be instantly whisked back to the Midrift and expected to bring justice to his murderer. Which is you!"

"Jeez, that's twisted. What a nightmare. Are you sure about that?" Marlo's heartbeat had risen just thinking about what would happen. "In that case maybe I should just turn myself in and confess, then rot in a Victorian jail for the rest of my life. Not much of a choice is it?"

"No, but you wouldn't have to worry about prison," re-assured Lillian. "You'd probably be hung."

"Oh well that's all right then. Hung? My God. Wow. That really is bad. I don't want to be…. but, hang on, that wouldn't happen, would it, because……because….. " he paused while his brain tried to catch up with him, "right, yes… as Walter's murderer, by being sentenced myself and given a punishment, I would still have met the resolver challenge so as soon as I was convicted and sentenced, before I was hung or went to jail I would disappear and be transported back to my normal life, so that's ok isn't it?"

"Yes, but who would you be bringing back with you?"

Marlo's face fell. "Oh my God, Walter! I'd be bringing the person I murdered back to 21st century Britain. Again, a nightmare!"

"It would be even worse than that. No doubt the first thing he would then want to do is kill you in revenge, then quite possibly come after me too if he realises I am there as well. To be honest I have had quite enough of being killed by Walter already."

He knew he shouldn't but Marlo couldn't help smiling. "I don't blame you. Then again, the chances of me coming across anything once owned by Walter are millions to one.... but stranger things have happened."

Lillian gasped suddenly. "Oh my, I've just had a thought. If I come back with you to the 21st century, I would also know how Walter died, so it could be me who is pulled back to The Midrift, to sort out justice for my own murderer! That can't be right. And I would be stuck there because if you were Walter's killer I could not bring you to justice or explain the death because you would not be there. No, the whole idea is a very bad one. Whatever you do, don't kill him, however much you might want to."

"I think Number Five should amend the Transition Conditions," mused Marlo. "You should be barred from becoming a transient if you have already killed someone. Seems common sense to me."

"I agree. Do you know what, I would hope that is something that FiveTwo might actually agree to discuss with Number Five. He is reporting back on us you know; I am told Number Five knows what is happening, he has heard about us. If we succeed he might get involved himself, who knows."

Marlo felt strangely proud but also anxious. Here was the creator of everything, out there somewhere in the cosmos busy with billions of stars and planets, yet he knew about Marlo Campbell and his quest to free a transient. No pressure then.

"Lillian, when we go back to the 21st century, we will still be able to remember everything, right? Won't that make us incredibly powerful with that kind of knowledge? You especially as you know more than me."

"Well, I've been thinking about that, and I've had a lot of time to think, believe me. It is a similar situation to that which you have now, as in we won't be disallowed from telling people, but it is a risk to tell them and possibly get accused of witchcraft or heresy and sent to the gallows. It just wouldn't be worth it. Also...."

Marlo interrupted. "That's not going to happen," he laughed "the state doesn't kill people any more. Well, not in Britain, at least. And you are also allowed to have whatever opinions or religions you want so we wouldn't be arrested, just advised not to be so daft, probably."

"Oh, right, good. Well that's helpful. The thing is though, when we go back to your time, the difference is that neither of us will have any knowledge of the future. We will know a great deal about a short period in the past of course but that won't be quite so impressive. What we will have knowledge about is how the world was created but as you have confirmed we can talk about that all we like but we have no evidence so can't prove anything."

"Like any other religion, basically," Marlo observed, his eyes scanning the ceiling as he lay there and alighting on a small black dot – a spider – trekking purposefully across it, absorbed in its own aims and no doubt unconcerned about the tribulations or indeed existence of the recumbent human just six feet below. "But you must know about things like life on other planets, don't you? You could guide scientists to look in the right place, that kind of thing, couldn't you? You did say that Number Five had created other life forms didn't you?"

"Yes, lots of them. That's partly what keeps Number Five occupied, he is creating life all over his domain. It is just so vast and so far away that we humans could never possibly ever know about it. Even if I could point out a star with life on it – which I couldn't, by the way, I don't know how – man would never be able to find it."

"Don't be so sure about that! We have satellites out there heading past Pluto even now."

"Pluto, what's that?"

"It's a planet in our solar system – the smallest one and the furthest away. Don't you know about that though? I know we discovered it after you died, but if the Priming told you about what is going on up there......"

"It didn't tell me the names that humans would give to planets in the future. Or anything in the future, remember, just how we got here and why. You said 'satellites', are they like the space machines you were telling me about the night before last, the ones that went to the moon?"

Marlo smiled at Lillian's description. "Yes, sort of. Just with no people in it. It takes years and years, you know, just to get to the nearest planets let alone Neptune and Pluto."

"I'm not surprised. Oh, and I do know about Neptune." Lillian sounded pleased with herself. "It was discovered about 40 years ago I think."

"That long ago? Impressive. Funny how man makes it sound as though it wasn't there until we found it. Anyway, I suppose you're right, however much we knew about the creation of our world and who created it, we couldn't prove it. Well, some people might believe us, I suppose, then we would become a cult, and that often doesn't end well. It is clever, isn't it? All that knowledge yet nothing we can do with it. Well, not that I can think of off the top of my head."

"I also think we are jumping ahead of ourselves a little bit here."

Marlo flung back the warm sheets and winced at the relative chill of the room. "Yes, you're right. I seem to be saying 'you're right' a lot these days. I had better not make that a habit."

"Nonsense, you should say that every time I speak."

"You had better not speak then. That would make me right more often."

"Only in your own mind. That's how dictators start."

"Well, I'm not, er, you....." Marlo stumbled, as he usually did, even when he had started well. It was like leading a 100m race with 20m to go, then tripping on your shoelace and watching everyone go past you. It was a feeling he was very used to. "Ok, you win. No doubt I'll be saying that a lot too. I think that is how the man-woman relationship works, not that I would know of course."

"You think I do? I step out with one man and he throws me off a cliff. Twice! I clearly know nothing about how to make a man respect my opinion." Lillian was joking but there was a hint of understandable frustration in her voice.

"Well now we have both got a chance to practice all that stuff, haven't we?" said Marlo brightly, as though it meant nothing but hoping it did. "Anyhow, let's get going. I'm getting up now, so you'll just hear the usual getting up noises."

"How exciting for me," Lillian deadpanned.

Once again no witty reply formed in Marlo's head and he found himself saying "Ha! Yes." Just another small stumble in the 100m there, painfully reminding him of his pre-Lillian struggles to appear confident and quick-witted in conversation. It was always the way - just when he thought he was getting better at the banter, it would let him down.

It wasn't as though he did not possess a sharp enough wit and so couldn't ever come up with a killer retort. It was just that he usually only thought of each masterful reply well after the moment had passed, particularly if a girl was involved. When obligated to at least say something quickly, the first thing to emerge from his mouth was often along the lines of "er, yes, I suppose so," which tended to mark him out as a witless dullard to whomever he was talking.

His theory was that our brains, having an element of muscle in them, behave like muscles in how they respond to stimulus. Some people have more 'fast twitch' fibres, others are 'slow twitchers'. But whereas with most muscles this can provide help when running for a bus, for example, or cycling to work, with brains it is all about how quickly they can fling out a witty response and 'come back at ya' with a killer line.

He had met many people who could maintain instant banter at a pace which was enormously frustrating for those like himself who were always a few seconds behind them, often with exactly the same comment or response or even a better one. His chance to shine in a group was continually snatched away by the sharper-witted chap next to him, such that he and others like him would all be silently thinking 'mate, will you please just go to the loo for an hour or so and give the rest of us a chance?'

On initial showing Lillian did appear to have a quicker twitching brain than he did, and could more often think of a snappy retort without thinking, if that made sense. The frustration was less with Lillian though, as she didn't seem to think any the less of him for it. Or was she just playing him along, keeping on his good side because she would be a fool not to? If they got back to his world, would she immediately abandon him? It was a thought he wished he would stop having.

Also, when you are bantering (was that a word?) with a girl, when did that cross over into flirting? Marlo had never experienced anyone flirting with him face to face and realised he probably never would, and of course for someone who looked like he did, it wasn't something he could ever initiate as it would just look creepy. He had to wait for someone to do it to him first, then maybe that gave him license to do it back. But if he mis-read the signs? What if they were just being generously friendly? He'd almost made that mistake before. No, his only experience of flirting would be to watch other people doing it while he was supposed to smile and feel pleased for them.

Sometimes it felt as though everyone else had become adults when they grew up but he had remained a child. They nearly all seemed relaxed and easy in the company of the opposite sex, while he was awkward and nervous, a fumbling, bumbling novice, and knowing that made it worse.

Forming relationships was like a big game with rules and procedures that everyone else had been given, but Marlo had somehow missed out. They were all in on it; he wasn't. He didn't have the handbook.

He continued to blunder nervously around, looking at others confidently and effortlessly pairing up, and being continually baffled as to how they did it. If he copied them in certain approaches that appeared successful for them, it never worked for him, but then he had nothing to offer. Everything had conspired against him. He was ugly, he was sensible, he was nice, he was dull. Nothing to see there, ladies, just move along. He was just a boring, useless excuse for a wimp in whom women could see no spark of possibility, and there was virtually nothing he could do about it other than continue to plod away, rely on luck, and hope that he eventually had some. God it was so depressing.

Maybe now, though, there was a tiny glimmer of hope. Fate had brought him Lillian, hadn't it? He knew full well though, that what for most people would be classed as a golden opportunity always lost its sheen when Marlo was involved. Opportunities for others were dreams for him: not a golden sheen or even a silver lining in sight. If only this time could be different.

Feeling mildly gloomy now, he washed, dressed, and shaved, the latter a new and slightly challenging experience, as his normal electric shaver was now what was basically a weapon in a sheath, being a very sharp blade which flicked out from its holder like a gangster's knife, albeit with the latest safety feature of a toothed metal guard.

He had bought it yesterday, having asked the man behind the shop counter for a shaving kit and been presented with a razor, a horse hair brush, some Viniola shaving soap which proclaimed that it caused "no blotches under the chin", and a strop, which was a leather strap for keeping your blade sharp.

Now he laid all the implements out on the bathroom shelf as though preparing for an operation, and got ready a towel and a bowl of water. Fifteen minutes and only two small cuts later he emerged from his lathered face with comparatively smoother skin everywhere except above his lip, which he had left alone in order to see what happened if those little dots managed to sprout into hairs worthy enough to be accorded the description of 'moustache'. At least then he would not look quite so non-Victorian. He knew there was no point trying to grow a full beard because, as he had already reluctantly intimated to Lillian in Seaford, his very efforts to grow one would illustrate to everyone that he couldn't. So better a small moustache and an otherwise smooth face than a tufty-fluff jaw that looked like some hairs had been randomly glued on by a small child.

The smell of Mrs Chomsy's bacon and eggs enticed him downstairs and it was only when he returned to his room and sat on his bed that he realised that he had left Lillian's diary in his jacket pocket.

"Lillian, could you hear me just now, having breakfast, talking to Mrs Chomsy?"

"No, it went quiet for twenty minutes. You left the diary in your room, didn't you?"

"Yeah, I did, I'm an idiot. Sorry about that. So it only works if I'm really close to it, as in, in the same room?"

"Yes, and don't ask me why, those...."

"...... are the rules, I know," interrupted Marlo with a manufactured sigh. "But hey, it has given me the kick I needed to sort myself out and not to do that again. Next time it could be important. You didn't miss anything though. It looks like Mrs Chomsy doesn't read the paper every day, or not all of it anyway. She still doesn't know about what happened to you."

"Ok, well I suppose there's no reason to tell her, it would only complicate things. I doubt anyone else would tell her either unless they knew about the source of her hats."

Marlo picked his own cap off the bedpost where he had hung it. "Let's hope she doesn't want a new hat any time soon then. But doesn't she have women friends that she gossips, I mean, you know, talks with? Two murders on a cliff top nearby, you would think someone might mention it?

"Well, yes, that's possible. She'll tell you soon enough though, when she finds out. Through gossiping, obviously."

Marlo swallowed the mild rebuke. "Ha, yes, naturally. Anyway, I might be gone by then." A sudden thought struck him. "What actually triggers the end of this task, though? I was thinking it was when we have managed to get Walter arrested and flung into a police cell awaiting trial, but is it going to be when he actually gets sentenced? That could be months away!"

"It won't be that long. The trial could be in a matter of days if we are lucky. Then again it could be longer. But it's about justice. If we got Walter in a police cell and then he was released the next day through lack of evidence or something, then we haven't done our job, and that isn't justice. He has to have a trial and be found guilty."

"But supposing he is found not guilty? Plenty of criminals escape justice through a good lawyer."

"True. But even a good advocate in court can't overturn a watertight case."

"Therefore we have to have a watertight case. Oh boy, we so need our plan to work."

Lillian chuckled unexpectedly. "You do talk in a funny way sometimes. Why did you put a 'so' in that sentence?"

"Did I?"

"You said 'we so need our plan to work'."

"Oh, right, yes. It's another way of saying 'really' I suppose, just gives it emphasis. People use 'so' all the time now, especially at the beginning of sentences when answering a question. Very irritating. Anyway, listen, more importantly, how long could the actual murder trial take?"

"Again not long, usually within a day. You have to wait, we both have to wait, until we hear the judge confirming that he is guilty and proclaiming the punishment - that is the trigger. It's only then that we know that justice has been dispensed and the conditions of our task met. So I'm sorry Marlo, but it might not be quite as quick an escape as you imagined."

"Actually that's not as bad as I thought. Just a few days to get a murderer to court and then a day to trial and sentence him? Wow."

"Is it not quicker now, in your world?"

"Jeez no, the exact opposite. The whole process can take years. Usually does."

"Years? Why have you become so much less efficient?"

"I suppose it is just to make sure that the accused isn't unfairly convicted. Everyone needs time to prepare their case. Also, we have too many criminals and not enough courts. But that's another story. Oh well, if it is just a few extra days or maybe a week or two after he confesses, then I guess that isn't too bad."

"I'm not making any promises, mind."

"I wouldn't expect you to!"

Marlo stood up again. "Ok. The quicker we get this done the better." He slipped his jacket on, patting the pocket with the diary in it, happy that it was snug and secure in there. "Right, I'm ready to begin the day. Let's enact the plan. First step – Operation Find Walter."

They had agreed that to track Walter down and make contact with him, it might be best to visit Lillian's family first, even though both were not sure whether or not they really wanted to. Lillian knew it would be heartbreaking to listen to her loved ones without being able to communicate back, and Marlo knew that he would have to be so careful not to give anything away and suddenly blurt out something only Lillian should know. But if anyone was desperate to know how Lillian was killed, it would be them, and if he needed assistance he knew he would be able to rely on them. For them to know who he was, he had to introduce himself – and have a reason for doing so.

Yet he could not use the best reason of all which was the truth. So the idea was to sow the seed of doubt in the family by pretending that Marlo had overheard Walter in a pub boasting to a friend about how he didn't love Lillian at all and was seeing a different girl at the same time but hoped for benefits from both, then when he saw the newspaper report he remembered the names, put two and two together and thought he ought to tell the family. It was plausible enough, they felt, and would certainly get the family on his side if they thought that it might lead to an explanation for their loss. Then he could explain how this wasn't exactly evidence, so rather than go to the police and put Walter on his guard and in the mode for revenge, it would be far better to try and trap him into a confession. Then Marlo would volunteer to engineer this, because he wanted to join the police force and he felt that if he could flush out a murderer who would otherwise have got away with it, then it would greatly aid his application. It was a bit of a flaky justification, but it was the best they could come up with and at least it wasn't beyond the realms of possibility, particularly as it was another reason for why he did not want to involve the police straight away.

As far as both Lillian and Marlo knew, Walter was an accountant. Lillian had never pressed Walter on his work as he always seemed reluctant to talk about it and changed the subject quickly – 'it's really very boring, nothing to talk about' he used to say – so she had no idea who he worked for or where he was based. She didn't even know where he lived as he had always come to her house to collect her. She realised now that this was almost certainly deliberate, but she wondered if her father had wheedled any more detail out of him in any of the 'man to man' talk the two of them occasionally engaged in when waiting for her to get ready.

Mr Jones, with his business background, may also be able to suggest a list of accountancy firms in Brighton that Marlo could investigate.

He set off and on the way there, took a little detour down to the beach because, well, it is what you do when you are by the sea, isn't it? He was also fascinated to see what it would look like, and it did not disappoint.

As soon as he came onto Marine Parade he was immediately struck by how much wider and more spacious the road and promenade seemed, possibly because everything using it was smaller. The broods of buses, lines of lorries, prides of people carriers, troops of taxis and convocations of cars were all absent, replaced instead by an oddball assortment of horses and carriages, bicycles, carts and pedestrians. A large percentage of the latter seemed to favour the road to the pavements, although Marlo soon realised that this was just people crossing the road in a casual and less direct way than you would if about to be mown down by a lorry. Of course you might always find four horses pulling a carriage trotting over you, but if the driver was paying attention that was a small risk, particularly as he was unlikely to have a mobile phone or a horse-mounted satnav to distract him.

Oh, and there were goats. Marlo could hardly believe his eyes when he saw a little allocated bay by the side of the road next to the omnibuses, the painted markings on the road not stating 'disabled' as he would expect in modern times, instead reading 'goat stand only'. It wasn't a mistake as there in the bay was a slightly startled looking goat with a tiny two wheeled cart strapped around its haunches, ready to give a ride to any child whose parent was for some reason prepared put their trust in a goat. A man in a checked shirt, scruffy suit, and a bowler hat hovered nearby eyeing up potential clients. It made a change from riding a donkey, although personally Marlo would have chosen the donkey, a decision no doubt to be welcomed by the goat.

He crossed the road and went down the little slipway that took him onto the seafront promenade. Immediately ahead of him was something he had never seen before that took him by surprise. He put his hand up to his mouth to speak. "Wow. Lillian, I'm standing looking at a narrow pier that looks like a little suspension bridge. Four little turrets in the sea. It has to be at least 1,000 feet long. I didn't know this was here."

"Oh yes, Chain Pier. I've been on it a few times, it's used for loading and offloading boats and as a tourist attraction too. It's not quite as popular as it used to be though."

"Oh right. Well, it's not there now. I mean now as in from my era. What a shame. Must have been a fire or something, that's usually how piers get destroyed."

"Or a storm. I heard it was quite badly damaged by storms in the thirties so maybe there was another one. That's sad if it has gone."

"I'll have to look it up when we get back to the future." Marlo smiled to himself. "Ha, that's funny, there's a film called Back To the Future and now that's what I'll be doing, hopefully."

"What do you mean by film?"

Marlo was a little taken aback by the question. "You don't have films yet? Cinemas, you know, where you go to see moving pictures?"

"No, I don't know. Moving pictures.... Is that like a magic lantern?"

Marlo had heard of magic lanterns but didn't know much about them. This conversation was starting to become like talking to a foreigner when neither of you spoke the other's language. "Do they show moving images?"

Lillian sucked in her breath a little. "No.... not really."

"Well, no then."

"Oh."

"Remind me, when we get through all this, to take you to the cinema as one of the first things we do. It will blow your socks off, I guarantee."

"What? Why would I want that?"

Marlo's face fell and self-pity enveloped him. "You don't want to come to the cinema with me? Well, that's something I'm used to I suppose. I just thought you might have liked to....."

"No, no, silly man," interrupted Lillian playfully, "I just meant I didn't see why I had to have my socks blown off."

Marlo breathed a sigh of relief and smiled. "Oh, right, yes, sorry. That's an expression, it means you will be amazed. Your actual socks will stay where they are."

"Well that's ok then, I would love to come and see a moving images film, whatever that means."

"Excellent!" Marlo was already envisaging snuggling up in the back row of the cinema with the girl of his dreams, something he had always desperately wanted to do but never had anyone to do it with. At the back of his mind, though, he knew not to count any chickens. These things never ended up actually happening. And let's face it, he was getting ahead of himself. He had only actually met Lillian two days ago – she might turn out to have all kinds of character flaws which she had kept hidden so far. He might end up not liking her at all. That wouldn't surprise him, it would be just his luck. No, he told himself, stop thinking like that. Try to be realistic as well as positive.

As he had been getting a few funny looks as he stood there with his hand over his mouth making noises, he left Chain Pier behind and started walking into town along the seafront. To his right he could see the large clock tower which indicated the quite recently opened Brighton Aquarium. He was sure that clock tower wasn't there now (it was indeed to be demolished in 1927), which was a shame because it was a very handsome structure. If he had a chance he would like to go back and have a look at the aquarium, especially as he could just make out a poster advertising 'a real live mermaid – half beautiful woman, half fish'. That would be amusing. This was like going on a business trip and factoring in some extra time to visit the tourist sights, although really, given his situation, it wasn't like that at all.

The biggest surprise was the beach. The section he was passing now was covered in sails and masts from all the fishing boats that had been dragged up the shingle and now lay like a dense pod of small beached whales, some of them listing slightly to one side. This was a working environment, with fishermen and helpers offloading their catch, tending to the nets and cleaning their boats. Up ahead he could see a fish market right on the beachfront, signposted by all the shrieking seagulls wheeling around above it and the shouts from the men advertising and negotiating prices.

There were sailing boats too, large white three-sided sails fluttering in the breeze, jostling for space with hundreds of little rowing boats the size of dinghies. He could see over-dressed families testing their reactions against the waves or just taking in the sea air as they walked awkwardly over the stones between the boats. Past one of the groynes that snaked into the sea he thought he could see a group of musical performers in red and white striped jackets and straw boater hats, putting down some wooden boards to make a platform on the stones, ready to entertain and accept coins from the punters looking down from the road above.

Although late September now and the sea starting to cool, bathers were catered for as well, evidenced by the rows of bathing huts lined up like carriages preparing for a society ball, their large spoked wheels providing sufficient ground clearance to allow them to be pushed into the sea far enough that the occupier could with much enhanced dignity and privacy step straight into the water. Some sported vertical blue and white stripes like a stick of rock, others were plain wood with 'Gentlemen's Bathing' in big white letters on the side, as though warding off women and impolite men.

The whole beach arena was a messy yet thriving scene of human activity rather than the dull empty expanse of pebbles that he had expected and was used to.

Further down the beach he could see that it became less crowded, yet small rowing boats were strewn about the shingle for as far as the eye could see, most a little distance from each other like beach towels reserving their own little spot. More little groups of wheeled bathing huts were clustered around the edge of the beach like oversized crabs testing the water.

Walking much more slowly than he normally did as he took in every detail of this semi-alien world that was carrying on around him, Marlo headed west along the seafront past the coastguard station, ready to cut back into town when Lillian told him to. As he strolled onwards, faces approached and passed by him, some glancing, others ignoring, all of them unaware that there was a time traveller in their midst, an imposter. It was a strange feeling, as though at any minute someone would point at him and shout 'this man is a fraud – arrest him!' even though he knew full well that this would never happen. Yet he felt so conspicuous, so un-Victorian, if that was a word, and so out of place.

He noticed how most of the boys seemed to be dressed in rough miniature suits with caps, like an army of scruffy pageboys scattered all along the promenade, and it set him wondering why humans in the modern era seem so keen to change clothing styles all the time. Why do we put so much effort into finding different ways of covering ourselves, and why does our society feel the need to radically change it at least every ten years? Well, that was as far as that thought was going. He had more important things to think about.

As he looked down the promenade it dawned on him that no-one was running – there were no joggers! He wasn't expecting lycra of course but you get used to seeing sweat-drenched runners everywhere these days and it was odd not to see them. Perhaps a stiff walk was considered sufficient to clear the lungs.

The sun was out and many of the women he passed held black umbrellas or parasols above their heads lest the slightest trace of sun should tint their alabaster skin, as a tan in Victorian times was the sign of someone of lower classes who toiled outdoors for a living. He recalled the rather amusing phrase he had come across in his research, written by some male arbiter of social norms, that 'it is generally preferable for a woman to be pale-faced, if her beauty is increased by it, no matter whether she be healthy or not'. Any man who said that in the 21st century would be best advised to get himself off social media immediately.

He wondered whether the phrase to 'bustle along', had anything to do with the bustles that it seemed all the women around him wore to widen and plump out their long skirts or dresses, as this caused the garments to sweep against the ground and swish as they moved, emphasising the movement of the owner. Skin was very comprehensively covered as well, there was barely an ankle on display. How different to today whereas at least an attractive woman would give him something he could work with in his imagination, seeing as that was as close as he was ever going to get. Out here they gave nothing away; every bit of skin was out of bounds to the keen observer. For men the excitement is usually in what they can nearly see rather than what they can see, but here it was neither. It was quite depressing for a man who could only get physical pleasure from ladies by looking at them and taking those memories home and imagining what might have been. Then he thought of Lillian again and cheered up. She was the carrot on the end of his stick, although perhaps that was not the most appropriate choice of words.

At the side of the road now stood a long train of horses and carts, the taxis of their day, patiently waiting for custom, the horses periodically shaking their heads as though irritated by the harnesses that you might think they would be used to by now. The smell here was particularly bad as the manure had mixed with the dirt on the road and was in some cases ground in by the wheels of passing vehicles. Maybe you got used to it but it really wasn't nice. He saw a child of about ten scooping some of it up into a bucket and running awkwardly off. Not something you would do voluntarily at that age so presumably someone was paying him to do it.

Up against the stone ramparts that stood between the beach and the road and protected the town from storms, Marlo could see a group of young men and boys playing pitch and toss, where players toss coins at a mark and the person whose coin hits closest to the mark tosses all the coins in the air and wins all those that come down heads up. He watched for a while as they played, ribbing each other and celebrating with a big cheer when a coin landed on or close to the mark or an 'oooh' as it just rolled past. Nowadays they'd all be on their phones not talking to each other, he thought, despite phones having been invented so that you *could* talk to each other.

He was now approaching West Pier, just twenty two years old and resplendent with its latticework of cast iron threaded columns and girders supporting over a thousand feet of walkway, which in itself provided home to numerous benches, kiosks and places of entertainment. The entrance was framed by gas lamp columns decorated with entwined serpents, and a central bandstand and a large pavilion at the far end of the pier emphasised its magnificence. It was hard to believe that it was now destroyed, storms and arson having ensured its demise over 100 years later. It was so sad, especially seeing it now in its heyday.

Marlo just stood, looked at it, and drank it in, before deciding to walk across to the entrance, through the gates and onto the wide decking. He could imagine when it first opened; no doubt many of the intrepid visitors would feel that they were walking on water, worried that they would fall through the slats in the wood through which they could see the rushing waves below. It was solid enough though; he knew it wasn't going to fall down quite yet!

He strolled over to one side and joined some other sightseers leaning on the rail and looking over the edge. From here he got an even better view of everything going on down below on the beach, and could see a couple of donkeys further down, competition for the goats. A lifeboat house, a sturdy wooden structure like a row of conjoined beach huts with boats in it, stood guard about twenty feet in front of the ramparts. Further on, between the beach and the road, was the esplanade, a genteel area for folk to 'take a constitutional', with bordered lawns, another bandstand, and wooden benches facing out over the sea. Marlo was amused to see that there were quite a lot of wooden benches actually positioned on the beach itself, unevenly lined up in little rows on the stones as though on a day trip and admiring the view. He could imagine that in modern Britain they would be gone by the next morning and wondered whether in 1886 they just trusted everyone not to steal them or whether someone came out every night and locked them away.

It had just gone ten o'clock and was already surprisingly busy, helped by it looking as though it was going to be a nice day. His hand almost went to his pocket to check the weather app on his phone but he was becoming quicker now at remembering he couldn't do things like that any more. But the emerging sun had brought people out to make the most of weather that would before long be pushed aside by the cruel breath of approaching winter.

As he stood watching the morning beach scene unfurling around him, he reflected that the people here were not really any different to the people he had grown up with all those years in the future. They had the same emotions, the same hopes and desires to better their lives and find happiness. They were just all dressed differently and the world they lived in was less advanced. Other than that, Marlo was the same as them really. As he thought about this, he felt the salty sea breeze caressing his face and ruffling his hair, heard the laughter of children playing on the beach below, and an inner peace enveloped him. "This is awesome," he said under his breath.

"What is?" Lillian was straight back at him.

"Oh, er, just the pier. It's beautiful. And looking at everyone going about their business or enjoying themselves. None of them know, do they?"

"Know about you, you mean?"

"Well, yes that, but also what is going to happen. When the queen will die, the fact that there will be two world wars, that man will fly to the moon. Even just how their lives will change, with all the inventions to come. The only person standing here on this planet, right now, who knows, is me. Jeez."

"That's true, but..... did I hear right? Two world wars? You hadn't mentioned that before! What happened? That sounds awful!"

"It was. But let's not spoil the day, I'll fill you in tonight. We got through them though, as you can tell, otherwise I wouldn't be here. Although I think if we had a third world war.... no, I'm not going there. Right! I need to get moving, much as I would like to stay here all day."

He turned back towards the town, the breeze tingling the back of his neck as he left the pier and climbed the steps back onto the Kings Road. "Ok, here we go then," he said more to himself than to Lillian, but she took that as a cue.

"You know which road to look out for?"

Marlo re-adjusted his thinking. "Preston Road?"

"Close. Preston Street."

"Right, yes, thank you. I think I can see it."

He was right, and after following further instructions from Lillian it was not long before he found himself in Challenor Street, approaching the shop marked 'Thomas Jones – Hatter'.

"How are you feeling, Lillian?" he asked softly as he approached.

"Really emotional," she replied with a nervous laugh. "I'm shivering with...well, I don't know what with. I want to hear them again, but not like this. Not when they are so upset. Oh gosh, oh gosh. I must take some deep breaths. Marlo, I'm sorry, I doubt I will be any use to you while you are with them, and just ignore me if you hear me crying, alright?"

"Ok."

He could almost hear her trying to pull herself together before she resumed. "But I will try to stay quiet and say nothing, I don't want to distract you. Right, just say what we agreed, and don't for goodness sake say anything that could give them any clues as to who you really are. This is probably going to be your hardest conversation."

Marlo was in front of the shop now. "I know. This definitely isn't going to be easy. But please feel free to prompt me if you can, if there's anything I should be saying."

"Of course. Good luck!"

"Thanks." Marlo walked to the front door and pulled the doorbell handle.

CHAPTER 38 : REVEALING THE PLAN

At just twenty-three, Frederick Jones had already begun to consider himself successful in life, even if some of that success had been down to good fortune for which he could take no credit. For example, he had grown up in a loving family who had worked extremely hard to make sure he went to a good school, so he was well educated. He judged himself reasonably good looking and had never struggled to attract the attention of the ladies. That was just luck, albeit luck that he had not been shy in using to his advantage.

Yet he had also made his own luck. He used the contacts of his parent's business to assist setting up his own enterprise renting out bathing huts on the beach. They were those wooden boxes on big wheels, looking a bit like a poor man's mini stagecoach, which the wealthy used to protect their modesty when bathing in the sea. It was hard work, especially in the summer, but was also rewarding and, despite its seasonal nature, was proving nicely profitable thanks to increasing tourism in the town.

He now lived in his own lodgings not far from the very large house of Mr Plundell, a boat manufacturer whose daughter Letitia he had been seeing for some time and for whom he worked during the winter running errands and helping with administration. It sounded menial but it gave him a lot of insight into how a wealthy man operated, and it fascinated him.

All things considered, life was good. At least, it had been. Now, his world was turned upside down. His sister, the sibling closest to him in age and so to whom he had the most affinity, and who, despite their many childhood arguments, he knew did not have a bad bone in her body, had been killed. It was Frederick's first experience of death. He never knew his grandparents; they were all gone before he was old enough to recognise them, and so this had hit him badly, not least because it came out of nowhere and to the person whom he would have least expected.

It was supposedly an accident, but Frederick wasn't so sure. He considered himself a good judge of character and when he saw Walter Threadwell for the first time yesterday, there was something about him he didn't like. He looked vaguely familiar for a start, although Frederick couldn't think why, and that familiarity seemed to have a bad association with it that he could not explain. Perhaps it was just that the man looked menacing. He supposed women, even Lillian, found this appealing but he couldn't see it himself. To him, the man just looked like a henchman, someone you might hire as a bodyguard or to exact a revenge on someone. The polite talk felt forced. Alright, he said he was an accountant and you should not judge a book by its cover, but he still felt uneasy, especially as Threadwell was the only person there when Lillian died.

And now he had read that another man had died on the cliffs too, the next day. There was no suggestion that Threadwell was involved in that but it did seem odd, a remarkable coincidence, particularly as Threadwell was in Seaford that day too. Something wasn't right.

And now here was this rather odd fellow Mr Marlo Campbell, turning up out of the blue, standing in front of all the family and claiming he thought he had heard Threadwell boasting that he had two women on the go and Lillian meant nothing to him. Frederick found himself unsurprised. Lillian's companion sounded like he was a damned gal-sneaker, a seducer who hadn't earned the right to take Lillian out to buy a loaf of bread, let alone escort her for a whole day.

On the one hand he felt vindicated in his suspicions of Threadwell, but on the other hand, and playing devil's advocate, why should he believe what Mr Campbell was saying? He could have mis-heard, misunderstood, or even got the wrong man – although to be fair his description of Threadwell was spot on.

He supposed he had nothing to lose by believing him, but should he also support this madcap idea he was now proposing to try to trap Threadwell into a confession? Provoking the man into admitting his guilt just didn't seem feasible. Why would he do that? Not just Threadwell, but Mr Campbell too. Putting his life in danger seemed unnecessarily cavalier, and he was sure that no-one in the Jones family wanted another murder to contend with. Not there was any meat on the bones of this plan anyway – it was much too vague for his liking.

There was silence in the room as they all mulled over what Marlo had just told them. William and Alice, the two younger children, were upstairs in their rooms and Maisy the maid was not around, so it was just Mr Jones, sitting very still on his favourite armchair and shaking his head slowly and gravely, Mrs Jones, perched dejectedly yet elegantly on the chaise longue, her eyes moist and mouth frequently quivering as they talked about her daughter, a permanent frown set hard to her brow, and Frederick himself, leaning forward on the writing table chair in the corner with his hands clasped over his knees. Marlo had been proffered the other armchair, and sat awkwardly in it looking expectantly at each of the family in turn.

Frederick would always defer to his father so he waited for Mr Jones to clear his throat and offer his response.

"Well, Mr Campbell," the older man began, his mouth fighting to be seen from under his forceful moustache, "I must thank you for coming. You will understand, we are still in shock and grieving, so if what you say is proved true about Walter's real feelings for Lillian, then that.....well, it doesn't make things any easier, you understand?"

Marlo nodded.

"But if it is true that he said these things...." Mr Jones continued falteringly, "I've still heard nothing to convince me that Walter had any reason to push her off the cliff. Why would he have done that, Mr Campbell?" He looked up suddenly and gave Marlo a piercing stare. Not accusatory, more desperate to know.

Marlo wished he could tell him, but he didn't know either. All he knew for certain was that Walter had pushed, then subsequently thrown, Lillian off that cliff. He was as puzzled as Mr Jones as to why he would have done that.

He fiddled with his cap, which he had been clutching nervously on his lap. "None of us know, Mr Jones. But were you all satisfied with his explanation?"

"No!" Frederick could no longer stay silent. "Papa, I've said nothing until now because you and Mama have enough to deal with and I was not sufficiently convinced of my own intuition to warrant it causing you further anguish. But now that Mr Campbell has raised the subject, I have to confess that I was vaguely troubled by Mr Threadwell's visit yesterday. As you know I had not met him before and to me there was something about the man, something dark. His account didn't add up for me, it felt unlikely. Lillian wouldn't have risked her life like that, she was always so careful. And then just before he left he clearly didn't want us to know where he lived, as though he had something to hide."

Marlo picked up on this. "Did he tell you eventually?"

Frederick nodded. "Yes, he did. I wrote it down, on the....the newspaper. Mama, where is yesterday's newspaper? It was here this morning, now this is today's copy." He looked urgently at his mother, who lifted her head with much less alacrity and looked at him as though she had not been listening to anything that had just been said.

"The newspaper? What of it?"

"Yesterday's edition. Where is it?"

"Oh, I took it downstairs, ready to go in the fire. It should be on the table in the scullery unless someone's already put it in the hearth. Why?"

"Never mind. Excuse me for one moment." And with that Frederick was out of the door and bounding down the stairs. An awkward silence ensued, broken a minute later by his return, clutching the newspaper in question and with a look of great relief on his face.

"That was close! I clean forgot I had written it down here. Anyway, it is.... 34 Southover Road," he said squinting at his shaky-hand writing. He looked up at Marlo.

"How will it help to know where he lives?"

"Well, it will mean I can track him to his place of work, see who he works for. Unless you already know, Mr Jones? Did Walter ever discuss with you which accountancy firm he worked for?"

Mr Jones smiled weakly and shook his head. "Goodness me no. He hardly said a word when he was with me. Most of our conversations involved the weather."

Mrs Jones suddenly came to life. "Then if you knew so little about him why did you let him take Lillian to......?" she started, her grief now turning to anger and wanting to find a target, but instantly realising that this was a futile avenue that they had been up and down at length already. She quickly held up her hand to ward off his riposte before he had a chance to fire it. "I'm sorry, dear, I know. It could not have been predicted. I just feel...well, you know what I feel." She turned to look at Marlo.

"That man was responsible for her safety. We trusted him to look after her, and he didn't. You do understand, Mr Campbell?"

Marlo nodded a touch too eagerly. "Absolutely I do. So if I can find out where he works and then befriend one of his fellow accountants, I might be able to find out a bit more about him. Walter, that is." He saw Mr Jones's doubtful face and elucidated "this is detective work, you see. If I can show in my application to be a police officer that I have used my initiative like this it could really help me."

Frederick was beginning to see an ally. He looked at his parents. "What have we got to lose? We've lost everything already. I think we should be very grateful to Mr Campbell for offering to help clarify exactly what happened. I'm sure it is what Lill would have wanted."

"Oh Freddie, I do love you. He is so right." Marlo heard Lillian's almost inaudible tear-filled voice in his head.

"Yes," said Marlo out loud, feeling he had to respond in some way, "I am sure it would be important to her, and I would be very pleased to assist."

Mr Jones looked over to his wife who nodded her agreement. He looked back at Marlo and simply said "Thank you."

Frederick relaxed slightly, pleased his father wasn't going to start getting all right and proper and insist they left everything to the police. If Mr Campbell was true to his word then whatever he did would be something that Threadwell would not be expecting, and that could be the key to catching him out. But he was still not convinced about Marlo's plan to trap him into a confession. He looked back at their visitor, this very plain looking chap who spoke a little strangely but seemed to have his heart in the right place.

"Mr Campbell, finding out more about Threadwell is one thing, but you said you were going to lure him into a position where he would admit to killing my sister, and in front of witnesses too. You did not specify exactly how you would do this, and I confess that I am struggling to understand how it might be achieved. Could you please elaborate?"

Marlo shifted a little uneasily in his seat. Frederick was right, this was the part of the plan that was more wishful thinking than calculated probability.

"Well, it is true that to actually make Walter confess is going to take luck, and involve risk, not least to myself." He paused to suck in some breath, as you would before making a grave pronouncement. As he did, he realised he was talking now in a formal language that bore little resemblance to office banter at Convestia. Well, that was good really, he was trying to blend in, so talking 'all posh and proper like' as his colleagues would no doubt describe it, was going to help him survive here.

"To fill in some of the details, I am going to pretend that I want to set up a business, and need some accountancy services. Mr Threadwell had been recommended to me so I will ask for him personally. I will arrange to meet somewhere quiet, and have at least one person hiding close by but within earshot, transcribing the key elements of what is said. I am not sure yet as to whether it is worth involving the police – without stronger evidence I doubt they would want to waste an officer's time hiding behind a curtain just in case. So it will have to be someone else, and I do have someone in mind."

A mental image of George Smith, the young man he had met on the train, flashed through his mind. If George wasn't up for it, he might struggle to find anyone else until he had been here long enough to make acquaintances. The problem was that Marlo knew he was not very good at making acquaintances. This plan really was clutching at short straws, but it was all he had, and he had to have something.

"After a while I will suggest a break and start to make small talk, asking if he is married, that kind of thing. That should allow me to engineer the conversation around to me suddenly asking him, as though I have just thought of it, whether he is the same Walter that I read about in the papers whose girlfriend fell off a cliff. I doubt he will be able to deny it, and at that stage why would he. Then I will get cold feet about using him and say that I found it hard to believe she fell on her own accord. He will get angry, then I will hopefully be able to trick him into an admission of some kind." Even as he said it he knew it sounded weak.

"Wait though....." Frederick interrupted, "I read that another man was killed at almost the same spot, the next day. Now Threadwell......" his speech slowed as he tried to phrase the words correctly, ".... was still in Seaford on Friday, as he did not come to see us until yesterday, claiming he couldn't because he was detained there the previous day helping the police. Could it be possible that once the police had finished with him he went back up the cliffs and killed that man too? Could you level that accusation at him as well?"

"Why would Walter have killed a stranger?" interjected his father, curious rather than dismissive.

"I don't know. Unless he knew him. But the man was a drifter so why would he? No, it doesn't make sense." Frederick scratched the back of his neck and scrunched up his face. "None of this does. Unless...." his voice quickened "unless the man witnessed Lillian's murder! Maybe he was out walking and came over the ridge just as Threadwell did it. That could be it, couldn't it? What do you think Mr Campbell?"

Marlo wasn't sure why Frederick addressed the question to him, as though Marlo was acting in the role of Hercule Poirot interrogating the family in order to collect evidence. He had in any case hoped he would not have to start bringing Jed into this at this stage despite knowing full well that Walter had indeed killed him, otherwise he might let slip a detail that he should not have known. Yet it was always going to be his intention to raise it with Walter, just to provoke him.

Conscious that all eyes had now turned to him, he ventured "I don't know about that. I think we should focus on Lillian and then who knows what will come out in the wash."

"Yes, perhaps you are right," conceded Frederick, although it was clear that his mind was still thinking through the implications of Walter being a potential double-murderer. "So Mr Campbell, what are you hoping that Threadwell will say when his word is doubted like this?"

"Although it sounds odd, I suppose I am hoping that he will start threatening me. Let slip something like 'do you want me to do to you what I did to Lillian', that kind of thing."

Mrs Jones shook her head. "I don't like this. It sounds too dangerous. There must be another way."

"I agree actually," agreed Marlo. "I would prefer a better way, I just can't think of it at the moment."

"How will you protect yourself?" asked Mr Jones, in a matter-of-fact way that sounded as though he was asking for a hat size.

"I'll have a large knife to hand. Not to use, you understand, just to keep him at bay should he try anything."

"I still don't like it. In fact I like it even less." Mrs Jones was trembling slightly now. "One, well, two if you count the other man on the cliff, people have died. We can't have a third. It's just too much."

Marlo could see that she meant too much for herself to bear, as well as too much killing in general, and he could see her point. The more he thought about this plan, the less chance there was he thought that it could succeed. If Walter did admit to anything, then immediately Marlo was a potential whistleblower and as far as Walter was concerned would have to be dealt with. And he and Lillian were the only people in this room who knew how Walter 'dealt' with people. The more he thought about it, putting himself in the firing line was perhaps not the plan of a mastermind.

"Alright," he conceded. "I'll take one step at a time, find out a bit more about Walter, then re-evaluate my next steps. I don't want to cause you any more distress than you have already been through."

"I think that is a wise strategy." Mr Jones nodded sagely, then looked around the room and clapped his hands together a couple of times to signal a change of tack.

"Right, let's move on. Where are you living young man?" he asked Marlo. "I assume it would be best if we are able to contact you should we need to."

Marlo smiled – he wasn't going to make the same mistake as Walter and get all coy about his address. "Yes, that's fine. I'm in lodgings in Arbuthnot Street, number seventeen."

"Thank you. Frederick?" The father looked over to his son, who was still lost in thought. "Would you care to write that down?"

"What? Oh, yes, sorry. The address, yes. I shall note it on one of my business cards this time instead of a newspaper!"

"You have business cards?" Marlo couldn't stop himself. A brief moment of panic subsided as he quickly realised that this could just refer to his surprise at Frederick having them as opposed to them being around in Victorian times. Before any other interpretation could be made he hurriedly turned it into a joke. "I didn't know you were that important!"

Frederick smiled briefly. "Oh yes, even my father looks up to me. He is doing it now, indeed!"

"Only because I am sitting down and you are standing up," replied Mr Jones wearily but with a sub-tone that indicated that he did realise that this was what son had been implying.

From his jacket pocket Frederick pulled a small wedge of what looked like playing cards and dealt two onto the table. On the first he carefully wrote down Marlo's address, but also that of Walter. He had to squeeze the detail between the printed lines, because the back of the card was filled by a map. Once done, he put the card into a small inside pocket. The other card he gave it to Marlo, explaining "Mr Plundell, whom I work for, was having a run of his own cards printed and as a sort of a gift he decided that I could have some too. As you can see, they often come in handy."

Marlo looked at the elaborately designed card, full of little squirly patterns and drawings of boats. It read:

Plundell Maritime Services Ltd
Luxurious Boats and Yachts (& Bathing Huts)
'We are as proud of our products as you will be to own one'
Main Office: 12 Brunswick Square, Hove
Frederick Jones, Senior Assistant

"You live in Brunswick Square?" Marlo was surprised, as if it was where he thought it was, it would be completely out of Frederick's price range even to rent a room. Turning the card over to show the little map confirmed he was right – it was an elegant regency square right next to the sea.

"Ah, yes, sorry, I forgot. That's a business card so it doesn't have my own address, just where Mr Plundell lives and runs the business from. If I could take it back for a moment, I will add my details."

Frederick retrieved the card, carefully wrote his address, and handed it back to Marlo, who squinted at the angled handwriting. It was all very neat, but almost too tidy and regimented in its flow, as though all the letters were part of each other. "Fifty-one, Narfall Road?" he checked.

Somewhat offended at Marlo's inability to read his splendid writing, Frederick corrected him. "No, Norfolk Road, you see the 'k' at the end there? And it is fifty seven, not fifty one."

"Oh yes, I see now. Sorry." Marlo didn't really see but it was easy to remember now that he had been told. "I will need to write down Walter's address too, though. Southover Road, you said?"

Frederick apologetically rolled his eyes. "Of course, I'm so sorry. My mind is all over the place." He took the card back for a second time, this time managing to fit 'Walter T – 34 Southover Road' right at the bottom of the card. He handed it back to Marlo.

"There you are. Now, if you need assistance, just let me know. We all want to know what happened to Lill, what really happened, you understand? If this Threadwell character has spoken as you report, and there is any possibility, any possibility at all, that he has had some hand in my sister's death, he must be found out, and he must pay for it."

Frederick realised his voice had risen and he cleared his throat self-consciously before resuming more quietly.

"Mr Campbell, is there anything else you need from us?"

He looked at his parents for reassurance that this was time for the closing question. Mr Jones gave a slight shake of the head, Mrs Jones lowered her gaze almost imperceptibly.

Marlo thought for a moment, giving Lillian a chance to interject as well, if she felt able to. But there was nothing, so he stood up as he said "No, thank you, I think I've said all I came to say. Although... there is one thing. I presume they have not found the body yet – can you have a funeral without a body? Forgive me, I don't mean to be insensitive, I just wondered?"

"It's alright my dear." It was Mrs Jones who answered. "It is a question we asked too, although we don't know the answer yet. You were going to find out, weren't you Freddie?"

"Yes, I'll be visiting the vicar later today to get that confirmed. You don't know with the sea, do you? She could be floating on her own little voyage somewhere, or washed up miles from where she went in. We want her back though, of course."

"Of course," Marlo nodded. The lack of a body might have explained why he couldn't find any newspaper reports of her funeral, but then that wouldn't explain Jed. Oh well, it was not important, and despite the family's measured reaction he wished now he hadn't asked. It seemed a bit too intrusive.

"I'll see you out," said Frederick, opening the living room door for Marlo. They descended the stairs, and as they walked through the shop to the front door, it occurred to Marlo that he might as well ask Frederick whether he knew of Southover Road, in case Lillian didn't know where it was.

"I'm not actually sure," replied Frederick, "I think it must be up in the north of town somewhere, otherwise I would know it. I wonder if he gave a false address though...."

"It's possible," conceded Marlo, "but if he did then that would be suspicious wouldn't it?"

"Yes you're right, there wouldn't really be any point him doing that I suppose. We'd get the police straight onto him. But then, they can't prove anything either can they? All we have is his word about what happened."

"I know, it's difficult. That's why we have to trap him, get him to make a mistake. One thing still puzzling us, I mean.... me, is what his motive was. Why would he want to kill Lillian? It doesn't make sense."

Frederick unlocked the front door and turned to look at Marlo. "No, it doesn't. As I said earlier, nothing makes sense at the moment. Why was this allowed to happen? Why take such a lovely person from her family, the people who loved her most, when she had her whole life ahead of her?" His eyes moistened, and he quickly extracted a handkerchief from his pocket and blew his nose, talking from under the material as he wiped. "Are you very religious, Mr Campbell?"

"No, I'm not, not at all." Marlo so wanted to tell Frederick what he knew, reveal to him what he now knew about Number Five. But he couldn't, so he said no more than that.

Frederick sighed. "I'm struggling, Mr Campbell, I have to tell you. My parents say it is all part of the good Lord's plan and we must trust him and be faithful, but I can't see how my sister's death can be part of a plan. Why would it be? What possible good can it bring? Why would a benevolent God want my sister to die at the age of twenty?"

"I agree with you," replied Marlo. "Unfair and early deaths like Lillian's brings no benefit, quite the opposite in fact. It makes no sense, which is one of the reasons why I do not believe in a deity who loves everyone individually. If there was such a thing, why would he allow so much suffering and evil in the world, including what happened to Lillian?" As he said this Marlo suddenly realised that this same argument should apply to Number Five, who was also evidently comfortable in allowing these bad things to happen on his watch.

Frederick dipped his chin, shaking his head sadly. "It is man who is the problem, not God – that is the answer that we are taught. But God is all powerful, so why would he not put a stop to such things? Why keep punishing man if you could lead by example and eliminate suffering and loss? There can be no reason to this circumstance, surely." He was leaning now against the front door, his head bowed, trying to keep his composure. "I'm sorry, Mr Campbell, at times like this it is hard to think straight."

Marlo patted him briefly on the arm, unsure of what the correct etiquette was. "Hey, come on. Railing against God won't improve things. Let's focus on what we can do."

Frederick looked up at him, desperation in his eyes. "We keep praying but nothing happens. It never has. It makes you wonder why we do it....." He trailed off, his eyes moistening again as the subject of those recent prayers came to the forefront of his thoughts once more. It was obvious that this shock to his world had triggered him to start questioning things he had previously just taken for granted because that was how he had been brought up.

Marlo now wanted even more to tell Frederick what he knew, but he couldn't. He absolutely couldn't.

"I think it is to make you feel better in yourself, give you a bit of hope. But I don't really know. But then I've never known, because I've never believed, and never prayed."

"Well, I suppose that has to be for me to worry about, not you." Frederick pulled himself up straight and shook his head, as though trying to whisk the conversation out of his mind. "I had better bid you good day, sir, and thank you once again for being so courageous in coming to see us at this difficult time and volunteering to help determine exactly what did happen to my sister. Please, though, be careful, won't you? And let us know what you find out about Threadwell."

"Of course, yes." Marlo felt a little uncomfortable with the thanks he was getting even though his deception was for their common good. "But coming here was the least I could do, given what I had heard," he mumbled. "Anyway, I shall say good day to you too, Mr Jones."

And with that very Victorian phrase he stepped out of the hat shop and headed down the street, waiting until he was out of earshot before exclaiming under his breath "Phew. Well, that was a bit stressful. Useful though. At least it is out of the way now."

For once there was no reply and he realised he might have been a bit insensitive. He wasn't used to having to consider other people's feelings. When you are on your own for so long you become habitually yet unavoidably selfish. "Hello Lillian? Are you alright?"

A pause, then "Sorry, yes, I'm just trying to compose myself. Hearing them all again, after all this time. And them not knowing I am so close, listening to them. It was hard. Hearing Mama talk about me like that.....I just wanted to call out to her, tell her I love her, tell her that I am alright. Except I'm not, of course."

"Yes, sorry, of course. I was so caught up in the moment that I forgot what you were going through. I'm not sure what to say really."

There was an awkward silence as they both pored over their own thoughts, so Marlo continued walking to the end of Challenor Street, allowing Lillian time to regain her composure.

Standing at the T-junction, he watched as a large besuited gentleman with a white moustache and a trilby hat cycled past on a tricycle that sported two huge back wheels and one tiny wheel at the front. Now that was something you didn't see in modern Britain, unless perhaps you were at a children's circus. The man trundled into the distance, followed by a fast advancing horse and cart that Marlo hoped would take steps to avoid running into the back of him.

"Are you ready?" he whispered as the noise of the hooves died down.

He heard a sniff. "Yes. Let's move on."

"Right. Operation Find Walter – step two. Scout out his house. Do you know where Southover Road is?"

"I think so. Vaguely, anyway. You know St Peter's Church, which you passed yesterday on your way to Mrs Chomsy's? I think it is a bit further north of that."

"Do you know what? I should just buy a street map. Do they have any in 1886?"

"Do we have maps?" Lillian managed a laugh. "No, we all just wander around asking each other for directions."

Marlo was pleased to hear her recovering her humour. "I'll take that as a yes then, but where can I get one?"

"Try the next bookshop you come across. If they haven't got them, they should know who has."

"Good idea. I'll head through town then, then cut back up towards St Peter's Church."

He adjusted his cap, put his hands in his pockets, and crossed the road as casually as everyone else, conscious that he seemed to be doing more walking in two days than he normally managed in two weeks.

CHAPTER 39 : WHO IS NEXT

Walter had settled back into his routine. Saturday was usually a productive day for collections as more people were at home, and so far today he had a one hundred per cent success rate. Mr Carberry had issued him with another heavy schedule, but he couldn't complain as it had been his own fault that he was now having to catch up, and half way through the day he was exactly half way through the list. If he could have patted himself on the back, he would.

As he manoeuvred the cart round Victoria Road and into Montpelier Street, he reflected on his more macabre achievements. Four murders to his name now – that was serial killer territory – and all in less than a year. Alright, the fourth wasn't planned but that didn't matter. If anything it was the sweetest because it was so simple. No disposing of the body or breaking and entering to worry about, just a snap decision, a stab of the knife, and an interfering old tramp was dead. Simple as that. And it felt just as good as the first two.

He had a different feeling about Lillian, a mixture of out-of-body elation in the process of doing it and regret afterwards that he had to. But Lillian's murder would not only provide him with further ongoing entertainment in how he would mentally torture her brother Frederick, it also proved that he was strong enough to put emotion aside when it came to it. He was ruthless. He was efficient. No-one was going to get the better of Walter Threadwell because he had already proved that he could do what he wanted and no-one could catch him. This was just the start. By Jupiter, he felt powerful.

Turning now into Upper North Street, a strange melancholy descended on him, a sort of floating consciousness that elevated him to the status of a mini god, impervious to human constraint. He liked that feeling, and he knew what had given it to him. So where should his attention be directed now? Who had displeased him recently? Then again, perhaps it did not need to be someone who had displeased him, otherwise he might be laying a trail of suspicion that would eventually catch up with him. Perhaps a random attack would be best. Or perhaps another opportunity would present itself.

He would lay low for a while though, give the dust time to settle. No sense in being greedy. He would bide his time. He smiled to himself and turned left into Dyke Road, past a church that could not save him.

CHAPTER 40 : WHERE WALTER LIVES

During the rest of the day, Marlo did a few things. He located Walter's house, and he found a good place to watch it from where he would not be seen – the doorway of an abandoned shop, partially and fortuitously shielded from Walter's home by a tree in the pavement. He would be back on Monday, as he supposed Walter would not be working on Sunday. He realised he had no idea what time Walter went to work, so resigned himself to getting up very early. He bought some more supplies. He found Sillwood Road, where his train friend George Smith lived, and walked down it, sighting George's house just so that if or when the time came to call on the young man's assistance he would know where to go.

Then he strolled around much of the rest of the town, comparing it to what it had turned into, fascinated by every aspect of the Victorian world he had entered, still struggling to believe that he was actually here, actually living in history. Lillian guided him around, answering questions and opening his eyes to a way of life that was both new and old at the same time.

He found himself noticing how everyone was actually looking where they were going as they walked along. No-one had their nose buried in, or ears attached to, a mobile phone and no-one was talking animatedly into a device, or shouting at it from an unnecessary distance. Rather they were focusing on the world around them, in many cases even actually talking to each other, rather than a little gadget in their hand.

No-one was taking a selfie – this was a world where taking photographs of any description was the preserve of well-dressed men carrying bulky apparatus constructed largely of wood and glass. Not that Marlo could see the point of selfies anyway. Why on earth would he want to ruin a photo by forcing the viewer to have to peer past his revolting features? Here's a lovely picture of the Taj Mahal, you can just see half of it behind the ear of that human eyesore taking up most of the screen. No, that would never happen.

Despite enjoying the fact that there were no mobile phones around, Marlo still wished he could have whipped out his own phone and started taking photos, just to see the reaction. But his phone was far away, in another century where it belonged, whereas Marlo was not where he belonged at all.

After lunch he found time to go back to the Aquarium and enjoyed a trip around the tanks and displays. He had been once before, but that was a while ago even though it was in the future – a concept he was still having trouble getting his head around.

Near the exit and positioned to provide a grand finale, the advertised mermaid reclined on a pedestal on a small stage with a tank beneath her, the fish tail submerged in the water but obviously a costume if you looked hard enough, or just looked, to be honest. Marlo had expected that so his only disappointment was that a flesh coloured body suit and long black hair covered the whole of the chest of the mermaid so that there was nothing to see there either.

Then again this was Victorian England so the chances of her going topless in front of children and the general public were less than slim. The poor mermaid sat there waving as seductively as boredom would allow, people gawped at her because that is what they are expected to do when faced with such a thing, and Marlo, having gawped along with everyone else, wondered whether there were different girls who took it in turns. Also what does she do when she wants to go to the loo? Possibly the same as surfers wearing a wetsuit he supposed. He hoped they changed the water in that tank.

He wandered around the outside of the Brighton Pavilion. He had told George he would be writing about it, but unless it was fundamental to Lillian's story, which Lillian had confirmed it wasn't, then he wasn't going to.

He came across a park, all beautifully tended ornamental lawns nudging beds of roses, with cast iron railings guarding large dark bronze statues of dignitaries portrayed in a permanent state of self-importance. He found an empty bench and sat down to rest his feet. Although surrounded by roads and houses, the air was quiet and fresh. It was pleasantly mild now too, provided you avoided a lazy wind from the sea which delivered a gentle air-conditioning effect along the east and west facing streets. Sheltered by the bushes behind the bench, he watched a couple of middle-aged ladies seated on the other side of the park catching up on each other's news, their voices just a distant babble.

He pictured himself holding hands with Lillian, strolling round the park in front of him, pointing out the brighter flowers, sharing amusing stories. Perhaps for another time, but at least he could talk to her even if he couldn't hold her hand.

"It is quite green, Brighton, isn't it? Plenty of open spaces with trees and lawns."

"It is now, yes." She was there, just not where he wanted her. But were she to suddenly appear in front of him now, what would happen? She would probably shake his hand, thank him for helping her, and skip off back to her family, leaving him back in his familiar role of lonely onlooker. At least when she was in his head she could not leave him.

And it was a relationship that suited him in one way because she did not have to look at his face, so with luck she would start to forget what he looked like and he could win her over with words. How likely was that though? Oh, this whole relationship stuff was just too hard, no wonder he was no good at it. And now he wasn't listening to what she was saying. Focus Marlo! Even he knew that not listening to a girl is a great way to persuade her that you are not interested in her. He tuned back to the words in his head.

"... and so much so that we were told in school that Samuel Johnson – you know him? – apparently once said about Brighton that "the place is truly desolate and if one had a mind to hang oneself for desperation at being obliged to live there, it would be difficult to find a tree on which to fasten a rope." I've always remembered that because it was so funny. Anyway, then they started a big tree planting programme about seventy years ago and now he would have plenty of options for his rope if he wasn't already dead."

"Yes but now it isn't desolate so he wouldn't have to hang himself anyway. So it is a win-win. Not for him though. What with him being dead and all."

"That's very true."

"Talking of quotes, have you heard the phrase 'if you can come up with a good quote you will be remembered for ever'?'

'No I haven't. Who said that?'

'Nobody knows.'

The little laugh he heard from Lillian vindicated the effort it had taken to retain that unused joke in his head all these years. He had finally been able to haul it out and employ it. But it was a good point at which to end the small talk and focus on what was most important. It couldn't be put off any longer. "Now, we do need to talk about this plan of ours."

"You're right, we do. How are you feeling about it now?" Lillian sounded tentative.

"Not good. In fact worse than I did before. Even as I was explaining it to your family I was thinking 'I know we don't have many options, and this is the best plan we could come up with, but it is still not a good one'. Their reactions kind of confirmed that. If my prodding doesn't put a stone in his shoe and irritate Walter enough to provoke a confession, then we are stuck, and I have blown my cover. If it does, I could end up dead. The chances of him confessing everything and walking casually away, leaving me to run off to the police, are probably zero."

"Yes, the more that I think about this, the more I think that we've got this wrong. There must be a better way."

Marlo paused as a small portly man puffed past in a bit of a hurry, looking very pompous in a smart grey suit with a waistcoat that was fighting to contain a generous belly. He was carrying a briefcase that looked as if it had been flung around a lot and was presumably on his way from one appointment to another. He passed by with only a fleeting sideways glance at Marlo that, despite its brevity, still managed to convey a hint of mild disapproval. It was a look Marlo was used to, but usually from the other sex. Once he was out of earshot, Marlo resumed.

"I vote that we see what comes out of me talking to one of his colleagues and take it from there. Maybe that will give us some more ideas. After all, a plan is only as good as the reality it encounters."

"That's quite profound, did you just think of that?"

"Yes!" said Marlo proudly, clutching at the credit like a delighted child. "Well, I think so, anyway. Don't think I've heard it anywhere else. Does that make me clever?"

He heard a giggle. "Well, one brick does not a house make."

Marlo loved this girl, what an amazing retort, and even better than his effort. He tried to squeeze out an amusing counter. "Well it's a good job I'm not.... building a house then," but realised after he had said it that this didn't make much sense. Once again he had been out-bantered. Maybe he would just have to accept his place in conversational society as the man who pulled the clay pigeons for other people to shoot them down in a blaze of glory. Probably best if he changed the subject.

"Lillian, I need to ask you a question."

"A situation I am not unused to, Mr Campbell."

"Well, yes, but I mean about you personally. If you don't mind, of course."

"No, of course not. Ask away."

It was a bold question, one he had never asked a girl before, but this was as good an opportunity as he would ever have. It could backfire, it probably would, but he needed to know.

"Ok, I just wondered, as a Victorian lady, well, girl, young woman, you know, what do you..... what do you look for in a man." Feeling that hadn't gone well and hearing a little intake of breath from Lillian, he attempted to clarify. "I know that Walter swept you off your feet, but how did he do that? Given that he has turned out to be such a monster, you know."

Lillian had obviously been initially slightly taken aback by the directness of the question but he felt he had rescued the situation by linking it to Walter. He had put his clumsy foot over the mark but drawn it back before he had completely overstepped it and fallen into a pit. Research, just research, that's all it is, nothing sinister or personal. Merely understanding the methods of the target, you see.

Lillian thought for a moment. "Alright then. When you are a young woman emerging from adolescence and being unfamiliar with young men, your emotions can be ambushed, Marlo. If a tall dark handsome stranger suddenly starts showing interest in a plain old shop girl, it is hard not to consider it a compliment."

Marlo was so focused on the nub of his question that he missed the opportunity to gallantly point out that Lillian was not plain.

"So if he had not been good-looking would you have allowed him to woo you?"

This was one question that Marlo was desperate to hear the answer to. His own experience told him that when you are very unattractive you can't ask a girl out as it looks like you think they are desperate, so you are effectively insulting them, which is something a polite chap would not want to do. You have to wait for them to approach you, but of course they don't. So was Walter's success solely down to his handsome manly appearance?

"If he was not a fine physical specimen then it may well have been harder for him to convince me, yes, if I am being honest. In the same

316

way that your head would be turned more by a pretty girl than an ugly one, wouldn't it? But that doesn't mean I would have turned him away if he had a face like a goat, he would just have to have been a bit more, well, captivating."

She was persuasive but Marlo was still struggling to believe her. "What was Walter like though? Was he nice to you or not, and if not, did you like that? Apart from his looks, what did you see in him?" He was trying not to get emotional or ask too aggressively yet the years of pent up frustration could not be entirely masked.

"I saw only good things when I first met him. I don't think any girl wants a man to be nasty to her, Marlo..."

"They do, though, they really do!" Marlo could not help himself and had to struggle to keep his voice under control. He was trying and failing not to make it personal to his own situation. "Don't a lot of girls confess that they would secretly rather have a rough man who doesn't treat them very well, one that they can try to tame, rather than a nice, kind man who doesn't excite them? It's just in their genes. They always go with the alpha male whether he is nice or not, as long as he isn't hideous. It's just a fact of nature, and I should know. I've seen it so many times."

"Now that's just being silly, of course they don't! Not unless humans have changed dramatically in the period between your era and mine. You just said it though: a man who doesn't excite them. Why would they want that? You can be nice and exciting at the same time – perfect combination! Girls will go for that. I thought that was what Walter offered. That and the good looks of course, that was just a bonus. What girl wouldn't be tempted?"

"Well I would bet good money that if Walter had a face like..." (and here he only just stopped himself saying 'mine'), "... a, well, I don't know, like a goblin, or even the goat you mentioned, then even if he was exciting you would have told him where to go, whether or not he really was mild-mannered and nice. That's what all girls do, isn't it?" It sounded more petulant than he had meant it to, and he was conscious that he was using Lillian to represent the whole female species rather than just herself. But weren't all girls the same? They all seemed to have the same reaction to him so why would Lillian be any different when it came down to it?

Lillian defended her corner. "All girls aren't the same, Marlo, whatever you might think. As I said, maybe they have become a bit different in the

21st century, I don't know. But I would not have stepped out with Walter if I had even the slightest doubt that he was not an upright, honest and good man who would look after me. Now we know that he was none of those things, so he must have been a good actor. But I would never accept an offer to go out from any gentleman who was nasty in any way, however handsome he looked. Never. Why would I? Why would anyone? Well, alright, some girls do, I will admit that, but they are very much in the minority and they are fools who you are best not to associate with anyway. I don't know where you've got these ideas about what all girls want, but they aren't true. You must believe that."

It was the answer Marlo had hoped for and needed to hear, but all his own experiences still told him something else. Or perhaps the excitement factor Lillian had mentioned was where he had been going wrong. He was offering sensible, reliable, logical, perhaps boring, and girls wanted spontaneity, emotion, spark, confidence – none of which he was familiar with. How annoying.

Confidence was particularly hard, as self-confidence implies self-satisfaction, which often comes across as boasting. It works though. How many rappers do you see in music videos doing their 'look at me, baby' raps on their own while a group of dancers get on with things in the distance behind them? No, the dancers are all over the rapper, loving his arrogance, lapping up his made-up boasts. The more gold chains the better. These people believe in themselves; Marlo had grown up with baked in inadequacy. But he had to give Lillian an answer.

"I'll try to believe that. It is hard though, when everything you have seen contradicts it."

He guessed Lillian must have realised that his questioning sprung from his own miserable situation but he did not want to directly admit it. If you confess that no girlfriends have ever troubled the scorers even though you have reached thirty-two not out, a potential partner would immediately wonder why, and not want to scrape the barrel by being the first person to go out with this loser. He desperately didn't want Lillian to think that. He wondered what she did think.

"Look at me, then, Marlo. How do you imagine I feel about men now? Why should I ever trust a man again?"

Lillian's unexpectedly emotional questions suddenly harpooned across his bows. "My only experience of a boyfriend is that it was all a sham and he only escorted me so that he could eventually kill me. Tell me, why should I ever want to entrust myself to a man again?"

"But you can Lillian! There are men out there, out here, who are not like that!" He paused as a sudden self-realisation came to him, then sighed, releasing some of his self-stoked frustration. "Sorry, yes, I get it. Not all men are the same, not all women are the same."

"Exactly. Do you think I would now want to look for a man with even an ounce of bile in him which could explode into violence? I wouldn't care what he looked like, if there was that risk, I would turn away. For me, 'nice' is good."

Marlo's stomach knotted. He so wanted to ask "do you think I'm nice, then?" but it was too soon for such a leading question and would put Lillian in an awkward spot. He also didn't want to hear the answer, as he was convinced it would be of the "Yes, but..." variety. Best to keep a dream alive rather than squash it with the dead weight of cold reality.

"Well I'm very glad to hear that. And sorry for getting a bit, you know, passionate. Well, not passionate in that sense... just, well, oh jeez, you know what I mean. Sorry."

Marlo was wincing even as he finished talking. He felt crumpled by his inability to always converse confidently like other men did when talking to someone they had designs on. It didn't matter which girl he was talking to, or however pleased he was with his utterances to that point, sooner or later he said something that came out wrong, sounded stupid, and made him look weak and ineffectual, while all he was trying to do was be polite.

Maybe that was the problem – it was always the impolite men, the brash ones who didn't care what they said, who had all the success. If they offended someone, it didn't matter to them, indeed they usually didn't even notice what they had done or the effect it had. Yet the object of their bad behaviour always seemed to brush it to one side, despite what Lillian had just said, as their eyes were fixed on the bigger prize of snaring this impressive and dominant hunter-gatherer who had the confidence to say what he thought without worrying about the consequences. Being polite, humble, self-aware, and apologetic appeared to be the worst traits a man could have, and Marlo was stuffed full of them.

As if to confirm what he was thinking, Lillian said "Don't be sorry, you don't need to be. It is good to ask these kinds of questions. We are all in the same boat really, none of us has all the answers."

She sounded wise beyond her years when given her age it should be her who was accepting wisdom from Marlo. Yeah, as if that would happen. Why was he such a poor excuse for a human being? It so frustrated him. He couldn't let that show though. He wasn't going to attract Lillian through constant self-criticism, and he guessed that pity, the best he could then hope for, would be unlikely to provide a firm basis for a long and happy relationship. Yet he could not hide a hint of sulkiness in his response.

"Some people do have the answers though. Plenty of them seem to have no problem at all, although to be fair it is a bit different nowadays in terms of promiscuity and attitudes to sex. There is no shame now in women saying they have had multiple partners. You should hear some of the female pop stars talking every few months about a new relationship they have just embarked on; they must get through dozens of men."

Lillian spluttered slightly. "Dozens? Gosh. That does seem excessive, to put it mildly. Where are their parents, and who are these popstart people you are talking about anyway and why do they behave like this?"

"Pop star, not start. Sorry, yes, that means someone who sings modern pop songs. I mean, popular songs, shortened to pop. They perform on stages with people screaming adulation at them and I suppose that is partly why they get so much attention from the opposite sex and can just pick and choose their partners. Hard to imagine what that must be like."

"Hard indeed. How odd. And why would the people watching the performance scream at them, surely then they can't hear the song? You should be silent and listen, that is just basic manners. Screaming at someone when they are performing for you is extremely rude."

"I couldn't agree more. I can't stand it when people starting shrieking and clapping when a singer hits a high note, but everyone does it now. There was a famous concert in America that the Beatles gave......"

"As in.... insects? Don't tell me you've managed to get insects to sing and give concerts now?"

"Ha! No, we haven't advanced that far. It is the name of a group, the most famous pop group ever. When you come back with me I'll play you their songs, they were brilliant. That will be interesting actually, to see if you like them despite never hearing pop music before. Anyway, they gave this concert where there were so many screaming girls that they couldn't hear themselves play, and they were going to all the effort of performing the songs even though no-one was really listening. It helped persuade them to give up doing live performances in the end."

"I still don't understand why they are screaming?"

"They were just trying to get the attention of the member of the group that they have convinced themselves they have fallen in love with, and when thousands of them are doing that the noise is deafening. But mostly nowadays it is just people wanting to encourage the performer. To me, they shouldn't need encouraging if they are good enough to stand up on a stage and sing."

"I agree. However, we seem to be talking about singing now. Perhaps we should focus now on what we do next....?"

"You're right, we should." In a way Marlo was glad to get away from the subject of sex and relationships despite raising the topic himself. He could not afford to show his entire hand to Lillian at this early stage by talking about things that could show him in a bad light. He realised though that he had laid so many clues now that only a fool would have failed to work out that he was no lounge lizard, and Lillian was clearly not a fool.

She was also being extremely kind in not mentioning it. But maybe that was because she did not want to start talking about Marlo's relationship status in case the conversation went in a direction she didn't want. Yes, that would be it. She didn't want Marlo to start talking about the two of them and their future, if they had one. It would be too awkward trying to rebuff him.

The trouble was, although it had only been a few days he really was starting to fall in love with the girl in his head. He wasn't sure whether his feelings for her were bolstered by the situation he was in or whether he would have fallen for her to the same extent if he had just met her in the street, but one thing he did know was she depended on him for her life, so if he made any overtures towards her, she could well say yes whether she meant it or not just so that he would be even more incentivised to get the job done. Then the usual heartbreak would ensue when he brought her back to his world only for her to say 'thanks very much' and go and find someone else. That was the script followed by all who had preceded her, so he had to find a way of writing a new end to the play.

Remaining professional and at arm's length had to be the best approach then. Allow her time to see that being that nice, sensible, slightly dull man wasn't such a bad thing after all, especially compared with Walter. At least he had time on his side for a change – she could not run away, leave him choking in the familiar tyre-squealing dust of rejection.

Lillian was talking now. "We have to be serious about this, Marlo; our lives depend on it. Let's just focus on talking to one of Walter's colleagues and see where that leaves us. So to confirm then... you are going to stake out his house on Monday morning and follow him to wherever he works, then see if you can make an appointment with one of his fellow accountants to discuss the business venture we dreamed up, then try to steer the conversation onto Walter."

"Yes, that's about the sum of it. I'm not hugely hopeful even with this part of the plan. Why is it always so much easier in the movies?"

"What's a movie?"

"Did I not explain? Oh hang on, I said 'film' before, didn't I. Well, movie is just another way of saying film really. It is short for moving pictures. I'm going to take you to so many movies when I get out of here." Realising as soon as he said it how presumptuous that sounded, he rushed to backtrack. "That is assuming you wanted to go of course, I mean you might not. I would fully understand if you didn't, or wanted to go on your own, you know, I was just thinking it might be nice, but it is entirely up to....."

"Shhhh," interrupted Lillian with a suppressed giggle, "You don't need to dig yourself a hole. I would love to come and see these movies with you, it sounds exciting. But maybe we are getting ahead of ourselves?"

Marlo felt a surge of pride mixed with relief at the thought of a real girl – assuming that Lillian *would* become physically real at the end of all this – actually wanting to go to the cinema with him, but he knew that this vision was dragging an anchor, and the anchor was the huge task he faced even to get back to a world where cinemas existed.

"Yes, sorry, back to Walter. When you think about it, the key to all this is finding out why he killed you, because that is the bit that makes no sense. Why would he kill his own girlfriend? You hadn't upset him in any way had you?"

"Absolutely not! If anything I was much too pleasant to him, always agreed with him and supported his decisions. When a man like that shows an interest in you, you don't want to do anything to put him off. Well, not initially anyway. So there was no possible reason why he should want to kill me as far as I was concerned, definitely not."

Marlo found himself feeling angry in a protective sense, still reeling at the thought that a man could have such a lovely girl as Lillian fall into his lap – a girl whose attentions more deserving yet unluckier men would have fought for – then callously murder her, for reasons that could not have been her fault, denying her the chance to find anyone else. It was so wrong, so unfair.

"There must have been some motive though," he said, "the fact that he came back and finished the job the next day – it wasn't a spur of the moment thing. He must have planned it. He's obviously an evil psychopath, but then why go to the bother of taking you out over the preceding months, then staging an accident? Why not just find a random person to kill who would have required less effort? He must have targeted you for a reason."

"And why not kill me straight away? None of it makes sense......"

"Possibly he was waiting for the opportunity to enact the perfect crime, and of course he so nearly got away with it."

"He still might."

"Not if I have anything to do with it. Which I do, of course." Marlo sighed. "I just hope my brave words turn into brave actions. I've not done anything like this before, you know." He realised as soon as he said it that this was a rather obvious declaration.

"Don't worry, nor have I," Lillian re-assured him, "although I appreciate your job here is marginally harder than mine."

"Heh, right. Just a little. The funny thing is, even though it didn't go entirely to plan, he must still think he has got away with your murder, so I suppose we have the element of surprise in our favour. He won't expect anyone to be on his tail, least of all a skinny time-traveller. Although it would help if I had a sonic screwdriver."

"A what?"

"A sonic..... ah sorry, that would mean nothing to you. We have a television programme called Dr Who and the hero is a time traveller who has a little gadget called a sonic screwdriver that gets him or her out of all kinds of sticky situations. Whereas I have nothing." He sighed again.

"You have your wits and intelligence, Marlo," encouraged Lillian, ignoring the Dr Who references for now.

"Is that a good thing or a bad thing?"

"Hopefully good. Also, you have my wits and intelligence too!"

"That's true. Even if we were both half wits that would make a whole wit between us, so we should be ok." Hearing a giggle, Marlo hoped that what was actually quite a half-witted comment has been interpreted by Lillian as knowingly witty instead. But in his usual misguidedly honest way, he felt he had to explain "Sorry, that didn't make sense but I'd started that sentence so I had to finish it. Sorry."

Lillian laughed. "Don't be, it was funny. Anyway, two heads are better than one, I think that is what you meant. So between us, we can do it!"

"Let's hope so. Right, time to head home I think. My feet won't thank me for any more tramping round the streets of Brighton." And with that he jumped up and made his way out of the park, and from there back to Arbuthnot Street.

CHAPTER 41 : SUNDAY

Sunday was a day of rest. Not just for Victorian England, but for Victorian Marlo too. After so much walking in the last couple of days, the lack of anything urgent to do inspired him to do nothing. He wrote some words in his writing book so that if anyone happened to look, he could show them that he was doing what he said he would do. Much of it was remembered from his actual novel about Lillian, so in effect he plagiarised his own work.

After lunch he wondered down to the beach, sat on the stones, and watched the sea. At least that hadn't changed. The waves still rolled in the same way that they did nearly a century and a half later, probably tumbling the same stones. Man would come and go but the sea would still be there, constantly and metronomically beating out time with the crash of each wave. He wondered why some of the biggest and most threatening waves petered out at the last minute and rolled in tamely whilst other smaller ones with no obvious potential suddenly built up a late head of steam and exploded more impressively onto the shore in a plume of spray. Big and menacing doesn't always deliver, he thought. Perhaps that could teach him something.

He talked to Lillian. Long, rambling conversations, opinions interspersed with revelations as each described their own world to the other. Marlo wondered how much of what he told Lillian was sinking in, how much of it could form shapes in her brain that translated those words into something tangible.

If someone from a hundred and thirty years in the future appeared in front of him and started describing what would no doubt sound like a sci-fi world of automation, would he find it so alien that he just couldn't relate to it? Or did he have the advantage over Lillian of having seen enough CGI and sufficiently realistic films depicting the future to allow him to better visualise and comprehend what the visitor from the future was telling him? For Lillian much of what he was describing to her about his life were things she could not possibly visualise.

He learned more about Lillian and what it was like to live in a reasonably well-to-do Victorian family. The dress, the formalities, the speak-when-you-are-spoken-to respect afforded to their parents. The strict education, the daily chores, the church attendance, the formal family mealtimes. Everything was manual, too; no vacuum cleaners or washing machines, it all had to be done by hand. It was a hard life. No wonder those that could afford it had servants and maids.

As Lillian told him more about herself it became clear to him that she was emotionally shaped by her father. He was a strict disciplinarian, Marlo learned, and Lillian had spent her short life trying to please him and be what he wanted her to be. That seemed to have become her approach to life in general and rather than developing and advertising her own clearly strong personality she had moulded it to fit what others expected of her. Not knowing how to relate to boys as she grew up, she had ventured few opinions, instead believing that her role was to agree with them and remain demure, which, to be fair, it very often was in that era.

She was brought up to believe that her main objective in life would be to find a good man and marry him. Marlo had winced at hearing another girl talk about finding a good man. So many women don't know a good man when they see one, he knew that much. They walk straight past them and fall into the arms of bad men. Here's a good man, Lillian, right in front of you. Well, figuratively speaking. Yet if you end up resurrected and back in my world you will no doubt fall into the same trap all women do and be magnetically drawn away from me and towards Mr Handsome Charisma-Magnet who will whisk you off on his white charger then dump you when he is done with you. And I will be left on the side of the road watching you disappear into the distance.

Rather than then realise your mistake and return apologetically to the good man by the side of the road, you will instead wait for another bad man on a white charger to turn up and leap up with him instead, repeating this cycle ad nauseum until you eventually get lucky. That's the way it works, isn't it?

Walter was her first serious beau ('boyfriend' sounded very un-Victorian) and she thought that the way for her to make him like her was to act politely and nicely and never contradict him. It seemed to work, she had thought, as he had never raised his voice to her and had always treated her respectfully. Until that awful day, of course, when all her illusions were shattered on that cliff top, the sharp shards of realisation striking her as she fell.

Now, in death, she understood. The wisdom she now held, the awakening of knowledge that had flowed from the Priming, her own experiences, even just talking to Marlo, had all added to her sense of realisation that life was more than just agreeing with and pleasing other people – you had to please yourself as well. Given a second chance, that is what she would do. And it was within Marlo's gift to give her that second chance.

Mrs Chomsy's shepherd's pie that evening tasted particularly good. "Hope the shepherd won't mind," she had twinkled as she served it up, showing that some jokes endured through the centuries however bad they were. From her conversation at the table it was clear that she had still not heard about Lillian's death, and Marlo was careful not to refer to it. The later she found out the better, it was less complicated.

That evening he sat in his room and contemplated just how little there was to do. No television, no radio, no phones and of course no computers. What did people do to keep themselves occupied? "You could play games, or read, mainly," advised Lillian, "or just talk."

"Ah yes, talking. Bit of a lost art now," reflected Marlo. "The mobile phone has taken over. It is supposed to be for talking but now everyone spends more time staring at that little screen and poking at it with their fingers."

"The world on a screen, then. Not that I know what this screen actually looks like. Is it shiny and hard like glass? Or is it soft and textured like a cloth?"

"Hard, and some are glass but some are synthetic materials."

"And you can actually see pictures of people and other things moving on them?"

"Yes. It sounds ridiculous I know, but it's true. But then I suppose if you told a stone age man that his descendents would be able to construct a huge wrought iron lattice tower over a thousand feet tall in the centre of a large city he would not have believed you either."

"What are you talking about?"

"The Eiffel tower, you know, in Paris. Surely you must have....oh hang on. Maybe it isn't built yet. I thought it was opened in the 1880s?"

"Must be the late 1880s then. I've not read anything about that. A thousand feet high? That sounds impossible. The wind would blow it over, surely."

"Believe it or not it is still standing, and is one of the most popular tourist destinations in the world. But of course it is not the tallest man-made structure in the world any more, not by a long chalk."

"Go on then, astonish me."

"Alright, what would you say to – oh wait a sec, I have to convert it from metres, that is all I know. What's 830 times 3.3?"

Lillian got there first, schooled as she was in calculating without calculators. "Just over two thousand seven hundred."

"Well there you are then. That high."

"Two thousand seven hundred feet? That's more than half a mile! Now that really is impossible. Are you pulling my leg?"

"No, really, I'm not. It's enormous. More than 160 floors, I think."

"Floors? So it is not just a structure, people actually walk around up there? I think in America they have some tall offices, perhaps 10 storeys, but 160? That is just absurd. Are you sure?"

"Yes, people have offices up there, they work there. Imagine the view."

"I'm not sure I want to. I would feel as though I was going to fall off. I'm going queasy just thinking about it."

"I thought you were ok with heights? You were happy to stand on the edge of that cliff, weren't you?"

"Not happy, exactly. I didn't get *too* close, just enough to see the waves, and only briefly before I turned back. Also, the fact that I was pushed off a cliff, twice, might have told you that my attitude to heights is slightly less contented than it once was."

Marlo mentally slapped his forehead. "God, yes, of course, I'm so sorry. I should have realised."

"Not a problem. That's what you say isn't it? Talking of the sea, you said earlier that you were going to tell me more about that big ship that sank in 1912. The Titan or something? What happened?"

And so Marlo related the tale of the Titanic, much of his knowledge of the incident stemming from the film of the same name, and then the conversation took him to submarines, what they were and how they operated in the war. Then onto weaponry in general, from guns to nuclear bombs, which somehow led him into describing the demise of the British Empire. It was strangely pleasurable, like telling stories to an appreciative child, and Marlo could sense the wide-eyed wonder of his listener even though he couldn't see it.

Lillian had been right – there was nothing wrong with talking as a mechanism for passing time. Before he knew it, it was time to get some sleep and Lillian's education had to be paused. Tomorrow beckoned, but it did so with a clawed hand.

CHAPTER 42 : CHANGE OF OCCUPATION

Marlo kept Walter at quite a distance as he trailed him nervously through the dewy early morning streets of a waking Brighton. This was not entirely an approach of his own making but rather necessitated by the unanticipated revelation that Walter was setting off for work on a pony and trap.

"Why didn't you tell me he had his own transport?" Marlo had hissed at Lillian as Walter was leading the horse out from the yard and hitching it to his cart. "I didn't know he kept it at home," replied Lillian, "I thought it was owned by the company and he just borrowed it. How was I to know? Not that many people in Brighton have access to a stable at home."

Marlo didn't argue, but as soon as Walter had mounted the cart, snapped the reins and the horse cantered off, he emerged from the doorway as nonchalantly as he could and began walking quickly in the same direction. The good news about this situation was that Walter would be too busy steering the horse to worry about looking behind him. The bad news was that the horse had twice as many legs as Marlo and was quicker than him.

So Marlo found himself trotting almost as much as the horse as he half walked and half ran in his efforts to keep up, re-doubling his exertions when his target turned a corner. He hoped that to anyone else he just looked as though he was late for work and so would not arouse any suspicions, but it wasn't helping that by the time he turned the final corner, ducking back when he saw that the horse had stopped, he was puffing and blowing like a child trying unsuccessfully to blow out a candle on a birthday cake. He really did need to do more exercise.

He had a vague concern that Walter would recognise him from the cliff top but convinced himself that he had been too far away, so once he had got some breath back while Walter was tying up the horse, he emerged into the street and slowly and as unobtrusively as he felt able, walked towards the man he was tracking, determined to see which door he would head for.

As he approached, Walter shook back his thick black hair, grabbed a bag from the seat of the trap and glanced up and down the road before crossing, completely ignoring Marlo. He strode up to a brown wooden door in a nondescript frontage with no signs other than a small brass plaque by the doorbell. Marlo heard the door tinkle as Walter went in and slammed it shut, but carried on walking past the horse and cart and a little further up the street before crossing over and turning back towards the office.

The street itself was dour and soulless, with no shops and just a few offices interspersed with small dirty tenement buildings from which people dressed for labouring rather than managing, were emerging. It did not look as though it was a hub for thriving businesses and certainly wouldn't get much affluent passing trade. Then again, Marlo supposed that people didn't choose accountants on a whim as they passed their office so perhaps footfall wasn't such a major factor.

As he got closer to the door his breathing, which was by now back to normal, started getting shorter again and he could feel his heart rate rising as he realised what he was about to do. He would, for the first time, be speaking to the man who had murdered Lillian and Jed. How on earth had he, meek and mild Marlo Campbell, ended up in this position, about to confront a double murderer? The closest he had ever previously got to any level of danger was traversing a pedestrian crossing without waiting for the little green man to light up. He took a deep breath to calm himself down, cleared his throat, and slowed his pace as he silently rehearsed his story and the arguments he would use to arrange a meeting on neutral ground. He reached the door and turned to face it, checking his collar was straight.

His eyes alighted on the small brass plaque. 'Threadwell and Carberry, Debt Collection'. Debt collection?? What the......? This wasn't an accountancy firm.

Quickly he turned on his heels and headed on past the office frontage. "Lillian!" he whispered urgently once he was safely past.

"What?"

"Walter lied. He isn't an accountant. He is a debt collector."

"No! Are you sure? A debt collector? Oh my. Why would he pretend he was an accountant? Oh wait, it's obvious isn't it. It was to impress me. It sounds less frightening, and it makes him sound cleverer than he is. Easier to impress gullible people like me. How could I have been so stupid?"

"You weren't, you really weren't. How were you to know? It's not as though you could set him an accountancy test or anything."

"No, well, that's true I suppose. A debt collector, though! That would explain a lot. Aggression probably comes with the job. But if I had found out he was lying about that I would have realised that he couldn't be trusted and I would never have gone with him to Seaford Head. Oh, that man is just… just…evil. He's a monster. I hate him!"

Marlo said nothing for a while, knowing that whatever he said probably wouldn't help. Then, as he turned into a quiet adjoining street, "You know what this means though don't you?"

Lillian had calmed down now. "Yes, our plan is no longer a plan."

"Exactly. Back to square one."

Back to square one. Tim sighed as he realised that he had written himself into another cul-de-sac. Why had he done that? Botheration, as his mother used to say. Anyway, he really ought to get up and have some exercise. Being sat on your backside all day was only ever going to exercise your backside, an area of his body that didn't really interest him, or anyone else probably, and certainly wasn't going to help him live longer however perky it was. What was the time? Ah, half past three. Perhaps a call to Claude or Jonathan, see if they fancied a quick frame or two at the snooker club. Wouldn't give him much exercise but at least he would be standing up most of the time.

As he contemplated the effort required to rise from his chair, he looked back at his last sentence. It wasn't really square one, he supposed, on a scale of one to ten possibly square four, but only because he hadn't really formulated a way round it. He felt as though he was a pot-holer exploring a cave system without a map, constantly coming up against difficult territory and being forced to find another route. But in a way that was part of the fun. After all, presumably pot-holers enjoyed the challenge of discovering new ways to get somewhere, and that was the same for him. Plotting in advance was for squares. Ha, squares, back to that again.

All he had to do was engineer Marlo and Lillian to find another way of trapping Walter. That shouldn't be too hard. In fact…..

He began typing again. The snooker would have to wait.

It was exactly an hour later than it had been an hour ago. Marlo was back on the beach. It was a good place to think, but also to talk to Lillian without having to whisper, as if he sat close to the waves the noise of the sea would mask his voice and crunching footsteps on the stones would alert him to anyone who approached.

He took an exaggeratedly deep breath of fresh salty air and exhaled slowly. "Ok ghost in my head, are you ready to re-plan?"

She laughed. "Wooo! Of course. I've had some thoughts."

"Fire away."

"Well, if you use a similar tactic, we need to get you into debt, or the appearance of being in debt, so Walter will come and visit you. In a way it is better as he is more likely to come to you rather than the other way around. You could ask that fellow George who you met on the train to claim he lent you some money and you won't pay him back. Then Walter comes to collect the debt, and you somehow trick him into admitting to the murders as a means of threatening you to get you to pay. He would think it would be his word against yours so wouldn't think he needs to kill you too. Although I suppose he might. Or he could just hit you. Oh, I don't know what he would do any more. I thought I knew him but I knew nothing."

"I don't really want to be hit, actually. Or killed."

"Well, yes, I know, you getting killed would be no good for either of us. But a little punch might be a price we have to pay to get Walter up before a judge."

"We? Do you feel my pain as I get hit then?"

"Well, no. I'll wince, if that helps."

"Thanks, very kind of you. I reckon it is academic though as if he is a debt collector then he'll just see this as business transaction; there would be no need to injure me even if he let slip that he had killed you, as he could argue that it was just an idle threat. But as you say, it would in any case be my word against his from his perspective, as long as he doesn't know we have a witness or two listening in. Talking of which, we still need a witness. How about I ask your brother to help out, maybe George as well, although that would look suspicious if Walter saw him. So just Frederick then, hiding and listening in the next room with a lead pipe in his hand or something just in case. But then he knows Frederick too, doesn't he? Well, we will just have to ensure that they stay hidden. Then....."

"Oh wait, wait. I don't want my brother attacked by this fiend as well. If he comes off worst I don't think my parents could take it. Nor could I. We can't involve Frederick."

Marlo sighed, pulled his knees up to his chest and wrapped his arms around them, as though this would help him think. He rested his chin on his knees and stared out to sea, hoping the vast grey blue emptiness of the choppily swaying waters in front of him would clear his mind of all distractions and facilitate some inspirational thinking. It didn't.

"Do we have any other option though?" was the best he could come up with. "I can't very well ask Mrs Chomsy."

Lillian couldn't help laughing. "Walter would have killed you, robbed you, tidied the room up and left before she could get through the door to help, and in any case he would probably hear her breathing heavily through the door."

"Ha, yeah, you're right. Just a hunch, but she might not scare him either. Ok, suppose we do everything we can to hide George and Frederick so that Walter doesn't see them unless things turn ugly. Maybe they could also wear masks so if they rush in then Walter would not only be outnumbered but hopefully scared out of his wits too. I can't see him trying to take us all on, he would probably just run. And if he did see George's face, it would really baffle him to see the chap who was owed the debt suddenly appearing by the side of his debtor. Ah but then he might start asking us angry questions, so that would be a bad thing, so....emergency masks or balaclavas if they have to rush in, that should do it. What do you think?"

He knew he had been rambling. There was a long pause. Lillian was weighing everything up, not wanting to put her brother in danger yet desperate to bring Walter to account for what he did.

"Very well," she said at last, "if you can ensure Frederick's safety by agreeing that he and George will only confront Walter if you are in mortal danger, then....." she trailed off, still wavering.

Marlo caught the mouse firmly before it had a chance to escape. "Agreed! One issue though – where can we meet him? I can't use my lodgings as I only have one room and I haven't got space in my wardrobe for Frederick and George."

"And we can't use my parent's house as that would give the game away."

"George?" They both spoke together.

"Well, I can try," said Marlo, "although I'm asking a lot of him. If George's parents were in the house Walter wouldn't dare do anything. I can pretend to him that they are my parents, and hopefully George can convince them that I am just a good friend who needs to borrow their front room to arrange a business deal or something and then keep them out of sight while Walter is there. It could work."

"I do believe we have a plan, Mr Campbell." Lillian sounded mildly triumphant. "Well, the threads of one anyway."

"Miss Jones, I concur." Marlo smiled, but it was a grim smile. The plan still gave him the willies, but he couldn't think of a better one, or indeed a better expression for how he felt. Now all I need to do is convince George to help, he thought, before remembering that Lillian couldn't hear his thoughts so he said it out loud too.

"Yes," she agreed, "and if you can't then we're in trouble."

CHAPTER 43 : PERSUADING FREDERICK

It was perhaps a little too convenient, too much like lazy writing, thought Tim. It could seem to the reader as though Marlo had fortuitously made George's acquaintance on that train only so that the latter could be woven into the story later. And of course that was true, from the author's perspective. But that didn't mean that it could not have happened. Indeed, it was perfectly plausible, wasn't it? And authors did this kind of thing all the time. Maybe he was getting too self-critical. Anyway, who cares, no-one is going to read this. He knew that the average human's proud assessment of their own literary achievements usually far exceeds the collective assessments of others, so he was under no illusions that his 'oeuvre' would lead to him being feted with prizes and invited to speak at international book fairs however pleased he might eventually be with what he had written. He wasn't pleased yet though, far from it, and at this rate he would probably be dead before he finished it. He chuckled. Then he would need a ghost writer. Better get on with it then.

Marlo presumed that George would be working during the day so there would be no point rushing over to his house yet. Between six and seven, Lillian had advised. But her brother Frederick should be more accessible, being more of a sub-manager than a worker under Mr Plundell and likely to be down at the beach working on his boats and huts, so Marlo set off for Brunswick Square initially, then down past all the proud white six storey bay windowed Georgian terraced homes concertinaed together in a line stretching down to the sea, and onto Brunswick Terrace, where more imposing white houses faced down the threat of the sea like a row of sturdy soldiers, shoulder to shoulder.

It was a Monday, so the promenade was less busy than at the weekend but those that were walking on it seemed slightly more hurried. It was mid-morning now, and although the sea carried with it a breath of salty freshness, it was otherwise calm, with an almost stationary patchwork of light clouds just occasionally allowing the sun to burst through and warm everybody up momentarily. He was reminded of a phrase his father had coined for these conditions: "When the sun's out it's hot, when it's not it's not." He smiled at the memory of his Dad first making this observation while strolling down the high street in Bangor in the middle of summer when on holiday in Wales, then realising what he had just said and being highly pleased with his own unexpected cleverness. "Did you see what I said there, did you? That's good that!" Happy memories of another time, now even further away it seemed.

Down on the beach Marlo could see the same random pattern of small row boats lying on the stones at all levels as though a giant had picked them all up in his hands and thrown them like dice on a table. An oyster seller had set up a mobile stall right below him, dressed in what looked like a train inspector's uniform with a flat peaked cap, enticing people to select from a pile of oysters piled up on the flat wooden surface of his two wheeled cart. A couple of small trays of fish provided an alternative for those not so keen on the shellfish. In the distance a thin forest of masts indicated the presence of fishermen at work repairing their nets and cleaning their boats from an early morning catch long since headed to the fish markets. Even from where he stood he could count perhaps twenty-five masts, and he knew there were more fishing boats further up on the other side of the pier. That was a lot of boats. He wondered if fish stocks were getting depleted even back in this era, or was the sea teeming with so much life that only the industrial-scale dredging of trawlers from future decades could decimate them.

Directly beneath him though, the ambience was more pleasure and leisure than work. This was the elegant side of town, where the well-to-do assembled and lived, but close enough to the pier to entice day trippers and holiday makers. Consequently, it was a sensible place for a bathing hut business, and as he scanned the activity below him, focusing primarily on the boxy little big-wheeled huts, he soon spotted someone who from a distance looked very much like Frederick hitching up a horse to the front of one of the huts in order to turn it round and bring it further up the beach.

"I think I can see Frederick," he informed Lillian, "I'll go and talk to him."

"Good, that was lucky," she replied "Are you sure it is him?"

"I'm pretty certain. I'll soon find out...."

Not being one to shout and wave or in any way draw attention to himself, Marlo headed quickly down the steps and onto the beach before crunching his way across to the man with the horse, in that awkwardly self-conscious gait that walking on large round stones entails.

Frederick had spotted his approach and hailed him before he even had a chance to get close. "Mr Campbell! How nice to see you! Have you any news?"

Marlo held up his hand in acknowledgement, but the last thing he was going to do was bellow his business to anyone within earshot so he just grinned and nodded, stumbling on some loose stones as he did so and falling embarrassingly onto his back like a small child in a sandpit.

He got himself up and had time to think of a wry comment before he reached Frederick. "Well, they do say sticks and stones can break your bones and they nearly did there," he announced as he went to shake Frederick's outstretched hand.

"It happens to us all," consoled Lillian's brother, "I've done it many time myself. You've not hurt yourself, I trust?"

"Thank you, I'm fine. I do have news though, and also a request."

"Pray tell."

Marlo jumped slightly as a seagull swooped past him with a loud shriek. "Well, our man Walter isn't what he said he was. He's a debt collector, not an accountant."

Frederick's eyes opened a little wider and Marlo could almost see his brain working to process the implications. "Are you sure?"

"Yes, I saw him go into his office and there was a plaque with his name on the door. It's true."

"The lying scoundrel! He entertained Lillian under false pretences from the start. It can only have been him who pushed my dear sister off the cliff. I'll kill him!"

"No! No, don't do that." Marlo immediately realised he had been a bit emphatic in his response, but of course he now knew that if he could not have Walter confess then bring him before a judge he would not be returning home, nor would he ever see Lillian again. Neither of those propositions bore thinking about. He backtracked slightly, taking care not to let on what he already knew.

"If you did that we will never know if he really did do it, or why. We have to get a confession, then get him in court, hear him explain himself, then let him face the punishment he deserves, don't you think?"

Frederick stared at him uncertainly, then nodded slowly. "Alright, yes, you are right, to the extent that if indeed he did do it, I need to know why. Then I'll kill him."

Marlo was surprised not to hear Lillian in his ear reacting to what her brother was saying. He felt his pocket. The diary was still there, it hadn't come out when he fell over, so perhaps she was just listening intently.

He shook his head. "No, please don't, even if just for me. If I can't bring him before the law it won't be any use for my police application. A dead man isn't going to impress anyone. Also, you could end up going to prison or the gallows instead of Walter, and I'm pretty sure Lillian wouldn't want that."

There was no confirmation from Lillian in his head and Marlo had a sudden moment of panic that somehow this ethereal connection had broken in the same way that an internet connection might do in the modern world. What if the link wasn't restored? What if he was left entirely on his own down here? No, no, that couldn't happen. Not if Number Five was involved. It must be a blip. He relaxed slightly, but nonetheless wanted Lillian to confirm she was still there.

Frederick was talking. "She wouldn't, I will give you that. Alright, for her I will restrain myself. You said you had a request, what is it?"

"I would like your assistance in trapping the man."

Frederick rubbed the back of his neck revealing a large sweat patch under his arm, but answered almost without thinking. "Of course. What would you like me to do?"

~

It was only once Marlo crunched his way back across the stones, having secured the promise of assistance from Frederick and now out of earshot, that he was able to hiss "Lillian? Are you there?"

A short silence and then "Yes, yes. Of course. I.... sorry, what did you say?" It was clear her mind was on other things.

"I didn't say anything. I was just expecting you to, well, say something while I was talking to Frederick, but you...."

"I was miles away, yes," she interrupted quickly, sounding rather excited, "sorry about that. But there is a reason. When Freddie started talking about killing Walter, it set me thinking. Now, listen carefully. We agreed before that neither of us could kill that evil man because we would disappear back to a different time zone, meaning that Walter's murder would be unexplained and we ourselves could then get a resolver chasing after us in the future."

Marlo nodded, somewhat unnecessarily. "Right."

"But what if someone else kills him on our behalf?" She let the words hang for a moment to allow time for Marlo to take in the implication of what she had just said, then continued.

"I can't believe I'm saying this but..... it would be quicker than waiting for him to get before a judge, it eliminates the chance of him somehow convincing a judge or jury that he didn't do it, and it would mean that our involvement ends nice and quickly and no-one could possibly chase after us through time to avenge his murder. We would just need to make sure that whoever killed him waited until the true facts behind my death are made known, and is also fully justified in doing so and will not get prosecuted themselves. We could engineer a justification for doing the deed, like self-defence, against which no-one could argue. But however he dies, whether it is by the hand of the state or an individual, for us at least that would still satisfy the criteria set by Number Five for a successful mission. After all, Walter will definitely be put to death as a punishment anyway as he killed two people, so all we are doing is hastening the process, which means we escape from this situation sooner. What do you think?"

Marlo could almost hear Lillian stepping back, folding her arms, and looking pleased with herself. His reply started slowly before speeding up as his thoughts caught up with his mouth.

"I think that sounds like, er, well, I can't see why we shouldn't be able to do that, other than perhaps the small problem of finding a way in which Walter could be justifiably bumped off, and finding someone prepared to.... oh, Frederick, of course! But surely you wouldn't want your brother doing this? Think of the risks..."

"I know, I don't want him involved at all. My parents have suffered enough already without seeing their son dragged into a murder situation as well."

"How about we make it look like an accident, which convinces the police? Then no-one would need to be implicated."

Lillian's laugh was brief and slightly dismissive. "Ha, no, we couldn't do that. We've already seen what happens when you try that, or at least Walter did and now he has us on his tail. The true cause of death has to be known on Earth, no subterfuge unfortunately."

"Right, yes, good point. Sorry. Really, then, we are talking about something like self-defence, like Walter attacking someone who has no option but to strike back. But we can hardly ask someone if they would be so kind as to goad a killer to attack them, then try to kill him before he kills them. I can't think of anyone other than Frederick who has any motive whatsoever."

Now it was Lillian's turn to acknowledge a point well made. "You're right. Wait though, what about Mr Attleborough's family? Did he have any? I know he lived on his own in that remote cottage but he might have had some distant relative who..... oh, this is hopeless. We just aren't going to find anyone willing to have themselves attacked by Walter so that they can justifiably kill him without getting hanged themselves."

"Also, as soon as Walter confesses, or the truth becomes clear to someone in authority, he will be arrested and frogmarched straight to the cells, won't he? There won't be any opportunity to take revenge anyway."

Lillian gave a little scream of frustration, the kind a teenager would give when told to go and tidy their room. "I hate him so much, I just want him dead as soon as possible, but we can't do it. We'll just have to let the law take its course and wait for as long as it takes."

Marlo sighed. This whole exercise was swimming with complexities, possibilities, and impossibilities, all of which overlapped and none of which seemed to help provide the perfect answer.

"Well, yeah, I guess so. Trap him and hand him over. That's all we can do. At least we have your brother on board for that now. Do we need to involve George too?"

"Safety in numbers. Walter is a dangerous man, Marlo, very dangerous. We know he has killed at least two people, it may be more. We can't take any chances."

"I was going to say the more the merrier but that sounds wrong. But you're right, if it turns nasty then we'll need backup. I'll pay George a visit this evening once he is back from work."

CHAPTER 44 : PERSUADING GEORGE

Once again Marlo found himself needing to kill time in a world with no mobile phones, internet, television or radio. This really was taking some adjusting to, although to be honest it was quite nice to have a break from it all. Just not for too long though. As he sat on a bench on the promenade and passed time by watching a fascinatingly different world go by, Marlo remembered how as a child he used to throw tantrums when his limit of two hours television a day was enforced, leading to his mother sternly folding her arms and reminding him that in her day she made her own entertainment, without ever actually being specific about what that entertainment was. He used to be so angry with her, so he was sure that she would be looking down on him now with some amusement. Well, actually, she wouldn't be looking down, given what he knew now. It was a sobering thought that even that slight comfort, that she and Dad might be 'up there' somewhere, no longer applied. They were just... well, gone.

At least he had Lillian to talk to though. That made up for a lot, but he was still wary. She seemed such a lovely person but was that just for show, in order to lead him along, make him help her? Once you got to know her she might have a mean streak, or have annoying habits as yet unrevealed. He might end up finding her incredibly irritating. He doubted it, but knowing his luck it was entirely possible. He also wasn't really sure what she thought about so many things, mainly because those things – upon which arguments are built and relationships can founder – were not common to them both. He did not have a view on how well the Marquess of Salisbury was doing as Prime Minister any more that she could take an angle on Donald Trump. They might be bitterly opposed on all types of topics. They could end up hating each other. No Marlo, think positive. And there is a positive, quite a huge advantage, actually. If and when they got back to his era, they would have a shared secret that would tie them together. Neither of them could really talk to anyone else about what they had been through. That must count for something, surely. Yes, that was a helpful thought, and he was pleased that he had had it as it perked him up.

He self-consciously adjusted his hands on his lap and reflected that he was one of those people who never knew where to put their hands,

343

making him appear even more socially inept. When standing up, do they hang loosely and awkwardly by your sides, do you clasp them at the front, behind your back like a dignitary, one hand in a pocket, both hands in pockets, folded arms? He never knew and wherever he put them it looked wrong. Yet the confident crowd seemed to have no problem forgetting they even had arms as their limbs just seemed to naturally fall into the right places. This lack of self consciousness manifested itself elsewhere too. Marlo used to watch enviously as his friends and colleagues lost all their inhibitions merely from the fact that they were in a club where music was playing and dancing was expected. As they flopped and wriggled to each other in time, or not, to the music, faces bright and wreathed in grins, part of a tribal mating ritual that Marlo could never join, he became dumbfounded at how anyone could not see how ridiculous they looked. Where was their self-awareness? Had they not seen those bored looking 1970s teenagers with long hair and brown jumpers on old Top Of the Pops videos, grooving awkwardly in a manner that surely no-one could define as 'cool'? Why did they do it? The whole concept of jiggling about in time to music only made sense to Marlo if performed by someone who knew what they were doing, as in a professional dancer. Perhaps one day people would.....

"Marlo?"

Lillian's sudden interruption to his thoughts gave him a start.

"Hello? Yes, sorry, I was daydreaming." He was getting better at his 'ventriloquist's mouth' now and so fairly confident passers-by would not see his lips moving, although admittedly 'daydreaming' had come out more like 'daydringing'.

"Oh, right, sorry. I only wanted to talk to you really. I haven't talked to anyone for so long, you see. These last few days, talking to you about so many things have been, well, so nice. You know?"

A warm feeling Marlo didn't recognise swept through him. "Oh, er, thank you. For me too. I've really enjoyed talking to you."

There he was, doing it again. Making an emotional moment rational and polite instead of from the heart. Why was he so useless at expressing himself? What would a real man do in these circumstances? He should rephrase that reply, make her know that he meant it.

But it was too late, Lillian was already talking. "Good, so let's talk some more! I was thinking about how my diary got into your father's house. Do you think we have a family connection?"

"Oh, jeez, I hadn't thought about that. Do you think so?" For one awful moment Marlo considered that Lillian might be his great-great-great grandmother or something, which would really complicate things, but then quickly realised how unlikely that was. For a start, his father had researched their family tree and he couldn't remember there being any Jones's in it. Also, Lillian had died without children, which to be honest was probably a clincher when it came to working out whether or not she had any direct descendents. He answered his own question. "No, that can't be it. Do you know what I think? When Dad got older he started going to boot sales, just to give him something to do. He probably bought something like a box of books or a storage unit that had the diary in it. Yes, that's probably it."

"That sounds feasible I suppose. But why would you be able to buy books and storage units at a place that sells boots? And do you not just call them shoe shops any more?"

People walking past and noticing Marlo suddenly grinning like an idiot would have been a lot more interested in him if they knew what had amused him, but he quickly composed himself and explained the concept of boot sales to Lillian, which took longer than it should due to her not knowing what a car boot was, which was not surprising given that Karl Benz had only just begun promoting the concept of his engine-powered vehicle a few months before she died.

They spent the rest of the morning talking, both learning more about each other's lives, which seemed a little strange given that one of them was officially dead. As they talked Marlo got up and walked slowly along the promenade right up to the far side of the Hove part of Brighton and Hove. After a lunch of some bread and a pot of whelks from a seafood stall, he headed away from the sea and back through the town. He saw new houses being built everywhere, terraced rows for the working classes but also large detached residences, almost all of which would still be there well over a century later. The sound of builders at work – shouts, bangs, crashes, whistles – rent the air as labourers kept up with the pace of a house building programme that puts modern Britain to shame. But then there was much more space here, with lots of gaps between buildings still just open patches of ground, ripe for development.

Away from the sea front he came across some desperately depressing streets too – rows and rows of small cramped tenement houses facing each other, built cheaply and with none of the architectural detailing the Victorians were famous for. He was pretty certain that none of these slums were still standing. Filthy poorly dressed children, some of them barefoot, played amongst the broken carts abandoned at the side of the street, watched by mangy dogs sitting on doorsteps. A jumbled pile of furniture outside one front door presumably indicated an eviction in progress. The families who lived in these areas knew poverty. This was not the poverty of modern Britain where you could qualify even if you had use of a car, a mobile phone, a flat screen TV and a supply of cigarettes. These slum dwellers clearly had nothing. Just their clothes, some basic furniture, and a roof over their heads. It looked dreadful and Marlo felt quite sick just thinking what these people had to go through every day. He didn't like it, and he felt exposed, out of place, and a little fearful. This was in no small measure due to Lillian telling him in a rather worried voice to move past quickly before he was noticed, advice he knew not to question.

The afternoon was spent back in the centre of Brighton, killing time by reading advertising posters and browsing the frontages of shops.

"Hey Lillian," he muttered under his breath as he passed an advertising hoarding, "there's a poster here from people opposing beer. Is that normal?"

"Are you sure?"

"Yes, it says 'Announcement: Anti Beer Adulteration Society Meeting. St Peter's Church Hall, Thursday evenings 9 till 10:30'. And they mix that with adultery, is that what it means? That can't be right…"

Lillian laughed. "I think you'll find you've mis-read it. They are protesting against the adulteration of beer, watering it down, that kind of thing."

"Ha, right, yes, sorry, of course they are. I've just read the small print underneath where it says that they are 'safeguarding the public from the partaking of unwholesome beer'. How would they do that?"

"Oh, I don't know, that's not really my area of expertise I'm afraid."

Marlo had already moved on as his eyes had alighted on a rather fortuitously placed flyer right next to it. "Alright then, how about this one. There's a brewer here listing all the beers they sell and one of them, a treble stout, says it is brewed specially for invalids. Really?"

"As I said, Marlo, not my area, but that does seem a strong claim, I'd agree."

"You're telling me! It's nonsense. Funny though. Do they think it will cure them or something?"

"Maybe it could help?"

"No, it definitely couldn't."

"How do you know?"

"Just from a basic understanding of health and medicine. You'd be amazed what progress we've made since your day, we can cure people of so many things now. They've even started doing things like face transplants."

"What? Don't be silly, how could you put someone's face on another person? What happens to the person who has lost their face? Or is it a face from a dead person? Eergh, no, you are pulling my leg. A face transplant indeed! The very thought of it makes me shudder."

"I know, it sounds ridiculous doesn't it, but it's true, honest. I'll tell you more about it later. Listen, I'm turning away from the wall now so I had better stop talking. I'm going to head for an interesting shop I've spotted."

It was an ironmonger across the street, so not that interesting really, but Marlo went to gaze at the window display and the cornucopia of tools and gadgets that were skilfully forged from metal and wood rather than the mass-produced plastic of today. They sat heavily on mainly wooden shelves, some of the tools being fiendish in their complexity and providing Marlo with a little game of 'guess the gadget', with assistance from Lillian, to pass the time. The shop even sold rat poison. A little box labelled 'Rough On Rats' with the somewhat odd strap line 'Don't die in the house' was right at the edge of one shelf, labelled at seven pence.

Every item in all the shops was served to you by the shopkeepers from behind marble or dark wood counters; self-service just wasn't a thing. He presumed shoplifting was not so easy so thieves would focus on swiping goods and property directly from the customers instead, as described by Dickens in Oliver Twist, for example. Living in 21st century London though, he was accustomed to being careful not to wave his wallet around so he kept his wits about him. The last thing he wanted was some scallywag bumping into him and accidentally acquiring his diary.

As he ambled past a haberdasher with a poster in the window announcing an unlikely 'Autumn Show of Novelties', he heard a sudden commotion. In the distance a bell had started clanging and it was getting louder. Further down the road, back the way he had just come, people were shouting urgently and there was a steadily growing rumbling noise.

He could see some flashes of gold, and as he strained to see what was going on the rumble became a thunder, and he realised that it was the thunder of hooves furiously pounding the soft road. He could see it now – a horse drawn fire wagon charging towards him, with seven grim faced fireman clinging on for dear life, all of them in heavy buttoned-up uniforms wearing shiny gold helmets that glinted in the sun.

There were three horses at the front all in a line and as they galloped past in a pall of dust Marlo had to stand back to avoid choking. Everyone on the road had sensibly pulled to the side allowing the wagon a clear run down the middle of the road, and as Marlo, like the rest of the pedestrians around him, followed the fire crew's progress as they disappeared from view, he could see a faint whiff of black smoke above the buildings in the far distance, presumably where they were heading.

Good luck to them, he thought. A fireman's job is tricky at the best of times, but not only did these guys have to make do with basic equipment, they also had to survive a chariot race before they even got there.

As the noise receded the road traffic started back up again, the pedestrians returned to their business, and Marlo went back to aimlessly meandering past shops for the rest of the afternoon.

By the time he once more turned into Sillwood Road and approached George Smith's house, the sun was close to dipping into the sea and the cool chill of a darkening evening was lowering its cloak over the town. The heavy front curtains in the bay window next to the front door were already drawn but he could see a thin sliver of weak light glinting between them.

"Here goes," he muttered under his breath as he ascended the four stone steps to a front door that could have done with a fresh lick of paint.

"Good luck," he heard Lillian whisper, even though she didn't need to.

"Thanks. I feel like I might need it."

It took a second knock but then the door was answered by a thin middle-aged woman with tied back brown hair and a deathly plain face that appeared not to have any eyebrows, giving her a strangely chilling demeanour. This was not helped by the fact that she was swathed in black and looked as though she had dressed for a funeral. She peered down the steps at him like a heron eyeing a fish, seemingly finding it hard to mask feelings of annoyance at being called to answer the door.

"Yes?" she asked rather fiercely.

Marlo forced a nervous smile and ventured "Mrs Smith?"

"That's me." Mrs Smith's pose remained as rigid as her face, her defences seeming to rise another notch.

"Ah, right, er, good. I've come to see George, is he in please?"

At this Mrs Smith appeared to ease a little, relieved perhaps that her role in this interplay could now be downgraded to simply that of messenger. But this did not encourage her to thaw her welcome at all.

"Who is asking if you please?" she demanded briskly, the politeness in her words not mirrored by her tone.

"My name is Marlo Campbell. George knows me." Marlo left it at that, thinking it best not to go into details in case it supplied Mrs Smith with the reason she was no doubt looking for to close the door in his face.

"Wait there please." With that she shut the door firmly and Marlo wondered whether it would open again. But after a couple of minutes the door knob turned and George's appeared, a broad smile on his face.

"Mr Campbell!" he announced, his hand outstretched. Marlo shook his hand warmly.

"Mr Smith!" he rejoined. "I'm impressed you remembered my name."

George laughed. "My great powers of memory were aided by you having just told my mother who you were," he admitted. "Anyway, come in out of the evening chill. How may I help you? Is it accommodation you need?"

Marlo followed him into the hallway, the polished wooden floor glinting in the gloomy light of a gas lamp on the wall.

"No, actually, it isn't, you may be surprised to hear. I am actually all sorted, you know, arranged on that front."

"Well that is a relief because I hadn't managed to find anywhere suitable for you anyway." As George turned to address him Marlo felt that he had the look of someone who may have not found anywhere primarily because he hadn't actually asked anyone yet, but he did not press.

He looked over George's shoulder and down the hallway but could see no-one there. "Are we alright to talk confidentially here?" he asked conspiratorially.

George looked at him quizzically. "Well yes, but...." without understanding why he was doing it he lowered his voice to a whisper, "...perhaps less chance of interruption if we go into the parlour? I don't think anyone is in there."

Marlo nodded even though he had no reason to know whether the parlour was any better than where they were now, or even what exactly the parlour was, but it seemed the right thing to do.

The parlour turned out to be the front lounge, and George led him in and closed the door behind them. He turned to look expectantly at Marlo, but Marlo was busy looking around the room and taking a moment to remind himself that he wasn't in a National Trust property.

The room felt smaller than it was, being muddled with furniture and cocooned in dark red swirly wallpaper that rather unadventurously exactly matched the hue of the dark red curtains, which hung from metal rails and looked heavy enough to stop cannonballs.

A single gas wall lamp like the one in the hall was working in tandem with an oil burning lamp on a small round table in the corner, the smell of them both combining to make Marlo feel slightly nauseous and between them giving off a dancing light that made the shadows gently wobble.

Opposite him the fireplace was large; ornate black iron with an inner frame of green and red patterned tiles blotched with soot, and a black cast iron mantelpiece shelf above it that supported an imposing black clock, vases of flowers and various small ornaments. A large aspidistra plant, tough and leathery, was attempting to smother an old upright piano in the corner, and on the faded patterned rug a selection of elegant single chairs filled as much available space as they could.

"Mother likes to keep the front room lit," George said, almost apologetically. "As soon as it gets dark she's in here doing the lights. She thinks people walking past will think we are well-to-do even though we no longer are, although why that matters is another question. It just wastes money we don't have as far as I am concerned."

Only because George had mentioned her, Marlo felt he could ask for a little clarity on the subject of his formidable mother. "I didn't knock at a bad time did I? Your mother seemed a little.....well....."

".... abrupt?" George interrupted with a grin. "Well, yes, you could have timed it better. She was just building up steam for an argument with Papa over... I don't know, something trivial I expect, it usually is. My father gets quite grumpy, because of his illness, you know, and the fact that he can't earn enough any more. I heard them from upstairs just starting to shout, and then you arrived. So don't take it personally. You may have inadvertently calmed things down actually."

Marlo remembered George telling him on the train about his father's lung condition and could understand why the poor man might not be cracking jokes all day. "Well that's a relief. I thought she had taken an instant dislike to me."

"That may have happened too," said George with a grin, "you never know with my mother. Anyway, we digress. Please, take a seat. Your purpose, Mr Campbell, in coming here. If it is not accommodation you no doubt wish to explain what it is? "

Marlo selected a polished wood chair with brown-at-the-edges pink upholstery that he hoped would be the least uncomfortable and was surprised to find it remarkably supportive. "I thought we had agreed to use first names?"

George flopped into the chair opposite, his chunky legs only just able to fit within it, ruling out any attempts at manspreading. "You are right, we did. How do you spell your first name? Just so that I know. I have not heard of a Marlo before."

Marlo smiled. "It is m-a-r-l-o. As in the town in Buckinghamshire but without the 'w'." This was an oft-repeated phrase that he now said almost without thinking.

"I don't know it, so that doesn't help, but the spelling does – nice and simple, as it sounds. Thank you."

"Good! Anyway, the reason I'm here. It is to ask a favour. Quite a big one actually. I know we've only just met but, I don't really know anyone else in Brighton and you seem like a really nice guy, er, chap, er, well, someone I can talk to about..... things and, well.....situations, like the one

I am in." He trailed off, realising he has started to waffle but unable to easily extricate himself from the verbal mess he had created.

"Sorry, let me start again and come straight to the point. George, I need your help to bring someone to justice."

George looked at him in the same way that a child does who has just been told to tidy his room: puzzled and slightly indignant disbelief that he could be asked such a thing.

"Well. That is not what I was expecting, and no mistake. You did just say bring someone to justice?" Realising his voice was raising and seeing Marlo's concern he lowered to a whisper. "Why? Who? How? And you can add 'when' and 'where' to that list if you like. Actually, no, don't. That would imply action on my part and I haven't agreed to anything. What do you mean by justice? I'm no use in a fight, and if you mean the courts then presumably you would already have involved the police? And what has he done, this man? I'm assuming it is a man?"

Marlo held up his hand to halt the torrent of questions and gave George a humourless smile. "Yep, I know, it makes no sense initially. Let me explain."

And so he outlined the story in the same way that he had told it to Lillian's family. He again embellished it a little with trinkets of compliments to the girl in his head, using the opportunity to say things that he would never have enough courage to say to her directly. How she was so well-loved, with such a nice personality, a special person to so many who knew her, and so on. The more he could make George feel sorry for her, hopefully the more pre-disposed he would be to help. And if he ingratiated himself a bit with Lillian while he was at it, then it was a double-bubble, as someone at work used to say.

Half way through his speech the door opened suddenly and a boy of about thirteen ambled in, saw George had a visitor, and immediately turned on his heels and marched back out again, trailing a 'sorry' in the air. George held up his hand to Marlo, let a few seconds pass then quietly got up and crept to the door, opening it quickly to find, as he expected, his younger brother with his ear to the frame of the door. Marlo heard a "get out of it, you nosy pest," and a scuffling noise and a yelp before George returned, straightening his shirt and apologising.

"Sorry about that. Robert is so predictable. I don't think he'll be back but let's keep it quiet so he can't hear anyway."

Marlo resumed his explanation of the plan that he and Lillian had formulated and George's proposed role in it. He finished, paused, and passed the conversational baton to George with a hesitant "what do you think?"

George didn't know what to think. He had only just met this young fellow, and that for all of thirty minutes at most, and now here he was a few days later asking him to get mixed up in some scheme to catch a murderer. Something didn't feel right. He studied Marlo's anxious face. "Why should I help you, Marlo, given that I am not obligated to do so?"

It was a question he and Lillian knew would be asked so Marlo had an answer prepared. "There is no reason why you should George. I am as you imply asking you to get involved in something that has nothing to do with you. But if we succeed, you will have helped make Brighton a safer place. If this man murders again, who will be next? It could be you or any one of your family. It could be a friend of yours. Or it could be someone you don't know, and if you read in the paper that Walter Threadwell has been convicted of another murder, you will no doubt wish you had helped. I'm not trying to emotionally blackmail you, just stating a truth. Also, think of the kudos."

"What's that?"

"Kudos? It's a sort of enhanced reputation, someone worthy of praise. People will pat you on the back and think highly of you."

"How do you know they don't do that already?" George's smile gave away the likelihood that they didn't.

"Then they will think even more highly of you. Where that is possible of course." Marlo played along with the shared pretence.

George toyed with his moustache and thought hard for a few moments. "Alright, so this is what I think......" he said slowly, his thoughts sorting themselves out and emerging now like suitcases on an airport carousel, ".... firstly, the risk. I could get hurt or even killed. Secondly, risking my family, in using this house for your scheme to trap him. Thirdly, getting my parents to agree, because I don't think they will. And also the practicalities of being able to hear what your fellow is saying if I and Lillian's brother are in the next room – it would be too muffled. We would have to be in this room, hiding behind a curtain or something. Again, too risky."

Marlo nodded as his heart sank, realising that George was right. Hiding behind curtains turned the whole thing into something out of a stage farce, with giveaway feet sticking out from underneath, or a sneeze revealing the subterfuge in an instant.

"Then there is the question of me having to claim that you owe me money when you don't, and making sure that this.... Mr Treadwell was it?"

"Threadwell."

"Threadwell, then, making sure he doesn't see me with you because if he does I would imagine he could become very angry, and who knows what he might do. I don't like that either. You are asking a great deal, Marlo. Too much, I'm afraid."

Marlo couldn't argue. He knew George was right and that was all he could say. "You're right, George. It was just that it was the only plan we had."

"We?"

Marlo thought quickly. "Well, you know, er, myself and Lillian's family. They are all in on it, although it was my plan initially."

In his head he heard Lillian breathe out a 'phew', followed by a quiet 'good recovery'. He smiled internally.

George didn't question Marlo's explanation. "I will tell you what I will do," he said slowly, "I want to be able to help you so I will assist you to a degree, because I can see that what you want to do is a worthy endeavour, albeit foolhardy. But not by using my parent's house, I cannot allow that. There is another possibility though. My employer, Mr Gradforth, he has a property that he lets out but at the moment it is empty, between tenants. Perhaps I could ask him........ actually no, I don't want to do that. I could get in trouble if anything goes wrong."

"Perhaps I could rent it for a day, would that be possible?"

"He wouldn't countenance a short let, too much paperwork for too little reward."

"Could it be done off the books, cash in hand?"

"No, I know Mr Gradforth, he wouldn't do it. I might be in want of a bit of the needful, so to speak, but he's an old miser so has plenty stored away, I'll wager. He doesn't need the tin. Also, supposing Threadwell pulled out and re-arranged, you would have to rent it again for another day, it would get too messy. No, the whole thing was a foolish idea, please forget I mentioned it. Have you thought of a different option though, one that is a bit more, shall we say, forceful?"

Marlo looked dubious. "Go on...."

"Get him on his own, then rough him up a bit, tie his limbs together, beat a confession out of him!" George was grinning disconcertingly but Marlo didn't know whether he was joking or not.

"You've definitely not seen him have you? He's a hulk of a man, probably twice my weight and three times as strong. Even with three of us we would be hard pressed to hold him down let alone tie him up."

George shook his head animatedly. "No, no, not us! Pay someone else, you know, a couple of prize fighters or villains, who would relish a scrap."

For a moment Marlo felt a strange breath of elation, as though this could be a quick and easy way out that neither he nor Lillian had considered. Then the female voice in his head brought him down to earth. "That's so tempting, but a bad idea, Marlo, it's too risky. You couldn't beat him up in front of the witnesses we need, because they would then have to testify in court at Walter's trial and perjure themselves by denying that you had him beaten up. Also, Walter would just claim he confessed just to avoid being killed, and then he would want revenge, and who knows how far he would take it. Well, we do know actually."

George watched as Marlo's expression slowly morphed from a piqued interest into glazed-eye consideration and finally, once Lillian had finished, to pursed lips and a frown.

"I don't think that would work, George. We couldn't use a confession extracted like that as evidence – he'll claim afterwards he only said it under duress. Then he'll come after me."

"Not if he doesn't see you!"

"Well he will because I'll need to be the one interrogating him really. You've got me thinking though."

George got up and opened the door suddenly, just to be on the safe side, but there was no sign of his brother. He closed the door and went over to the curtains, peering through into the partially-lit gloom of the street outside as though this would bring inspiration.

"Alright, here is my final suggestion," he said as he returned to his chair. "Befriend a debtor, one of Threadwell's clients. Get him to say to

Threadwell that you owe him enough money to clear the debt but are threatening him, and also tell Threadwell that if he comes back at an agreed time he can catch the two of you in the house and get the whole thing sorted there and then. If he is the bully you describe he might find that a tempting opportunity to throw his weight around and frighten you, if you prompt him, by revealing that he has killed people. Give the debtor some money as a reward, so you get them on your side."

At first this sounded feasible to Marlo, apart from the bit about Walter throwing his weight around. He and Lillian would have to think of ways to mitigate that. "So then we hide the witnesses in the house, maybe not behind the curtains though, and then I get him to confess, this time maybe by goading him about how he can't be that tough because he wouldn't know what it is like to kill someone whereas I used to be in the army and have done it – how about that? Then on the basis that he will think no-one can prove anything, he will hopefully point out that he has killed someone, possibly two people if he is feeling bold, and with a bit of luck he might name Lillian. I'll prompt him if he doesn't, based on what I read in the paper. Then I'll say that I haven't got the money on me but will bring it to his office the next day, something like that."

George was warming to his plan. "Yes, and the reason you will do that is because you are obviously now very clear that Walter means business after what he has told you, so naturally you are going to do as he asks. His civilian killing far out-trumps your army service duty in terms of menace. In the meantime, you go to the police with your witnesses and get him arrested."

"This all assumes I can get that confession out of him, of course."

"Well, yes, but if you goad him enough, as in why should I fear you, what have you ever done that should make me scared of you, that kind of thing. This all sounds quite exciting!"

Marlo harrumphed a little. "For you maybe, me, I'm bricking it."

"You're what?"

"Oh sorry, that's er, a local expression where I come from, it means I'm really frightened."

"Why would it mean that? Oh never mind. The point is, I think you have a workable option now." George sat back and looked rather pleased with himself.

Marlo knew that what he was about to ask could change that expression on his face. "Would you still be happy to be one of my witnesses?"

George was brought back down to earth. "Ah, well, I'm not sure that..... you know..... given what you have told me........and the risk if something goes wrong. I can't really commit to...." He trailed off as he saw Marlo looking at him with the most earnest and hopeful countenance he had probably ever been subjected to.

"Please?" Marlo's tone of desperation was genuine. He needed someone who unlike Frederick did not have a vested interest and George was his only option.

George mulled over the pros and cons. Yes, it was potentially dangerous, but he would be hidden and would make absolutely sure that Threadwell could not possibly see him, so theoretically he should be safe. Otherwise he wouldn't do it. Things could go wrong, of course, but on the other hand if he could say he had helped to catch a murderer that would give him a story to dine out on for years to come, especially when courting. But he was at work six days a week and valued his day off. Then again, it was only one day. He would have to give evidence in court though. But he worked in a solicitor's office – that would help. And it would be quite an experience. He came to a decision, perhaps a little too quickly.

"Alright, I'll help."

Marlo leapt up and shook his hand before he had a chance to change his mind. "Oh, thank you George, so much. I really do appreciate this."

George attempted a smile but it was dimmed by the thoughts still clouding his mind and sprinkling some loitering seeds of uncertainty as to whether he had done the right thing. Marlo could see this and so tried to move things on.

"Right then, next steps. I ought to introduce you to Frederick. He's a really nice chap, I'm sure you'll like him. Perhaps we could meet at a pub, er, tavern one evening this week? I'll pay."

"There's a good beer house just around the corner," said George, perked up by the thought of a free drink, "its run by Mrs Sapworthy, a friend of my mother."

"Right, I'll speak to Frederick and let you know." Marlo realised as he said this that what in today's world would take him five minutes to arrange with a quick call on the mobile, was now going to require a lot of walking, and a lot of time.

"I can make any evening this week," said George, "just put a note through the door in a sealed envelope – I don't want my family knowing what I am doing, you see."

"Of course, yes, no problem. And I'll have a think about exactly how this plan would work so we can all talk it through when we meet."

"Right, good."

George had replied almost automatically, as though he had stopped listening. Marlo could see the doubts starting to creep back into his face so he moved towards the door. "I won't take up any more of your time. You have been so helpful George, you really have."

George steered Marlo into the hall and out of the front door. "Not at all, dear fellow, not at all," he replied unenthusiastically, well aware that he may have just committed himself to something that he would subsequently fervently wish that he had not.

CHAPTER 45 : AN UNEXPECTED CATCH

The music was beginning to be a distraction. Tim normally enjoyed a bit of background classical music while he was writing – at a low volume, mind, just enough to take the edge off the silence and help relax his mind. Mahler's fifth symphony was a favourite, but today he was finding it hard to concentrate and the music was diverting him away from the complexities of his rapidly spiralling plot into a simpler, floatier world of aural pleasure. In the old days, which were not actually that long ago, he would have had to get up and lift the needle off the LP or pause the CD, but now he had been shown how to use YouTube, all he had to do was switch windows on the computer and press pause. No legwork required. It was easier, he supposed, but easier isn't always better for you.

The sudden silence re-calibrated his focus. Now, what to do about Marlo and Lillian and their plan to catch Walter. In the same way that you can talk yourself out of something, he had written his way out of something - his original plot device of using George's home as the honey trap location. Or was bear-trap a more appropriate term? If it had been Winnie the Pooh either would have worked. Anyway, concentrate Tim, concentrate! The plot......

Finding Marlo a debtor to ally with might have been feasible but it wasn't quick to write unless he skimmed over important elements. And he was very conscious that by this time, either the reader would be completely engrossed in his bewitching tale and wanting more, or they would be checking how many pages were left and wondering why they had bought this confounded book. Keep it short, said all the advice, don't waffle. Long books by first time authors won't find a publisher. But so far he had reached 133,000 words, and surely that wasn't too bad compared with Watership Down at 156,000, or then Jane Eyre and Great Expectations at 183,000, or even Moby Dick with 206,000. Then if you really have time on your hands you can sit down with Anna Karenina (376,000), or Gone With The Wind (408,000), or of course War and Peace (587,000). Topping them all was the best selling first novel of Vikram Seth, About A Boy, which weighs in at 591,000 words, presumably stretched out just enough to take the title from War and Peace. That did alright, didn't it?

He had found all this information on the internet and it comforted him a little. He certainly wasn't going to try and challenge Vikram Seth, but if he could keep it within the boundaries of a Dickens classic, that would be quite acceptable, he thought, particularly as it was set in the same era and had a similar tone in places. Not that he could compare himself to Dickens of course. He chuckled at the thought of The Mysterious Fall being on the school curriculum in twenty years time and teachers earnestly describing to pupils what the author meant when he wrote key phrases even though they had no more idea than he did when he wrote them. They just came out of his head, it wasn't really explainable. But he remembered his English Literature lessons at school and the ability of the teacher to dissect every sentence of Hamlet and find hidden meaning, aided by a library of scholarly studies from esteemed academics who quite often disagreed anyway. Shakespeare probably just wrote each sentence as he thought of it and made some of the language quite obscure so that if there was hidden meaning in there, that was a lucky coincidence that would provide gainful employment for literary intellectuals for years to come.

Tim decided that whichever way the writing took him, he would continue at this pace, and if he ended up producing a book that was too long, so be it. All he had to do was write his way out of the corners he kept writing himself into.

It had just started raining outside and the gentle rhythmic patter was more suited to writing, he realised, than the less regular strains of an orchestra. Not that they were straining as they played, of course, but..... no, come on, getting sidetracked again. Concentrate....

Back at his lodgings that night Marlo sat in his room and talked over the situation with Lillian. It seemed as though the huge prize ahead of them was attached to a rope which someone kept sadistically jerking away from them just as they thought they had made a significant step forward and could almost reach it.

Yet they couldn't think of any better plan than the one George had diverted them on to, so Marlo was faced with no other options than to find out who Walter's debtors were. Marching into his office and asking to see the records wouldn't cut it. There was only one way – follow him again and see where he called on his rounds. Then hope that one of his sorry customers will help.

If Marlo had to chase after that horse and trap again it would not be easy, so Lillian suggested acquiring a 'safety bicycle'. This turned out to be a recently invented type of bicycle, plain and simple and much more like today's design, but so named as it was safer to ride than the large wheel / small wheel penny farthing. Marlo had seen a few of them amongst the larger machines, but with their solid rim tyres and judging by the grim, stoic expressions of the riders, they really did look uncomfortable and extremely bumpy, so he suggested trying to follow Walter by foot initially and if that failed then he would look at using two wheels.

So it was that early the next morning, with the town waking up to a grey, damp overcoat of dreariness for which Britain is famed, that Marlo found himself loitering in a doorway about a hundred yards up the road from Walter's office, shivering slightly in the early chill due to his having dressed sparingly, on the basis that he might be doing a fair bit of light jogging very shortly and didn't want to overheat. A light misty drizzle had now started, depositing glistening fields of little droplets on his jacket. A few men passed by, most in rough clothes and caps, head nestled down in their scarves, walking purposefully to work, many of them no doubt preparing to toil for long hours of manual labour in conditions that the authorities of modern times would condemn and shut down immediately. Some glanced curiously and slightly unnervingly at him as they went, suspicious of a stranger just standing there but perhaps just miserable with their lot and wondering why Marlo wasn't doing anything except hiding in an alcove. But as far as Marlo was concerned, he had a job, a very important one.

He peered round the doorway again, not wanting to miss his man. He had seen Walter arrive about ten minutes ago and heard the bell tinkle in the distance as the door slammed with a force that he suspected was not strictly necessary. Unfortunately for Marlo his target had indeed arrived with the cart, and tied the horse up outside. Marlo shook his legs a little to keep himself loose and prepared for some exercise.

But when the door tinkled and Walter emerged a few minutes later with a case in his hand, Marlo saw him take a brief look up and down the street, turn up his coat collar to keep his neck dry, and set off on foot in the opposite direction to Marlo, walking straight past the horse and cart.

"Target sighted!" Marlo whispered to Lillian, "and he's going on foot, thank God, he must have a local appointment. I'm following him now."

"Good, but keep well back. We don't want him to see you."

"I was planning to catch up and walk beside him, actually," Marlo said before he could stop himself, realising too late that his amusing sarcasms normally ended up being mis-interpreted as rudeness by those not on his wavelength or who he had not got to know well enough. He tried to redeem himself. "Sorry, I was just joking. It maybe didn't come out sounding too funny though. Sorry."

"No, but then I suppose I was stating the obvious. I just don't want you to be hurt." Marlo breathed again; Lillian had taken it better than most, but it was still a mistake to say it. You have to know someone for more than just a few days before mocking them, he scolded himself, even in jest. Why did he keep doing that, he was such an idiot. "Thanks," he said.

Walter had now turned the right-hand corner at the end of the street, into Montpelier Road. Marlo hurried forward, not wanting to lose him. It was all very well keeping your distance but then every corner becomes a risk. The spits of misty rain bit into his face as he scurried forward against the wind and reached the junction with Clifton Place. Peering round the edge of the building he was relieved to see the large figure of Walter striding down the near pavement towards a resplendently large structure that looked like a temple, which kept guard over the junction with Victoria Road.

Marlo was just about to emerge when Walter suddenly looked round. Marlo instinctively ducked back behind the wall. Damn, he thought, he's seen me. Perhaps he didn't though. Maybe he just wanted to cross the road and was checking all was clear. Slowly he eased his head round the corner again. There was Walter, further away, but now on the other side of the road. That was all it was then, he was ok. His heartbeat now recovering, he walked into the road and continued down the near side, keeping watch from afar but walking quickly to reduce the gap back to a sensible distance.

Lillian had heard Marlo utter a startled swear word under his breath when he thought he had been spotted and had hissed "What? What's happened?" Now he could answer her.

"It's alright, I'd thought he had seen me but he was just looking back so he could cross the road. I had to duck back."

"Even if he does spot you, he doesn't know who you are does he? He wouldn't recognise you from the cliff top, surely? So it doesn't matter really, as long as he doesn't see you trailing him every time he looks round."

Marlo felt a bit stupid. He doubted that the best secret agents evaded detection and blended into their backgrounds by peering round corners and guiltily ducking back every few minutes when the target looked round.

"Well, yes, that's a fair point, but I would rather he doesn't see me at all - less risk."

"But if he sees you acting suspiciously...."

"I know, I know. This 'following a suspect' business is harder than it looks."

Walter reached the junction and turned left into Victoria Road. Marlo upped his pace a little and crossed the road. The fine dampness in the air was easing off a little now, which was good; he wouldn't have to keep wiping his glasses.

This time he turned the corner without peeking round, acting as though he was heading off for work like everyone else. It would have looked odd anyway, as there were more people around now, so he did not want to draw attention to himself.

As he entered Victoria Road he thought for a moment that he had lost him, but then saw Walter emerging from behind a parked cart on the other side of the road – he must have crossed over as soon as he turned the corner.

Walter reached the junction with Powis Road and stopped, looking left and right as though getting his bearings. Marlo slowed his pace right down, not wanting to get too close, and fell in behind a group of three labourers who were joshing and jostling with each other and so not moving very quickly. Up ahead, Walter turned right and disappeared up Powis Road.

As Marlo reached the same junction and turned the corner, his heart leapt into his mouth as he saw a now stationary Walter just fifty yards ahead, taking a sheet of paper from his case. This time Marlo had no option but to instinctively veer back to his left in order to cross the road and resume a straight line across the junction, heading back into Victoria Road. Walter was side-on to him and concentrating on his piece of paper so hopefully he wouldn't have noticed anything amiss.

Playing it safe and once out of sight, Marlo crossed to the other side of Victoria Road and came back the other way to re-cross the junction on the far side, glancing up Powis Road as he did so. Through the traffic he could see Walter still standing there examining what was probably an address, looking around briefly, then quickly putting the paper away and striding down a side road.

As soon as he was gone, Marlo jogged back across the junction and into Powis Road again. He couldn't afford to lose him now. He reached the side road – the road sign said Powis Grove. He was just in time to see Walter turn off the pavement into a side alley or footpath about seventy yards ahead.

Quickly he reached the narrow alley, the entrance of which adjoined a house fronted by a hedge above a low brick wall. He stopped at the end of the hedge and peered round the corner. His eyes met those of Walter, standing less than four feet away, staring back at him.

"Oh! Sorry!" mumbled Marlo, backing away as a slow horror enveloped him.

"Not so fast," said Walter, stepping forward and grabbing Marlo by the arm, then dragging him back off the street. It was quiet here, off the beaten track. Either side of the passageway were the solid brick and windowless side walls of houses, and he could see that further down it led to a gate, possibly a back garden or allotment.

Marlo realised now that Walter had known he was being followed and had been deliberately leading him to this trap.

With one easy movement Walter twisted Marlo round and pushed him robustly up against the wall, his large saturnine head leaning forward and glowering over him. Marlo was immediately petrified; he knew that this man killed people.

There was a penny sized stain the colour of weak tea on Walters's collar and Marlo found himself focusing on that in order to avoid looking directly at him. The voice was deep, rough, and laced with threat, the breath sharp and acrid. "Care to explain why you have been following me?"

"I wasn't," was all Marlo could think of to say, sounding too much like a defiantly naughty child. But as this denial was demonstrably untrue he realised that he would have to think of something else quickly. His mind raced, simultaneously realising that he still had Jed's whittling knife in his jacket pocket, but that if he tried to get it out Walter would probably just grab it off him and use it on him instead.

"Ah, I see. You weren't," growled Walter, his odorous breath now far too close to Marlo's face. "Well that explains everything. So that wasn't you running after my cart yesterday morning, then walking past my office first one way and then the other? Oh yes, I could see you out in the street about to ring the bell. It is easier looking out than looking in you know."

He smiled humourlessly, clearly enjoying the feeling of superiority. "And that wasn't you peering around a doorway as I came out of the office this morning, and then following me all the way to this alley? And this isn't you that I have pinned up against a wall in front of me? Because that is the person that needs to give me some answers, but if it isn't you then of course I will immediately let you go."

Now that was sarcasm at its finest. Marlo could hear Lillian repeating 'oh my gosh, oh my gosh' in a frightened whimper in his head. It possibly wasn't helping. He had to think of something, quick. His breaths were short not just from panic but from the force with which Walter had him pressed against the wall.

"Alright, alright! You win. Yes, I was following you."

The sudden admission appeared to take Walter a little by surprise. He relaxed his grip and the whole of Marlo's shoes touched the ground again. In his head, Lillian was crying "No, Marlo, don't admit it! He'll kill you!" and Marlo felt sure that Walter would be able to hear her.

But Walter simply moved his head even closer to Marlo's so that their noses almost touched and hissed "Why?"

"I was under instruction." Marlo was aware that the voice coming out of his mouth was not that of a film hero who would be able to growl manfully and articulately even when being throttled, but instead that of a fourteen year old boy having his private parts squeezed. However hard he tried, he sounded as petrified as he was feeling and of course he knew that this would just further strengthen the superior power dynamic of his aggressor.

"What are you talking about," spat Walter. Lillian was just crying uncontrollably now, the emotion of hearing Walter's voice again, the awful memories bursting back, and the situation Marlo was in and how Walter was talking to him; it was too much for her.

Marlo was, for the first time, trying to ignore Lillian. His brain was working furiously, formulating a story as he went, thinking of films he had seen for inspiration. "I'm working for my uncle."

He paused, not for effect but to give him time to come up with something plausible about this uncle he had now invented.

Walter re-tightened his grip. "And....?" He was like a wolf, homing in on its prey.

"....and.... he's a rich man. So he's got some enemies, people trying to get his money off him, you know?"

He had had a thought, a story that might work. He took a gulp of air, talking more quickly now.

"So in the early days he was a bit naive, leant some of them money, often large sums for what they told him were guaranteed get-rich-quick schemes which would bring huge returns for everyone. Some did, but a few didn't, and where they didn't he's still owed money. A lot of money actually. And he's lost patience. If he trusts you, he's good to you, but if you break that trust, he doesn't forget. And now with those people who tricked him and now avoid him, he's reached the end of his tether. So now he's angry and, well, you wouldn't like him when he's angry."

Marlo glanced at Walter's eyes and was almost surprised to see him not register the provenance of that particular phrase even though he knew he wouldn't. Ironic that Walter was a hulk of a man himself. He continued.

"He can be ruthless. But he's clever too, doesn't like involving the authorities in his business but also doesn't like getting his hands dirty. So he said to me, 'Find me the best debt collector there is. An enforcer, you know? Someone who knows how to get money back off people. Someone who doesn't take prisoners'. And I heard on the grapevine about you."

Marlo could see his assailant processing this information, debating whether or not to believe him but no doubt also mildly pleased that his reputation had spread.

Walter drew his head back a little. "So why, then," he said in a slightly less pugnacious tone, "didn't you just walk into my office and ask for me?"

It was a good question. Think, Marlo, think. "My uncle.......doesn't do business like that." Ah man, that was lame. Now what? How does he do business then?   Ah right, yes, of course, got it..... "He knew that you would just sing your own praises wouldn't you? So he wanted to get the picture from the people you dealt with, understand your methods and how they felt about dealing with you. How frightened they were, how likely they would do as you requested. Some customer research, if you like."

Walter released his grasp of Marlo's jacket. "Go on."

"As I said, he told me to find some of your debtors and talk to them. I couldn't just walk into your office and ask for their names, could I, so my only chance was to follow you and see who you visited, then once you had gone I would knock on their door and talk to them. Then I would report back to my uncle."

"Who is this uncle of yours?"

Marlo was warming to his theme now. "I'm under strict instruction that he should remain anonymous and all communication should be through me. He doesn't want anyone finding out what he is doing. Element of surprise, you see."

Walter nodded thoughtfully, cautiously taking it all in as one would when perusing a menu. "How many debtors are we talking about? And how much money do they owe?"

This was good. They were talking business now. The focus had changed, and Marlo had to keep it this way.

"I think five. Perhaps six. But a lot of money involved. He doesn't tell me everything. He doesn't tell anyone everything. That's why he is successful." The short sentences were giving Marlo time to think between each one.

"What business is he in that makes him so successful?" Walter's aggressive impatience was morphing into tentative interest.

Marlo took a risk. "He doesn't want you knowing that."

Fortunately this had the opposite effect to that which Marlo feared. Walter stood back, one eyebrow raised. Rather than being angry he seemed impressed by how this fictitious uncle operated. The picture Marlo was painting was of a person Marlo suspected Walter might aspire to himself.

"You're not from round here are you?" Walter suddenly changed tack. "You have a funny way of talking."

"No, that's right. I'm from a little village near Salisbury. People often say we speak a bit oddly, it's a local dialect."

Thankfully this seemed to satisfy the bigger man. He bent down to pick up the case that he had put down against the wall when preparing to apprehend Marlo and drew himself up to his full height. He was certainly built for scaring people.

"So what happens now?" he asked, ceding the initiative to Marlo.

Marlo smiled, trying to appear relaxed despite knowing that he only had to say one stupid thing and his achievement in talking himself out of a life or death situation could be for nothing.

"My uncle is not going to be happy that you've caught me out. Then again, perhaps that would convince him that you are the man for the job. You outwitted me - that must count for something."

Marlo could see the flattery was working, but Walter's satisfied slow nods were less about being grateful for the compliment, more that it was being confirmed to him what he already knew. Marlo had an overwhelming sense that here was a man who was full of himself, not a shred of self doubt. The very opposite of Marlo, in fact. It was another reason not to like this brute, as if he did not have enough of them already.

"I could ask you for some names, of course, and visit them as I had planned, but you could get there first and put the frighteners on them."

"The what?"

"Frighteners. Er, frighten them basically."

"Well I guessed that but it's a daft way of saying it. Its true of course, I could pay them a special visit before you get there. But I don't need to."

"But you might. My uncle wouldn't want to risk that. In any case, I don't think there would be any point now. I've seen at first hand how you can threaten people and it was very effective, I can tell you."

"Oh, you've seen nothing, believe me." Walter's response was suitably chilling.

Marlo didn't want Walter providing any more details about his ability to threaten people until there were some witnesses around so he didn't dwell on Walter's response. "Well, yes, I'm sure. But from my perspective at least you've passed that test. So I'm going to suggest to my uncle that we move straight on to stage two."

He knew the original plan of teaming up with a debtor in order to catch Walter was now dead, so he needed an alternative. And one had suddenly popped into his head, courtesy of his newly acquired non-existent uncle. All he had to do was steer Walter into the trap. First the carrot.....

"By the way, there's also the matter of payment. What are your fees, your commission rates?"

"That depends."

"On what?"

"The amount to be collected, the type of customer, the number of visits, that kind of thing. I have a partner, Mr Carberry, he normally deals with all the details and the...." Walter paused himself, suddenly realising what he was saying. He resumed quickly "But for this job, where maybe a more personal service is required, and depending on the fee, I would be the only contact. I will need all the details though."

He thinks he's being clever by deceiving his partner, thought Marlo, but all he is doing is digging himself nicely into the hole that would become his grave. There was only one person doing the outwitting now, and it wasn't Walter.

"I think we can kill two birds with one stone," he announced brightly. "I can arrange for you to meet my uncle so he can assess you directly and ask all the questions he needs to. He would remain incognito though, you understand. And at the same time you can discuss fees directly without going through a middleman. Yes, I think that makes much more sense."

Making a contact as successful as this rich uncle seemed to Walter like a wise move. Not only could he get himself a nice piece of business which he wouldn't have to split with Carberry, but it might lead to further work. And if this uncle was as angry with the debtors as was being described, he might even encourage a little rough treatment and let Walter engage in a few 'questionable' interrogation and fund retrieval techniques. That would get the juices flowing. He needed something to stimulate him after the excitement of dispatching his previous four victims. It was a habit that needed feeding. The incompetent and frankly pathetic squirt in front of him, who had made such a pig's ear of following him, was lucky; he had been looking forward to meting out a bit of punishment and leaving him in a heap in this alley. But circumstances had changed. An opportunity had to be taken.

"Alright," he said slowly, careful not to look too eager, "when and where?"

"I will have to speak to my uncle first, then get back to you. Should I call at your office?"

"Yes. Actually no, best to keep this private between us. I assume you trailed me from my house the other day so know where I live?"

Marlo felt guilty as he replied simply "yes."

A large frown appeared on Walter's brow. "How did you find out?"

Marlo immediately realised that he could not mention Frederick or Lillian's family so would have to think of something else quickly. He paused, giving the impression that he was debating whether or not to reveal his source. Then, giving a deliberate 'ok, so what?' face, he said "Once I had your name, I asked my uncle to help find out where you lived. I don't know how he found out, but he has people that find things out for him. He told me."

Walter looked him in the eye, looking for signs of an untruth, but Marlo didn't look away and held his gaze, more confident now.

To Marlo's relief Walter relented, moving the conversation on. "Right. When you have the details, knock on my door. If I am not in, leave a note. I will need to get back to you though. What is your address?"

Lillian instinctively cried out "No, don't tell him." Marlo agreed, the last thing he wanted was to worry that Walter might turn up at his lodgings at any time of the night or day. Quick, think of something....

"I live.... with my uncle," he lied, "so all the details will be in the letter I give you once I have agreed the details with him."

This seemed to satisfy Walter, despite the fact that Marlo seemed to be pinning every one of his answers to the uncle who didn't exist. "Very well. It was unfortunate that our meeting got off to a less than cordial start." He didn't look or sound very sorry about that but Marlo didn't care.

"My fault." Marlo held up his hands. "I shouldn't have put myself in that situation. But at least we have put everything straight now." He just wanted to get out of there now; his heart felt as though it was beating faster than an electric toothbrush.

He pulled his jacket back into position and stepped past Walter and quickly back out into Powis Grove, still worried that Walter would suddenly see through his story, grab him again, and give him a demonstration of how fists can break faces. Even out on the street, though, there was no-one about, so he still wasn't entirely safe.

Walter slowly followed him back onto the road, turned to face him, and to Marlo's surprise grabbed and shook his hand, the unnecessarily firm grip almost breaking his fingers. It was another alpha-male signal, as if he had not already exerted enough dominance for one meeting.

"I shall wait to hear from you then. Good day." And with that he turned and headed off up the road, presumably to visit the client on his piece of paper.

"Good day," replied Marlo and immediately turned in the other direction and started heading as fast as he could walk back into the more populated Powis Road.

"Wait!" Walter's voice boomed up the street. Marlo jumped internally, a combination of surprise and fear. Has he just rumbled me? He fleetingly debated whether or not to run but instead turned slowly to see Walter striding back towards him. He flinched, waiting for the first blow.

"Your name. I never asked your name."

It was a request, not a statement, but in his relief that it was not a physical assault, he didn't even think before replying "Marlo Campbell."

"Marlo? Right. Strange fellow, strange name. Makes sense." And without further ado Walter turned on his heel and strode off again.

It was only when Marlo had turned three or four corners and was amongst pedestrians again that he could start to relax and realise just how close he had come to disaster. It was a feeling he never wanted to have again.

CHAPTER 46 : THE POST MORTEM

"Has he gone?" Lillian asked, as Marlo manoeuvred himself around a couple of ladies wheeling two prams side by side on the pavement and hurried forward in any direction but the one he had just come from. He waited until he was out of earshot before replying.

"Marlo?"

"Yes, sorry. Just moving out of earshot. I'm still shaking."

"So am I. But Marlo, you were magnificent. I thought you were doomed, and me with you, but you talked your way out of it. How did you do that? It was brilliant. I'm so proud of you."

It was almost worth what Marlo had just gone through to hear what Lillian had just said. Almost. He had never had a girl praise him like that before, let alone one he had designs on. It was a really, really nice feeling. Maybe he wasn't always a loser after all. Maybe somewhere inside he did have qualities that others would appreciate. He perked up.

"Thank you," he replied a little inadequately.

"I was no use at all, I was just a blubbering nervous wreck. As soon as I heard that voice... it was such a shock."

"That's hardly surprising after what he did to you, so don't worry about that. I was just lucky, I guess, that something plausible popped into my head and Walter swallowed it. Oh my god, that was not fun, not fun at all."

"The way you built the story, though, all that stuff about the rich uncle. So clever! And under pressure like that too. I would never have been able to do that."

"I didn't think I could either. But thank you for your compliments, that's....er.... really nice. Sorry, I'm not used to receiving them so I don't really know what to say."

Marlo was as usual making a mess of any conversation that involved even the smallest hint of a discussion about himself, his least favourite subject. Yet Lillian really did sound proud of what he had done, and that was great. But rather than agree wholeheartedly that he had played a blinder and deserved all the praise that could be poured over him, Marlo's innate insistence on self-depreciation, bolstered by the fact of

372

birth that he was resolutely it-was-nothing-old-chap British, meant that he wasn't really taking full advantage of the opportunity to bask in some well earned glory. But wasn't it better to be modest? Tell that to a peacock fanning its tail. Sometimes when you are trying to impress someone maybe that tail needs to come out. Cash in while you can. It was too late now anyway, Lillian was moving the conversation on.

"Don't worry, I won't give you any more compliments! I won't forget that though. Anyway, we'll need to do some more thinking now, though, like for example where you are going to find an imaginary uncle?"

Marlo was on more solid ground now. "Exactly. Very good question. And we still need a location, somewhere private to meet Walter and extract his confession."

"Gosh," said Lillian, "every time we make progress our goal seems further away. It's odd how this is working out, isn't it?"

Marlo kicked a small stone back into the road as he walked. "Yup, sure is. I suppose one way to look at it though is that the further you are away from something you want, the more you want it." He knew only too well how this felt.

Lillian made the kind of approval noise one makes when tasting a good wine. "I like that! Yes, the harder it becomes, the more we re-double our efforts because we want it even more. A good way to look at it. I like your positive thinking."

Marlo hadn't really meant it like that but he wasn't going to sacrifice a brownie point for no reason. "Exactly. We are hungrier for success than ever now. I think I need to sit down first though."

He found himself walking north, heading towards the Seven Dials junction. On his left was a nursery with greenhouses and squares of land sprouting roses, small bushes and other ornamental foliage. To his right was a sweeping crescent of grand Georgian three storey houses, uniformly white and with stone pillar gateposts that imposingly announced 'wealth lives here'. So different to the slum houses not too many streets away.

A small half-moon shaped park shielded the affluent occupants from the main thoroughfare, and there he found a bench and flopped down with a sigh, in the way that older people do.

He surveyed the bush opposite. "We ought to have a secret code, you know," he said suddenly.

"What? Why?" Lillian wasn't expecting that.

"I was just thinking – I couldn't converse with you while I was in that situation with Walter. You couldn't get a response to any questions and I couldn't give you any signals as to what was going on apart from what you could hear."

"Well, yes, but that's just how it is. Isn't it? We just have to live with that."

"What if I click my teeth once for yes and twice for no? Like I'm making a clip-clop horse noise, like this." He demonstrated, simplifying to a clip without the clop, as though now attracting his metaphorical horse to a handful of sugar lumps.

"Won't people think there's something wrong with you if you suddenly start clicking in front of them?"

"Nervous tic? Or should I say nervous click. I don't know, it was just a thought. But if I am in a tight spot and need you to help without giving the game away, better I sound mad than not be able to communicate at all."

"Alright! You've convinced me. Once for yes, twice for no. Maybe three times for 'any ideas Lillian?' if you need some help. Oh, and four for 'I can't talk right now'."

"I'm going to sound like a Swahili tribesman if I'm not careful. It might be academic if we don't need it but I thought it would be good to have it in our toolbox."

"Fine! Now, we need to discuss your Uncle Whatshisname. He ought to have a name really. How about....um..... Sampson Borthwell?"

"Where did that come from?"

"Oh I just put two names together from some of the wealthier clients we used to have. Another combination could be, er... Edmund Philpott."

Marlo weighed them up briefly. "I think I prefer Sampson Borthwell. It has a ring to it. Uncle Sampson. Yes, that will do. Right, it is all very well naming him but he doesn't exist. Where are we going to find my Uncle Sampson?"

"The problem is, he can't be you with a disguise, or George, or Frederick. All too young – the voices would give it away. Unless he talked through an intermediary, but that would be silly. It isn't as though he is foreign or something. No, you'll need to find someone who can act the part."

"I don't know anyone." Marlo felt useless. It seemed as though his clever plan was already collapsing around him.

"But you do know people who know people," Lillian reminded him. "Speak to Freddie. He moves in higher circles now. His employer Mr Plundell is on the council, he can pull lots of strings and knows plenty of older men."

"Ooh matron!" Marlo responded automatically, quickly realising that this would mean absolutely nothing to Lillian and deciding not to try and explain Carry On films to her. "Ignore me, sorry, that was just a modern cultural reference to what you said but... so, yes, he might be able to help."

Lillian remained oblivious to any unintended double-entendre. "Yes, but whoever he found would have to be up for acting the part. That won't be easy. I think the thing to do is speak to Freddie. And George of course. One of them might also be able to suggest a venue for this meeting with Walter."

"Yep, agreed, that sounds the best option. I'll head off to find your brother in a minute, then George this evening. Man, it's such a pain not having a phone!"

CHAPTER 47 : THE THREE MUSKETEERS

It was Wednesday evening, the day after Marlo's brush with Walter. Marlo, Frederick and George were meeting together for the first time and were hunched around a jug of beer over a rough wooden table in the corner of Mrs Sapworthy's beer house, George's local. Not that it was called Mrs Sapworthy's Beer House – the faded sign over the door declared that it was simply 'Western Ale House', in deference presumably to the name of the road it was in rather than any association to cowboys or ales from the west country.

This was not the elegant Victorian pub that Marlo had been anticipating. There was no mahogany bar with intricately carved surrounds, stained glass inserts and oval mirrors. There were no private booths, not even any chairs. This was one big, open, noisy, smoky room with an uneven wood plank floor and a big open fireplace on one side of the room.

Wooden tables were laid around the edges of the room, with empty beer barrels replacing legs where this had become necessary. Punters sat on uncomfortable wooden benches or stools with no back to them; those without tables just stood around in groups in the middle.

In one corner a booth had been constructed next to a door to the next room, from which jugs of beer, and not much else it seemed apart from the strange mix of pewter tankards, china mugs and pint glasses to drink it from, were being dispensed.

Mrs Sapworthy was the custodian, stout and shiny-faced, keeping order and barking orders at her two assistants who were collecting glasses and replenishing supplies. It appeared chaotic but she seemed to be in control.

The whole place looked as though someone had just converted their front two rooms into an open space, but it served beer and that seemed to be all that mattered.

Frederick looked a little uncomfortable, having in the last few years become more used to establishments that provided a slightly more welcoming environment, and feeling perhaps a trifle overdressed in his breeches and mustard coloured corduroy jacket.

The three acquaintances had managed to secure a small table in the corner and so had at least a modicum of privacy. George and Frederick had completed all the formalities of a first introduction and the three of them were getting down to business. The general noise of raucous background conversation ensured that, provided they didn't shout, their conversation would not be overheard.

"What did Mr Plundell say?" George was asking Frederick.

Frederick put down his mug and wiped some foam from his lip. "Well, good news, gentlemen, I hope. He knows someone who might fit the bill precisely."

Marlo had caught up with Frederick yesterday, shortly before lunchtime, and brought him up to speed with what had happened earlier that morning in that alley. The way that Walter had conducted himself during that interaction with Marlo had convinced Frederick even more that the man was a wrong 'un, and he had readily acquiesced to bringing Mr Plundell into play. They had agreed that there was no reason to hide anything from his employer as they would need his full confidence, and Frederick was confident that this would not be a problem. Now it seemed that he was right.

"Who?" Marlo asked the obvious question which Frederick was theatrically waiting for.

Frederick milked the moment, knowing he was about to drop a nugget of gold into a prospector's pan, and looked slowly at each man in turn before revealing "The assistant town coroner."

Marlo and George looked at each other and in unison looked back at Frederick. "You're joking!" declared Marlo. "Aren't you?"

"Absolutely not!" Frederick sat there with a large grin and with arms folded, delighted to take credit for his employer's help. "He's really keen on amateur dramatics, apparently. Mr Plundell suggests he would be up for anything that involves a bit of acting, and especially if there is a connection with his job."

"Even if there is danger involved?" George did not seem convinced.

Frederick's smile dropped a little. "Well, yes, I agree that is the one small possible hiccup. He has to be willing to do it. However...." his smile returned, "more good news. Given that it is my beloved sister that we are talking about, my employer has very kindly agreed to donate a small sum as a reward should this venture lead to the successful prosecution of this man. That can be the carrot that we offer to Mr Babington."

"That's his name then," asked George slightly unnecessarily.

"Yes, Ezra Babington. He is in his fifties so he sounds ideal."

Marlo patted Frederick on the back awkwardly, something he immediately realised he had no experience of doing so it felt all wrong. "Well done Frederick, you've played a blinder there. What a result. Well, once he has agreed to do it, of course."

Frederick appeared pleased yet at the same time confused. "Played a what? What's a blinder? I thought it was one of those street robbers who blind you to rob you. You have some very odd phrases, Mr Campbell."

"Sorry, yes, where I come from it just means you have done a great job. Which you have." Quickly he changed tack. "So when will we know if Mr Babington is up for it?"

"Tomorrow I hope. My employer has a function tonight and Babington will be there. But Mr Plundell assured me he would be very surprised if he refuses."

"Brilliant. Things are moving now. Ok, what about a venue. We need somewhere to meet Walter, an office or something ideally. For this kind of meeting it wouldn't look right if we all met up in someone's front room."

"And it needs hiding places," interjected George. "Good ones, too, where I won't be found. Or you, Frederick, of course," he added hastily.

Frederick nodded. "Mr Plundell will discuss that with Mr Babington. Between, them, I am sure they can come up with something."

A thought occurred to George. "If you have the coroner involved, you won't need me then!" he said brightly to Marlo.

"Oh, we will, George. We still need you. The more witnesses the better, and also, if anything does happen to Mr Babington – not that it will of course – then even more so."

"You think Threadwell could kill Mr Babington?" George looked horrified.

Marlo backtracked a little. "Not really, no. I'm just trying to cover all eventualities."

They looked up as someone started shouting at the far end of the room. A minor altercation was kicking off, possibly caused by someone barging in through the front door and knocking into a man drinking with his mates. "Oy, watch what you're doing, will ya?" was followed by "well don't stand so close to the door then, you bufflehead...." at which point the pushing started and others started to intervene to separate the pair.

As the excitement calmed down, Frederick smiled ruefully. "That reminds me of a little incident I had once," he confided, "except it was me spilling a drink on someone else! Ended up in a scrap on the floor and I knocked him clean out! Big chap too. Now I come to think of it....." A slow realisation of horror spread across his face. "Wait....no, no, no! It can't be! No!"

George and Marlo looked at each other, more than slightly alarmed. "What is it Frederick? What's the matter?" asked Marlo.

Frederick's shock at what he had just realised was now subsiding into incredulity and grief. He slumped forward and held his head in his hands, elbows on the table, and started sobbing. "I don't believe it," he mumbled between sniffs, "it was him. I knew I'd seen him before. It was Threadwell. He was the fellow I hit."

He looked up suddenly at his two companions, a new anger in his eyes. "It was revenge. Revenge, that's what it was, pure and simple. That monster took the life of my sister to get back at me. I'll kill him. I'll kill him!"

As his voice raised people looked round. "Perhaps not quite so loud, eh?" George tried to impart the advice in a consoling tone.

"Sorry, I just....." Frederick had started shaking now as he tried to control the rage and anguish coursing through him, his fists clenched white and pressing down hard on the table.

Lillian had let out a short gasp when her brother realised who it was he had punched all those months ago. But as the three men each wondered what to say next, Marlo heard the girl in his head tearfully spit out words so filled with hatred that he was a little taken aback.

"So.... that miserable, evil wretch, that devil on earth, killed me not because of anything that I had done, but just to get his own back on Freddie? *To settle a score?* So to him I meant nothing, I was just a means to an end, nothing more than that. I had no value. Marlo, promise me that you will catch him and make him suffer. Really suffer. As long as we get that confession, what happens to him after that.... well, I don't care."

Marlo softly clicked his teeth once. It was once for yes wasn't it? He hoped he hadn't just said no. But what Lillian had said made him think what she was probably realising too – if they could get a confession out of Walter in front of someone representing the coroner, that surely fulfils the requirement that the true cause of death should be known and documented by officialdom. Then what happened to Walter after that... well, that was up for debate. He looked at Frederick.

"I'm so sorry," he said. George nodded, both of them unsure what to say next.

Frederick continued to stare down at the table. He rubbed his eyes but they were already red and there were tear streaks on his face. "It was my fault, Marlo. If I hadn't hit him, Lill would still be here today. It's my fault!"

Lillian was straight into Marlo's head: "No! No! Definitely not! Tell Freddie, Marlo. Tell him it's nothing to do with him, I don't want him feeling guilty for this. Tell him!"

Marlo grabbed one of Frederick's arms and held onto it to keep his attention. "What would Lillian be saying to you now, Frederick? Would she be blaming you? Would she?"

He knew the answer of course but it prompted Frederick to look up. "Well, no, she wouldn't. I know that. But that doesn't mean I don't feel responsible."

George butted in. "But Frederick, that is exactly how Threadwell wants you to feel, don't you see? If you blame yourself, he is winning. There's only one culpable person here, and that is Walter Threadwell. You are not in any way responsible, you must accept that."

Frederick nodded weakly but did not appear convinced.

"He's playing on you feeling guilty, that is part of his revenge," chipped in Marlo. "But there's only one person who is guilty of anything, and that is him. And now we are going to do something about it."

They all nodded solemnly but a silence ensued as they each mulled over the implications of Frederick's revelation. No-one was drinking now.

George broke the silence. "I hate to say this......." he spoke softly and carefully "...but, we still don't actually know, for certain, that he did it. I mean, it's clear to us that he did, but we've no proof, have we?"

Marlo was torn. He of course knew that Walter did it, but he couldn't say so and give away the reason he knew. He also didn't want any vigilante style revenge until Walter had confessed, otherwise the true cause of Lillian's death would be taken to the grave with Walter, thereby ending Lillian's life, and his own, at the same time. It would be a catastrophic conclusion. They just had to get that confession out of Walter.

Frederick suddenly straightened up. There was a new steely resolution about him. "We don't need proof. No-one else could have done it. He was the only one there at the time of her death. He had a motive. We also now know he's a thug and intimidates people for a living. What more evidence do you need? We need to catch him and kill him."

"Catch him, yes. Kill him, no. The state must do that." Marlo couldn't let Frederick's emotions drive the argument. "If you or any of us kills him and ends up getting the punishment that Walter should have got, how is that going to help? How would your parents feel, losing not just one child but two?"

The reminder of his parents was enough to throw a handful of sand over the embers of righteous defiance that had been starting to spark and burn inside Frederick.

"You're right," he conceded with a sigh, "that would devastate them. I can't put them through it all over again. But, let me tell you, that man will pay for what he has done. Make no mistake."

Marlo nodded – he certainly wasn't going to disagree with that. But his overwhelming emotion was that of relief that Frederick had agreed not to take matters into his own hands, and he heard Lillian whisper a 'well done' to confirm that, unsurprisingly, she felt the same.

"Threadwell missed a trick, you know," George said suddenly.

Marlo and Frederick looked up at him in surprise.

"Well, why didn't he just claim that the other fellow who was killed up on that cliff was the one that murdered Lillian, then Walter stepped in and killed the man in self-defence? Or something like that? That might have been an easier story to believe."

"The police said that the other man was small and old, and Monday's paper said he was a harmless drifter who lived down by the beach," said Frederick, "so I think the police would have had a hard time believing that he would have randomly tried to kill two people, one of whom was a man twice his size, for no reason."

"Well, yes, when you put it like that......." conceded George.

Marlo felt it was time to bring the evening to a close. "Gents, I think we should reconvene once Mr Plundell has got Mr Babington on side, and they have hopefully come up with a venue for us too. Frederick, shall I call at your place tomorrow evening?" He finger-and-thumbed into his top jacket pocket and brought out the business card with the addresses on it.

Frederick glanced at the card. "Yes, that is probably best. You know where I am. Then we can meet up again, although I would suggest we will need to involve Mr Babington this time. His role in this is crucial and the plan needs to be watertight. Actually, I'll need time to arrange for us to meet him. It's Wednesday now, so how about you call round on Friday evening? Hopefully I will have everything in place by then."

The thought of two more days doing nothing, two more days that he was away from getting back home with Lillian, caused Marlo's heart to sink a bit, but he knew he had no choice. It had to be done properly.

"Alright," he said, "then after that on my way home I'll call in on you, George. You'll be in?"

"Yes, I should be. Remember I work on Saturday though. And of course we have church on Sunday morning."

"Of course," said Marlo, keeping his thoughts to himself.

They scraped back their wooden benches and walked slowly out of the ale house in a sombre mood not normally associated with this kind of establishment. As they parted, Marlo felt it prudent to remind George "Not a word of this to anyone, George? Even your own family. No-one else must know what we are doing."

George did not need the advice. "I don't look as stupid as I am, Marlo. No, that's not right, I meant, I'm not as stupid as I look. Is that it? Anyway, the point being, I'm not stupid, although based on what I just said you could be forgiven for thinking it I suppose. If my parents knew I was involved in something like this they would try to stop me. You can rest assured that I won't be telling them anything."

Marlo smiled. "Good, and point taken. Probably a good thing that you stopped drinking when you did though."

George shoved him in the side, purely to unbalance him. "Careful what you say, Mr Campbell. I'm not as weak as I look either."

Frederick joined in, trying to raise his own spirits a little. "So now you look weak as well as stupid? You must be a real hit with the ladies, my friend."

George realised he had not only been digging himself a hole but had then handed the spade to his friends, so metaphorically took it back. "Enough with your joshing, please gentlemen! I fear the ale is talking for all of us at the moment. Perhaps our focus should be returned to the task ahead of us?"

There was a new reason for George's commitment to the cause. He had quietly noted Frederick's announcement that Mr Plundell was putting forward a reward for anyone involved in bringing Walter to justice, and although not knowing how much this would be, had just realised that this presented an opportunity to avail himself of a part of it. The more he helped, the greater his claim. And after all, he was sure Mr Babington was in far less financial penury than he was and that any split of the money might favour he who most needed it.

Humour was a release but it could only be temporary, and Marlo and Frederick could not disagree with George's request. So after a few less personal pleasantries, the three men each headed off in different directions, each lost in their own thoughts apart from Marlo, who had someone else's thoughts in his head too.

CHAPTER 48 : MR BABINGTON

It was Friday now, and already October. There had been no letter through his door. Walter turned away from the front door and went to get some breakfast. He was beginning to wonder if that Marlo Campbell character he had pinned to a wall on Tuesday morning had been making the whole thing up. That would be very disappointing, as he could otherwise have enjoyed himself beating him to a pulp.

His story was convincing though, he would have done well to make up all that stuff about the rich uncle on the spot, and it all seemed to add up. He had to take the risk that it was true. The problem is, the man had been clever, not leaving an address, so unless he bumped into him in the street he couldn't chase him down and find out what was going on.

He was keen to meet this uncle, but at the moment he didn't even know his name. He couldn't do any research, nothing. It was very frustrating. Walter liked to be in control, and now he wasn't, and he didn't like it.

However, assuming that Campbell bloke got back to him soon, and assuming that the meeting took place, Walter knew that the cards would start to turn in his favour. This could be very lucrative. If he could put in a good showing here and impress this uncle, he could potentially then branch out into other enforcement services working for someone prepared to pay well to keep himself in business, and Walter could do very nicely out of it.

Human nature can often take a promising situation and, using all the best case scenarios at once, weave an imagined ending which is big on optimism but short on pragmatism. Stir in a large dollop of self-confidence as Walter was doing, and already the vision had projected five years into the future to see Walter taking over the rich uncle's business empire and ruling it with an iron fist, frightened minions scurrying to his every command. All he needed was a foot in the door, and this could be it.

Perhaps his recent foray into bloodlust was a substitute for a different type of dominance, one that was less about hands-on murders but more about threat, and the thrill of being respected through fear. Respect has to be earned, he had been told once, but that didn't say how you earned it. Respect through fear was total, any other kind was just a substitute. But until he had that, he wouldn't know what it felt like and whether or not it gave him the same intense highs that personally ending another person's life had done previously.

He fried an egg, piercing the yolk to let it spread across the pan as blood would seep from a wound. It was strangely satisfying, though not as much as the real thing. The heat congealed it and stopped the flow much too quickly. He slid the cooked egg onto a slice of bread and admired it in the way that a fox would admire a chicken, then devoured it in a style that would have done the fox justice. A bottle of beer washed it down.

As he locked the front door he glanced up and down the street, but there was no-one hiding in a doorway, and no-one approaching clutching an envelope. He went around to the side gate to get Gertie, hitched her up, and trotted off in the direction of the rising sun for another day of pleasant intimidation.

Tim wondered whether he should take a break from writing. It had been so intense, and he had been so involved in it all that he felt his brain needed a holiday. How some authors churned out book after book, often within the same year, he just couldn't fathom. But then they were professionals, he was just an amateur. He had been chipping away for months now since Liz died and it was slow going.

Perhaps he should take out these autobiographical inserts as well. It was all very well trying to explain his thought processes to the reader by describing himself in the third person and detailing the ways in which his life had shaped the narrative, but did the reader want to know all that? No doubt critics, should there be any, would argue that it was a boring distraction from the story, and would be nodding in silent agreement even now as they read this sentence. But did it not add an extra layer of icing to the cake? And that is all it was, just a thin smear of additional flavour and colour, even if that colour might be seen by some as a bit grey. It was contrast after all, a rest break from the world of the past, thereby sweeping the reader back and forth through time, as neatly demonstrated by this little musing in that now, with one bound, we head back once more to 1886.

Mr Babington was comfortably proportioned. Not a tall man, but not short of padding, and with arms that stuck out from his sides a little because there was not enough room to let them hang straight. His pate was smooth and shiny apart from a band of tufty white hair that ran from ear to ear around the back of his head and connected itself to a crinkly grey-white cropped beard that had been subject to some careful topiary, ending as it approached the bottom of the mouth in a rather odd half moon curve that revealed an unnecessarily bald area of skin. This matched the top lip, which was also hairless. He reminded Marlo of an Amish elder, but neater, as his suit was smart and the gold buttoned waistcoat was complimented by a natty bow tie.

The Assistant Coroner's wide face smiled patiently as he waited for George to sit down in one of the chairs arranged in front of him.

"Sorry I'm late, we were especially busy today," George apologised breathlessly. He turned to Marlo. "I did say it might be difficult......"

"Don't worry, we're all here now." It was late on Saturday afternoon, just gone half past six, and they were sitting on plain wooden chairs in a waiting area in the coroner's office. An hour and thirty minutes had been set aside though none hoped it would all be needed. Marlo turned to Mr Babington. "I understand Frederick has explained the situation, sir?"

Mr Babington nodded in unison with Frederick. His hands were on his knees, his fingers drumming out a silent rhythm, almost as he could not wait to get started. "Yes, yes, yes, I am fully appraised. A very rum affair all round, don't you think? Most irregular. But we can't have murderers roaming the streets of Brighton, can we? No no no. Something must be done. And I can see that without hard evidence, something that Superintendent Weddall informs me that we do not have in this case – then we cannot proceed. So it appears that we need to grab the bull by the scruff of the horns, as it were, do we not?" He scanned his small audience, eyebrows raised despite the rhetorical question.

Marlo smiled to himself. This chap was quite a character. He suspected that acting a part would come quite easily to him.

Babington did not wait for the three men in front of him to respond but ploughed straight on. "I am satisfied that the circumstantial evidence that Frederick here has relayed through my friend Mr Plundell, and what he has just told me this evening about his previous encounter with the suspect, presents a persuasive argument. This man you are accusing had motive and opportunity to kill Miss Jones, and if you ask me I suspect that poor Mr Whittleborough stumbled across the deed being done and was dispatched, shall we say, in order to eliminate a witness. Now, in my position I would not normally become involved in a police investigation, or any other investigation for that matter. But given the situation, my position in society, as it were, and the impact it has had on your family young man...." – he looked sympathetically across at Frederick, who quickly looked up from his lap and gave a grateful nod – "... and of course the opportunity to hone some of my amateur, and the emphasis should be on amateur here, dramatic skills, I have agreed on this occasion to lend my assistance."

"Thank you sir," said Marlo, "we really do appreciate it."

Mr Babington nodded gravely as though this was the least that he would have expected. "I have some concerns, of course, about the...er... operation, shall we say, and also some thoughts about how it should be enacted, based on the rather sketchy outline my friend provided. But I would be surprised, indeed disappointed, if you have not already formulated a more detailed plan worthy of the name, so perhaps you could be so kind as to elaborate, then I will comment as appropriate as we proceed." He looked in turn at each of them. "Who would like to begin?"

Two heads looked at Marlo, who looked at Frederick. It was a silent vote, and with the expected result, so Marlo turned to Mr Babington, who was leaning forward expectantly, still with his hands on his knees, eyebrows raised in anticipation.

An hour later and they had taken Marlo's suggested approach, which although perhaps lacking the details that Mr Babington had expected, was then adapted to resemble a workable plan. They would use a neutral venue not connected with the coroner's office so as not to arouse suspicion. Mr Babington had already arranged with his friend Mr Tilcott, an undertaker, to borrow one of his preparation rooms, ensuring first of course that it had no inhabitants.

The advantage of this arrangement was that although the room offered no hiding places in itself, Frederick and George could be easily concealed in two of the empty coffins that were stored there, as it was extraordinarily unlikely that Walter would consider it possible that the coffins were occupied.

This might have been an advantage in terms of tactics, but it offered no advantage to Frederick and George, who had unsurprisingly not immediately taken to this idea and indeed protested vigorously, neither of them having harboured any previous ambition to emulate a corpse for an evening.

"We must be able to find a room with some closets or cupboards, surely?" cried Frederick, "and for me to clamber into a coffin so soon after my dear sister's death, well, it just isn't right. There must be a better option!"

Mr Babington assumed a face that he hoped combined empathy with authority. "My dear Mr Jones, I entirely respect your predicament. Believe me, if at such short notice I had been able to arrange something more suitable, that I would have done. Unfortunately no alternatives presented themselves and I was obliged to accept the generous offer that Mr Tilcott was, ahem, persuaded to make. I realise the venue is insensitive, and I apologise to you most sincerely for that, but it is my considered view that in this case the end justifies the means, and the quicker we apprehend this dreadful man the better it will be for all of us."

He looked pointedly at Frederick, who frowned back at him. "I'm still not sure, sir."

There followed further discussion around the lack of alternatives and the practicalities of squeezing into coffins (for example keeping arms rigidly by your sides whilst being attacked by an itch on your face), at the end of which the two nominees were finding themselves running out of arguments.

"What if one of us sneezes?" pointed out George.

"Well it is better than coughin', isn't it," pointed out Marlo, drawing a brief shriek of welcome laughter inside his head from Lillian but less mirth from within the room, so he tried to back down with a quiet "sorry," which he didn't really mean.

A brief hint of a smile had flitted across Mr Babington's face but then he had shifted uneasily, aware of the risk of unexpected noises from unexpected places. "Well, then we will see what kind of stuff this Threadwell character is made of, wouldn't we. But no, there must be no sneezing, no noise. If there is, it will have to be explained away somehow. I'll think of something, heaven knows what. I would hope you would not have to be in there for long though, gentlemen; I would expect matters to be concluded fairly swiftly once we have extracted a confession. You two just have to stay still for a short period of time, and keep your ears open. That's all. It strikes me that you might actually have a slightly easier time of it than those of us facing this... this... nasty piece of work." He turned to briefly glance at Marlo, the mere act of doing so in his eyes gaining an ally and thereby cementing his argument.

Frederick and George looked at each other. The finality of Mr Babington's tone and the sense that he had a good point was enough for the two men to finally shrug, accept defeat and reluctantly agree to their fate. It was all in the greater cause, after all.

Marlo noted how the Assistant Coroner, schooled by years of experience in imparting statements authoritatively, was far better suited to driving forward this enterprise than he was, so was more than happy to let him get on with it. Marlo would slink into the background as usual.

As if on cue Mr Babington had affected a serious face and held up his hand to stop any voices that did not belong to him, not that there were any at the time but the gesture also served to indicate that all previous discussion was ended and he was now starting a new one. "Gentlemen, we must move on. I am sure none of us have time to waste – in fact, time wastes for no man. Ha! I believe I have just invented an amusing aphorism there - I must remember that one, as should you."

He smiled benevolently at his audience as though he had just gifted them something of great use, before realising that he had only managed two sentences before steering himself off track and so needed to get back to the point. He cleared his throat importantly.

"Now, I must make it very clear to all of you, that on no account are you..." and here he looked at Frederick and George as though peering over invisible reading glasses, "... to reveal yourselves in any sense, at any time, or prevent Mr Threadwell from leaving. The aim of this operation is purely to extract the confession and hear it being said. I do not have the means or wherewithal to arrest the man at this point, and I could not persuade Superintendent Weddall to deploy his officers to hide outside and await a signal. There was too much risk to that approach anyway, both for the success of our plan but also to ourselves physically. Once we have the confession, in front of four witnesses including myself, and Threadwell has left, I will then report back to the superintendent, and he will arrange for Mr Threadwell to be safely detained. Does everyone understand?"

They had all nodded, although Frederick and George were still internally questioning the wisdom of agreeing to squeeze themselves into a defenceless position in a wooden box just yards from a murderer.

Earlier it had been agreed that Mr Babington, in the guise of Uncle Sampson, would do most of the talking with Walter, as one might expect this supposedly rich and powerful man to do. Marlo would just do the introductions and chip in where necessary.

To maintain the illusion that the uncle did not want his identity revealed, they would not reveal his fictitious name, and Mr Babington would wear a mask. Fortunately his amateur dramatics group possessed a selection he could choose from, so this would not be a problem. Even if Walter whipped the mask off it wouldn't matter as there was no reason why he should know the Assistant Coroner, but it was best to maintain the tale that Marlo had spun.

They had agreed on a date and time convenient to all of them, guessing that Walter would amend his schedule to fit given the potential reward on offer. It would be at eight o'clock in the evening, this coming Wednesday, the 8th October. Meanwhile Marlo would write the note to Walter and post it early tomorrow morning, so as not to waste any time. They were all set.

CHAPTER 49 : GOING TO AN UNDERTAKER

That evening, Marlo lay back on his bed and reflected on what was to come. He had written the note to Walter and would be up early to post it through his letter box as unobtrusively as he could, the aim being to avoid any contact with the man until the meeting with Uncle Sampson.

"I suppose I could have posted it tonight really," he sighed, unwilling to raise himself from the bed, so knowing that he wouldn't do that now.

"I wouldn't risk it," advised Lillian, "it will be very dark by now, and I don't think there are many street lights up where Walter lives. You never know who might be lurking in the shadows."

"Possibly Walter."

"Oh, I would hope not. Surely he has not taken to hiding in hedgerows or alleys and dragging people off the street?"

"Well we don't know do we? It is clear that none of us really know what he has been doing as a hobby over the years – he could be a serial killer like Jack The Ripper but in Brighton.... Walter The Ripper! Although that sounds terrible, he would need a better moniker."

"What's a ripper?"

"Well, it was his name, because, well, he....... well he must have ripped something. I don't know actually. Ripped their throats? Eeugh, not nice. Anyway, Jack The Ripper - have you not heard of him? I thought he was of this era."

"No, never heard of him, and I'm not sure I want to." He could almost hear Lillian shuddering. "Spring-heeled Jack, yes, but not Jack The Ripper."

"Spring-heeled Jack? Who was he?"

"No-one's sure. He attacked a gardener about 50 years ago up in Round Hill, then others up in London, dressed as a bear, or a devil, or some such monster, and with claws and glowing eyes. He ran on all fours too, and could leap around like a cat, so they say. They thought he came back about ten years ago but they never caught him."

"I'm not surprised, if he had spring-heels. How bizarre. Anyway, maybe Jack The Ripper didn't start until a few years from now, I'm sure it was the 1880s. You've got all that to look forward to."

"Well I haven't really."

"Why…. ah, right, yes, sorry, of course. I'm an idiot. Anyway, sorry, I shouldn't be banging on about murders either, I wasn't being very appropriate there. But it is a point though, how do we know Walter had not killed anyone before you?"

"We don't, but we might be about to find out……"

They both fell silent for a while.

"Lillian?"

"Yes?"

"We might be nearly there."

Lillian let out a long deep sigh. "Oh I really do hope so. But I am not counting any chickens just yet. Walter might not confess to anything, however clever Mr Babington is with his role playing. Then what do we do?"

"Think of something else I guess. But we're short on options. This whole business feels like I'm performing a delicate medical operation on a waterbed - one false move and it's over. It's a shame you can't make yourself heard though my nose or something and tell everyone who killed you. That would be so much easier."

"I'm not sure I would want to be coming out of your nose. Mouth would look wrong. Ears, perhaps? Any other orifice, definitely not."

Marlo laughed. "I really would be talking out of my you-know-what then, wouldn't I? Well, you would at least. People would have to gather round the back of my trousers."

Lillian found this thought hilarious, and for them both the conversation was a welcome break from the serious stuff.

There was more serious business at half past seven the next morning, as Marlo set off, too early for a proper breakfast, to post his note to Walter. He was still remarkably keen to avoid meeting Walter again, which perhaps was not surprising given the circumstances of their last encounter, and so his instructions included a request to Walter to place two candlesticks in his window to confirm he had accepted the meeting. No candlesticks would mean no attendance, although of course it could mean that Walter did not have any candlesticks, unlikely though this might be. Well if he didn't he would just have to buy some then, or make them out of sticks or something. Marlo had indicated in the note that his uncle would look elsewhere for assistance if Walter could not attend, as he was a busy man. That should do it.

He walked quickly, being determined to slip the note through the door and hasten away before Walter got up, or, worse still, emerged from the house for some reason just as Marlo was approaching. Daylight was rising, easing its way through the thick grey cloud that sat heavily and stubbornly in the sky as though it had nothing better to do. Even though it was Sunday a small but steady trickle of working men were heading into town as he headed outwards, making him feel even more self-conscious as the eyes beneath every flat cap gave him a passing glance.

He reached Southover Road, where Walter lived. It was quieter here. He kept to the even-numbered side of the road until he reached the door marked 34. Quickly he removed the envelope from his jacket and was just about to lift the letterbox flap when he heard a loud cough from what sounded like the other side of the door. He froze. Was Walter about to burst out of the door? What should he do?

Mild panic overcame reasoned thinking and cemented his feet to the floor. The door didn't open though and a few seconds later he heard another cough, further away. It looked as though Walter had just happened to be moving around in the hall near the front door as Marlo arrived. He was up though, clearly not one for a Sunday lie-in.

Slowly Marlo opened the flap, pushed the envelope hastily inside, turned sharply, and walked away as quickly as he could without running. He kept expecting to hear a shout, but there was nothing. He turned the corner and relief swept over him.

"Right, it's done," he whispered to Lillian. "I'll go back tomorrow afternoon to check for candlesticks."

"Well done. I suspect that is a sentence you never thought you would utter."

"Ha, yeah, you're right there. Although almost all the things I am saying or doing at the moment are things I never thought I would say or do. It's mad, this whole thing is mad. Right, I have time to kill. I'm going for a walk along the beach again. I might have a mosey along that Chain Pier that isn't there any more unless you have any better suggestions."

She didn't, and so Marlo Campbell, a twenty-first century boy, spent another day wandering about the nineteenth century while simultaneously wondering at it too.

By mid afternoon he was sitting once more on the stony beach, cap by his side and hair being tousled by the wind. Being Sunday, the promenade was especially busy, a tide of spruced-up humanity milling and spilling onto the beach to enjoy a fresher dose of sea air. It was funny how almost everyone was in comparatively drab colours. It meant that distinguishing figures from a distance wasn't so easy as they all merged into each other. No hipsters wearing lime green trousers, no girls with blue leggings, no men with pink t-shirts, no bright colours at all. It was all mainly brown, black, grey and some white underneath. If a lady sported some red or purple it was dark and reserved, nothing garish, just blending in. Gentlemen's jackets were similarly restrained. Well, history was so often portrayed in black and white so maybe it was appropriate that in real life people dressed with less colour. He hadn't even spotted a daft logo on a shirt either - Victorians didn't do words on clothes.

Once again he watched the glassy, frothy waves thrumming away, throwing themselves repetitively against the beach, wearing it down and never giving up. There was a lesson for him there somewhere, although he did not have millions of years to achieve anything, just a few days. It made him think about the passage of time.

"I've been here over a week now, you know."

"This is your eleventh day actually, so that's a week and a half." Lillian was evidently keeping count.

"Well, yes, you're right. A week and a half. In 1886." He shook his head, still finding it hard to comprehend. "I can't have been dreaming for that long."

"You're right, you haven't, you've been living."

"Hang on though, you said that when, well, if - no, it has to be 'when' - I go back, with you, to my old life, it will be as though nothing has happened and no time has passed?"

"Yes, that's right. No-one will know you were ever away."

"So doesn't that mean that this eleven days, and any other time I am here in 1886, is extra life for me? Eleven more days that I would not have lived normally? That's good, isn't it?"

Lillian didn't reply immediately, which Marlo didn't take to be a positive sign. "Well, the length of your life is less about where you've been and more about what you do," she said carefully after a while. "The lifespan of your body won't change because you are here. So if biology dictates that you will drop down dead in a year's time, that could happen whichever time zone you are in."

"Ah, ok. So what you're saying," said Marlo slowly, "is that I don't magically gain an extra eleven days of life, or however long I am here for. Which actually means that I should die eleven days earlier than I would have done previously in my normal world if I were to return home today."

"Yes. But none of us know when we are going to die anyway do we, so it is not as though it would make any difference to you."

"That's true, but what if I end being stuck here for five years trying to pin down Walter, wouldn't I look older? So when I returned, people would get a real shock and think I had seen a ghost or something. Which, in a way......"

"I'm not a ghost," interrupted Lillian in mock admonishment, "I'm a transient. Very different things, remember."

"To you maybe. But you'll need to take off that white sheet with the eye holes when we get back to my world."

"Very funny." For once Lillian did not have an instant and witty response. Had Marlo finally won a battle of the banter or was it because his comment wasn't actually that funny and Lillian was just being ironic? Probably the latter, on reflection.

"But to get back to your question, you will never look older when you return however long you are here for. Internally, though, your body will be older. Your heart will have taken more beats, your stomach digested more food, your joints moved more times, and so on. And you will die earlier as a result."

"Nice. But fair enough, I suppose. I was thinking my internally aged body could confuse doctors but then lots of people have bodies that have been measured as more than their actual age – I've seen it on TV."

"I'm looking forward to seeing one of these 'TVs' you keep talking about." Lillian was the first to go off on the tangent that their conversations so often did. "I still can't picture it, what they look like."

"Well, picture is the right word to use. The way to picture it is to just picture a picture. A moving one. You're going to be gobsmacked when you see it!"

"That doesn't sound good. You're talking gibberish again. Why would I want to be smacked like that?"

"Ah yes, that almost certainly isn't a word in 1886 is it? Gobsmacked means amazed."

"Well I don't really like it. It sounds violent. I would rather just be amazed, thank you."

"Very well, you shall be. But we have to get back to my world first."

"We do indeed. And all we have to do to get there is trap Walter."

It sounded so simple, but much of it was now out of their hands, and in the hands of an amateur dramatics enthusiast who happened to be an assistant coroner.

~

Walter opened the envelope and read the instructions left by Marlo. Well, at least it looked as though Campbell had been telling the truth. The meeting with the rich uncle was on. But they were going to a funeral parlour? He didn't like the sound of that. Or maybe this fellow owned a chain of undertakers! Now that would be a result. What better way of disposing of bodies! Walter wished he had thought of this before. Well now, this was a much greater opportunity than he had envisaged.

He took two candlesticks off his mantelpiece and put them in the front window. He would definitely be there.

That morning, as he busied himself giving the stable area a bit of a clean-out, he whistled happily, already planning in his head for the day that he would running the undertaker's and bringing back bodies overnight to be cremated before anyone was any the wiser.

It was only towards lunchtime that he realised that it was actually more likely that just because they were meeting there didn't mean that this was necessarily the man's profession. In fact it probably wasn't. At the first meeting he probably wouldn't want to give away his identity so this could just be to throw Walter off the scent. His good mood rapidly tumbled into a gulley of apprehension. Maybe this was just Campbell luring him into a trap. They would cosh him over the head and tip him into a coffin, seal him up and bury him alive, because perhaps, perhaps, Campbell had been following him for a different reason than the one he gave under duress. Did he know about any of the four murders? Was he a relative of one of them, out for revenge?

Walter now didn't know what to think, or whether even to go. All afternoon he agonised over which part of his head to believe. Eventually, logic started to win over emotion. He knew he had covered his tracks so well that no-one had witnessed any of his murders. No-one could know it was him. The story given by Campbell still made sense, nothing had changed there. The potential opportunity he would be giving up by not turning up would be huge, and he would forever regret it if it turned out to be genuine and he missed out. As long as he kept his wits about him and did not allow himself to become drawn into any potential traps, like standing next to an empty coffin or something, he should be alright. He knew he could handle himself. Yes, he would go. The candlesticks stayed where they were.

~

Sunday turned into Monday, as it so often does. Marlo had three more days to fill before the Wednesday evening appointment at Mr Tilcott the undertaker's preparation room. He was already nervous and the anticipation would only increase. So much was riding on this encounter.

He did a bit of reading in his room, then went to check on Walter's window. Sure enough, to their great relief, the candlesticks were there. Then he headed down to have a look at Brighton Pavilion. He felt he ought to, seeing as he had told George that it would have a starring role in his book. How much cleaner and grander it looked, laid out in its elegant gardens, without roads throttling it from all sides and vehicles spraying exhaust particles over it. Its domes and minarets looked like those iced gem biscuits he used to eat as a child, biting the coloured icing off first before nibbling the biscuit base, sometimes the other way round. Funny how there are some thing you no longer eat as an adult without really knowing why not.

The relative silence helped too; the background growl of thousands of engines replaced by the clop of hooves, the occasional shouts or conversations of people, and the overhead cries of the ever-present seagulls, waiting for tourists with a loose grip on their fish and chips to become more commonplace.

This was all Lillian had known, he thought. This clean air, this gentler noise level, this social media and phone-free world. But also the poverty, the chores, the long working hours, the poor healthcare, the dim lighting, the manual labour required just to wash your clothes or clean your house. He knew where he would rather be, but perhaps that was because he was used to it. Would Lillian find the modern world too much? Would it be so alien and overwhelming to her that she could not adapt and would constantly yearn for her own life back again? He could not ask her, because she would not know yet, but hopefully he would find out soon enough, and the answer would be to his liking.

After meandering around the Pavilion and chatting periodically with the girl in his head about what he was looking at, he headed off down St James Street in order to explore the east of town a bit more. He was expecting the houses and wide roads to pretty soon turn into fields and tracks but this end of town was surprisingly well populated. St James Street turned into Bristol Road, which curved round past a church and into St Georges Road. He finally reached a crossroads with Paston Place. Ahead, more houses. To his right he could see the sea in the near distance, to his left, an equal distance away, a very large building sat imposingly at the end of the road.

"That's probably the hospital, the Sussex County," advised Lillian.

Marlo was slightly taken aback. "It looks like a stately home!"

"Well, it is an important building. It's been there for, I don't know, about fifty years I suppose. A long time, anyway."

"It's huge. It does look Georgian, certainly." Marlo went to have a closer look. Half way there the houses gave way to two small open fields bordered by low wood pole fences, which helped to set the hospital apart from its neighbours and enhance its grandeur, as did the fact that it sat up a slope a good twenty feet higher than the road it faced. He could see as he got closer that two wings had been added, as the stone was a different shade, turning the building into an enclosing angular horseshoe. At the front were two kidney shaped areas of grass flanking large stone entrance posts that signposted the required ascent of a number of wide stone steps leading up to the huge front door. No concept of being disabled-friendly here, even in a hospital! People struggling for breath or with a bad leg were faced with a small assault course before they even got inside. There were also no car parks of course, just horses and carts waiting outside at the front in the street without a yellow line or a traffic warden in sight.

Marlo knew that it wouldn't look like this now. There would be extensions, prefabs, perspex canopies, car parks, ambulances, taxis and all the usual hectic paraphernalia which accompanies every hospital these days. The aesthetic value would have been strangled by the practical realities of running a health service in the 21st century. As he watched, the odd person negotiated those steps, some quicker than others, but there was no feeling of urgency or panic. It was just a very big building with some people going in and out.

He decided not to try and go in, as he was not sure he wanted to. Don't want to catch anything, he thought, or maybe pass some modern germs onto them. No, he would just observe from a distance and pass on.

He was now on Eastern Road and this did seem more rural. There were fewer people around and hardly any road traffic, just the occasional cart. A weather-beaten man leading a weather-beaten horse trudged past him, his shoulders hunched and his face fixed into an expression reminiscent of someone who had just stepped in something that smelled. The two small fields at the front of the hospital were the first of many now as he continued out of the town, interspersed with larger houses and lodges. A group of three young women, perhaps in their late teens, passed him coming the other way, their lengthy swishing dresses billowing as they walked. He stepped into the road to let them past and they giggled and nudged each other. Marlo was never sure what this meant. In his head, they were laughing at how unattractive he was, mocking his barely visible half-grown moustache, judging him in some negative way. Look at that guy, what woman would want anything to do with him? That was his default assumption, but of course they may have just been sharing a joke about something else, or were amused that they had effectively pushed him into the road. Either way, he never liked it when women he didn't know were coming towards him in the street; it made him uneasy, whichever era he was in. He thought better about asking Lillian to give him some feminine insights here; it was a confession he didn't want her to know.

He knew he wasn't just imagining how women looked at him either. He could submit as evidence any number of occasions where he had been with a group of colleagues having a drink or a meal and an attractive girl would come to take the order, laughing and joking in a flirty way with them all. However, the minute she turned to Marlo he could see her face fall and the 'service flirt' mechanism immediately switch off in case he got any signals he shouldn't have. She would seriously and professionally take his order, then turn to the next man and the smile would return. He had seen it time and time again, usually when ordering drinks at the bar, so it could not just be coincidence, and he knew for a fact that he was the only one it happened to in every group that he had been in. Girls as a species really did just find him repellent.

This partly explained why back in the modern world he had never tried a dating app or agency. Marlo knew that others would assume he was so desperate that he would try anything, but he could think of nothing worse. For a start, how can you sell yourself when you have nothing to sell? And of course most people selected partners based on a photograph, so that would rule him out straight away. Even if matches were made on personality type, a photo would have to be provided at some point and as he did not have a single photograph of himself that he could bear to look at, it was hardly worth bothering submitting one of them only for his profile to be routinely laughed at and then ignored by all potential suitors. Or at least, all those who were not desperate. No, actually, all those who were desperate as well. Everyone, basically. And then even if it got to the stage of meeting someone, and he did actually like her, it could only go the same way as every single encounter he had ever previously had with a girl he was chasing - crushing failure and rejection. They say you make up your mind about someone within the first five seconds of meeting them, so that first impression would immediately seal his fate, then he would be tongue-tied and verbally inadequate, as he always was with girls, and before long he would be walking home alone again. So he had convinced himself that dating agencies were a pointless waste of money for people like him, and would only bring big wet dollops of added disappointment and frustration. If you have no pride, best to hide. His conundrum had always been that you only find someone by meeting people, but meeting people always led to humiliation and rejection, and he couldn't take any more of that. That's why this opportunity with Lillian was just too good to waste, but he had to make the most of it. He had to impress her, and that might be a lot easier while she wasn't looking at him.

He walked on past a few more clusters of dwellings amongst the fields and open ground, the houses now intruding on the land rather than the other way around. But then some more concentrated large buildings loomed up ahead. The road sliced between them and as he emerged on the other side he was surprised to find himself suddenly confronted with a quite magnificent crescent of enormous white houses, such as you would find in the most expensive parts of London. Five storeys high with giant Corinthian pilasters, Doric columns and porches, fronted with iron railing balconies along the first floor, they swept round a central park, a half-moon of grand opulence with views straight out over the sea and overlooking an ornamental square that must have been two or three hundred feet wide. It was not what he had expected at all. There were no large trees obscuring the view so Marlo could see that half way down, the houses on each side spread even further apart, fanning out in curves like the top half of a wine bottle.

"Wow," said Marlo, "that's just amazing. Look at those houses. Jeez." He started walking down towards the sea a little, taking it all in.

"I presume you've reached Lewes Crescent?" Lillian didn't really need to ask.

Marlo checked the road sign. "Yes, that's it. I wasn't expecting that. I've never been this far east of town before. How come they are out here, this far from the centre?"

"Well you're in Kemptown now, it was supposed to be like Hove but on the other side of Brighton. Lewis Carroll, the author, stays every summer in one of those houses, you know. Mrs Cavendish told me, she lives three doors down from him. Quite proud about it she was, and who can blame her. I had to deliver her some bonnets for her daughters once."

"So he probably wouldn't be here now then, seeing as its October? That's a shame. Imagine me bumping into Lewis Carroll, that would be amazing. But I'm well impressed by these houses. When we get back to my world we will have to come and visit it, see how it has changed. Not much, I expect."

"They were built to last, those houses, so it wouldn't surprise me that they have. There's a tunnel, you know, from the gardens down to the beach. They reckon that is how Mr Carroll – well it's the Reverend

Dodgson really, that is his actual name - had his idea for Alice falling down a rabbit hole and into a tunnel in Alice In Wonderland."

"You know your stuff, don't you? How do you know what you know?"

"I just do. Mostly from talking to customers I suppose, and delivering around the town. Also I do always..... did always read the local paper. And there is always something new happening in Brighton. It was a nice place to live."

Lillian's drift into the past tense had muted his enthusiasm a little, so Marlo walked on, turning in slow circles as he went in order to take in the full majesty of his surroundings. He continued across the central park space and back onto the road that dissected the crescent. Ahead, through the gap between the houses on the other side, he could see that it was now mostly fields but also some hulking shapes on the horizon.

"What are those huge constructions up ahead?" he asked Lillian. "They look like gasholders."

"That's because they are. It's the gasworks. There's nothing much beyond them."

"In which case, I'll head down to the sea and come back along the seafront."

"Marine Parade," said Lillian, "it's a nice walk. You'll see Chain Pier as you turn back onto it. Oh, and the little railway too, Volk's Electric Railway it's called. It's only been open a few years. It's for tourists, with little trains, it runs up and down the front, you must have a look."

Marlo smiled at Lillian's pride in her town and eagerness that he should see its attractions. He didn't like to break it to her but he had to "Believe it or not, I've already been on it. It's still running today."

"No! Really? Oh, I'm so pleased. Well, you can see what it looked like when it was nearly new then."

"I certainly can, and I certainly will." And Marlo headed down towards the seafront, his trousers flapping in the fresh salty breeze.

Tim stopped and stretched his arms out sideways, wiggling his fingers to shake out the repetitive rigor of typing. This was getting boring, surely. Just describing Marlo traipsing round old Brighton town might be of interest to a history aficionado, but to the reader waiting for action, nothing was happening. He was just describing Marlo killing time. No, he had to move it on a bit. And explaining his own thoughts like this, as though someone else was writing a book describing how he was writing a book about someone who, co-incidentally, had been writing a book, well, it gave him the opportunity to explain why he was taking the odd short cut like the one he was about to take now.

It was Wednesday. The big day had arrived. Much of Monday and all of Tuesday had been spent getting a guided tour of virtually all of the safe areas of Brighton, courtesy of tour guide Lillian. The unsafe areas – the backstreets, dens, areas where gangs or robbers could hang out, even the workhouse up by the racecourse, were carefully avoided. Instead Marlo was directed to all corners of the town, from the County Cricket Ground to the east right next to Hove Station, to Preston Barracks in the north.

It had occurred to Marlo that without really realising it he was being presented with a huge opportunity here. When he got back to his former life, assuming that he did, he would be able to write about the Victorian landscape of the 1880s in a way that no-one else could. No-one would be able to challenge his observations. He would make a name for himself not as a general historian – as surely their workload increases with every day that passes from now into then - but as a Victorian scholar. So it was sensible to take in as much as he could, see everything around him in recording mode, trying to imprint it on his memory so that he could recount it later. As an aide-memoire he had begun spending a lot of time each evening just writing down what he had seen during the day. Lillian had pointed out that he shouldn't get too above himself about his visions of being a twenty-first century expert about Victorian society as he would be bringing back someone else who knew a huge amount more than he did, and who had lived twenty years of it, not just a few weeks, so who was likely to be the greater expert? This was a fair point, but even if he was only second in the pecking order it would still be better than nowhere, and in any case, he had hoped, although of course he didn't say this, that they would become a team, dispensing historical wisdom together. Not that he had any idea how this would work practically, but he would think about that when he got back. For now, the long shoe-destroying walks every day were worth the effort.

But today, Wednesday, could be the last opportunity. Could be, probably wouldn't be, as if it all went to plan then it would be some time before Walter was punished after being arrested and charged. Just for this one evening, though, the future was unknown. And, like on the morning of the day you are due to give your first public speech at work, he just wanted it over and done with.

And so, as is traditional in these situations, the day dragged. On Lillian's suggestion, he went down to the beach in front of Brunswick Square to see if he could find Frederick, just to make doubly sure her brother had not had second thoughts on doing anything silly, but he wasn't there.

"Why not go and watch a trial at the county court?" suggested Lillian as Marlo shuffled back along the beach through the stones. "That might be entertaining and take your mind off tonight."

The county court was a stout square-ish building in Church Street, near the Pavilion. Marlo approached with some caution, worried in case he was stopped and questioned. He still felt he was an imposter – which of course he was in so many ways – and that proximity to any official of the law could somehow result in his secret being quickly revealed. Before you could say 'game over' he would find himself clapped in leg-irons, or whatever the procedure was, and carted off to a dungeon. Maybe he was going back in history a little far with that analogy, but he knew that Victorian justice was a little less thorough than he was accustomed to, and he was wary of getting too close to it.

But Lillian told him not to worry, just walk in, head up the stairs, and you can sit in the public gallery, and she was right. There was no jury in this particular set up, just a judge - or maybe he was a magistrate - either way looking splendidly officious in his wig and gown. There was only a scattering of fellow voyeurs, and Marlo watched as a succession of sorry looking characters were hauled into the witness box and presented with their charges. Then a barrister would take a few minutes to outline the case for the prosecution, perhaps an accusation of obscene language, or partaking in a fight, or petty thieving, after which a defending barrister would explain the sad circumstances that the defendant had found themselves in which led them to commit the crime despite their normal exemplary good character, and the defendant would conclude proceedings by mumbling a hopeless plea for clemency. After a short summary of what had been heard and the conclusion to be drawn, the judge, with the weary air of a man in need of a new purpose in life, would invariably announce them guilty and hand down a surprisingly harsh sentence that seemed to bear little relation to the crime.

Marlo left the court to find some lunch, which turned out to be a rabbit pie from a street vendor which had more pastry than meat, although given that the meat was mostly gristle this was a blessing in disguise. He then returned to watch a few more court cases in the afternoon before heading back to his lodgings and writing some notes on what he had just seen. He gave Lillian quite a lengthy exposé on how modern justice works and the sometimes ridiculously long trials that can drag on for years in big city fraud cases. Open prisons were something Lillian had trouble understanding too, where prisoners could just walk in and out as long as they were there when they were supposed to be. "That's just like lodgings then, isn't it? And they don't have to pay? Why isn't there more crime in your world then, if the punishment is free board and lodgings?" It took a while for Marlo to explain that one, and he wasn't sure he had done a very good job of it.

Before they knew it, his pocket watch was reading five o'clock. Three hours to go. They had agreed that Mr Babington and George would aim to be there between a quarter past seven and half past, in order to allow time to set up the room and refresh everyone on their roles in the drama. Frederick and Marlo, though, would arrive even earlier in order to avoid any risk of Walter turning up early and spotting Lillian's brother, as this would completely give the game away. This would be especially important if Walter had somehow rumbled them and was lying in wait. After all, it would be dark by then and ideal conditions for being pounced upon, so best not to take any chances. Because he and Frederick came from different directions, they would meet at the Pavilion at ten to seven and go on from there together.

And so after trying to read some Robinson Crusoe and finding that his eyes were looking at the words but his brain wasn't, he filled the time to half past six telling Lillian about holidays he had had and the experience of flying, although he suspected she wasn't giving him her full attention and could completely understand why.

As he spoke he reflected that in all the time they had been talking since he had arrived in 1886, they had both steered carefully along conversational paths that did not stray into anything personal that could be misconstrued. They probably both silently recognised that for this whole adventure to work, the two of them must not create any traces of awkwardness or ill feeling. So although both had asked the other about their background, and Marlo had told Lillian about his parents and where he grew up, when she asked 'Are you married or with someone?'

he just said no and left it at that. And she left it too. But was that in fact because she was not interested, or did she not want to ask in case that was interpreted as an interest in his eligibility? He hoped it was neither but feared it was both.

As the time approached, Marlo fell silent before musing "We are going to need to be lucky this evening. It's not just about the planning."

Lillian agreed. "That is very true. Luck is a funny thing. I remember as a child sitting on a grass verge by the side of the road. I was watching a trail of ants. There were hundreds of them, and their route crossed the road. They moved so fast, those little legs scurrying them along, all bumping into each other as they tried to keep up. Then a man on a bicycle came along, and I watched as he rode right over the line of ants. But there was a bit of a gap in the line, and after he had gone I could see that just one ant was squashed. And I remember thinking, that was such an unlucky ant. Of all the hundreds, possibly thousands of ants who could have ended up under those wheels, just that one did. That must be the definition of bad luck." There was a pause. "I can't remember where I was going with that story now. Oh yes, I remember, my point being, with all the planning you have done you would have to be really unlucky, like that squashed ant, for it to all go wrong. Think of all the other ants, happily trotting along, not that they trot of course, more like racing really with the speed they go, anyway, they are all racing along probably oblivious to what happened to the unlucky ant and all achieving whatever it was they set out to cross the road for. Oh my, I need to stop talking. Sorry, I'm just so nervous."

Marlo laughed. "Don't worry, me too. Well, we will just have to hope we don't get crushed by a bicycle wheel tonight."

"Exactly, what would be the chances of that! Very slim, I would wager. So we'll be fine! I'm convinced of it."

Marlo wished it was that easy, or that they did not have to go through with it at all, but nothing could stop the onerous crawl of time, and at the appointed hour, he had no option but to set off.

Mr Tilcott's funeral parlour was on Richmond Street, near Queen's Park. It was a detached house, but not in the grand sense, more like two small traditional terraced houses welded together. A line of four identical sash windows on the first floor were the unseeing eyes above the gaping black mouth of the shop front beneath, where a black curtained display window attempted to convey sympathy with two vases of dried red flowers flanking an expensive looking wooden casket. An illustrative wreath, a little faded now, adorned the wooden lid. The shop sign above the window simply stated 'J.J. Tilcott & Sons', as though no further explanation was needed which, given that there was a coffin in the window, there probably wasn't. For the avoidance of doubt, though, 'Funeral Undertaker' was discretely etched in gold on the obscure glass panel of the front door.

Marlo and Frederick cautiously opened the door and went in. Marlo noticed that pretty much every establishment of these times announced your entry with the annoying tingle of a bell above the door, something he particularly disliked because it drew unwanted attention to the owner of the hand on the door handle, which in this case was him, as it usually was when he was the one entering the shop. "Look out," it informed the shop owner, "that potential thief Marlo Campbell has just entered, so take a good look at him as he walks in. While you are at it, have a good silent snigger at his hideous face." This was the last thing Marlo wanted, but those damn bells were so trigger sensitive that even if you eased the door open as gently as a latin lover, it always jangled as though you had just thrown a rock at it. Mind you, there wasn't much you could steal from a funeral parlour so he did not feel quite so potentially guilty this time.

He quickly eyed up the room as they walked in. There was wood panelling everywhere, another luxurious casket on a table on one side of the room as an illustration of how impressively the deceased could see out their rotting days, a couple of shiny top hats and a black umbrella on a wooden hat stand in the corner next to a chair, and a few framed advertisements and notices on the wall – that was about it. One of the notices had the headline 'Reasonable Prices' and proceeded to list six different classes of funeral ranging in price from 21 pounds for a first-class burial down to 3 pounds, five shillings for the sixth class. Even these prices could be reduced further by dispensing with the funeral cortege. Choose your quality of grief, effectively. Another notice sombrely pronounced that this establishment "keeps on hand and furnishes to order coffins, caskets, burial cases, robes and shrouds" - a reminder to clients in case they were not already sufficiently depressed by the heavy hand of death that had steered them through the front door. It certainly wasn't welcoming, but then frivolity or fuss were not the objectives. Solemnity and seriousness were what it was all about. It was what was expected.

Standing behind a counter, fountain pen in hand as he paused and looked up from writing in a large leather bound book, was a gentleman who Marlo assumed must be Mr Tilcott. He was probably in his late forties, and had been blessed with a large lugubrious face that hung off his cheekbones in a manner that perfectly suited his chosen profession. Marlo could imagine him in twenty years' time with jowls like a bulldog. His hair was receding, and what there was of it was dark but flecked with grey. Large bushy sideburns framed a face dominated by a nose that could have given a vulture a run for its money, such was its dominance and pronounced curvature. As if reading Marlo's thoughts he sniffed loudly, wiped his beak with the back of his cuff, and stood up to his full height, which wasn't actually as high as Marlo was expecting given the size of his head. "Good evening, gentlemen," he announced sonorously in a voice strained of all positivity from a lifetime of talking to dead people's relatives. "I trust you are the two young men that my friend Mr Babington described?"

Frederick answered first. "I presume we are, sir, yes."

Mr Tilcott nodded. "I understand that you wish to make use of my facilities for an hour or so this evening."

As Marlo opened his mouth to reply, Mr Tilcott continued, evidently not requiring confirmation. "I must say it is a little inconvenient, but I value my friendship with the assistant coroner, and it can be helpful to occasionally scratch each other's backs with a favour now and again, which is why I have agreed to it. I will stay here until he arrives because, you will understand gentlemen, I do not know you from Adam and will need him – the assistant coroner that is, not Adam - to give me the absolute assurance that you are who you say you are."

Although Marlo felt that despite the humorous aside, this was said with a degree of unnecessary pomposity, he and Frederick nodded gravely, assuming that Mr Tilcott had more to say, which indeed he did. "While we are waiting for him to arrive I will show you into my preparation room and you can....." he chuckled softly to himself realising what he was about to say "..... prepare yourselves. Although not for the reasons I normally use that room, of course."

Marlo and Frederick exchanged glances, now realising that they were actually unsure as to whether Mr Babington had told his friend Mr Tilcott of the plan to hide Frederick and George in coffins or even the actual purpose of the enterprise.

"Thank you," said Marlo, after forcing a functional smile to indicate that he found Mr Tilcott's unintended word play about preparation appropriately amusing. "Did Mr Babington explain the situation, regarding our, er..... well, the reason we need to......."

Frederick could see that Marlo was struggling and cut in. "Did he tell you precisely what we needed the room for, sir?"

As the question hung in the air, they exchanged a nervous glance, both realising too late that maybe this was something they should not have asked.

Mr Tilcott raised an eyebrow, then smiled, revealing a glimpse of yellowing teeth that Marlo was pleased to see looked even less appealing than his own brown ones. "He did. Ezra is an old friend, we go back a long time." He lowered his voice conspiratorially and raised his eyes heavenwards. "I had to withhold some of the finer details from Mrs Tilcott upstairs but I also share his desire to rid of streets of undesirables, and told him I was willing to play my part. Provided of course..." he coughed slightly "... that my public spirited assistance is duly noted."

What this meant Marlo could hazard a guess but wasn't going to ask. No doubt it was related to the earlier 'scratching of backs' reference. He guessed from the mention of his wife that the Tilcotts lived 'above the shop', so it had to be said that allowing a suspected murderer to be entertained at close quarters to his family must have taken some persuading by the assistant coroner.

Mr Tilcott put down his pen, clapped his hands suddenly together as though catching a fly and eased himself out from around the counter. "Right!" he announced, "let me show you gentlemen into the room. It is just here, through this door."

He led the way to an adjoining back room and Marlo was immediately struck by the warm smell of musty wood which pervaded the air, a bit like his old woodwork class at school. In the centre were two plain tables about six feet long and two feet wide. On one of them lay a freshly sawn coffin lid with rough edges that still needed sanding. Around it were dotted little chunks of freshly hewn wood sitting on a mist of sawdust. On the other table was a small white coffin with lead handles, no more than three feet in length. Seeing Marlo staring at it, Mr Tilcott moved over to it and carried it over to a corner of the room, stacking it on top of another three that were on the floor. "Child's resting place," he sniffed, "tis a shame but there you are, that's life. Or not, as the case may be. One of our most popular models, that one, always in demand. Plain but respectful."

Marlo wasn't sure what to say. To Mr Tilcott it was just business but so many children's coffins? That just didn't seem right. This was certainly a different age.

The room was busy with the accoutrements of death. Next to the little tower of small coffins were a row of adult ones leaning against the wall - an assortment of caskets and coffins in various states of completion. On the other side of the room was a long bench-like table divided into sections for material and cloth, small cardboard boxes with handles, studs, and nails. A smaller table held a selection of flowers which brought some much needed colour to the room.

"You'll be needing to arrange the furniture to your liking, I take it," said Mr Tilcott, "but nothing too dramatic if you would be so kind. There are chairs over there, see, under the window. You can use this table now I've cleared it. I'd best go and mind the shop now, ready for Ezra and the other fellow he mentioned."

"George," said Marlo.

"Yes, probably. I don't recall exactly. Anyway, make yourselves at home gentlemen."

And with that, his business done, the undertaker was gone, closing the door unnecessarily quietly behind him in a manner befitting of his profession.

Marlo looked at Frederick, who was rather desperately scanning the room in case a secret closet or other alternative to hiding in a coffin could make itself apparent. It didn't take him long to realise that, as Mr Babington had already assured them, it wouldn't. Four walls, a door, a window with no curtains. That was pretty much it.

"Is the room alright?" Lillian had been silent up until now but obviously wanted a re-assurance. Even now Marlo still had trouble adjusting to the fact that no-one else could hear her, but Frederick's expression had not changed, which it certainly would have done if he had just heard his dead sister talking in an undertaker's room. The voice in his head needed answering though, so he made a little horse clop noise – one click for yes – and disguised it by immediately pretending it was a tut, adding "I'm not sure about making myself at home, but we need to get this place ready. Give us a hand with this table."

They manoeuvred the table sideways a bit and put two chairs on one side of it and one chair, for Walter, on the other. A traditional interview format, thought Marlo, although it looked sparse enough to be a police interview, which in a way it was. The coffins proved more problematic. They needed two that could accommodate Frederick and George, and with Frederick being quite tall only the largest one would do. He pushed it completely upright and stepped tentatively into it. It was a sturdily fashioned affair, presumably destined for a first or second class funeral for the lucky recipient, assuming luck is something still available to you when you are dead. Frederick backed tentatively into it with about as much enthusiasm as a novice non-swimmer descending the silver steps of a swimming pool. The coffin had a surprisingly heavy hinged lid which Marlo heaved slowly closed on its unwilling occupant, leaving a gap for ventilation and, almost as importantly, sound.

"I don't really like it in here," came the muffled voice from inside. "It's dark and cramped, and it's going to get quite hot after a while."

Marlo ignored him and sat down on the chair assigned for Walter. "Can you hear me?" he said in a normal voice.

"Yes," came the muted reply "I don't think hearing things is going to be the problem."

The lid swung back open and Frederick carefully stepped out, shaking his head. "I knew we shouldn't have agreed to this. It is madness. I could feel myself wobbling slightly as well; surely Threadwell will notice the coffin moving. That could spook him, if you will forgive the pun. I don't like it, I really don't. How long are we going to have to be in those things?"

Marlo may have been more sympathetic if he himself was shortly also to enjoy the confines of a coffin, but given that he was instead to sit face to face with the man he least wanted to see of anyone in this world and his stomach was tying itself in ever increasing knots, he found it hard to feel much pity for Lillian's brother. He would happily have swapped places.

"I don't know, Frederick, not long," he said distractedly as he focused on looking round the room and making sure that he would have a quick escape route should he suddenly have to take flight.

411

"What about George's coffin?" prompted Lillian in his head, keeping involved.

"Ah yes, George," said Marlo without thinking, but immediately thankful that what he had just said wouldn't sound that odd to Frederick if he quickly added "we need to prepare a coffin for him too."

Frederick nodded, happier to turn his attention to someone else's temporary incarceration. "A George-sized coffin should be a bit easier. Look, there's few over here that he should fit into."

"Don't forget the width though," Marlo reminded him, "you know, for down below."

Frederick turned and looked at him with some incredulity. "He isn't that well endowed, is he? My goodness."

"Oh no, no, I meant his legs. You know? He is sturdily built, isn't he. In the leg department...." He trailed off, wishing now he had never mentioned it. It is not as if Frederick wouldn't have noticed George's chunky lower limbs too.

Frederick flashed a smile. "Ah yes, of course, I see what you mean now. I'll see what I can find then."

By the time the door opened and Mr Babington stepped briskly in, both coffins were propped up against the wall behind where Walter was to be seated. They had decided that positioning them here would reduce the chance of him spotting any movement and also make it easier for the two pretend-corpses to hear what Walter was saying. Conversely, he would be more likely to hear them too if they made any noise, but that was a risk they would just have to take.

"Good evening, gentlemen!" announced the assistant coroner with a bright smile, clapping his hands and rubbing them together in a businesslike fashion. He had on the same smart attire that he was wearing when they last saw him, and looked for all the world as though he was about to convene a meeting to discuss Christmas holiday arrangements, rather than risk his life trying to trick a murderer into a confession. "Is everything ready?"

"Yes, we think so," replied Marlo.

"Think? Think? No dear boy, we must 'know'! Nothing must be left to chance." He looked round quickly and before Marlo had a chance to reply tutted slightly, strode to the table and pointed at a spot on it. "Just here, a glass of water for our guest. Oh, and one for myself too I think.

Hospitality, you see? We must give the impression of it even if we do not feel it. Other than that...." he paused for a final look round the room "....I think that this should be sufficient. Now, what say you to this?"

He reached inside his jacket and with a theatrical flourish pulled out an appropriately theatrical mask. It was black, and might have been something that Batman could have worn were it not for the fan of coloured feathers splayed out above the eyes. There were holes for all the requisite facial features and orifices, affording the wearer the luxury of seeing, breathing and speaking, which is all that was needed. "Don't know what this was used for, probably some French renaissance play a few years back, but I found it in the costumes trunk and it rather suits me, don't you think?"

He stretched it over his face and tilted his head in a manner that would be described as coquettish if modelled by a lady.

To Marlo it looked ridiculous and he could see Frederick struggling to suppress a smirk but they did not have time to debate the qualities or otherwise of a mask so he just replied meekly "yes, very good," then, "have you seen George?"

Mr Babington wrestled the mask off, revealing a look of mild surprise. "Is he not here yet?" Quickly realising that this was a silly question, he qualified it with "Well, no I suppose he isn't, that much is obvious. Is the boy always late?"

Marlo shrugged. "I don't know him well enough. I hope not."

"Hope is the enemy of planning, dear boy, the enemy. We do not have long, especially if Threadwell turns up early. If George is late and our subject is already here, I will just have to make up some story about him being an employee of mine or something and he will have to sit next to you." He nodded at Marlo.

Frederick bristled. "Wait, no, I am not having that. I get here on time and am bundled into a coffin while George arrives late and as a result doesn't have to? That, sir, is not fair."

Marlo chipped in with what he thought a much more important point. "Also, if Walter is faced by three people he might be less likely to spill the beans."

"Spill the what?"

"The beans. Oh right, sorry, it means tell us what we want to know, where I come from."

Mr Babington gave a little shake of the head to indicate that the effort of trying to understand someone else's linguistic peculiarities was not worthy of his attention. "Strangely expressed, but that is a salient point. Now, perhaps we should....."

He was interrupted by a knock on the door in the front reception room which gave them all a start. "That is either George or Threadwell," said Mr Babington, checking his pocket watch. "Twenty two minutes to the hour. I sincerely hope it is George. I locked the front door you see, I have the keys now."

He strode towards the door to the front room, stopping and turning briefly to say to Frederick "Young man, best you climb into your coffin" – a phrase he had probably not uttered before and hoped not to have to do so again.

As Marlo ushered the still unhappy Frederick back into his wooden box, they could hear voices, then just as Marlo had managed to get the lid correctly adjusted, in walked Mr Babington, closely followed by George. "We are safely delivered of our last accomplice," announced the older man, "who without further ado needs to take position in his, shall we say, accommodation for the evening." Seeing the look George gave him, he added "just to ensure a good fit, you see. Then we wait for Threadwell."

Frederick, awkwardly emerging once again from his assigned hiding place, threw George an empathetic glance that involved a raised eyebrow. "Not exactly an armchair," he pronounced sharply. But George was a little more phlegmatic and quickly tested out his coffin, successfully accommodating his legs as well as the rest of him into it and declaring himself happy with the fit, even if not with the imminent prospect of temporary incarceration.

"Good!" barked out Mr Babington. He looked at Frederick. "Now, Mr Jones. Perhaps you could be so good as to go through to the kitchen and get two glasses of water." Marlo pointedly cleared his throat. Mr Babington harrumphed a little. "Three, then, three glasses of water please Mr Jones. I need to go through our story with Mr Campbell here, make sure we have all eventualities covered, as well as getting myself into character of course."

And slowly but surely eight o'clock moved closer.

CHAPTER 50 : WALTER MEETS THE UNCLE

Walter had planned to be in Richmond Street no later than half past seven, half an hour early. He had realised that even if this rich uncle was going to meet him in some form of disguise, he would be unlikely to arrive at the venue looking like that, so Walter would be at an advantage if he could see him arriving, before the disguise went on, by keeping watch on the premises. He had done his research and had a look around JJ Tilcott and Sons a couple of days earlier, spotting a path down to an allotment with chest high hedges that he could crouch between.

But he had had a bad day at work. Two debtors were not in and he had to return later in the day when they were. So he finished late and then to cap it all on the way home, Gertie, his horse, had started limping. He had to take a detour to see Mr Furdle the vet, who had been busy seeing to a whimpering dog and by the time he had diagnosed a wedged stone in Gertie's hoof and removed it, something Walter could have fixed himself if he had thought to check, it was already twenty minutes past seven o'clock and virtually dark.

He just had time to get home, grab something to eat, then hitch up the long suffering horse again and set off for Richmond Street, arriving just a few minutes after the hour. So he was not in a good mood as he tied Gertie's reins to a lamp post and marched up to the front door of the undertakers.

He tried the door but it was locked. Well that would just about put the tin lid on his day, if this turned out to be a wasted journey. He knocked hard enough on the glass to cause the maximum noise without breaking it and stamped his feet impatiently. After a short wait and to his relief, the door was answered by Marlo Campbell.

"Come in, Mr Threadwell, please!" he said, waving the larger man through with an expression that could be generously described as lukewarm. Walter nodded with a similar lack of bonhomie and made his way into the dark, wood panelled entrance room, the coffin in one corner given a more ominous presence by the flickering shadows from the one gas light above it.

Marlo closed and locked the door, then brushed past Walter as confidently as he could muster and beckoned him to follow. "Through here please. My uncle is waiting for you."

They emerged into the preparation room, lit more brightly and containing a cornucopia of coffins and tools of the trade which so diverted Walter's initial attention that he was not as polite as he should have been in recognising that there was an important man standing on the other side of the table. Once acknowledged, though, he found it hard to take his eyes off him. The man had a most bizarre mask on, covering most of his face and with the top of his head obscured by feathers. It took some effort not to burst out laughing. He definitely hadn't expected that. One thing was for certain – the man would not have worn that disguise to get here, and if Walter had arrived when he had planned to, he might have seen who this fellow really was, although of course he probably would not have recognised him anyway. Walter could see white hair at the sides and a grey-white beard below, and he was smartly dressed, as he would have expected. Apart from Marlo Campbell, there was no-one else in the room.

"Mr Threadwell, welcome." said the comically masked man, extending a hand and shaking Walter's with a clutch almost as firm as his own. "You will forgive my use of the disguise; I believe my nephew has explained. Please, sit down. There's water there if you would like it. Nothing stronger, I'm afraid, not when doing business, you understand."

Walter nodded, unsure what to make of this rather peculiar situation. He checked round the room once more. There was one other door in the corner. Could there be a group of accomplices behind it, ready to leap out and accost him? Before sitting down he walked slowly over to it and tried the handle. The door was locked. Good. If there was anyone behind it he would hear the lock first. But then it was unlikely to have been locked if to be used as a means of attack. He turned and walked slowly back to his seat, easing himself down opposite Marlo and his uncle.

"I don't know what is behind that door either, Mr Threadwell. I have no need to." He guessed that the uncle was smiling behind the mask.

"I leave nothing to chance, Mr......?" asked Walter, leaving the question hanging.

The uncle made a short snuffling noise that was probably a chuckle. "You need not know my name yet, young man. All in due course. For the moment you can call me whatever you wish, provided it is not offensive, of course. But to make things easier for now, what shall we say....” he looked around the room for inspiration ”... how about Mr Wood?”

Walter felt as though he was being gently mocked but he bit his tongue. The prize could be worth it. “Mr Wood it is for now then,” he said without emotion. “Mr Campbell here told me you had some debtors who needed attending to.”

He gave Marlo an unnecessarily prolonged look as he spoke, laying down a marker. If a game was being played, he would be on to it. He wanted them both to know that.

Marlo maintained eye contact without blinking but felt like an antelope facing off a hungry lion and was relieved when Walter blinked first and returned his gaze to the man by Marlo’s side. He trusted that Mr Babington was feeling a lot more confident than he himself was, and was re-assured by his co-conspirator’s firm-voiced reply.

“Ah, yes, indeed, sir, indeed. A sorry tale, and not one that I enjoy recounting as it does not paint me in a good light. I was taken advantage of, you see. Not something that happens any more, I can assure you!” He wagged a finger energetically as he spoke, to emphasis this important point.

“The past is gone, Mr, er, Wood, all that matters to me is the future. These people who have your money, who are they? Why have they not paid you back?”

“Too big for their boots, sir! Jumped up popinjays, the lot of them! Think themselves more impressive than they are and just have to throw their weight around a bit to scare me off whenever I approach them or threaten proceedings. Well now it is time for me to throw a bit of weight too. My patience is at an end. They have had enough warnings. My problem, Mr Threadwell, is that I do not have the necessary, shall we say, muscle. My nephew here, trusted assistant though he is, does not present – and I am sure he will not mind me saying this – an intimidating presence. Nor do any of my other employees, as most of them are women. I need someone to do, shall we say, the dirty work.”

 “Most of your employees are women? What business are you in? Not funerals then?”

“Unfortunately not, young man. A good business to be in though, in this day and age. Never a shortage of customers, eh? And from what I understand......” and here Mr Babington lowered his voice and leaned forward slightly, as though Mr Tilcott upstairs might be straining to hear through an upturned glass on the floor "…. the bereaved are often led into spending more than is either necessary or desirable, paying inflated prices for no purpose other than to increase profits, although I had better keep those thoughts to myself whilst I am in this particular establishment, don't you think?"

Walter nodded. "I've heard they take hair off the dead and sell it for wigs," he said, as though this was a clever thing, before adding "most disrespectful, of course."

"Indeed, indeed." Mr Babington, now rather wishing he had not veered down that line of conversation, sat up straight again and resumed his normal volume, pulling at his cuffs as he did so. "No, clothing is my game. I have factories up north, clients in London, the south, and to some extent abroad. A large operation. That should tell you how important this is to me, that I have come here this evening to meet you. But I need assurances. Before we talk about the, shall we say, financials, I need to know you are the man for the job. If you are, this could be a very profitable arrangement for us both. Yes indeed."

Walter could see the mask nodding assertively, as the man whose face lay behind it sat back in his chair, finally taking a breath. Walter could see his eyes but only in the same way that a bank teller could see the eyes of a robber in a balaclava, making it very difficult to gauge emotion. He wanted to cut to the chase, though. Although he knew that this fellow had accumulated some wealth, he could already see that getting quickly to the point was unlikely to have been a contributing factor.

"What do you need to know?" he asked, still wary of this whole set up. Was it a trap? So far, it didn't seem so. But many times over history a great many confident men have fallen into traps that hindsight made obvious, and he wasn't going to add to that role call. He would not let down his guard. He would continue to analyse every word spoken, every gesture made by the odd couple in front of him.

Mr Babington, in his role as Mr Wood the rich uncle who wasn't really Mr Wood or indeed a rich uncle, took a sip of water from his glass and placed it carefully and deliberately back on the table, then steepled his hands and began a slow twiddling of his thumbs. Marlo felt the sudden urge to also take a drink but realised that this would look a little synchronised so held back, instead continuing to watch the over-confident brute on the other side of the table with a mixture of fearful hatred and reluctant admiration. Why could he himself not emulate and manufacture this aura of superiority and strength? He wondered how many ladies Walter had charmed over his short life and had his way with. Probably dozens. He started to hate him even more.

"Well now," said Mr Babington at last, "the job that I would be looking for you to do for me contains a number of elements. I doubt there are many that could do it to my satisfaction. This is why I must exercise considerable judgement, Mr Threadwell, and not leap to any fast decisions."

There was a sudden loud creak from behind Walter which caused him to start and Marlo's heart to leap into his mouth.

"What was that?" cried Walter, twisting round. Behind him, nothing moved. The coffins, some stacked horizontally, some vertically, remained still and silent. He turned back to Mr Babington, who appeared to be unmoved, although obviously it was hard to tell.

"These are freshly made coffins, Mr Threadwell. The wood is still curing, as it were. The occasional creak is not unusual, I can assure you. Perhaps you feel uncomfortable in the presence of death?"

Walter settled himself back in his chair. "No, of course not, quite the opposite. Continue, please."

Mr Babington had done well there and thought on his feet, and Marlo breathed an internal sigh of relief. He could imagine his hidden colleagues doing the same, only more so. Whoever's coffin the creak had come from would not be transferring weight from one foot to the other again, he was sure. He also guessed that they were fervently willing Mr Babington to get on with it and not engage in too many theatrical flights of verbosity, but Marlo suspected that this was about as likely to happen as asking a child alone in a room to look at a sweet without eating it. As if to confirm this, Mr Babington took a deep breath and began his next soliloquy.

"I have already satisfied myself that you are an efficient debt collector, Mr Threadwell. That much is clear. The incident, shall we say, with my young nephew here, well, that ended up being a useful exercise in a way that we had not intended. It was clear from that that you possess the ability to threaten, and are able to execute this attribute quite effectively. Clearly, when dealing with the men who owe me money, a great deal of that characteristic will need to be utilised. However, I need to tell you, Mr

Threadwell, that two of these men will be hard nuts to crack, so you may need to, well, crack some nuts, shall we say."

Despite becoming increasingly irritated by Mr Wood's verbal 'shall we say' tic – an itch he couldn't scratch - Walter had to smile. He knew what was meant.

Mr Wood continued. "So it is important that I know how far you are willing to go. Whether you will be up to the job should things become a little more, shall we say, challenging. I should say of course, although I am sure I do not need to, that I will not be officially suggesting anything that would contravene the laws of this great country. Not officially. Do you understand, Mr Threadwell?"

It was clear what was being suggested. A few 'extra-curricular' activities. Walter like the sound of that. He nodded. "Of course."

"Excellent. Now, I mentioned two men. I shall not give you their names yet. Both could be difficult but one of them, let us call him Mr X, particularly so. He has used my money to good effect and made himself a much richer man. But he used the money nefariously, Mr Threadwell, not for the purpose he promised me, but to set himself up offering 'protection' to businesses in return for money and favours. Not a pleasant way of doing business. So he employed associates who now work for him and apply the extortion. They also protect him and he thinks this makes him invincible, even from the law, let alone me. I would like to disavow him of this illusion. Make him realise that he is not the only one who can throw his weight around."

Mr Wood suddenly pushed back his chair, eased himself to his feet with a leisurely grunt, and started slowly walking up and down the room as he spoke, hands clasped tightly behind his back.

"Can't sit still for long these days, sir, age catches up with you. You will discover this one day, as will young Marlo here." He paused, extracted a handkerchief from his jacket pocket, and went to dab his brow, only to find mask feathers in the way. He quickly placed the handkerchief back in his pocket and resumed his stride with the air of someone who didn't want to wipe his brow anyway. "As I was saying, it is time to fight fire with fire. So I need to ask you a question, Mr Threadwell."

He stopped again, turned to face Walter, and insofar as you can ask a serious question when wearing a mask topped with feathers, asked him a serious question. "How much of a *hard* man are you, sir?"

"Hard?"

"Yes. Unafraid of danger, ready to instantly defend yourself, or indeed cause someone to need to defend themselves against you. Willing to take a risk if it the occasion demands it and face up to another man without flinching. Is that you, sir?"

Walter looked up at the feathered mask but he was no longer distracted by it. "My job depends on me being able to do that," he said simply.

"Good, good." Mr Wood resumed pacing. "But how far would you go, Mr Threadwell, should the occasion demand it? This is what I need to ascertain. With all due respect, I doubt that you will have encountered in your current role the situations I am anticipating with the work that I am proposing. This will be at another level. Compensated appropriately of course, but we will come to that. Let me be blunt. Have you ever punched a man, sir?"

Walter laughed. "Have I punched a man? I could not tell you how many times, sir, because there are too many to count. No-one has bested me in a fight and I intend to keep it that way."

Marlo could hear Lillian, silently listening until now, gasp in disbelief and mutter despairingly 'how could I have ever fallen in love with this brute.....I was such a fool'. At the same time he thought of Frederick, the man who knocked out Walter in a fight, listening from barely four feet away to the man boasting that such a thing had never happened and, being a man, probably itching to step out and put the record straight.

But Mr Babington picked up on this. "That is not what I heard, sir," he said. Marlo knew this was coming. It was a risk, and they had discussed it at length, but they had all concluded that it was a risk worth taking.

"What do you mean?" Walter looked accusingly at Mr Wood.

"I know a bit more about you than you think, Mr Treadwell. Some time ago a friend of mine, who just happened to have made use of your services a while earlier, was taking a drink in his local tavern when he was distracted by a scuffle. Then he saw you, sir, sunk by a punch from a young man not even your equal in size. Knocked you right out, he did. My acquaintance told me all about it the next day, and no mistake. So unless there is another Walter Treadwell matching your description....?"

Walter stared at his accuser, trying to disguise his anger. He wished he was wearing a mask too, that could have helped. This was something he had not seen coming, but how could he have done? What else did this man know? Quickly he weighed up whether it was best to deny it or hold his hands up. He took a deep breath.

"Alright, it is true, that did happen. But I did not count it as I was very much intoxicated at the time. If I had been sober, there would have been a very different outcome."

"And the young man who felled you, did you let him get away with it?"

Marlo tried hard to maintain an ambivalent expression but underneath his heart was racing. This could be it. He looked back to Walter, who had assumed the kind of smug, arrogant expression he recognised from his least favourite bullies at school.

"Of course not. He got his come-uppance, believe me, but not in the way you might expect."

"You got your revenge then?" prompted Mr Babington, trying to sound impressed in order to eke out some more crucial detail.

"Yes, with interest. Let's just leave it at that, shall we."

Marlo's heart sunk and he could hear Lillian groan. So close, so close. He wondered what Frederick was going through just a few feet away. The poor man must be going through hell, not just physically, but listening to this thug taunting him without realising and as good as admitting to murdering his sister but not actually saying the words they needed him to say.

But Mr Babington would not let it go. "There is a reason I am pressing you to the detail, Mr Threadwell." He paused, walked back to the table, then slowly settled back into his chair, making a satisfied grunt as though he had achieved something in doing so. "I have not been entirely truthful so far, and should I be so, I would like your word, in front of my witness here ...." he glanced sideways at Marlo "... that not a word of this discussion will ever be repeated outside of this room. Do I have your solemn undertaking on this, sir?"

Walter had raised an eyebrow in interest but it quickly lapsed back into a neutral expression. "Of course."

Mr Babington smiled humourlessly, matching his foe for lack of emotion. "Good. Good." He looked across at Marlo as though seeking his confirmatory approval for what was about to be revealed. Marlo, happy to let his partner continue to do all the talking, nodded his agreement, though of course it would have been more than a mild surprise to Mr Babington if he hadn't.

"Very well. The spirit of honesty will spin both ways, Mr Threadwell. Anything I say will remain confidential, as will anything you say to me. So just to confirm absolutely, is that understood?"

Marlo studied Walter's face for signs of his guard being dropped, but his dark, confident expression gave nothing away. It felt wrong to Marlo to be promising confidentiality when this was the exact opposite of their intentions, but that seemed a small moral price to pay for catching a murderer and none of them would lose sleep over it.

"Yes," replied Walter, still guardedly, and now shifting in his seat, getting comfortable for whatever revelations he was about to hear and wishing that the old man would just get on with it.

Mr Babington took a deep breath. "Mr X, who I have previously mentioned, has not just created a protection racket, with my money, he has actually had the nerve, the barefaced cheek, if you will, to turn his heavies on to my businesses too. So not only does this scoundrel take my money, he then uses it to extract more of my money! Can you believe that?"

Mr Babington's voice had risen dramatically as he pumped emotion into his performance, but Walter just looked at him dispassionately. "Well, yes, given that you are telling me that it is so."

"Indeed," said Mr Babington, slightly deflated by the response. "It is indeed so. The police are not interested as they need hard evidence that I cannot give them. He is clever, this fellow, I'll give him that. Leaves no trace back to him, does everything through third parties. My factory managers are scared of what he might do next. I need to stop him, Mr Threadwell, by whatever means necessary. But, to give him a taste of his own medicine, whatever happens to him must not be linked to me."

Forgetting he had a mask on, Mr Babington went to touch his nose with his forefinger in a conspiratorial fashion, but the mask got in the way so he abandoned the attempt and needlessly scratched his ear instead.

"And so what, in your opinion, should happen to him?" asked Walter, wanting to hear this without prompting.

Mr Babington glanced at Marlo again, building up the tension, then back at Walter. "Well, he needs to be stopped, if you grasp my meaning.

Now, how he is stopped is not my concern. But however it is done, I shall not care, to be perfectly truthful. And depending on the, shall we say, permanence of the solution, I am willing to offer a considerable reward."

"How much?"

"Four hundred pounds, sir. Subject to conditions of course. And this is just to deal with Mr X. The other debtors will be a separate negotiation, although of course far less lucrative, you understand, as they do not pose the same threat."

Marlo's initial reaction was that this was a derisory sum but he quickly realised that not in 1886, it wasn't. Four hundred pounds could buy you, well, a lot. He wasn't sure what, exactly, but certainly more than the set of four dining room chairs you could get with it today. Probably a stable of horses at least.

Of course Walter did not know that Mr Babington could have offered any sum he wanted because he had no intention of paying it, so he was a little taken aback by its generosity. He was expecting he would need to drive a hard bargain. Surely if this man was a successful businessman then he would have tried a lower opening gambit? But then perhaps all his verbal diarrhoea was just a facade and underneath there was a sharp business brain that did get straight to the point and didn't want to faff around arguing endlessly about fees. But that didn't stop him trying his luck.

"Mr Wood, I can't deny that is a good sum of money. If I were to take on this challenge, and was successful, I have one further request. I would like a share in your business and the possibility of a role in it too."

Mr Babington gave the appearance of thinking hard about this. He drummed his fingers on the table, then carefully stroked his beard, always a sign of great thought for reasons no-one seems to know. He cleared his throat. "Very well, Mr Threadwell, I am sure we can come to some kind of arrangement on that score. The details can be agreed in due course. However, there is one important question that we have not yet broached, and I need to know the answer before we take things any further." He placed his forearms on the table and leaned forward, light blue watery eyes staring fiercely through the mask at the man before him.

"Mr Threadwell, do you have the capacity to kill another human being? Do you think, when push comes to shove, that you have it within you? I cannot commit to any form of arrangement with you without

425

knowing that you have this in your armoury, so to speak. In fact, have you ever ended someone's life before? That would be the ideal proof."

He sat back, both he and Marlo watching Walter intently. This was it.

Walter sat perfectly still, staring back at the mask in front of him, glancing twice at Marlo. Could he tell them? Was it worth revealing his secret for what could be a life-enhancing amount of money and potential opportunity? If he didn't tell them, they might look for someone else. If he did tell them, then firstly he had their assurances of confidentiality – although they weren't really worth anything if they weren't written down, which of course they wouldn't be. Secondly, and more importantly, he could just deny everything afterwards. That snivelling wretch next to Mr Wood would soon succumb to a bit of roughing up if necessary, and if Mr X had managed to get this Wood fellow over a barrel he was sure that he could do the same. Yes, the cards were in his favour really. He would take the chance.

"I have ended someone's life before, yes. More than one, actually." He didn't move as he said this, and his face continued to display no emotion. Marlo marvelled at how anyone could be so matter-of-fact about such an awful revelation. It was as though he was proud.

Even though this admission was not totally unexpected, Mr Babington was glad his mask was there to hide his fleeting expression of horror and disgust at what he had just heard. He immediately regained his composure and went for the kill. "Was one of them not the young man who hit you, then? You said he got his come-uppance in a way I might not expect. Is that what you did then? Killed him?"

Walter sneered. "Ha! No, better than that. I killed his sister. And an old man who was in the way at the time. You will not find anyone who crosses me and avoids a consequence, you can be assured of that. That idiot will suffer now for the rest of his life."

He realised as soon as he said it that he had said too much. Admit to killing a man, but killing a woman, that was not going to go down well. He didn't have time to think about anything else though, as suddenly from behind him there was a blood-curdling scream of rage which caused him to jump out of his chair and swivel round, just in time to see the door of a coffin behind him fly open on its hinges, and a man spring out clutching a small knife.

Walter didn't think he could be frightened any more but it would be difficult for anyone not to get a shock if an angry screaming figure suddenly leapt out of a coffin right behind you. His heart leapt uncontrollably into his mouth and his body was infused with a surge of instant adrenaline, but this enabled him to immediately turn fright into fight. He had to defend himself. As his attacker, who he instantly recognised as Lillian's brother, raised the arm with the knife, he grabbed hold of it with both hands and twisted it hard, causing the knife to clatter to the floor.

Marlo and Mr Babington watched in horror as the two men, carried by the momentum of Frederick's attack, tumbled to the floor, pushing the table to one side as they fell. Great physical alacrity was required from the two observers to push their chairs back and leap instantaneously to their feet.

This was exactly what they did not want to happen, for Frederick to be overcome by his emotions, understandable though that may be. The fact that he had a knife as well, showed that he had come prepared. But now their cover was blown. Walter would know that this was a set-up.

Marlo didn't know what to do. He hated any form of physical violence or confrontation, but this was real. Two men were fighting in front of him, but he was too weak and cowardly to do anything other than try to get out of the way. He had his own knife but he wasn't going to use it, he just couldn't. Even if he did, knowing him he would end up stabbing Frederick by mistake. He stood transfixed, back against the wall, frozen by the horror of what was happening in front of him.

"Kill my sister, would you?" Frederick was screaming as he wrestled Walter on the floor in a re-enactment of that scene in the tavern all those months ago. "It's your turn now, you evil....." but he was cut off by a thick arm grasping him round the neck and pulling tight, while the other arm twisted Frederick's body round so that he faced away from him. Walter's legs were now tight around the legs of the lighter man, his stomach pressing into Frederick's back, one arm holding the left arm of his opponent, the other round his neck. This did not look good.

Mr Babington had hurriedly kicked the knife to the edge of the room and followed it into the corner, where he had begun jabbing his arms in a sort of 'pummelling a pillow' fighting motion, in that hope that his exertions would somehow assist Frederick in defending himself. A sudden moment of self-realisation then helped him to regain control of his arms and, instead of using the knife at his feet to assist Frederick, he instead resorted to barking 'Gentlemen! Gentlemen!", as though this would bring both men immediately to their senses and re-assert his suddenly emaciated authority.

Lillian was panicking, crying out in Marlo's head, "No, no, no! Stop them Marlo! What's happening? No! Frederick! Tell him to stop!"

Everything was chaos, but amidst this, the other coffin lid opened, a little tentatively. George's head poked round it. He saw what was happening on the floor just in front of him and immediately stepped out and skirted round the two writhing figures, heading straight for the table stacked with coffin wood. Grabbing a slab of teak about the size of a toilet lid, destined for a premium casket no doubt, he wheeled round, raised it high above his head to one side, and brought it down as hard as he could in a sort of a golf swing motion, smack into the back of Walter's head.

There was a loud crack, but not even a cry of pain. Just an immediate relaxation of grip and a body that went limp as quickly as though it had been shot, rolling slowly onto its back. Frederick, suddenly able to breathe again, gasped wretchedly as he threw Walter's arm to one side, crawled onto his hands and knees and crouched there panting like a dog, strings of thin saliva hanging from his mouth.

"What's happening? What happening?" Lillian was crying.

"It's ok!" Marlo whispered, not caring too much now if anyone heard him. What if Walter was dead though? What was going to happen? Why hadn't it already happened? Would he be going home or stuck here forever? He needed to know what was going on; he needed to check with Lillian, but right now he couldn't start a detailed conversation and arouse suspicion, even being so close to a conclusion of some kind.

Mr Babington, judging he was safe to do so, stumbled over and warily crouched down to check Walter's pulse. "He's alive, I think," he said. "Very faint pulse though, probably fractured his skull at the very least." He turned to George, who was standing legs apart, mouth open, still holding onto the piece of wood and with a look of mild horror on his face. "Young man, well done. You saved the day there. That was quite a strike."

George looked at him almost as though he hadn't heard him, a delayed shock settling in at what he had just done.

Mr Babington stood up, happy - now that the immediate danger was over - to assume command again. He pulled the mask off his face and wiped his forehead. "I won't be needing that any more, thank goodness. Now, we need to move quickly. This is not the result we had planned for." He looked pointedly at Frederick, who was pulling himself to his feet with an expression of surprise on his face that reflected his luck at escaping a suffocating death rather than anything else.

"Mr Campbell, could you please find something to tie our suspect's hands and feet together. There must be some of that rope they use to lower coffins into the grave around here somewhere. Ah, wait, here's Mr Tilcott!"

The undertaker, hearing the commotion downstairs and fearing for his business, had come running downstairs and burst through the door. "What the blazes is going on here? Why is that man lying on the floor? Ezra? What's happening?"

"No time to explain, my friend," said Mr Babington brightly, "other than to say that this is the man I told you about and we need to tie him up quickly. Have you some rope?"

Mr Tilcott, not being phased by the sight of a body even if not actually dead yet, and quickly sizing up the urgency of the situation, nodded and disappeared back out of the room, returning no less than twenty seconds later with a short length of rope.

He and Marlo then heaved the motionless Walter over onto his front, being surprisingly careless in failing to ensure that his damaged head did not hit the floor, and used one end to tie his hands behind his back and the other to tie his feet. The rope was a little too thick so they did the best job they could in tightening the knots.

"Right!" declared Mr Tilcott as he rose to his feet. "Now what?"

They all looked at each other. This was a situation none of them, even the two older and hopefully wiser gentlemen in the room, had previously encountered.

"Put him on the table?" suggested Marlo.

"The table is well suited to the purpose," observed Mr Tilcott, no stranger to seeing bodies occupying its surface. "I'll take the legs, if two of you gentlemen can take an arm and shoulder each. Careful now, if he's not the best part of fifteen stones then my name's Ermintrude. One, two, three, hup!"

And with a considerable effort Marlo and George helped Mr Tilcott heave the dead weight of the injured murderer onto a table that was thankfully easily sturdy enough to support him.

This at least qualified as having done something, but in reality they were no further forward as to what to do now.

"Am I in trouble?" asked George quietly, almost reluctant to ask in case he got the answer he didn't want.

Mr Babington shook his head vehemently. "Good lord, no, lad! Quite the opposite. It was a clear case of self-defence, although admittedly on behalf of another. You saved Mr Jones' life, if I am not mistaken, and for that the only response should be gratitude."

"Hear hear!" said Frederick, realising that he had not thanked George for what he did. "George, I owe you a great debt. You are a friend for life." He walked over to George and gave him an unexpected hug. "Thank you."

George brightened, and in the true British spirit attempted to downplay his heroism. "Well, I had to do something."

Marlo smiled but internally was cursing the fact that he had showed himself to be useless again. A real man could act in a crisis, use force where necessary, not shy away from danger. George had showed those qualities, Marlo had not. He had bottled it, as he knew he would when it came to the possibility of violence of any kind. It should have been him striking that blow on Lillian's behalf, not someone she didn't even know.

But then again, as they had discussed, it would have complicated things if he had done that, so alright, maybe he had done the right thing, but it didn't feel right, and irrationally depressed him. Talking of Lillian, he still needed to speak to her, not only to fully explain what had just happened but also to discuss what they can do next and what would happen to both of them if Walter, who was still out for the count and looking paler by the minute, suddenly died now.

Suddenly there was a low, quiet, barely imperceptible moan. "Sssh! What was that?" said Marlo. "Was that him?" They all looked at Walter. A small trickle of blood was crawling from one nostril, but apart from the slow rise and fall of his chest, nothing else moved. Marlo didn't like it. He wouldn't put it past the man to have just recovered consciousness and now be bluffing, pretending to be more badly injured than he was. He'd seen that so many times in films. Any minute now he would leap up and start fighting them all as though nothing had happened. But then again his hands and legs were tied so that might be tricky.

"We need to be careful," he said, "this guy could be like Rasputin."

"Who?" his companions queried in unison.

"You don't know him? Ah, right." Marlo, not for the first time, attempted to back track. "Old Mr Rasputin. William, his name was. He was a chap in my home town with, er, Russian ancestry. Wouldn't die. He suffered all sorts of, er, accidents, and kept recovering when no-one thought he would."

Frederick looked puzzled. "Why would we have known him?"

Marlo cursed himself internally. He knew he mustn't blow his cover now, not when they were so close. "Er, I just thought you might have read about him, as.......as.....he kept appearing in our local paper and was in the national papers a couple of times because of his....his... accidents. You didn't read about him?"

Frederick looked at the others, who all shook their heads, then turned back to Marlo. "No."

"Ok. Sorry, I just thought you might. Anyway, the point being, Walter isn't dead yet, and we don't even know how badly hurt he is. He might just have a sore head."

As Marlo had hoped the thought of their trussed up captive being potentially able to imminently recover and assault them quickly diverted their attention back to the room.

"Ezra, could I suggest you call for a doctor for this gentleman?" suggested Mr Tilcott. "That will at least answer our young friend here's concerns."

"Not without a policeman in attendance," replied Mr Babington, "that should be our first port of call. Who knows what this.... this... beast might try to do if he recovers suddenly. I will need to get word to Superintendent Weddall. And after what Threadwell has just admitted to, I have to say my sympathy for his welfare is stretched thin."

"You might need more than one officer," pointed out Frederick. "You know, just in case. Although on reflection, and looking at the wretch, even if that was him moaning I'd say his days, or hours even, could be numbered. I don't agree with Marlo. Look at his colour. And that was some clout that George gave him, as hard and true as I would have administered myself, and may still do so given the chance. The man would have to have an iron skull to emerge from that with just a sore head. My head was close to his at the time and even I felt it! Even if he starts to recover though, is it really worth it trying to take him to the courts? I'm not sure Threadwell qualifies as human after what he has done and so does not deserve to be treated as such. My position, gentlemen, is that he is close to death anyway by the look of it, so why not help him along? End his suffering, and ours. It would save everyone a lot of time and effort."

Mr Babington surveyed the four other men in the room, and they all looked back at him. There was a collective moment, a silence as they all weighed up the implications and wrestled with their consciences to varying degrees of intensity.

"I am the Assistant Coroner," pronounced Mr Babington at last. "I have a duty to uphold Her Majesty's rule of law. I cannot be seen to condone the ending of someone's life if not done through the correct channels, which is the courts."

Mr Tilcott, who had no personal axe to grind other than the prospect of conveniently having a dead body already on his premises and so not requiring transport, nodded sagely, obliged to support his friend.

Frederick shook his head. "This man deserves nothing. Not after what he did to Lillian."

Mr Babington stared at him intently, nodding slowly. "I understand your feelings, young man. Nevertheless, we have the confession now, in front of multiple witnesses, which is enough to convict him. We know indisputably that he killed her, and that other innocent man. We also know why he killed her, although I swear I cannot occupy the mind of a man who would plot and undertake such an endeavour purely for revenge over such a small trifle as a lost scrap in a tavern."

He paused, then sighed deeply. "Alright. I might regret this, but I am going to suggest that we all make our way into the adjoining room to consider our next steps, except, perhaps, yourself Mr Jones. You may like to have a last word, as it were, with the man who killed your sister. A man whose death will be justice for your sister and old Mr Whittleborough up on that cliff. And if he happens to pass away from his injuries while you are having a final word with him, well, that would be a terrible thing, wouldn't it?"

He gave Frederick a look that conveyed the essence of a wink without actually winking. Frederick's expression of dawning realisation, then surprise, turned to one of gratitude. Mr Babington ushered the rest of them out of the room and into the front reception area, closing the door behind him as though this would absolve him of whatever went on in there. As Marlo followed them all out, Lillian started talking quickly.

"Alright Marlo, I know you can hear me even if you can't speak to me right at this moment, and from what I have picked up, Walter is injured but not dead. But Mr Babington has left Freddie alone in the room with Walter, after which that situation might change. But I think we are alright! If Freddie gives Walter the final push, it sounds as though neither Freddie nor George will suffer any consequences as Mr Babington will just record the death as self-defence, which effectively is what it was, and Walter's death will not be unexplained so he will not become a transient. But the fact that I was murdered by Walter is now to be recorded so will be official, and the perpetrator will have been punished. Whether it is death now or death later doesn't matter. So everything is coming together - I think we are nearly there!"

Marlo clicked his teeth once in confirmation that he had understood, his excitement rising.

Mr Babington, his adrenaline having done its job and now passing the baton to a slow realisation of what had just happened and the situation they were all in, turned to face the others. He pulled out a silk handkerchief from his breast pocket and wiped his brow much as an actor might after a performance.

"Well, gentlemen!" he announced, "as I said, that did not go quite as planned, I must admit. Nonetheless, we have a result, due in no small measure to our hero of the hour." He smiled benevolently at George, then glanced at the door to the preparation room.

"Now, let us assume that Mr Threadwell does not live long enough to attend court, which strangely enough I am suspecting may be the case. My feeling, and I trust that all of you here will agree with me on this, is that it might be prudent to hold our counsel, shall we say, should anyone from the journalistic fraternity happen to pose any questions in their understandable desire to report on a death. I think the less publicity we attract on the circumstances of tonight's events, the better for all of us. If any of you are approached for comment, just refer straight to me, but I see no reason why you should be, as long as no-one knows you were here. Mr Holdsworth – he is The Coroner, you understand, and my superior in terms of rank – is a close acquaintance of all of the owners of all the local papers and I will ask him to, how shall we say, have words, and to advise them that this particular case warrants no comment in their columns. However, as Assistant Coroner I shall follow my civic duty and record the death, of course, and I will not be untruthful, just perhaps economical with what is recorded on the certificate. I suspect that 'accident' will suffice, because none of us had planned for this to happen. It happened, well, accidently." One hand toyed self-consciously with his beard. "Although I may have to work on that. I will also ask the superintendent to notify family, work colleagues etcetera so that they can arrange a funeral."

Mr Tillcott harrumphed quietly.

Mr Babington raised an eyebrow at him. "Don't worry, my old friend, I shall recommend you for the job!"

Mr Tillcott nodded approvingly. His back was being scratched as promised.

Marlo made his way over to George, whose strands of once neatly greased hair were now hanging randomly across his forehead. He still had a 'what have I just done' expression that no doubt reflected a whole lot of thinking going on inside, none of which was yet brightened by the prospect of a potentially significant share of a financial reward.

Marlo clasped his hand and shook it firmly. "George, I just want to say thank you for what you did. Well, everything you've done, really. I barely know you, but you trusted me, and you got involved in my scheme, even though you didn't have to. On top of that, you have just saved Frederick's life, and possibly saved other people's lives too if that evil man had been allowed to carry on as before. You're a star."

George looked pleased but also slightly confused. "A star? Why...?"

"Er, yes, well, in the sense of a beacon, a shining light, an example to others. Thank you!" Marlo knew it didn't mean exactly that but it would do.

With a final shake of George's hand, he turned to Mr Babington, who was possibly now questioning his previously unshakable belief that verbal dexterity was sufficient to extricate oneself from almost any given situation.

"Mr Babington, could I shake your hand too. You were magnificent in there. Played the part to perfection. You got the confession! That was brilliant!"

Mr Babington beamed, self-belief starting to return. He was not used to receiving praise but, whoever it came from, he would take it if offered. "I take it that I am a planetary object too then?"

"Of course! Where I come from, you would definitely be called a star."

"Where *do* you come from, Mr Campbell, just out of interest?" asked Mr Babington, "I've noticed you have a strange turn of phrase...."

But before Marlo could answer there was a loud crack from next door which made them all jump. Despite there being four of them, and despite being perfectly aware of the respective physical and mental states of the two individuals in the preparation room, in unison they instinctively backed away from the door, watching it nervously in the unlikely event that they had made a terrible misjudgement and a rejuvenated and snarling Walter came bursting through.

But instead there was a silence. Then, a repeated slapping noise accompanied by some rough grunting. The four men, looked at each other, gained collective courage from strength in numbers, and edged back towards the preparation room. Mr Babington, finding himself pushed reluctantly to the front and thereby nominated to open the door, did so with the initial caution of a man expecting to reveal a lair of waiting tigers.

Marlo stayed at the back, hoping and praying something might happen to him that he did not want the others to see. Over the shoulders of his companions he could see as the door opened that Frederick was punching the unconscious Walter's bloodied face repeatedly, muttering "that's for Lillian, and that, and that," as his fists flailed. The large piece of wood that George, and now presumably Frederick himself, had used as a weapon, was beside him on the floor.

As Mr Babington and Mr Tilcott rushed forward to pull him away, Marlo felt something. His stomach was moving. He clutched the outline of the diary in his jacket pocket, confirming, as he had been doing so many times every day, that it was still there. He heard Lillian call out "Marlo, can you feel it? Has Walter died? Do we have finality? Is this it? I can feel something!"

"So can I, I think it might be!" he whispered, conscious that the others were pre-occupied with Frederick, "please let this be it...."

It was as sudden as the first time. A blinding light forcing his eyes closed, then the sensation of rushed movement, his stomach on a rollercoaster, up then down, then, nothing. No bang this time. Just silence.

The smell hit him almost before he had opened his eyes. It was familiar, a warm taint to the air that he could not describe. As his eyes focused and adjusted from the bright light, he could see a dirty window in front of him and outside a big palm of cloudy grey sky being pointed at by fingers of concrete and glass buildings. Car horns were sounding, a helicopter buzzed in the distance. He was home.

In the reflection from the window, something white caught his eye. He wheeled round.

"Lillian!"

"Marlo." She smiled, those big brown eyes filling with tears, and rushed towards him, grabbing him, hugging him in a way he had never been hugged before. "You did it! Freddie did it! We made it! I'm alive again, can you believe that? Look, here I am! I am so happy! Thank you, thank you, thank you!"

She released him, stood back, and beamed excitedly, then looked at her surroundings. "Is this where you live, is this your home? On my! Look at all these strange things! And oh! Look! Marlo, look how high we are, and all those huge buildings outside, just like you said there were. We are as high as the birds! Are we safe? Oh my goodness!"

She backed away from the window and sat down on the sofa, her simple white dress spreading around her. "I feel quite giddy."

Marlo's emotions were suddenly as mixed up as they had ever been. What did he do now? He was deliriously happy. His dream had come true. The girl whose diary he had found, whose story he was writing, who he had effectively brought back from the dead, was here in his flat. Marlo Campbell had a girl in his flat, and he had decided that he was most definitely in love with her.

But how did he keep her and try to win her over? She had been really nice about what he had done for her, but in reality he hadn't done very much – it was George and Frederick who had finished off Walter. If he had followed convention, the way it works in films, he would have found some inner strength, overcome his inner demons, and amazed everyone with a show of manly aggression against the evil bad guy.

But apart from when he came up with the story of the rich uncle while being crushed up against a wall, he hadn't done any of that. OK, he had organised things, set the wheels in motion, but he had relied on others to help him, and been very pleased that they had. He was still a wimp. When Lillian reflected on it, she would realise that, wouldn't she? Could this be the pre-cursor to the biggest disappointment of his life yet when she encounters the first man who isn't him and decides she would rather switch to someone better?

In any case, he still had no idea what she felt about him and if the past was anything to go by he certainly wasn't going to be able to correctly interpret any positive clues unless they were presented on a silver platter by a troop of footmen playing trumpets. Fear of doing the wrong thing would always outweigh the risk of making the first move, and asking her directly what her feelings were could also go horribly wrong. She might be grateful to him, see him as a friend, but that's probably as far as it would go. But then they have such a huge shared secret, surely that will be enough to keep them together?

All of these heated thoughts flew through his head in an instant. But then they were gone, put in the pending tray. Let's forget all that for now, Marlo, just deal with the present and enjoy it.

He walked over to the sofa, realising as he did so that he was back in his own clothes, and tentatively sat down next to Lillian. It was something he would never normally do as he always knew that no girl would want him to, but, given the circumstances, he hoped she wouldn't mind. Jeez, she smelled good. No perfume other than her own. To his delight she didn't even shift to one side. She just looked at him with all the sweet enthusiasm of a child on Christmas Eve, a wide smile that wasn't going anywhere.

He smiled back, relief merging with elation. His eyes were as bright as hers. "What happens now?" he asked her.

She put her arm around his shoulder and gave him a squeeze. "Marlo, that is entirely up to you."

EPILOGUE PT 1

Tim had found himself slightly at a loss for things to do since he finished the book. It had taken him such a long time to do, but now he had an accomplishment to his name, something that wouldn't just be lost in the corporate sinkhole of false attainment that occupied your entire working life yet which meant pretty much nothing to anyone else. So you negotiated an extra three per cent off a service contract to clean the toilets. Who cares? Is it something you will proudly tell your grandkids? Will future historians be documenting your achievement, recording your name for future generations to revere?

No, in most jobs you just did what you had to do, then came home again, and however brilliantly you did your job and however much you achieved, no-one outside work could give a monkey's. But writing a book, this was a thing, a real legacy. Well it would be if anyone read it of course.

Having said that, he did find it a bit odd that he, along with so many other people, felt the need to bequeath a legacy of some kind to a grateful population given that the nature of a legacy is that the originator will not be around to bask in any consequent glory, but hey, the human psyche is a strange creature.

So now he had his book. The only problem was that it was no good to anyone if it just remained on his computer and never saw the light of day. He had to get it published somehow, and he had been struggling to decide which was the best way of doing this now that self-publishing was a thing. Working out what to do was almost harder than writing the damn thing in the first place. He'd ended up taking the easier option and sending off manuscripts to some literary agents, but five of them had come back with a 'thanks, but no thanks', and the other three had not yet replied and of course might never do so. Now he had to decide on next steps.

It was June now, the days were nice, long, and warm, and the front lawn of which he was so proud was like a small child in that it wouldn't stop growing and demanding attention. Today was a Saturday, and although this made no material difference to him now that he was retired, it did mean that there was sport on the telly and he had got into the habit of adjusting his schedule to fit. At least now there were no light-hearted arguments with Liz about how pointless it was to watch people kicking a ball around or running in circles round a track and why didn't he go and do something useful instead – now he could watch whatever he wanted, whenever he wanted. Was it wrong to say that there were some small compensations to Liz not being around anymore? Probably.

He pottered into the kitchen to see what he might rustle up for lunch. Just as he opened the fridge to remind himself of what possibilities lay within, the doorbell rang. Strange, he thought, I'm not expecting anyone. Maybe it's a parcel. He shuffled to the front door and peered through the spy-hole. A young man and woman. He opened the door.

The young man was clean shaven and quite plain looking, the girl definitely not so. This chap was undoubtedly punching above his weight. The man spoke first. "I'm really sorry to disturb you, but we were just on a drive through the country and our radiator sprang a leak and we've ground to a halt just outside there. I've called the breakdown services but we were wondering if you would mind if we pushed the car into your drive just to get it off the road. Would that be ok?"

Tim's initial wariness was eased by the young man's polite demeanour and the lovely smile of the young lady. This didn't seem like a scam. Always have to be on your guard these days, he had heard a lot of tales on the radio about door-steppers duping elderly folk, but these two weren't offering to tarmac his drive or anything; they seemed genuine.

"I don't see why not," he replied, "I'm not going to be using the car today. Can't give you a hand though, I'm afraid. The knees wouldn't take it. Will you be alright?"

The man looked at the woman, who shrugged. "On second thoughts," said the man, "perhaps if I could borrow some water to fill up the radiator, that will be enough just for me to drive it round the corner."

"A much better idea!" laughed his companion, "as long as this kind gentleman doesn't mind?"

Tim couldn't help smiling. "My dear, I don't mind at all. Please, come in, we'll find a jug or something."

A few minutes later and the man, furnished with what ended up being a small bucket of water, was out in the road attending to his car. The young lady had gratefully accepted Tim's invitation of a cup of tea and they were both in the kitchen waiting for the kettle to boil.

Tim dropped some teabags in the cups. "I hope he's alright out there."

"Oh, he'll be fine," said the girl, "Marlo said he has had this problem before, so he knows what to do. He said that last time he couldn't afford to replace the thingamajig that needed replacing, so he did a temporary repair which....... sir, are you alright?"

Tim had turned round suddenly from putting the teabag box back in the cupboard, his mouth had dropped open, and he was staring at the girl as though she had just told him that some aliens bearing a selection of cheeses had landed in his garden.

"What..... what did you say his name was?"

"Marlo. It's quite unusual, apparently."

Tim leaned back against the kitchen worktop, suddenly feeling the need for some physical support. "It certainly is. I've just written a book, and the main character is called Marlo Campbell. I thought I had made it up. That's an amazing coincidence!"

Now it was the girl's turn to look incredulous. "But.... Marlo is called Marlo Campbell too. How did you..... oh, this is too strange."

Tim shook his head in disbelief then looked up suddenly and fixed the girl with a curious eye. "Your name isn't..... Lillian, is it? Lillian Jones?"

"Yes! Yes, it is! How did you know that? Have we met you before? No, we can't have done. This doesn't make sense. We need to get Marlo."

And with that Lillian ran out of the kitchen and Tim could hear the front door being opened and fast footsteps on gravel. She was obviously as flustered as he was. She was right, this didn't make any sense at all. These were his characters, that he had made up, and now here they were, or at least their namesakes, at his house. He wasn't dreaming, he knew that much.

Perhaps it was actually just an incredible coincidence, akin to that poor American fellow who was struck by lightning seven times. There were plenty of examples like that over history, but this, well this just seemed impossible. Well, there was only one way to find out. He made his way slightly unsteadily to the open front door and saw that Marlo had managed to get his car onto the drive. It was a scruffy looking dark red VW Polo. Wasn't that the car he had described Marlo as having? He couldn't remember, it was so long ago that he had written that. He had a nagging feeling that it was though, and it wasn't helping.

Lillian was with Marlo, animatedly recounting the conversation she had just had with Tim. They were just too far away for Tim to hear what was being said, but then Marlo turned to look at the house and saw Tim. He looked back at Lillian, grabbed her hand, and the two of them crunched up the drive towards him, both with expressions of intensely puzzled apprehension.

"It sounds as though we need to talk?" said Marlo simply as he approached.

Tim beckoned them both back in to the house. "Yes, yes...we certainly do. Come into the lounge."

Marlo and Lillian took the sofa, Tim perched on the front of his armchair. All thought of cups of tea were forgotten.

Marlo was in first. "Lillian says you know our names even though we've never met. Well, we can't have done, can we? What is your name?"

"Tim. Tim Jenkins."

Marlo and Lillian looked at each other and face shrugged. They looked back at Tim, who was studying them closely. "Do you know," he said, "now I think of it you even look like my characters, how I had imagined them. It's just remarkable. Marlo, can I ask, do you live in London?"

"Yes. Yes, I do. Although so do a lot of other people." Marlo was not prepared to stop clutching at straws until they had all gone.

Tim took a deep breath. "Alright, I have to ask this. Lillian, are you Victorian?"

Lillian gasped and turned immediately to Marlo. "How could he..... oh my. Marlo, what's happening?"

Marlo had continued to stare at Tim, and just shook his head slowly. "I don't know," he replied softly under his breath.

Tim wasn't going to stop there. "Marlo, you wrote a book about Lillian based on her diary. You went back to 1886 to solve the mystery of her murder. You found her murderer, got him to confess, and he was killed. This enabled you to come back with Lillian. That, in a nutshell, is what I wrote in my book. Oh, and a whole load of stuff about how the world and the universe was created which I just sort of made up." A look of mild horror crossed his face. "That isn't true as well is it?"

Marlo turned slowly to look at Lillian, the two of them struggling to process the implications of what they had just heard.

"What did you write about creation?" Lillian stalled for time.

"Well, I invented this concept of Number Five, who is one of a number of immensely powerful creators that we as insignificant humans cannot comprehend. But Number Five is responsible for......"

"Stop! Stop!" cried Lillian suddenly. "You don't need to say anything else. He knows, Marlo, he knows. Everything. What does this mean?"

Her eyes were moist, and Marlo could feel the same fear, the same feeling that everything they thought they knew was being uprooted and in a direction that they could least have expected. Were they actually just characters in Tim's imagination, thinking they were living a real life but in reality fated just to do whatever he decided, their back story just a necessary lead-up to where the action started? But how could they be when they were talking to him now, in real life?

Marlo had a thought. "Your book, when does it end? It is finished, isn't it?"

Tim nodded. "Yes, in as far as it could be. Marlo and Lillian, well, you two, I suppose, had just returned from 1886. I had to stop it somewhere, so it finished moments after you returned. Both of you were in your flat, Marlo."

"That was last autumn. So everything since then, you've not written about?"

"No."

That put Marlo slightly more at ease. He did have some free will at least, and perhaps this meant that once the book finished, that was it, he could go back to living his own life. But who was this Tim Jenkins? Was he Number Five in disguise, playing with them?

Lillian was clearly thinking along similar lines. "So Mr Jenkins, is there anything we should know about you? You obviously know all about us, but we don't know anything about you. Are you....do you......is there more to you than meets the eye?"

Tim wished there was. "Just call me Tim, please. No, I'm just a boring old ex-civil servant who wrote a book. That's it, I'm afraid. I have no more insight into this situation than you do."

For a moment a heavy silence descended as they all sat there in disbelief, thoughts tumble-drying around in their heads, each trying to work out where all this led. Tim in particular was struggling to believe that he appeared to have written a work of fiction that was fact, and solved the mystery of creation while he was at it. That was ludicrous. It just couldn't be. Yet here were Marlo and Lillian in front of him, telling him it was so. But then they would do, wouldn't they, if he had invented them? But no, he hadn't invented them, they must have been around before he started describing their lives in his book. Nothing made sense, he was just going round in circles.

Marlo was first to speak. "Ok. So you wrote a book about me writing a book, yes?"

"Yes, and I even put in passages that made it look as though someone else was writing a book about me writing a book but towards the end it turned out it was me all along... is that right? Oh lord, I've confused myself now."

Marlo sat forward. "Right, well that's actually along the lines of what I was thinking could be an explanation. No, actually, forget it, it wouldn't make sense."

"What wouldn't?" asked Lillian.

Marlo pursed his lips, glanced at the other two, then took the plunge. "Ok, what I'm thinking is that if you wrote about us, and what happened in 1886, and now here we are in a situation that you haven't written about, who is to say that what is happening now isn't just part of someone else's book? So although we think we are real, and...." he grabbed Lillian's arm and shook it gently "... we are real, aren't we, as far as we are concerned, but maybe actually we are just players, all three of us, in another dimension created by another author, a sort of fictional reality."

Tim raised an eyebrow. "So what you're saying is that when an author writes a work of fiction that somehow creates a parallel dimension where the world that author has created actually happens?"

"Well, to the characters, yes."

"And so that is the reason that we have been brought together like this. Your car could have broken down anywhere but it just happened to be outside my house because that was a plot device engineered by someone writing a book about us. But meanwhile I've been doing the same to you. But only because someone else was writing about me doing that. Oh my goodness, my brain hurts."

Marlo scratched his head fiercely. "You're not the only one. I don't know why I just thought of that, but..."

"I'm not sure that could be right though," interjected Lillian. "After all, how far back could this 'author writing about an author' thing go? It is like asking who or what created Number Five, and who or what created them. You've just said that someone could be writing about Tim writing about Marlo writing about me, but what if the person writing about us isn't real either, but the creation of another author? That could stretch back to an infinite degree, couldn't it?"

"I don't know," admitted Marlo, "I haven't had time to think all this through. It's only a theory, anyway."

Lillian tried to answer her own question. "Actually that would be a pretty challenging read, wouldn't it? Who's going to want to read a book with multiple layers of authors all writing about the one below them, as it were. One or two layers is enough, surely. Even someone writing about Tim writing about us seems a bit far-fetched. Who would want to read that? It would get the reader really confused. So I suppose it is self-limiting."

Marlo nodded slowly. "I guess that means that whichever author is at the top of the tree – the one who has no-one writing about him or her – that author is the only one who lives in a world that really does have a proper creator, like Number Five, or a god. Or not, of course, if you are an atheist. Theirs is the real world."

"How can any of us know what's real any more," said Tim, shaking his head.

Lillian looked at him for a while, digesting this. "But then.... that means that the Number Five that we know about, and that Tim wrote about, might not exist? Well, to us he does of course, but not in the overall scheme of things. Unless the author writing about us lives in a world where Number Five really does exist and that is why he or she has written about him. But then how would they know that, unless Number Five has revealed himself to mankind, which isn't likely is it? Or maybe.... oh, I don't know."

She trailed off, and all three of them were silent for a while, once again lost in a jumble of competing mental tangents that they all wished would somehow converge. Outside a blackbird was singing, its bright and glorious trilling an incongruous backdrop to the weighty, burdened conversation taking place within the house. None of them really heard the birdsong though; every pause in conversation was overwhelmed by all-consuming reflection and rumination.

"There's another thing," said Tim suddenly. "No writer details every minute of their character's lives, do they? So the life both of you led before I started your story, that all happened didn't it, without anyone writing about it? And my life, too, I suppose, if someone is right now typing what I am saying. How would that work?"

Marlo scratched his head again. "It wouldn't. Unless....."

"Go on," prompted Lillian.

"Unless we come pre-programmed with memories. As soon as someone starts writing our story, we appear fully formed, as it were....." he trailed off, already internally questioning his own logic.

Tim thought for a while. "So you, Marlo, would have come into existence sitting at your computer typing "Lillian, grab this rope" and you, Lillian, would have first appeared in your world hanging from a cliff. A nice way to start!"

Marlo turned to Lillian apologetically. "You can thank me for that."

"On the contrary!" objected Tim kindly, "I think you will find that it was me. I can only apologise, my dear. I made him do it."

A hint of a smile played at Lillian's lips. "And someone might have made you do it too! I don't think it mattered either way, so I forgive you both. But in any case I can't believe what you are saying, I just can't. I know I have lived my life, every day of it. It was real! That last day..... well, it just felt as though that was just another day like any other, all twenty years of them."

"It must be seamless then," said Marlo, "as I feel the same. As far as I'm concerned, I've lived every minute of my life. To be fair, it would sound stupid to say anything else. And what about you, Tim? If our theory is true, you don't even know when your written story and therefore your actual life started, and I'm guessing that you've not felt anything, experienced anything unusual?"

Tim shook his head. "Nope. Nothing." He thought for a second. "You would also have to ask 'why'? Why create all these parallel worlds every time someone wrote a book? And think of all the books that are written, there must be millions of them; some of them have outlandish plots and settings. Take science-fiction for starters, are all these recreated and lived out in another dimension?"

"Remember though that we aren't talking about books in this world – they are in another, and there may not be many of them. Also it could just be selected books? If a being like Number Five is controlling all this then he can do what he likes, can't he? He may restrict it to certain types of book only, like just ones set on earth. Or conversely, he might use the imagination of humans to create new worlds that he hadn't thought of."

Tim perked up. "Now that is a thought! I like that idea. It would be a very easy way to indulge your fantasies too. Oh hang on, no it wouldn't because it would be the characters in your book that experience them, not you. But then that would mean you would have complete power. If I had known this I could have changed your lives in so many ways."

"You already have," chorused Marlo and Lillian.

"I meant for the better," replied Tim with a wry smile. "Assuming that the author writing my story allowed me to, of course."

Marlo nodded. "Whether what you write is what you are thinking or what the author above you is making you think, that might be the key. Of course Lillian and I am at the bottom of this particular food chain so we have no say in the matter!"

"Especially me," pointed out Lillian with a mock pouty lip. "Although less so now as Marlo won't be writing about me any more, will you Marlo?" She wrapped her mouth around the last three words to make it perfectly clear to Marlo that he wouldn't.

"No dear," he said, exaggerating a henpecked husband voice.

Tim butted in. "Back to our dilemma? If your theory about our memories is wrong, Marlo, then the only other thing I can think of is that time has to run backwards and then forwards again for us to have lived the life that leads up to the bit that is being written about. That seems a bit unlikely."

Lillian chipped in. "Oh, but time can go backwards, can't it? That's what I was able to do when I was in the Midrift! Turn back time!"

"Cher can do that too," smiled Marlo, unable to resist.

"Ah, now.... I've heard of her. She's a singer isn't she? Is that right?" Lillian looked at Marlo hopefully.

"Well done, yes she is. She's not going to help us here though. That was a song not a talent."

She looked down at the floor, missing the humour. "No.......no, she won't in that case. Also, thinking about it, if we are right then I could only turn back time because Tim wrote that I could." She glanced up at Tim with a face that reflected the confused and slightly deflated feelings that this realisation had brought.

Tim felt briefly powerful until he remembered that his actions were probably no more of his own volition than Lillian's were, however much it felt like it. He stood up and stretched.

"Well, I don't think running time backwards and forwards just to fill in the gaps is even remotely possible. Think how much chaos that would cause. And it wouldn't easily explain memories. No, I would suggest that at the moment, Marlo, your theory about someone writing about us and creating our world, and our memories being fully formed when we appear, is the only one we've *got, whether it has a few logic gaps or not. It might be implausible but I can't see any other plausible explanation for the situation we are in."*

Marlo shrugged gently. "I agree."

They fell into another silence, digesting it all. The blackbird had flown off and so now the only sound was the gentle tick-tick of the mantelpiece clock. Tim didn't normally hear it – it was such a constant that his brain usually just merged it into the background, there but not there. Now it felt amplified, almost as though it was trying to encourage someone to speak so that it could quieten down again. It was Lillian who obliged.

"Oh my. Oh my goodness." Her mouth had fallen open and she looked at the two men with an expression of shock that Marlo hadn't seen before. "Do you know what this means? If you are right, Marlo, do you know what this means?"

It was a rhetorical question of course but both men shook their heads as convention dictates.

Lillian blinked fast and her words sped up. "Alright, this is what I am thinking. If someone is writing about this scene we are in, together, here in your house Tim, they are writing our conversation, are they not? If not word for word then at least summarising. Just like you presumably did with us, Tim."

Both men now switched to careful nodding.

"Right, well, what that means is the solution we have just come up with is the one that the author wanted us to come up with, as it must be what he has written. Therefore, it is the correct one! So we must indeed have started our lives at the point that the book started, with all our memories pre-installed in order for our characters to function properly. Yes?"

Marlo clutched Lillian's arm briefly before immediately letting go. "Yes, yes. That could be it. But that means we have no free will. Everything we are saying is the product of some author's imagination, even what I am saying now. That can't be right. It doesn't feel right. I'm saying what I want to say, aren't I? Supposing I suddenly say 'penguin' for no reason. What author would think that was something a reader would want to read? Some bloke randomly saying 'penguin'. I had free will there didn't I, to say it, proved by the fact that I did!"

Tim let out a sigh. "We don't know. This is all supposition. I would just point out though that I didn't write down every single conversation you two ever had, and I am sure the same applies to whoever might be writing about us. So in between what is being written for us, we must have a bit of leeway. How all that knits together is anyone's guess. Maybe you saying 'penguin' will be cut for editorial reasons."

Marlo smiled. "I hope not. It is not often I say 'penguin'."

"That's three times now already," pointed out Lillian.

Marlo's grin suddenly morphed into to an expression of shocked realisation. "Hang on, hang on, I think might have an answer!"

"To what?" asked Lillian.

"To everything! You know, the situation we are in."

"Go on then."

"Ok," he said slowly, as though still forming it in his head. "Have you heard of simulation theory?"

"Possibly," ventured Tim hoping to sound more informed than he was. Lillian unsurprisingly shook her head.

"It says that we could all be living in a simulated world, like we are part of a computer programme, you know? So somewhere, a far more intelligent race than us has been able to recreate consciousness and run imagined worlds on computers, or whatever equivalent they have, and we are just characters in one of those worlds. It is not as cranky as it sounds either, lots of intellectuals have supported it."

"Hence why it was called 'The Sims'" mused Tim.

Lillian glanced him a look of exaggerated incomprehension. "I was struggling just to follow Marlo but now you have lost me completely."

"The Sims was an early computer game," explained Marlo, "where you created your own simulated world of little people and buildings. So Sims as in simulation, yes. But this is on a totally different level."

Tim's face was now screwed in concentration as his brain tried to keep up. "So you are saying it might not be Number Five, and it might not be an author writing about us, but instead it is just some teenager playing a computer game in the future. Well, not in the future I suppose, but in an upstairs universe somewhere."

"Well, yes, but also no," replied Marlo enigmatically. "What I'm saying is that maybe within the Simulation Theory our author theory still holds true. So in this upstairs universe, as you call it, someone has written a book about everything that happened to us, and just by typing, or thought transferring, or whatever method they use, this story onto their computer, the computer turns it into an imagined reality, the one we are in now."

As Tim and Lillian continued to look blankly at him, he continued. "So what I mean is, the Simulation Theory helps explain how our own theory could be less fantastical than it sounds. There is still someone or something who created this adventure, but the way it came to life was through the Simulation Theory."

"Ok...." said Tim slowly, "but it is just a theory, however many intellectuals have proposed it. I'm guessing there is no evidence for it and no way of proving it?"

Marlo shrugged. "No, but look at the progress we've made over the last 30 years alone and what we can do with computers. Imagine where we will be in 100 years. Creating virtual worlds within computers will be old hat by then. In fact... we might actually be part of a virtual world created by humans of the future, not some upstairs universe space beings – I wouldn't rule that out. If so, I'm impressed, they've done an amazing job."

"I could do with a software patch for my knee though," said Tim.

Marlo smiled. "I'd want a complete upgrade. Far too many bugs on me."

Lillian, who had managed to understand approximately half of what the other two had been talking about, could no longer remain silent. "Bugs on you? What are you talking about?"

He grinned at her. "Software bugs. It means things that are wrong, need fixing. Don't worry, I'm not covered in insects."

"Well that's a mercy at least. This theory of yours though, it is becoming extraordinarily complicated......"

Marlo shifted uneasily. "I am quite probably completely wrong with this whole suggestion and there is a perfectly sensible explanation for all this. It is just that my brain is leaping all over the place."

"You're not the only one," said Tim with a nervous chuckle. He suddenly clapped his hands as though summoning a servant. "Right! Before we twist ourselves into any more knots, would you like to see the book?"

"Absolutely!" said Marlo. They all needed a break from this, although it was not exactly changing the subject.

They spent the next couple of hours hunched over Tim's computer, homing in on all the key passages, and Marlo and Lillian were able to confirm that, as far as they could recall, every word Tim had written had *indeed taken place, right down to the conversations – further confirmation of their theory.*

Realising the potential implications and feeling it didn't really matter right now, Tim was careful to skip past all of Marlo's background story regarding his lack of success with women, although he was confident that by now Lillian would not keel over in shock if she were to read it. Us losers have to stick together though, he thought, whatever situation we find ourselves in.

There was a brief interruption when the mechanic turned up and fixed the leak in Marlo's radiator, advising him to replace it as soon as he got home, but this was a distraction from what had suddenly become a lot more important and the repaired car stayed where it was.

As they turned to the last chapter and re-lived the couple's arrival back in the 21st century, Tim left them reading and wondered over to the window to stare vacantly at the apple tree in the garden.

"I was thinking of writing a sequel, you know," he said. "About how you adjusted to modern life, Lillian, and then the possibilities of more adventures. Written from your point of view this time, as I didn't do that at all in this book otherwise it would have been even longer. I also realised that almost all the main characters apart from you were men, and these days that kind of thing gets pointed out, so I could put that right in the next book. I'm not sure what to do now. I don't know if I have to rely on someone else to be writing about me doing that or can I just crack on?"

"Crack on what?" asked Lillian, looking up from the screen.

"I'd just crack on if I was you. See what happens!" said Marlo.

Lillian ignored the fact that she had been ignored and smiled brightly at Tim.

"Well, I could tell you my point of view, so you wouldn't have to make it up."

Then her face fell. "Oh, but that would have to be after the event, though, wouldn't it? If we are to have another adventure then you would have to write it first. The writing dictates everything, according to our theory. Alright, well, I could give you some upfront advice at least. Although.... I'm not sure I really want any more adventures quite yet."

"I'm with you there," said Marlo, before adding "isn't there is still a big plot hole in all this though? Tim didn't write about the last six months and we still lived through it. Ok, you could argue it wasn't all necessarily interesting

enough for a book, but it didn't need Tim to have written about it for us to have gone through it and experienced it, did it?"

Lillian frowned. "That's true, but supposing everything that has happened since we arrived back at your apartment in October didn't actually happen, but was just memories again, like we said before. You know, just to get us to the point we are now, where we are being written about. Assuming that we are, of course."

Tim stepped forward from the window, wagging a pointed finger in validation. "Yes, yes! That could be it. Basically, everything that is not written down by the author at the top of this writer's chain is determined by them to be inherent in their characters, which means that we all, in this dimension, feel as though we have experienced whatever life we need to have lived for it to make sense in the book that is being written about us, but we don't actually know what is being written down and what isn't. To us it is just our lives, flowing along in a normal fashion, hour after hour, day after day - even if it isn't. Does that make sense?"

Marlo scratched his neck and winced. "Just about. Still seems implausible though." He looked at Lillian. "What do you think?"

"I think we are doing too much thinking. In trying to find the end of the string we are tying it round ourselves. Maybe we should just let nature take its course, not worry about who is writing what and what is real and what isn't. It is too tiring for the brain. Don't you agree?"

Marlo and Tim looked at each other, looked back at Lillian, and in unplanned unison said simply "Yes," then shared a laugh that helped to dissipate some of the mental tension that had overwhelmed them all since they first realised they had something in common.

Marlo turned towards Tim and raised an eyebrow at him. "Wait a minute, though, Tim, there could be an upside to all this. If you write about us again, how about you give me some super powers? Invisibility maybe?"

Lillian looked at him with a frown that needed no explanation.

"Well perhaps, for a small fee," replied Tim. "One thing in return though, and I hope you don't mind me asking. I just have to ask whether you two..... are you, well, together now? Properly together?"

Marlo looked at the floor and Lillian smiled shyly. She gave Tim a little shrug. "If you want to know that you'll just have to write about it, won't you?"

EPILOGUE PT 2

And so the tangled web I've woven collapses in on itself and should any reader have had the fortitude to reach this point, they may find themselves trying to extricate their brains from a journey that took them in directions even the author didn't see coming.

Marlo was right. Someone was guiding what was happening to him and Lillian, and ultimately it wasn't Tim. It was me. But is anyone guiding me? Or you?

BONUS CHAPTER: MARLO'S CHALLENGES

There is another chapter, should you be interested. It gives some background on Marlo's early years and his struggles with how he looked. Warning: It's a bit depressing as it details what it is like to find yourself seemingly unable to ever attract a partner, so read at your own risk or if you have ever wondered what that is like. If you are seeking to be offended by what Marlo thinks during his times of despair (as I have already had comments of this nature), please bear in mind that his mental state is shaped by his experiences. If you cannot handle that please stay away! ☺

You can find it at:

www.angussilvie.com/writing

What Did You Think of The Mysterious Fall?

First of all, thank you for reading my first novel, I really appreciate it. There are millions of books to read out there, but you picked this book and for that I am grateful, and I hope you are too.

It you liked it (but not if you didn't, of course!) it would be great if you could share this book with your friends and family by posting through social media or even through that old-fashioned method of talking to them.

I also really hope that you could take some time to post a review on Amazon – it makes all the difference, and I am always checking the website. Thank you so much! Your feedback and support will help this author to improve his writing craft for future projects and make the next books even better, should that be at all possible of course.

You can reach me on angus.silvie@outlook.com. I apologise in advance if any reply is slow, as it relies on me remembering to check that email account. I will get there eventually though!

Also Available By This Author

The Slightly Mysterious Death

The sequel to the Mysterious Fall. Lillian is alive again, but now she is in the 21st century, and astonished by what she finds. With Marlo by her side she has to learn how to adjust to an alien future she thought she could never have dreamed of inhabiting, a future that is wonderful yet very confusing.

To his dismay, though, she decides that she wants to go back in time and rescue someone else who was in her position. They both know how they can do it, but it is a lot easier said than done. As they soon find out.....

This is a supernatural crime thriller unlike any other. Well, there is one other book that gets close to it, but you have already read that, and the sequel has a very new dimension. By the time you finish it, you could be thinking not just about the characters in the book, but also about your own existence too.

Printed in Great Britain
by Amazon

63479678R00272